Greenbeard

At EXTERMINATING ANGEL PRESS,
we're taking a new approach to our world. A new way of looking at things.
New stories, new ways to live our lives.
We're dreaming how we want our lives and our world to be...

Also from
EXTERMINATING ANGEL PRESS

The Supergirls: *Fashion, Feminism, Fantasy,*
and the History of Comic Book Heroines
by Mike Madrid

Jam Today: *A Diary of Cooking With What You've Got*
by Tod Davies

Correcting Jesus: *2000 Years of Changing the Story*
by Brian Griffith

3 Dead Princes: *An Anarchist Fairy Tale*
by Danbert Nobacon
with illustrations by Alex Cox

Dirk Quigby's Guide to the Afterlife
by E. E. King

A Galaxy of Immortal Women:
The Yin Side of Chinese Civilization, by Brian Griffith

Park Songs: *A Poem/Play,* by David Budbill
with photos by R.C. Irwin

THE HISTORY OF ARCADIA SERIES
by Tod Davies

Snotty Saves the Day
with illustrations by Gary Zaboly

Lily the Silent
with illustrations by Mike Madrid

GREENBEARD

Richard James Bentley

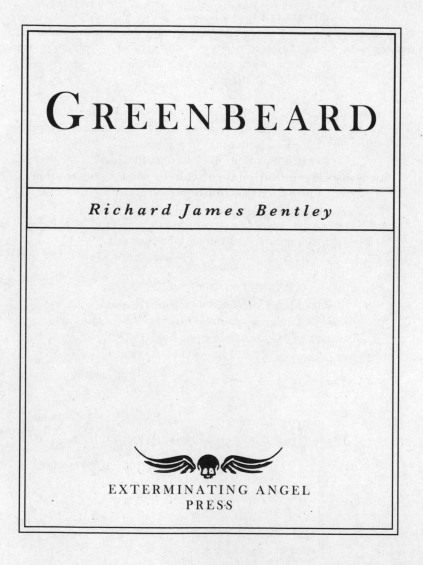

EXTERMINATING ANGEL
PRESS

Portions of this book first appeared, some in different form, on the
Exterminating Angel Press online magazine at www.exterminatingangel.com
Exterminating Angel Press
"Creative Solutions for Practical Idealists"
Visit **www.exterminatingangel.com** to join the conversation
info@exterminatingangel.com

Exterminating Angel Press book design by Mike Madrid
Layout and typesetting by John Sutherland
Cover art by Stephen Player - *playergallery.com*

ISBN: 978-1-935259-21-3
eBook ISBN: 978-1-935259-22-0
Library of Congress Control Number: 2012950070
Distributed by Consortium Book Sales & Distribution
(800) 283-3572 *www.cbsd.com*

PRINTED IN THE UNITED STATES OF AMERICA

For my mother, and in memory of my father.

Captain Sylvestre de Greybagges was growing his beard, which was to say he was idling and drinking rum. If someone should ask him "What are you doing this afternoon?" he would say "I think I shall just sit and grow my beard." Growing his beard would necessarily involve the drinking of rum, of course. And a fine beard it was, too! Lustrous and as yellow as Spanish gold, it reached nearly to the belt that cinched the black broadcloth of his coat over his hard flat belly. The belt from which hung his heavy cutlass in its black leather scabbard, the wide black belt that had three knives and two flintlock pistols thrust into it, easy to hand, for Captain Sylvestre de Greybagges was a pirate.

In this business of growing his beard, and drinking rum, he was ably assisted by Israel Feet, his First Mate, right-hand man and partner in many a villainy. Bulbous Bill Bucephalus was there too, the porcine sailing-master of Captain Greybagges's ship *Ark de Triomphe*, and Blue Peter Ceteshwayoo, the giant African who was the Master Gunner. The four buccaneers were sitting around a wobbly table in the back room of *Ye Halfe Cannonballe* tavern, which was conveniently close to the quays of Port de Recailles, that nest of sea-wolves whose name would be first in any Baedeker of infamy. The back room was pleasantly cool, whilst the lane outside baked in the heat of the late Caribbean sun and the eponymous half-cannonball hung on its rusty chain with no breeze to make it swing and creak. Captain Sylvestre de Greybagges's beard grew and the rum bottle passed around. Blue Peter lifted his little finger as he sipped his rum delicately, for although his face was decorated by tribal scars - the face so black it seemed blue in certain lights - and his teeth were filed to points, he aspired to be an English gentleman, an ambition which would have caused hilarity among the rough crew of the *Ark de Triomphe*, except that any such merriment would have been instantly fatal. His companions at the table were fellow officers of the ship, and so his equals, and accepted his cravings for refinement as no more than an endearing eccentricity. Blue Peter dabbed at his lips with a fine white lawn handkerchief, then tucked it into his sleeve.

"As Aeolus denies us his zephyrs we may surely take our ease, my friends," he rumbled, "but we may with profit turn our thoughts to such stratagems and ploys as the future will surely require. Especially before we purchase another flask of this fine sugarcane distillate."

"A-who? Zebras?" piped Bulbous Bill, his high-pitched voice incongruous coming from so obese a body.

"Arr! You fat fool! He means there ain't no wind, but we oughter be a-plottin' for when there is. Be. For when wind there be! Arr!" Captain Sylvestre de Greybagges's ambitions were in an opposite direction to those of Blue Peter. He was a man of some education, but yearned to speak as though he had been born in a Dorsetshire hovel and schooled on a bumboat in salty Poole Bay. "Speshly afore we gets blootered. Arr!"

"Har! 'Ee do have the right of that, and you 'as me affy-davy on't! Cheerly messmates all, look'ee! Har!" Israel Feet downed the rest of his rum and splashed some more into his tarred leather drinking-jack.

The pirates sat for a moment in silent contemplation, firstly at Israel Feet's effortless grasp of the sea-rovers' argot, for he hardly ever made more than a blurred kind of sense, but then at the implications of Blue Peter's words. They were indeed running low in funds. Plunderable treasure had been scarce in recent times.

Captain Sylvestre de Greybagges, to cool his brain and thus aid ratiocination, removed his black tricorn hat, revealing a shiny pink bald pate, in contrast to his ever-growing yellow beard.

"I could check out my newspaper contacts..." Captain Greybagges mused, adding "Look'ee" as an afterthought. He wrote an occasional gossip column upon piratical affairs for the *Port de Racailles Gleaner*, which was syndicated in the *Tortugas Times*, the *Port Of Spain Plain-Dealer* and even, to his delight, the *Poole Advertiser*, where the infamous Harry Paye would surely read it, or have it read to him at least. The recompense was welcome, of course, the prices of rum, tar, hempen rope, gunpowder and shot being what they were, but the main attraction of the arrangement was not the one-eighth-of-a-*Reale*-per-word but the quantity of scuttlebutt, rumour and chat that came to his ears. It was also pleasant to practise what the tutors of Eton and the Fellows of Cambridge had taught to him in the days of his more-or-less innocent youth. The *scritch* of goose-quill upon vellum had a comforting sound, and the influence of that pen – oh! but the Bard was right! – ensured that even cutthroat villains like Eddie Teach and that bloody

2

jumped-up Welshman Henry Morgan were at least polite to him.

"Har!" Israel Feet cleared his throat, "There's many that goes to Madame Zonga's for lovesome sport and frolicking, ye'll ken, and there's many of them as 'as loose tongues, look'ee, an' damn yer eyes!" The company only wrestled with this for a second, for it was one of Feet's more intelligable utterances. It was also known that Madame Zonga had a soft spot for Israel Feet, since he had been kindly to her in the early years of her career, when she had been merely Dottie Pigge. They nodded their understanding.

"Avast! Methinks we shall visit Madame Zonga's betimes, after a bottle or two and a mortress of beef to settle the vitals. Ye can work your wiles and cozen some secrets out of the old trollop then, Izzie. Blast yer liver and vitals if ye cannot!" Captain Greybagges took a reflective sip of rum from his chased-silver goblet. The four were silent for a moment as each considered, in his own way, a vision of the rat-like first mate working wiles upon the well-upholstered Madame Zonga.

"The plantations of His Majesty's North American colonies are supposed to have enjoyed much prosperity of late," opined Blue Peter Ceteshwayoo, "and they may be ripe for plunder and rapine. A raid by land would be necessary, but that has not been unknown to gentlemen of fortune such as ourselves, surely?"

"Arr!" said Captain Greybagges, fixing Blue Peter briefly with his grey eyes, and said no more. The first mate and the sailing master sympathised with the African, for he was an escaped slave and regarded slave owners with a natural distaste - and indeed who of the Free Brotherhood of the Coasts did not? - but even with his elegant tact he had still reminded their captain of the celebrated success of Bloody Morgan in taking the City of Panama, a hugely-profitable land operation that Captain Greybagges had refused to take part in, thinking it ill-judged and foolishly risky. He had been proved wrong, and had not shared in the enormous, the almost-unbelievable plunder. But who could have foreseen that the Spaniards would have left Panama's western approaches undefended? A bloody jumped-up Welshman, that was who. They kept their own counsel and avoided Blue Peter's black eyes, their whites yellow and blood-shot, as he looked to them for support.

"Arr!" squeaked Bulbous Bill Bucephalus, eager to change the subject. "I buys me hot peppers from a half-breed cove name of Denzil." The searing chillied stews that the sailing-master made were much appreciated by the piratical crew of the *Ark de Triomphe* as a sovereign cure for hangovers. He could not be expected to maintain his vast bulk on an unvarying diet of oatmeal burgoo and salt-horse and pease, after all, so even the ship's cook did not object too much when he was booted out of the galley to let Bulbous Bill perform culinary experiments. It was true that Bulbous Bill's cookery was not always entirely successful – when he had simmered a hyena with pot-herbs, for example, he had made himself a laughing-stock – but any additions to the menu were usually welcome. They sensed that there was more yet to come, and waited patiently as Bulbous Bill sipped rum from his *lignum-vitae* beaker and knotted his brows to concentrate his thoughts.

"The man Denzil, ye sees, he gets his hottest peppers from them Spanish Americas. Goes down there in his little boat, a-sailin' an' a-fishin'. One o' them double-ended canoes with a littler canoe on the side on two planks, it be. At the first he got them peppers from Cayenne, of course, but he likes 'em hotter an' hotter, so he sails up and down the coast, and sometimes he wanders inshore a-ways. Looking fer them peppers." Bulbous Bill took another pull of his rum. "Anyways, being a half-breed, his ole Carib indian mother taught him the Carib lingo. Wasn't the right lingo to talk to them Cayenne indians, ye ken, but it gives him the advantage of not bein' civilised as are the likes of us so he picks up a lot of those Cayenne indians' lingoes fair quickly, and now he speaks their lingoes pretty well." The pirates were paying close attention now. "Seems to me, iffen we was to be friendly, and axes him nice, and gives him some money, he may keep his ears open for things that may be to our advantage. Them indians hates them Spaniards like poison, so they do. They'd give us the nod outa sheer devilment an' spite, an' be damned pleased with theyselves for doing so."

"That," said Captain Sylvestre de Greybagges musingly, "is a very good idea. A very good idea indeed." He blinked. "'Pon me life, ye rascal! A blasted fine piece o' headwork it be, and here's me hand upon't, damn yez!" He roared, pounding the wobbly table so that the pirates all grabbed for their drinks. "A fat fool ye may be, but ye be a fat fool with a headpiece upon yez! Blast me vitals, else!"

"Bill, old chum, I am in admiration of your sagacity!" agreed Blue Peter. "That is indeed a capital lucubration! A cerebration of the very first order! I observe, in passing, that was exactly the strategy that Sir Francis Drake utilised in his matchless endeavours to relieve the Dons of their coinage, specie and bullion back in the days of Good Queen Bess, and I can give no higher praise than that!

Let us refill our glasses and raise them in a toast to Bulbous Bill Bucephalus, that paragon of incisive analysis!"

Blue Peter filled Bulbous Bill's *lignum-vitae* beaker with rum, the bottle nearly lost in his huge blue-black hand, then Captain Sylvestre de Greybagges's chased-silver goblet, then Israel Feet's tarred leather drinking-jack and lastly his own tumbler of precious diamond-cut Bohemian crystal, and the buccaneers toasted Bulbous Bill Bucephalus, who simpered modestly, his many chins and jowls wobbling. Israel Feet then proposed a toast to Great Good Fortune, with many a "Har!" and many a "Scupper me gizzards, else!" and so the rum bottle was empty. Captain Greybagges looked at his officers fondly.

"So, messmates, we have our duties for the morn. Bulbous Bill shall proceed with his wily plan to sound out this Denzil cully, softening his heart towards us with sweet words and golden coins. Izzie here shall cozen Madame Zonga for the secrets that sleepy satisfied coves may have murmured in the shell-like ears of her girls. I myself shall write letters to my correspondents and snitches," and here he smiled at Blue Peter, "and Blue Peter may plot fire, ruin and plunder upon the slave-drivers of Virginny and Kentuck, for his plan to raid by land may be useful in days to come. I am not agin the notion, ye sees. No, I only wish to see it happen when it is timely and we are well prepared, for the Colonials can be rare plucked-uns when they be a-riled-up."

A feeling of harmony and piratical brotherhood came over the four buccaneers with these well-chosen words. Captain Sylvestre de Greybagges placed his black three-cornered hat back on his shiny bald pate, signalling that the plotting was over and that the roistering should begin. He pounded the table with his meaty fist. "Wench! Bring us rum! Damn ye eyes! Bring us RUM!" The serving-wench peered round the corner from the tap-room and nodded. "And can we have some nibbles, too?" said Captain Sylvestre de Greybagges.

———

In the morning, the late morning, Captain Sylvestre de Greybagges woke from deep slumber in the Great Cabin of the *Ark de Triomphe*, the high sun shining in his eyes through the tall stern windows. He yawned and rubbed his eyes, the hanging bunk swaying on its ropes, then roared for his servant Mumblin' Jake to bring him hot water and a cannikin of coffee. As he sipped his coffee and Mumblin' Jake shaved his head Captain Greybagges recalled the previous evening. In the event, only Israel Feet had taken himself to Madame Zonga's establishment, with a foremast jack to carry the lantern and protect the drunken First Mate from footpads and ruffians. (What was the town coming to? Upon a time it had been safe for an honest pirate to walk the streets at night!) The Captain, the sailing-master and the Master Gunner had felt too logy with food and drink to climb the hill, so had settled for a game of *Bezique* and a few glasses of Smoking Bishop to round the evening off. The mortress of beef had indeed been very good, the Captain recalled, a little bland perhaps, what with the goat's milk and soppets of sourdough bread, but surely that only enhanced the flavours of the meaty skirt-of-beef? He felt sharp-set and ready for breakfast at the mere thought of it.

After Mumblin' Jake had helped him into his freshly-brushed black broadcloth coat and spit-shined black top-boots Captain Greybagges sent his servant to call the officers to join him for breakfast in the Great Cabin. He buckled on his wide belt with the cutlass, tucked the knives and pistols into it and carefully placed the black tricorn hat on his freshly-shaven head; a pirate captain should look like a pirate captain, even at breakfast. The other officers joined him at the table as the ship's cook and Mumblin' Jake set out the gleaming cutlery and brought bacon, eggs, lamb chops, sausages and grilled tomatoes in chafing-dishes, toast in a rack of silver and a tureen of Bulbous Bill's fiery chilli. Blue Peter Ceteshwayoo was the last to arrive. He had drunk the least during the evening and had been up with the lark to ensure that the pirate crew were not skimping on their duties, skiving or otherwise swinging the lead. Slushing the yard-arms with rancid tallow was a dirty job even if one was supervising, so he had taken time to wash and change. Blue Peter liked to be informal in the mornings and so he wore only a white silk shirt and sky-blue knee-britches and not the turquoise *moiré* coat, white lace stock and powdered periwig of the night before. Informality only went so far, however, so a short cutlass with a brass knuckle-duster grip and a horse-pistol like a small cannon were thrust into the multicoloured sash around his waist.

Israel Feet had perhaps drunk the most and looked even more rat-like than usual, his eyes red and watery and a hangdog expression on his face. After a plate of eggs and mixed grill, a bowl of chilli and a quart of black coffee his looks improved and some colour came back to his narrow pale features.

Captain Greybagges kindly waited for his First Mate's recovery to proceed a little, helping himself to buttered toast and marmalade, then questioned him gently on his cozening of Madame Zonga. Israel Feet answered at length and, in amongst a barrage of "Hars!", a number of "Scupper me gizzards, elses!" and even a solitary "Rupture me kidneys if I should tell a lie, messmates!" they understood that the First Mate had been hospitably received by Madame Zonga, that because of his consumption of rum he had only been able to complete the first of her famous Six Lessons, that the Lesson had been free because she liked him despite this amatory *faux-pas*, but that she had not been forthcoming with any information useful to buccaneers eager for plunder.

"No mind, Izzie, me ole fighting-cock," said the Captain. "Maybe she'll hear of something in days to come. Let's see if Bill here can't glean something from his mate Denzil."

"Aye-aye, Cap'n. I'll go over s'arternoon," piped Bulbous Bill. "I needs summa them peppers anyways."

Blue Peter drank the last of his coffee and wiped his lips fastidiously with a linen napkin. "Mr Feet and myself shall keep the crew at their labours, methinks. The futtock-shrouds need serving and parcelling, the harpins are quite poorly catted and there are always cannon-balls that need to be chipped, alas."

When his lieutenants had gone about their tasks and Mumblin' Jake had cleared the remains of their morning repast from the table Captain Sylvestre de Greybagges took out his writing-case from beneath the bunk. The teak writing-case opened along a brass piano-hinge to form a sloped lectern, its green leather surface lifting to reveal sheafs of paper and vellum. An inkwell, sealed with a brass lid, contained blue-black oxgall ink and a compartment held goose-quills. Captain Greybagges was very fond of the writing-case, which had previously belonged to some hoity-toity Austrian aristocrat (whom the Captain had so disliked that he'd been glad when the ransom was quickly paid, as he would have otherwise have killed the stuck-up sod and been out-of-pocket) and he admired it as he whittled a fresh goose-quill into a nib. For the most part of half a dog-watch he composed letters to his informants, the *scritch-scratch* of quill on parchment audible to his servant polishing the silverware and mumbling in the Captain's pantry. There was an occasional *crash*, *thud* or shouted order from the deck above, but these were the normal sounds of a fighting ship and did not disturb his concentration in the least. He read the letters through again after he had sanded them and the ink was dry, nodded to himself and wrapped them carefully in vellum packets closed with great blobs of red sealing-wax squelched down with the black onyx stone of his ring. He took a small key on a fine gold chain from around his neck, opened a secret compartment in the writing desk and took out a small booklet. With scissors he cut squares from the booklet. Each paper square was printed with an image of a death's-head blowing a post horn, the horn muted with a bung, and the inscriptions *Ten Reales* and *Postage Paid*. He glued the squares to the vellum packets with gum arabic. The Captain seemed a little furtive while he did this, glancing over his shoulder to ensure nobody was looking through the stern windows and keeping an eye on the door. Some of a pirate captain's secrets are best kept even from his officers and crew, and the Tristero company's clandestine postal service was surely one of them. He tucked the packets into an inside pocket of his coat and called for Mumblin' Jake.

CHAPTER THE SECOND,
or the Captain's Great Good Fortune.

Captain Sylvestre de Greybagges ambled along the quay of Port de Recailles, flanked by two bully-boys armed with oaken cudgels who glared aggressively at anybody within range. The Captain was not unduly worried about being robbed, but the two ugly thugs enhanced his stature in the eyes of the townspeople. Being a pirate captain was about three-quarters public relations, he estimated. That show-off Eddie Teach and his ridiculous trick of tying sputtering fuses in his beard! The Captain shook his head in wonderment; he had once been obliged to hurl a bucket of water over the fellow, before Teach had learned to soak his beard in alum to fireproof it. There was no doubt that the trick had worked, however, and now treasure-laden prizes would heave-to the instant that Teach's Jolly Roger rose above the horizon rather than risk his wrath by running or giving fight. What a saving in powder, shot and wear-and-tear on the ship and crew that would give. And now the fellow was calling himself Blackbeard! He was fond of Eddie Teach and enjoyed his subtle sense of humour – that night when Eddie had blown his first mate's kneecap off with a blunderbuss concealed under the table! How they'd laughed! – but he wondered if he might not go too far one day. Teach did not have the benefit of a university education, ruminated the Captain, whereas he himself had taken the Cambridge course option *Ye Art Of Showinge A Fine And Charitable Face To Ye Worlde, One Hundredd And One* and so knew the advantages of restraint in self-publicity; nobody would find Captain Sylvestre de Greybagges calling himself Yellow Whiskers!

The Captain turned up a narrow alleyway and came to a small dingy shop so decrepit, its wooden beams so crooked and its stucco so cracked that it might have levered out of a previous and wider location with pry-bars and pounded into its present space with mauls. The Captain gestured to the bully-boys to stay by the door and entered. A bell jangled as he opened and closed the door. The interior of the shop was dark and crammed with junk. Broken furniture, cracked dishes in stacks, piles of malodorous old clothes, unrecognisable things in tangled heaps. A path between the rubbish led into the interior of the shop, where an ancient pantalooned man in a filthy peruke sat smoking a churchwarden clay pipe. He might have been a corpse except for the occasional wisp of smoke from the pipe.

"Do you have a *waste* bin?" asked the Captain. The ancient indicated with a glance of his rheumy eyes to a dark corner. Behind a statue of a blackamoor there was a wooden box with a slot in its lid. It was marked with the symbol of the muted post-horn and the letters W.A.S.T.E in paint so faded that it was barely legible. Captain Sylvestre de Greybagges took the vellum packets from his pocket and slid them into the box. He hadn't spotted the box at first because the blackamoor in front of it was a new addition to the shop's contents. He examined it idly. A life-size statue of a Negro holding a tray on an outstretched hand; wealthy people kept them in the foyers of their mansions for visitors to leave their cards on, should the master be absent. With a start the Captain realised that it wasn't a statue but a real black man, dead, but stuffed and mounted like a hunter's trophy. He made an involuntary snort of disgust and the ancient man smiled a slow evil smile. Captain Greybagges made to leave. The ancient man reached into the breast of his greasy coat and handed Captain Greybagges a bundle of packets tied together with string. He put them in his pocket and threw the ancient a coin. After he had turned his back on the ancient man the Captain made the horns sign with his fingers to ward off evil.

In the alleyway outside Captain Greybagges strode quickly away, taking deep breaths to clear the musty air of the shop from his lungs as though it were a poisonous miasma. Tristero's secret mail was very useful, but its postmasters could be very creepy. The two bully-boys trotted after him.

Captain Greybagges spent the remainder of the afternoon strolling from tavern to low dive to shebeen in Port de Recailles, meeting friends, acquaintances and informants and drinking coffee and the occasional glass of beer. No useful information had come to him, but he hadn't entirely wasted his time. When he entered a drinking-house his bully-boys would hold back and follow him only after several seconds, and meanwhile he would surreptitiously watch the other drinkers. Although all his clothes were black and the dives were dimly-lit it was still apparent that he was a wealthy man, so he would watch for men who looked as though they were thinking of jumping him, but who appeared to lose interest when his bully-boys followed, and he would memorise their faces. A pirate captain was always on the lookout for crew, and a fellow who would think immediately of robbing him despite his muscular build was the kind of man he needed. Quick-thinking, not shy and definitely thievish. If they didn't give up the idea when the bully-boys followed they were too stupid. If they didn't think of robbing him at all they would never be pirates. Of course, there were some who would conceal their interest, hoping to follow him and ambush him outside later, but he didn't want fellows who were too wily, either; they could be trouble. Several possible candidates had been noted by him, and he would recruit them as and when it was convenient. He would, of course, point out to them that they'd thought of mugging him, so giving the impression that he could read their thoughts, which would establish him as their superior in quickness of mind and thus their natural leader. A simple trick, but effective. Doctor Quaestifuncula, the Captain's tutor at Cambridge for Law, had called such things *nousology*; the science of being clever.

As Captain Greybagges ambled back along the quay to the *Ark de Triomphe* he remembered Doctor Quaestifuncula with affection. Law was, of course, absolutely the best training for a pirate, and the good Doctor had been a master of it. Few who had not been up to university were aware of the sheer viciousness of the infighting amongst academics. Those old fellows in their black gowns and tatty wigs would go at it hammer-and-tongs at High Table, yet to the casual observer they would appear the best of friends as they stuffed themselves with roast baron-of-beef and passed the port around. Battles of intelligence, memory and wit, and Doctor Quaestifuncula was the master. An old bent-backed beanpole with a long nose, thick spectacles and a kindly smile, yet he would have made a fine captain of pirates. He would still plead the occasional case, despite his age, and the Silks and Stuffs would quake as he shuffled into the court with his clerk stumbling along behind him carrying a vast stack of law-books and briefs tied with pink ribbon. The Captain remembered once climbing out of a racing-shell, he and his team glowing with exertion and eager to raise hell in the taverns of the town, when he had overheard Doctor Quaestifuncula as he passed by remark to a colleague "there's the rowing-eights, getting out of their sculls again." What a wit the man had! The Captain had been a rowing Blue, and he wondered if that hadn't been his first step on the way to piracy. From little boats to bigger boats, maybe.

Captain Sylvestre de Greybagges strode up the gangplank onto the deck of the *Ark de Triomphe*, his bully-boys huffing after him. He stopped and looked up into the rigging at the crew about their work and for an instant nearly said "Good work! Good work! Keep it up, lads!" but that would never do, so he roared "Ye scurvy knaves! I catches a man slacking and I'll see the colour of his liver and lights! An' yez may lay to that, wi' a wannion!" and was gratified to see them all try to look busy. One day he would find out what a wannion was, he promised himself.

The thoughts of rowing on the Cam had made him nostalgic, so he threw his coat and hat to Mumblin' Jake and clambered down the ship's side into the skiff. With powerful strokes he pulled the light craft across the harbour of Port de Recailles, around the end of the stone-built mole and across Rum Bay to Sruudta Point. There he hove-to, enjoying the sun on his bald head, the skiff bobbing in the slight swell. He reached under his yellow beard and removed his black silk cravat, unbuttoned his shirt and rolled up the sleeves. He folded the cravat carefully, for it was from Saville Row, London, and had cost as much as a case of decent claret. Nobody could see it under his beard, of course, but *he* knew it was there. He sniffed the air and looked at the little puffy clouds on the horizon. The dead calm would end soon, he was sure.

He spun the skiff with a single pull of an oar and rowed back to the harbour, slower now, with easy strokes of the oars. He'd seen Calico Jack Rackham in Y*e Petty Mountmartree Froggie Wyneshoppe And Grille* earlier, and clanked tankards with him. He'd always been plain Jack Rackham before. Was every freebooter adopting a *nom de guerre*? Perhaps *nom de pillage* would be more accurate. Jack Rackham had got his nickname from the haberdashery stall he'd used to run in Petticoat Lane market, Captain Greybagges recalled, but he supposed that made it easier to remember, and not many would recall him from those days. It would be a shame if one forgot one's pseudonym: "Har! Shit yer britches ye weevils, for I am ... oh! A pox on't! What was it now? ... Ah! That be it! ... For I be Cutthroat Cecil Cholmondleigh!" Captain Sylvestre de Greybagges shook his head and grinned. That ass Billy Bones had tried to call himself The Pirate With No Name, but, never the brightest of buccaneers, he had spoiled it by roaring "Hear my name and shiver, ye swabs! For I be Billy Bones, The Pirate With No Name!" just as he was boarding a prize. The defending crew had been sore a-feared, but when they heard that they'd all howled with laughter and Bones's boarding-party had retreated in confusion, followed by jeers and hoots. The silly sod had been forced to skewer his quartermaster and two foremast jacks to restore discipline, and by then the prize had made sail and cleared off, of course.

Mind you, thought the Captain, this fashion for bloodthirsty nicknames might not go away. If it did not he'd have a problem, for one could never buck a well-established trend. He couldn't call himself Yellowbeard, for that would seem like he was aping Eddie Teach, and he was damned if he'd call himself Yellow Whiskers, as that just sounded silly. And yet his trademark was his long yellow beard, and all the more apparent in contrast to his all-black apparel. He would have to think about this some more, maybe.

He tied up the skiff and clambered up the tumblehome onto the deck. While rowing back he'd noticed that the ebb and flood of the tide had left the harbour with clean clear blue water, and that the bottom was visible. He was also sweaty from rowing.

"See yez any sharks?" he shouted to the look-out up in the cross-trees.

"Nary a one, Cap'n!" The look-out waved his hand from side to side and shook his head to emphasise the absence of sharks. Pirates feared sharks, for they believed that sharks could be spookily possessed by the souls of those they had eaten. Given the number of people who had been fed to sharks by pirates there was a worrying possibility that a possessed shark might well recognise a jolly buccaneer as the one who had encouraged his human incarnation to step out along the plank by jabbing a rapier in his bottom, should they happen to meet whilst swimming in the sea. It was also said by some that sharks would never attack lawyers out of professional courtesy, but Captain Sylvestre de Greybagges had no notion to put that to a practical test. The harbour was clear, though, so the Captain stripped off, clambered onto the rail and dived into the blue water. He swam along the length of the frigate and back, the great tattoo on his back visible to the crew in the rigging; a depiction of Old Nick sitting upon his dark throne, shaded by his black bat's wings, staring down upon the Earth with a look of resigned distaste on his long face. There was a *boom* as Blue Peter Ceteshwayoo bombed into the water beside him. "Ye swab!" roared the Captain and splashed him. There was a smaller plosh and Israel Feet slithered underneath them through the clear water trailing bubbles, as agile as an eel. The three freebooters larked about in the salty seawater until Captain Greybagges shouted "Race yez to the harbourmouth!" Although Captain Greybagges was a strong swimmer the small sinewy First Mate had an easy fast crawl and overtook him. They trod water until Blue Peter arrived, swimming a sedate breaststroke. "Arr! Blue Peter shall buy the drinks tonight!" roared Captain Greybagges.

The three pirates stood upon the deck of the frigate *Ark de Triomphe* laughing and pouring buckets of cold fresh water over their heads, as naked as jaybirds. There was a murmur of amusement from the crew in the rigging. Captain Greybagges looked up, a scowl on his face.

"Was I not speakin' aforetimes about the livers and lights of them as might be slacking!" he roared. There was a sudden stillness among the crew. The Captain grinned. "Har! Har! Har! I caught you out there! Har! Har! Har! I do loves my little jest! Har! Har! Har!" The crew in the rigging and on the decks looked uneasily abashed. "No, me hearties! Yez bin working like riggers, ye has, toiling 'andsomely like, but too much graft and not enough roistering makes for a mumpish band o' buccaneers. You may finish up and knock off for the day." There was a pleased mutter from the crew. "Finish what yez is doing with a will, mind yez all! I will tell quartermaster to broach a cask o' rum and a couple barrels o' beer and ye may have yeselves a jolly evening. Let yez hair down. Grow yez beards a bit." The crew cheered. "BUT!" and the Captain spoke this in a voice of brass, "BUT, I will obliged if yez shall drink matey-like." He paused and let his grey eyes rove over them. "For there are fresh breezes a-coming as the season o' storms approaches, and them winds has been known to blow good *fortune* to gentlemen of *fortune* such as we. T'would be a great shame and a pity iffen we should miss a handsome bounty because some knavish swab had a sore head and did not attend to his duties in a proper and seamanlike fashion. So ye'll drink easy-like, and play a hand o' cards, mebbe, and roll the bones for Crown and Anchor, and play upon the squeeze-box and fiddle, and yez may even sleep late o' the morning, but I'll not stand for fighting amongst yeselves, nor drinking yeselves into a stupor! No, I will not! When them winds freshens up we shall go for a little sail, we shall, an' we may find what we may find. Now finishes up yer duties, me hearties, with a will."

The crew carried on, with a cheerful mutter of voices from the rigging and the deck.

"T'were a fine piece o' speechifyin', Cap'n, damn me, but it was!" said Israel Feet in a low voice. "T'will set the lads up 'andsome-like. That an a few jars o' ale."

"Why thankee, Izzie! That be praise indeed," said the Captain, wringing water out of his beard.

Mumblin' Jake brought the Captain and his two lieutenants towels and stood by holding their clothes. As he stepped into his breeches Captain Greybagges told Mumblin' Jake to fetch the boatswain and crew of his longboat, who were the largest men in the crew. When the seven hulking sailors came they formed a line on the deck, slid their right feet forward and knuckled their brows respectfully.

"Bosun, I wishes you and your lads to stay sober tonight." The bully-boys looked aggrieved. "Here is something to ease yez disappointment." whispered the captain, winking, and dropped a thick silver coin into each of their hands. "Ye shall roister tomorrow. I needs yez sharp to make sure no silly sod gets hisself fighting-drunk, that no clown lights his pipe in the powder-magazine and that no sly strangers slips onto the ship to do mischief while the jacks are a-quaffing. Ye may let some trollops come aboard, no more than three at a time, mark yez. Nobody else at all. Do yez ken?" The bullyboys nodded, "Aye-aye, Cap'n!" said Loomin' Len Lummocks the boatswain.

"How now, me buckos," said the Captain as the bully boys lumbered away, slipping the Joachimsthal thalers into their pockets. "Is Bulbous Bill come back yet?" His lieutenants shook their heads. "Well then, Izzie, yez takes a wander around the messes and makes sure they all got my meaning. Peter, you do the same with yer lads on the gun-decks. Make sure no sod 'as skimped his duties to get a-quaffin' quicker, too." He buckled on his belt over his black coat. "I shall joins yer in a while. Take a mug o' grog with 'em and show me face, like. Then I may grow me beard for a bit up at the *Halfe Cannonballe*, and you may accompany me and welcome. We'll leave word for Bill to catch us up."

Captain Sylvestre de Greybagges, Israel Feet and Blue Peter Ceteshwayoo walked down the gangplank and onto the quay, dressed for a night out. The Captain was in his customary black attire. Blue Peter sported a coat of deep-pink silk with gleaming gold buttons, yellow knee-breeches, white hose and gold-buckled shoes the size of small boats on his huge feet, gemstone rings twinkling multicoloured on his fingers. Israel Feet was dressed in the traditional pirate rig of calico shirt, fustian waistcoat and knee-breeches with no hose and black leather pumps on his feet, a bright-coloured knotted kerchief covered his hair and a gold hoop dangled from his ear-lobe, an English Tower-of-London flintlock pistol and a Venetian poniard in his belt.

"Look you, boyos!" came a voice with a strong Welsh lilt. "It is Captain Yellowbeard the Pirate with his pets, the rat and the raven!"

Captain Greybagges spun round. "Why! Iffen it ain't my ole shipmate Bloody Morgan – or shouldn't that be bloody Bloody Morgan, har-har!" He grinned at Henry Morgan with every appearance of amiability. "Yez is surely looking wealthy these days! 'Tis small reason to insult my friends, mind yez, especially when ye have dressed yer own fellows like they be performin' monkeys o' the sort that the Eyetalian hurdy-gurdy men has by them to caper and pass the hat round." Morgan's four bully-boys were dressed in short red bumfreezer jackets, and looked put-out at the Captain's comment.

"You are surely jealous of my finery, Greybagges" sniffed Morgan, twirling around to show off his plum-coloured coat and its gold buttons, epaulettes and braid. "If you had possessed the good sense to accompany me to Panama you would be as grand as myself, surely you would."

"I be merely a humble gentleman of fortune, Morgan, and I seeks not glory at the cost of the lives of my jolly buccaneers. I am not a captain in the Navy, that has Admirals to please and pressed men to fritter away to get a mention in the London *Times*." Captain Greybagges shrugged eloquently.

"If you don't please anyone but yourself, boyo, then nobody will want to please you. Why, King Charles himself has asked me to come to London. I hear he wants to dub me Sir Henry Morgan and make me Governor of Jamaica, on account of how my little expedition to Panama has discountenanced the Spaniards so."

Captain Sylvestre de Greybagges eyebrows went up. "Well, and there is a wonder!" he said. "A gentleman of fortune to be Governor of Jamaikey!" The Captain looked thoughtful. "It may be that the king wants a poacher for a gamekeeper, rather than to reward you for upsetting the Dons, belike. You will not be Sir Henry Bloody Morgan Governor of Jamaikey and yet still be in good standing in the Free Brotherhood of the Coasts." He indicated Morgan's bully-boys with a wave of his hand. "And yer jolly boys will be dancing a hornpipe for yez one day, and dancing a different hornpipe for yez the very next day. At the end of a rope, methinks. Such is the price of a knighthood, given to yez by King Charles himself with a dab of his little sword on yer shoulder-boards."

Morgan's face flushed red with rage. "You always were a churlish cully, Greybagges! A mere scribbler for the scandal-sheets! I bid you good-day!" He and his bully-boys swept past them. Israel Feet had to jump back so as not to be jostled.

The three buccaneers watched them as they went. The small Welsh pirate captain strode confidently, his nose in the air. One of his bully-boys looked back at them uncertainly before the crowd closed behind them.

"Damn! Damn! Damn! Damn the jumped-up Welsh fool!" muttered Captain Greybagges, making no attempt to speak like a pirate. "And damn me for not being able to keep my mouth shut."

"I thought you spoke well and to the point, Captain," said Blue Peter. "I believe that you planted a seed of concern in the minds of his men, too."

"I did, but that means he will be able to deal with it, as I have tipped him off in time to what people will say, and that in turn means that he will go to *London* and see the king." Captain Greybagges sighed. "There was a small chance that I could have talked him out of it. He did trust my judgement in times gone by, when we were shipmates under Captain Flint. If I could have kept my own counsel and then seen him later alone I might have swayed him, but now it's as though I've challenged him publicly, so he will go to the king, damn him. And the king will dub him Sir Henry Bloody Morgan. And the king will make him Governor of Jamaica. And the king will have hired himself a fine poacher as a gamekeeper, a very fine poacher indeed. And the Free Brotherhood of the Coasts will be broken. And England will be united with France and Spain to rid the oceans of the scourge of piracy, which is us."

"England, France and Spain united?" said Blue Peter. "I thought they all hated each other."

"They do." Captain Greybagges sighed again. "Bloody, *Bloody*, Morgan sacked Panama, though, and thus the Spaniards are so weakened on their own Spanish Main that they must make peace with the cursed ungodly English. King Charles, meanwhile, has inherited a bankrupt nation from Noll Cromwell and so must make peace with Louis *le Roi Soleil*, who knows it well, but who cannot take advantage of Charles's penury because he has his own troubles at home in *la belle France*. Thus they can all make common cause against the wicked pirates for a while, and feel a great warm glow of righteousness, the hypocritical sods. They will fall out again soon, of course, but that will be too late for some. We need a treasure now more than ever, my lads. We will need to either retire or keep our heads down for a while, and that will need gold."

They came to Ye *Halfe Cannonballe* and entered into its dim cool interior.

Bulbous Bill Bucephalus was already seated on a settle at their usual table in the back room, his posterior being too wide for a chair. He was sipping Madeira and chewing on pieces of smoked dried squid from a dish of assorted snacks. The three buccaneers joined their colleague with gloomy expressions on their faces.

"What cheer d'yez bring us, Bill?" said Captain Sylvestre de Greybagges. "We are in need of some good news to hearten us. And some Madeiry to wet our whistles, too." He poured himself a glass of the rich brown sweet wine.

"I seen the man Denzil," said Bulbous Bill, "and got some o' them peppers. Some very special peppers. Very hot, they be." He sipped the Madeira thoughtfully. "Very hot indeed." He lowered his voice and tapped the side of his nose. "An' we spoke of the other thing, too."

Blue Peter got up and walked casually to the taproom door and peered in, then to the door to the front bar. He sat down again and nodded.

"Denzil is agreeable to our suggestion. Grateful for them gold coins, too," continued Bulbous Bill in a low voice. "He says that he has become pally with a fellow down in them Spanish Americas. The kind o' cully they calls a *brujo*, which is to say a sorcerer or medicine-man. He says them fellows claims to be able to fly like witches and to talk to gods an' devils an' spirits an' the like. He thinks it's all my eye and soft soap, but that all them *brujos* sticks together so they knows a lot of what's a-goin' on, even if it be miles away, d'ye see?" He sipped the Madeira. "Anyways, he says he's a-goin' down there this next week and if anybody knows anything to our advantage it would be them sorcerer fellows, and no mistake. We'll know in a week, mind yez."

Captain Greybagges looked thoughtful. "Well, messmates, we be hopin' that he comes up trumps, but still keep yez ears open. I reckons we'll take the *Ark de Triomphe* out tomorrow, wind and tides permitting, and sees that everything is shipshape and Bristol-fashion. Something will come along, you marks my words. We must be ready when it does."

The lieutenants of Captain Sylvestre de Greybagges nodded in agreement, then all four buccaneers sipped their glasses of Madeira in silence, each lost in his own thoughts.

———————————

Captain Sylvestre de Greybagges stood on the quarterdeck of the *Ark de*

Triomphe as it slipped into the harbour of Port de Recailles, conned with great skill between the stone pillars that flanked the harbourmouth by Bulbous Bill Bucephalus, the sailing-master. The morning light gave a blue tint to the scene, and the air had a slight chill remaining from the cold of the cloudless night.

"Away the sheets!" cried Bulbous Bill, and the sails flapped loose and the frigate slowed. There was a *splash* as the longboat was launched over the side, and soon the frigate was towed to the quay and secured with singled and doubled mooring-cables to the squat stone bollards. There was a purposeful scurrying in the rigging as the crew lashed the furled sails and loosened the stays to put the masts and yards in a shipshape fashion for port.

Captain Greybagges was pleased. The ship and crew had performed well during the six days that they'd been at sea. They had not encountered a fat merchantman to board and plunder, alas. Only a fishing boat, from whom the Captain had purchased a couple of tunny and a swordfish (only a foolish pirate would rob a fisherman; they were the great gossips of the seas and it was best to have them on your side) and very good eating the fish had been, too. The Captain was satisfied, though. The *Ark de Triomphe* and its crew of jolly buccaneers were fit and eager for piracy upon the high seas. If information was received, if a tip-off came their way about treasure suitable for the plundering, they would be ready to act upon it, he was sure.

The Captain retired to the Great Cabin to write the ship's log, after leaving word that the crew could go ashore in parties of six when their duties had been completed. He was writing an article for the newspapers about Morgan's forthcoming knighthood and governorship when Bulbous Bill tapped on the cabin door.

"I shall go and see if the man Denzil is back from them Spanish Americas," said Bill. "He said he'd be gone a week or so."

"Aye, Bill, you be about that. Any information about some fat galleons a-waitin' to be plucked would be right welcome. The crew be eager and the barky be shipshape, so the sooner we be sailin' off to meet with fortune the better."

Bulbous Bill nodded and left, and Captain Greybagges continued with the article, *scritch-scratch*. He needed to pitch it just right; he must not sound carping or jealous of the bloody jumped-up Welshman's success - in fact he must wish him well - but he did need to point out the possible danger to the sea-rovers of the Free Brotherhood of the Coasts, and yet the writing must be humourous and light. It really ought to be in the post today, too, lest some other scribe scoop him. *Scritch-scratch.*

That evening Captain Sylvestre de Greybagges sat in the back room of Ye *Halfe Cannonballe* tavern sharing a jug of ale with Blue Peter Ceteshwayoo. He reached into the pocket of his black coat and pulled out a pistol.

"Here," he said, pushing the gun across the table to Blue Peter. "Clap yer eyes on this, shipmate."

Blue Peter examined the pistol. It was a flintlock, but quite lightly built with a smallish bore and a longish barrel. Blue Peter's thick index finder would barely fit through the trigger guard.

"Hmm, is it a woman's gun?" asked Blue Peter. "It is a very light weapon. Very finely made, though. Beautiful chasing, and very elegant, I do declare."

"It is called a Kentucky pistol," said Captain Greybagges, "and it is not built for a woman, although a woman could surely fire it. The gunsmiths of Kentuck have their own ideas about guns. They believe that a light gun with a longish barrel is more accurate than a great cannon with a shorter barrel and a great charge o' powder, and so more likely to kill at the first shot. They makes a fine lightweight rifled musket, too. Some calls 'em *squirrel guns* because the Kentucks loves squirrel pies like we loves rabbit pies, d'ye see? I came across it today in the market when I was out posting a packet to the *Tortugas Times*."

"I think I see, Cap'n," said Blue Peter slowly. "You are informing me that the British North American Colonies not only make good firearms, but are so confident of their craft that they will make innovations to suit themselves and their particular circumstances. Furthermore, one might deduce from that that they are dangerous opponents and not to be trifled with in a blithesome or nonchalant fashion."

"You hits upon my meaning straight off, Peter," said Captain Greybagges. "Keep yez the pistol to think upon it. If we raids the Colonial fellows we must be well prepared, and will need inside information and a good plan to succeed. I'm sure the ship's smith can braze a bit into the trigger-guard so's you can get yer finger through it."

The Captain and Blue Peter talked idly about firearms - the difficulty of obtaining pyrites chips for wheel-locks these days, the poor quality of Spanish musket balls, the dubious superiority of Damascus-twist jezail barrels - until Israel Feet and Bulbous Bill Bucephalus arrived. The First Mate was bright red in the face and apparently incapable of speech.

"I gave him one of Denzil's peppers. The new ones what looks like a little Scotsman's hat. Them peppers is awful hot," said Bulbous Bill. "I warned him, but he just said 'Har! Har!' an' et it whole."

Israel Feet filled a mug with ale and drank it all, then drank another. His face became less red and his eyes less bugged. "Arrrrgh!" he said in a hoarse voice. Tears streamed down his face. Captain Greybagges called to the serving-maid to bring another jug of ale. The buccaneers watched Israel Feet as he slowly downed yet another pint of ale, wiped his eyes and blew his nose on a cotton handkerchief and said "Arrrrgh!" several times more.

"Izzie, me ole fighting-cock, we all knows that ye be a hairy-arsed matelot and as hard as a Chinese riddle," said Captain Greybagges kindly, "so yez don't need to prove it, especially by fighting with vegetables." Blue Peter and Bulbous Bill chuckled and Israel Feet looked daggers at them through still-teary eyes.

"Well, Izzie cannot speak yet, but he can listen," said Bulbous Bill, "so perhaps I might tell yez what the man Denzil had to say, though it be not great good news."

Blue Peter got up and checked the taproom and front bar for potential eavesdroppers and sat back down, nodding for Bulbous Bill to continue.

"The man Denzil has spoke with his *brujo* pal," Bulbous Bill said in a low voice, his fellow-buccaneers leaning forward to listen. "It would seem that them sorcerers are just as fond o' a golden coin as anybody else, so he was willin' to pass along anything he might hear. Trouble is, he's only heard of a fleet carryin' crockery. Seems to me that crockery is hardly worth our effort to plunder, but yez may think otherwise."

"Hmm, crockery," mused Blue Peter. "It has a ready market, that cannot be denied. It is not of great intrinsic value, though, even if it is fine porcelain from far Cathay, embellished with blue-painted scenes of that mysterious land. Bulky and breakable, too. Not the easiest of loot to plunder and transport."

"Tell me, Bill," said Captain Sylvestre de Greybagges slowly, "did your friend Denzil actually say 'crockery'? Did he use that precise word?"

"Why, no, Cap'n," said Bulbous Bill. "He said it were plates."

Captain Greybagges looked at Bulbous Bill for several seconds, then he began to laugh. He laughed until his face turned red, he laughed until he had a coughing fit and Blue Peter had to pound him on the back. His three lieutenants stared at him in amazement. At last he gained control of himself, blowing his nose on a black silk handkerchief pulled from his sleeve. He shook his head, still grinning, and put a finger to his lips.

"Oh, Bill! But you are a caution, and no mistake!" He gestured for them to lean closer to him and whispered "It is surely the Spanish Plate Fleet. Plate meaning silver, from the Spanish *plata*. Oh, my! This is a great good fortune indeed!"

The Captain's three lieutenants stared at him open-mouthed, then, as the meaning of his words came clear to them, their open mouths curved into great smiles. Great wolfish piratical smiles.

"Oh deary me!" whispered Blue Peter, "I am ashamed that I did not spot that. Plate, of course, from the Spanish *plata*, meaning silver, from the Greek *plato*, meaning wide. Obvious when one sees it."

"How come wide gets to mean silver? Look'ee." said Israel Feet in a hoarse voice, his throat still burning from the pepper.

"It is because the minting of coins involves taking little lumps of silver and bashing them flat with a hammer. Thus they are made wide, and the word has come to mean all silver in Spanish when once it meant just coinage." said Blue Peter. "The silver of the Plate Fleet will be mainly in ingots, though, each one weighing sixteen and one-half pounds. I've seen them before, and they are a very cheery sight to a gentleman of fortune, a very cheery sight indeed. The Spanish Plate Fleet sails once a year and takes the whole year's production of silver from the Spanish Americas to King Carlos's treasurehouse in Bilbao. That is a large quantity of silver by any standards."

The four freebooters considered this in silence for several minutes, occasionally sipping their mugs of ale and staring into space.

"Tell me, Bill," said Captain Greybagges at last, "did your pal tell you the times of the sailin' and the routes that the fleet may take?"

"Nope, but he did say that the fleet will be anchorin' overnight in Nombre Dios Bay on the third of next month."

The Captain favoured Bulbous Bill with a smile and a nod. He reached inside his black coat and brought out a small book. A Jolly Roger and the words *Ye Lett's Pirate's Diary* were tooled in gold on its black leather binding. Captain Greybagges thumbed through the diary.

"Well, shiver me timbers, here is luck!" he exclaimed. "That night is a night of no moon. It's just before the autumn storms, too, so there's a good chance there will be an overcast sky. A moonless clouded night, and the silver fleet will be anchored over the bones of Sir Francis Drake, who was buried at sea in Nombre Dios Bay, stitched into his hammock betwixt two cannonballs, it is said. These are indeed good omens, me hearties!"

The buccaneers sat back and grinned at each other, the prospect of plundering a vast pile of silver bars warming their piratical hearts like pints of hot rum-toddy.

"Let us enjoy this moment," said Captain Sylvestre de Greybagges, "but let us not become complaisant. The treasure is vast, but it is not yet in our hands, shipmates. There is much plotting and planning to do if we are to take possession of this great fortune. To be sure, the King of Spain does not really need it, he has much wealth already, and he would only waste that fine silver paying Irish mercenary soldiers to keep Flanders in the Catholic faith. The quickest way of turning the Dutch Protestant is to tell them they must be Catholic, of course, but I wander from my point. The Plate Fleet will be at anchor in a secluded bay on the darkest of nights, thinking themselves safe because nobody knows that they are there. By careful planning we can take each ship in turn by stealth alone, and thus we need involve nobody else. We shall need no partners to ensure the success of this venture. No partners to share the booty. No partners to gossip and yakkity-yak, either, and that is important. The only ones who knows about this are us four - Bill's mate Denzil and his witch-doctor both thinks the fleet carries crockery - so let us keep it strictly to ourselves until we are at sea. Look miserable, too. No grinning, no laughing, no dancing of jigs. Keep our good fortune hidden to yourselves alone until we are at sea again. If we does this venture right then we are in clover. Blue Peter will be able to raid the slave-masters of Virginny and Kentuck until he is satisfied that they are contrite, and pay for the expeditions out of his small change without thought of profit."

"You jest, Captain, because you have never endured the pain and humiliation of slavery. I may very well do just what you suggest solely for the sheer vengeful joy of it," said Blue Peter, a wicked smile revealing his pointed teeth.

"As I say, Peter, we must first take possession of this great bounty. That must be foremost in our minds from now on. If we thinks too much of the spendin' of the loot we will not be thinking enough about the plunderin' of it. I meself could easily waste hours thinkin' about how a certain jumped-up Welshman's nose will be put properly out of joint, but I will forego that pleasure until the silver bars are safe in my hands. Well, then, let us drink a draught o' rum to toast this venture," said Captain Sylvestre de Greybagges, "then return to the barky and gets ourselves an early night, shipmates, for it is now my intention to sail on the mornin' tide."

CHAPTER THE THIRD,
or a Foregathering in Nombre Dios Bay.

The frigate *Ark de Triomphe* slowed as the foremast jacks cast off the sheets and the wind spilled from the sails. The night was as black as Indian ink. No moon. No stars. Two dim glimmers of red light showed from the loom of the land to the west, where the pirates had mounted lanterns in the jungle two days earlier as navigation beacons. The lanterns had four-gallon oil reservoirs to burn for a week, and were shielded with black-painted canvas so that they were only visible from a particular bearing. When both lanterns were to be seen the *Ark de Triomphe* was in position for the raid on the fleet, with Nombre Dios Bay to the north just around a concealing point of land.

"Let go the anchor!" hissed Bulbous Bill Bucephalus, and the anchor was slid into the water slowly and carefully, without making a noise.

Captain Sylvestre de Greybagges was clad entirely in black, even more black than was his normal custom. His beard was wrapped in black cloth, his head was covered with a black knitted cap and his face was blackened with soot. In the dim light from the dark lantern by the wheel only his pale grey eyes were easily seen. There was a low mutter of voices and a soft splash as the skiff was lowered over the side by black-clad pirates.

"Less of the chatter, ye swabs!" hissed Captain Greybagges. He turned to Bulbous Bill Bucephalus and spoke softly. "I shall make me reconnaissance quick as I can, but I cannot hurry. Maybe half an hour. Maybe an hour. Keep the men at readiness until I return, then we'll go quickly. Try and keep the swabs from talking or making a row. If I am gone more than three hours, or iffen you hears a shot, then I will have been taken. In that event make sail at once, Bill, and no argument, for this venture requires complete surprise and without it you too will be taken."

Bulbous Bill nodded, and Captain Greybagges climbed over the side. The skiff was difficult to find in the dark by the side of the frigate, for it had been painted black. The Captain found it with his foot and climbed in. The oars were also painted black and muffled with black rags tied around the blades. Blue Peter Ceteshwayoo and Israel Feet looked down from the ship's rail, but the Captain was almost invisible in the moonless starless night. They heard a soft splashing and sensed rather than saw him row away towards the headland.

The night was black as pitch and silent, occasionally a bird's call could be clearly heard from the jungle by the shore. A seaman by the compass-binnacle coughed. Bulbous Bill reached across and grabbed him by the ear.

"Iffen yez coughs again, cully, I shall quiet yez by a-squeezin' yer throat," he whispered.

Time passed slowly. After a seeming infinity had passed there was a soft thud as the seaman at the binnacle turned the hour-glass. One hour. Bulbous Bill, Blue Peter and Israel Feet said nothing, waiting by the rail in the silent darkness.

Another infinity of time passed. Another soft thud. Two hours. Blue Peter shifted himself uneasily. The three buccaneers glanced at each other, but still said nothing.

Blue Peter walked to the binnacle and looked at the hour-glass; the third hour was nearly passed. Suddenly Israel Feet hissed and pointed. Neither Blue Peter or Bulbous Bill could see anything at first, but they began to hear a rhythmic splashing, then a faint white blur became visible in the darkness. As the blur came nearer it resolved into a naked man rowing. A little nearer and they could see it was the Captain, the great tattoo of bat-winged Satan upon his back. He was pulling on the oars of the skiff like a man possessed, the little craft almost leaping out of the water with each heave of his broad shoulders. When the skiff came to the ship Captain Greybagges dropped the oars, stood up, turned and hurled himself onto the side. He scrambled up the tumblehome of the wooden planks like a great white spider, his eyes and mouth like three black holes in his face in the dim light of the dark lantern. He stood on the deck completely naked, shivering as though with the ague, and his three lieutenants stared at him in shock. The Captain took a step forward and seized Bulbous Bill by the arm.

"Make all sail now. Waste no time. Cut the anchor loose and go. Now!" he hissed. His pale grey eyes bulged from his head and his face was etched with dark lines from some awful horror. Slowly his eyes rolled up under his eyelids and his knees buckled. He would have collapsed onto the deck but Blue Peter slid a mighty arm around his shoulders to support him, then the other arm under his legs as he fell backwards and lifted the Captain and carried him like a baby down to the Great Cabin.

Blue Peter carefully laid the Captain into his hanging bunk and wrapped blankets around his shivering body. The Captain's eyes were open again but they seemed sightless, as though he stared into a different world. By the dim light of the single candle Blue Peter could see the Captain's lips moving soundlessly as though in prayer. Captain Sylvestre de Greybagges looked older, as though he had been gone several years and not three hours. From overhead came the tramping of feet on the deck as the frigate made sail, then the ship heeled as it caught the wind to flee from Nombre Dios Bay.

Blue Peter sat by the Captain all through that long night. Several times he tried to give the Captain water to drink, but it just dribbled out of his lips. The Captain said not a word, and his eyes still seemed to stare into some other place. As he watched the Captain's face Blue Peter became convinced, to his great unease, that the Captain had aged several years. His face was more lined, different somehow.

The worst horror, though, waited for dawn, for as the sun rose and clear light streamed through the tall stern windows into the Great Cabin he saw that the Captain's long beard was no longer the bright yellow of Spanish gold but had become *green*. As green as spring grass.

———

Blue Peter Ceteshwayoo nursed Captain Sylvestre de Greybagges with great tenderness as the *Ark de Triomphe* sailed dolorously back to Porte de Recailles, unburdened by silver ingots, its commander shocked into catatonia. On the second day he managed to get the Captain to eat. Bulbous Bill Bucephalus made a special burgoo, seething milk with a strip of cinnamon bark before pouring it onto the oatmeal, sweetening the burgoo with honey and a mashed roasted banana as it simmered. Blue Peter held the Captain with an arm round his shoulders and spooned the burgoo into his mouth as though he were a child. Bulbous Bill then made a medicinal grog. He put a double handful of camomile flowers, a handful of African rooibosch leaves and two teaspoons of poppyseed into a pot with water and set it to simmer. He melted a large lump of butter in another pot, waited for it to foam and added a cup of brown Demerara sugar, stirring it rapidly with a wooden spoon. He added the herb infusion to the caramelised sugar and butter a little at a time, straining it through a cloth and stirring continuously. Then he added rum, a very special dark rum that he had been keeping in his seaman's chest, a black syrupy rum of great strength that has only ever been drunk by pirates, and which has not been made since the time of Captain Flint. Blue Peter lifted the Captain and held a mug of the grog to his lips. The Captain drank the mugfull. Then another. Then a third, and then his tormented grey eyes closed at last and he slept.

Blue Peter sat by him through the night as he slept and dreamed. The Captain's slumbers were riven by nightmares and he ground his teeth and cried out. Once the Captain spoke in his sleep as though revisiting some scene from the past:

"Welcome, sir! Welcome to the Mansion of the Glaroon! The boy will park your skimmer, sir. Let me take your helmet and cape, sir. Follow the footman, sir, and he will lead you to the festivities. Welcome, sir! Welcome to the Mansion of the Glaroon! Why, Great Cthulu, sir! How pleasant to see you here again! And Mrs Cthulu, too! Why, you are looking in the pink, my lady! Or should I say green, har-har! And your daughter, too! Why, Miss Lulu Cthulu, you look lovelier each passing week, I do declare! Har-har! The Glaroon is in the Games Room, Mr Cthulu, sir, I am sure he will be delighted if you join him there. Welcome, sir! Welcome to the Mansion of the Glaroon! The boy will park your skimmer, sir ...." The Captain's voice trailed off into unintelligible mumbling.

How can this be? thought Blue Peter Ceteshwayoo. He has been away three hours and yet he has been away years. And he has known the pain and humiliation of slavery, too, which I would not have wished on his noble freedom-loving pirate's soul for all the silver in Spanish America. And his beard is turned green. Not dyed green, but *turned* green, for it is growing green out of his skin. How can these things be?

———————

The pirate frigate *Ark de Triomphe* was safe at last, moored to the quay of Porte de Recailles. Blue Peter Ceteshwayoo joined Bulbous Bill Bucephalus and Israel Feet in the officers' wardroom, where they were gloomily drinking rum.

"I believe he is on the mend," said Blue Peter. "He has slept now for three days, and the colour has come back to his face. He is no longer dreaming nightmares, but sleeps easily and restfully. I think we should leave him until he awakes of his own accord. Loomin' Len is sitting by him, and one of the bully-boys guards the door. It is best that the crew do not know that his beard has turned green just yet. They are naturally restive that a great fortune in silver has disappeared from before their eyes. Anything strange may cause mutiny. A Captain with a long yellow beard is one thing, a Captain with a long green beard is entirely another thing."

"Iffen it ain't the damnedest thing I ever did see," said Israel Feet, "an' iffen it ain't you may boil my arse in oil, you may. An' I will lay to that, else, messmates!" He took a drink of rum.

"Indeed, there is much about this whole affair that I find strange and unnatural," said Blue Peter. "I should have been wary when a medicine-man was involved. We have those fellows back in Africa, you know, and I wouldn't trust a one of them as far as I could throw him uphill. They are always talking to spirits and devils and suchlike, and that cannot be right, no matter which church you worship in."

"I don't think it were the *brujo*'s fault," said Bulbous Bill Bucephalus slowly. "I was asking some questions of the man Denzil, to try and get this straight." He sipped his rum. "I think it were more a problem of translation, like."

"How do you mean?" said Blue Peter, pursing his lips.

"Well, Denzil he reckoned he translated that indian lingo as best he could, and it were a crockery fleet, just like I said at first. T'weren't Spanish, either. Some other bunch I've never heard of. It wasn't the Spanish Plate Fleet," he sipped his rum again, "it was the Martian Saucer Fleet."

CHAPTER THE FOURTH,
or the Captain Has A Banyan Day.

Blue Peter Ceteshwayoo rode a Percheron mare down the winding path to Porte de Recailles. The plough-horse was quite old and he had bought it very cheaply, but it was big enough and still powerful enough to carry the weight of his huge frame with ease. A smaller horse would have been overloaded, and Blue Peter abhorred cruelty to animals. It was the early morning and the air was still cool and crisp, which was pleasing to both man and horse. The late-summer day would soon become bakingly hot as the sun rose high over the Caribbean island.

Nearly a year had passed since the beard of Captain Greybagges had been turned green by the horrors he had encountered in Nombre Dios Bay, and these months had been very good to the pirates of the frigate *Ark de Triomphe*. The disaster in Nombre Dios Bay – the sad failure to take the Spanish plate fleet, the mysterious greening of the Captain's beard – had seemed like a terrible portent, but the pirates had been extraordinarily lucky in the aftermath. Captain Greybagges's bright green beard had not made him an object of mockery, but had instead given him a fell and perilous aura of the supernatural. Ships that could easily have out-run or out-fought the *Ark de Triomphe* had hove-to at the first sight of Captain Sylvestre de Greybagges standing grim-faced on the quarterdeck, his sombre all-black clothes emphasizing the brilliant grass-green of his long beard. The mystery of how his beard had become green was now a legend across the Spanish Main, and he was feared in a way that no ordinary captain of buccaneers could emulate. The fortunes of the *Ark de Triomphe* had prospered accordingly.

The horse whickered and tossed its head, and Blue Peter patted its neck affectionately.

Blue Peter Ceteshwayoo had invested a small part of his treasure in a cottage high in the hills above Porte de Recailles. He spent time there when the frigate was in port, adding to his growing collection of books, improving his grasp of Greek and Latin. He even wrote poetry occasionally, seated at an inlaid oak escritoire by a window with a view down onto the smoking chimneys and the squalor of Porte de Recailles, over the forest of masts in the harbour and out over the clean blue of the sea. In a small way this satisfied his desire to be a gentleman; a true gentleman would surely have such a refuge in which to write and to study, away from the cares of the world. A true gentleman, thought Blue Peter, might also have a groom, so he wouldn't have to chase his own carthorse up and down the field himself, for the old mare had been frisky that morning. He patted its neck again.

The larger part of Blue Peter's treasure remained in the keeping of Captain Sylvestre de Greybagges, as did the bulk of the treasure of the rest of the *Ark de Triomphe's* crew. This was unusual, to say the least. Buccaneers were not by nature or experience trusting creatures, and would commonly demand that all plunder and loot be divvied up as soon as circumstances allowed. Captains of pirates who kept all the boodle, telling the crew with a wink "I'll keep this safe and sound fer yez, shipmates, and there's my affy-davy on that, wi' a curse!" were viewed with darkest suspicion, for amongst the brotherhood of pirates the Seven Deadly Sins were not unknown, and Greed was almost a celebrity.

But when Captain Greybagges had given each man only a portion of his share of the loot nobody had complained. The pay-outs had been substantial, it was true, but the Captain had not pretended that they were complete. Nor had he offered an explanation.

Blue Peter mused upon this as the old padnag plodded on down to Porte de Recailles in the cool morning air. There was no doubt that Captain Greybagges had been changed by his strange and unearthly experiences in Nombre Dios Bay, and not just in the colour of his long beard. The Captain had possessed a whimsical sense of humour and an almost boyish sense of mischief, but now he was grim and distant. In the times before the Captain's beard had been turned green he would not have been able to hold back treasure from an open division of the spoils under the strict rules of the Free Brotherhood of the Coasts. If he had tried then it was certain that a voice from the back of the assembled crew would have made a smart-alecky comment, Captain Greybagges would have made a witty rejoinder and so the reasons for keeping back the loot would have been teased out of him with good humour. But now the crew - and a crew of lusty pirates, too – accepted it without question or comment. It was very odd. The crew of the *Ark de Triomphe* were more disciplined, more efficient, under the cold grey eyes of this grim new Captain Sylvestre de Greybagges, but Blue Peter Ceteshwayoo found this unsettling. In truth, he feared for his friend.

Captain Greybagges was reading some very unusual books, too. The Captain was a literate man, and had always enjoyed reading a good rollicking yarn – Tobias Smollet was a favourite, or that hussy Aphra Behn (a *woman* writing books, what a disgrace!) – but lately the Captain had been nose-deep in Professor Newton's *Philosophiæ Naturalis Principia Mathematica*, Robert Hook's *Micrographica* and other such rum stuff. He had even been reading the works of the heretical monk Giordano Bruno, who had claimed in his *De l'Infinito, Universo e Mondi* that the stars in the night sky were suns like the sun of daytime, but very far away, and who had been burned at the stake for cherishing such offensive and blasphemous thoughts. Blue Peter recalled that the deranged monk had even suggested that those far-away suns could have planets like the Earth itself and that creatures might live on them, even races of intelligent beings. Blue Peter had seen many wonders since leaving Africa as a child, and learned many things in his extensive reading, but planets of strange beings orbiting distant stars? That was such a disturbing idea that he wasn't really surprised that the Inquisition had torched the monk. Why was the Captain delving into such arcane stuff?

Blue Peter's conscience prodded him; it was not just Captain Greybagges's loyal and thievish crew, *you* did not *yourself* object when he didn't share out the loot, it said. It is true, thought Blue Peter, but I felt that if I had, then I couldn't be sure if he'd burst out crying, shoot me, or curse me with the evil eye.

The old plough-horse plodded on down the path to Porte de Recailles, with a thoughtful Blue Peter Ceteshwayoo riding bareback upon it.

Two of the smart-alecky voices that might be heard from the back of any assembly of the crew of the *Ark de Triomphe* were conversing companionably, sitting on the cross-trees of the frigate's mainmast, high above the deck. Jemmy Ducks, keeper of the ship's ducks, chickens, pigs and goat, and Jack Nastyface, cook's assistant, both holding honorary job-titles in lieu of their real names, were skiving-off, and their idle discussion had been following the same path as Blue Peter's thoughts; what was the Captain doing with the loot?

"Ay-yoop! 'Tis the Blue Boy!" said Jemmy Ducks, "on his trusty charger."

"Where away, cuz? Where is the dark knight on his Arabian steed?" said Jack Nastyface, whose eyesight was poor.

"End o' quay. Just come round corner o' timberyard," said Jemmy Ducks, slithering from his perch onto the ratlines. The pair climbed down, warning the other foremast jacks of the Master Gunner's approach and bickering, Jemmy Ducks averring that Jack Nastyface's myopia was the result of onanistic practices, Jack Nastyface replying that he did indeed practice onanism but only once a day and only to spill his seed into Jemmy Duck's morning porridge.

Captain Sylvestre de Greybagges, sitting at his desk in the Great Cabin in the midst of a chaos of account-books and ledgers, heard the two still bickering as they went down the companionway, and heard his servant Mumblin' Jake mumble at them to shut up and not disturb the cap'n, look'ee. Blue Peter will be here presently, he thought, knowing that the livestock-keeper and the cook's assistant would not otherwise have ended their mid-morning smoke and yarn. He called to Mumblin' Jake to make fresh coffee.

Blue Peter knocked and entered the Great Cabin, followed by Mumblin' Jake with a tray bearing a steaming tin coffee-pot, mugs and a plate of biscuits. Jake set out the mugs and poured the coffee, placed the plate on the edge of the desk, and mumbled off to his lair in the Captain's pantry. Blue Peter sat down opposite Captain Greybagges, who smiled a grim smile at him in welcome, his grey eyes far-away.

"Let me finish with these damn' books, curse 'em. I'll be a whore's half-hour, no more. Here, read this while I figure." The Captain handed him a printed broadsheet, folded in the fashion of the stock-jobbers in crowded London coffee-houses to show only the article of interest. Blue Peter unfolded it to find the broadsheet's name; the *Tortuga Times*. He refolded the broadsheet, and glanced at the Captain, who was in his shirtsleeves, checking entries in the ledgers, clicking an abacus and writing, *scritch-scratch*, with a quill, his face impassive.

Blue Peter turned his attention back to the newspaper. The article was a poem. Blue Peter read it through with mounting amusement, having to choke back guffaws of laughter as it was so bad. He looked at the Captain, but the Captain's eyes were on the account-books, and his pen went *scritch-scratch*. Blue Peter could bear no more; he snapped the folded broadsheet to flatten it, cleared his throat and, in his deep voice, with an artful theatricality, read the poem out loud...

"CAPTAIN GREYBAGGES ALIAS 'GREEN BEARD'
by Mungo McGonagall.

Sylvestre de Greybagges came from Recailles, and sailed from that port
On board the good ship *Ark de Triomphe*, in search of sport,
As Captain, long had he held that station,
And for personal courage he had gained his crew's approbation.

'Twas in the spring, Captain Sylvestre de Greybagges sailed to Providence
In the continent of America, and no further hence;
And in their way captured a vessel laden with flour,
Which they put on board their own vessel in the space of an hour.

They also seized two other vessels and took some gallons of wine,
Besides plunder to a considerable value, and most of it most costly of design;
And after that they made a prize of a large French Guinea-man,
Then to act an independent part Captain Greybagges now began.

But the news spread throughout America, far and near,
And filled many of the inhabitants' hearts with fear;
But Lord Mondegreen with his sloops of war directly steered,
And left James River on the 17th November in quest of Green Beard,
And on the evening of the 21st came in sight of the pirate;
And when His Lordship spied Green Beard he felt himself elate.

When Green Beard saw the sloops sent to apprehend him,
He didn't lose his courage, but fiendishly did grin;
And told his men to cease from drinking and their tittle-tattle,
To see to their dags and cutlasses and prepare for a battle.

In case anything should happen to him during the engagement,
One of his men asked him, who felt rather discontent,
Whether anybody knew where he had buried his pelf,
When he impiously replied that nobody knew but the devil and himself.

The Captain Has A Banyan Day

In the morning Lord Mondegreen weighed and sent his boat to sound,
Which, coming near the pirate, unfortunately ran aground;
But Mondegreen lightened his vessel of the ballast and water,
Whilst from the pirates' ship small shot loudly did clatter.

But the pirates' small shot or slugs didn't Mondegreen appal,
He told his men to take their swords and be ready upon his call;
And to conceal themselves every man below,
While he would remain alone at the helm and face the foe.

Then Green Beard cried, 'They're all knocked on the head,'
When he saw no hand upon deck he thought they were dead;
Then Green Beard boarded Mondegreen 's sloop without dismay,
But Mondegreen 's men rushed upon deck, then began the deadly fray.

Then Green Beard and Lord Mondegreen engaged sword in hand,
And His Lordship fought manfully and made a bold stand;
And Green Beard's cutlass *clang*ed against the sword of Mondegreen,
Making the most desperate and bloody conflict that ever was seen.

At last with shots and wounds Mondegreen fell down in a swoon,
And his men thus dismayed laid down their pistols and spontoons,
Green Beard laughed grimly and marooned them all ashore,
And went back to Recailles to fritter his loot on rum and whores.

Green Beard derived his name from his long green beard,
Which terrified America more than any comet that had ever appeared;
But wicked pirates thank the Devil that in this age all be a'feared,
Of the mighty buccaneer who possesses the eldritch Green Beard!"

Blue Peter Ceteshwayoo, with magnificent fortitude, managed to read to the
end of the poem, but then could no longer keep control. He laughed until his eyes
ran tears and his ribs hurt, slapping the folded broadsheet on his thigh, wheezing

and whooping trying to catch a breath. Captain Greybagges had sat back in his captain's chair and was watching Blue Peter with a smile. As he watched the grimness slowly departed from his face and the smile grew wider, until he too was laughing, a great booming laugh. This continued for some minutes, as each time one would try to stop he would catch sight of the other and so fall again into helpless merriment.

"Oh, bugger!" said Captain Greybagges, wiping his eyes and shaking his head. He pulled the black silk scarf, knotted pirate-fashion, from his shaven pate and blew his nose on it, which triggered Blue Peter into a further fit of laughter. Blue Peter was a giant, and Captain Greybagges was not a small man, so their combined laughter was very loud. Up above, on the deck and in the rigging, the crew were frozen, exchanging startled glances, only continuing with their work as the gales of rumbling hilarity from below subsided to inaudible giggles.

Captain Greybagges wiped his eyes and blew his nose again on the now-sodden black scarf, and managed to curb his mirth enough to take sips of coffee. After a while Blue Peter did, too, hiccoughing and spilling some.

"Oh, God! I needed that!" said the Captain, "I have been very mumpish of late, I know."

"I was beginning to be concerned. Unremitting solemnity is unbecoming even in a preacher of Calvin's credo, let alone in a captain of buccaneers," said Blue Peter, dipping a biscuit in his coffee and eating it swiftly, before it disintegrated.

"You know, when I gave you that paper I had not the notion that the wretched doggerel was so amusing. I was merely going to comment upon how the plain facts of the matter were so sadly misrepresented," said the Captain, refilling his mug, and carefully selecting a biscuit from the plate.

"Yes, indeed. My Lord Mondegreen is a terrible buffoon, is he not? Do you think he paid that poet to write it? ... on second thoughts, no, let us please talk of other things, or I shall start again, and I feel that it would kill me."

"You are right. We cannot sit here chortling like tom-fools, yet I am deeply loath to lose this pleasant lightness of spirit..." Captain Greybagges drummed his fingers on the desk-top for a moment, then roared for Mumblin' Jake.

"Look'ee, Jake! Makes you me a picnic-hamper! A great fine picnic-hamper!"

"A picnic-hamper, Cap'n, sor?"

"A basket o' wittles for a shore-goin' party o' two hungry fellows. Bread - the soft tack and not the ship's biscuit, mind yez! - butter, cheese, cooked meats - if there be any left wholesome in this damned heat - boiled eggs, pickles, fruit, some bottles of beer, some sweetmeats. Tell Len to fill a water-bag from the pump on the quay. Put it all in the skiff. Smartly now, ye lazy hound!" Mumblin' Jake scuttled out of the door.

Captain Greybagges stood up, rubbed his hands together and started slamming the ledgers and account-books shut.

"Away, dull care!" he cried. "School is over! Out for the summer!" Blue Peter stared at him as he packed away the books, abacus, quills and inkpots, humming under his breath.

"He is a terrible ass, though, is Lord Mondegreen," said the Captain, musingly. "D'you remember him singing in that church in New Amsterdam? That Christmastide? Getting all the words of the hymns wrong? What a jackanapes!"

"Good King wants his applesauce, at the feast this eve-ning!" sang Blue Peter in a rumbling bass, grinning hugely, showing his filed teeth.

"Kept by thy tender care, Gladys the cross-eyed bear!" sang the Captain, in a light tenor. The two buccaneers struggled against a new attack of mirth.

The Captain rummaged around in a chest and found a ragged straw hat, which he clapped on his head. Another rummage in a cupboard produced a brown canvas bag. On a whim, he pushed back the desk and rolled up the rug and threw it over his shoulder.

"A banyan day for the captain!" he roared. "Come, let us picnic, shipmate!"

Captain Sylvestre de Greybagges rowed the skiff across Rum Bay with long easy strokes of the oars. He ran the skiff onto the beach below Sruudta Point. The two freebooters hauled it ashore by its gunwales, then tied the painter to a long iron spike tapped into the sand with the butt of an oar. The day was calm and sunny and the waves mere ripples, but good seamanship is good seamanship and cannot be gainsaid, even by the most temerarious of buccaneers.

"Har! Place you your trust in Allah, but tie your camel to a tree, as the Moors are wont to say," said the Captain. "Look! There is a capital spot!" He pointed to a knoll where the ground started to rise up before the tor on the point. They carried the things from the skiff. There were two stunted trees on the knoll,

Captain Greybagges unrolled the carpet on the coarse salt-grass and hung the canvas waterbag from a branch in the shade. A sailcloth fire-bucket, half-full of seawater, was hung from another branch as a beer-cooler, the basket was hung from yet another branch to preserve the food from ants.

"Not a sylvan glade, exactly, or even an Arcadian grove, but a small oasis or *caravanserai* at any rate, with a Turkish rug, too!" laughed Captain Greybagges. "Now, how about a game of cricket? Get an appetite for lunch, eh?"

"Cricket..." Blue Peter said softly, "I have long wished to play cricket. Surely it requires two teams of eleven men, though?"

"It does, but we shall play a practice game with made-up rules, as I did so often as a boy."

On a flat stretch of beach the Captain put down the brown canvas bag and undid its straps.

"Here, Peter, this is the club, or bat," he handed it to Blue Peter, "and here is a ball, and here are the stumps and bails. How much do you know of the game?"

"I have only read of it, so treat me as an ignoramus."

"Firstly, the pitch is twenty-two yards long between the wickets."

Captain Greybagges pushed three stumps into the sand and placed the two bails on top. He then counted twenty-two paces and put up the second wicket.

"The crease is a short step afore the wicket," he said, using a bare toe to scratch a line in the sand by each wicket, "and the batsman stands thus." He took the bat from Blue Peter and demonstrated. "The bat must stay touching the crease until the bowler starts his run. Opinions vary about this from cricket-club to cricket-club, but it is a good strategy anyway to cover the wicket, as the bowler is trying to knock it down." He gave the bat back to Blue Peter, who tried the batsman's stance, having to bend and crouch to touch the bat to the crease. "I will bowl the ball, but I will bowl it slowly. Don't hit it hard, not at first, get the feel of the bat and just prevent the ball from hitting the stumps, for if a bail falls off then you are out."

Captain Greybagges bowled slow balls to Blue Peter, then Blue Peter tried bowling slow balls to the the Captain. Occasionally the Captain would stop and explain a rule, or an aspect of the game-play. The *thwack* of the hard leather ball on the wooden bat was loud in the quiet of the beach, and echo'd faintly from the cliffs on the other side of Rum Bay.

"What-ho! I'm hungry," said the Captain, "Time to pull the stumps! How do you like it then, Peter? The game of cricket?"

"I am intrigued. I think I could become enamoured of it. The over-arm bowling is more tricky than it looks, especially when there are two pistols and a cutlass in one's belt. I wish to practice it more."

"One thing, Peter. When the game is finished the team captains must shake hands." He offered his hand to Blue Peter, who shook it solemnly. "I am ever pleased to shake hands with you, Peter, but you must remember that the captains must *always* shake hands. If the other team's captain were to be a blackguard, your worst enemy, had boasted in the pavilion of swiving your sister, has beaten your team by bare-faced cheating, and was grinning at you like an ape, then you must *still* put a good face upon it and shake hands. It is the finest of games, but it is still a game, and not something to fight duels over. That is its greatest value, perhaps."

They walked slowly back to the knoll, the Captain swinging the cricket-bag.

"Might I not kill the blackguard for abusing my sister *after* I have shaken his hand, Captain?"

"Why, of course! As long as it's not about the cricket, and doesn't inconvenience the cricket-club committee, then it would certainly be quite the right thing to do."

Seated on the rug, reclining in the shade, leaning comfortably against the trunks of the trees, they cut the waxed string from the necks of beer-bottles, eased the corks out carefully and poured the cold beer into glasses.

"Oh, my! That is good!" said Blue Peter, wiping the back of his hand across his mouth. "Captain, would you be good enough to pass me those crustaceans?" Mumblin' Jake's picnic-basket included a damp cloth full of boiled shrimps.

"Surely, Peter!" the Captain passed the shrimps and a pot of pepper relish, "but you may call me Sylvestre, or even Syl, as this is my banyan day." He took a bite of a sandwich of cold roast pork and mustard, then took a gulp of beer. The grim cast which had darkened his face for a year had faded, and he looked at ease. They ate in companionable silence for a while.

"I will speak freely, then, Sylvestre," said Blue Peter. "I suspect that you have a hidden purpose in this, your banyan day, and that you wish to converse with me without the possibility of eavesdropping, yet to conceal that purpose within an apparent madcap lark, to prevent invidious or far-fetched conjectures among the crew."

Captain Greybagges turned to look at Blue Peter.

"You should have been a lawyer, you scoundrel!" He took a draught of beer. "You are right, for the most part. The idea of the madcap lark came first, as I looked at those damn' ledgers, but I had been seeking such an opportunity anyway. Do not underestimate the roborative effects of a madcap lark, though. This day, my banyan day, has already taken a great weight from my oppressed spirits..."

The Captain would have continued, but Blue Peter raised his hand.

"Indeed, Captain ... Sylvestre ... I can see that. I can also sense that you are going to discuss affairs of great importance. May I give you advice? In the land of my birth such matters were discussed with due ceremony, and that usually involved an exchange of information and compliments; 'do your father's feet still stand firm upon the earth? and does the sun still shine upon your seemingly-endless maize fields? and does your mighty heart still encompass the love of ten wives?' That sort of thing. It's all nonsense, of course, but it seemed to work. Perhaps we should colloquise for a while longer, enjoy your banyan day a little longer," Blue Peter ate a shrimp and took a swallow of beer, "before plunging into matters profound and weighty."

"In England we are not so different," said the Captain, helping himself to a sausage. "In fact, there's a phrase; 'less of the old how's-yer-father' meaning 'stop trying to cozen me and get to the point.' As pretty maids are often the ones being cozened it has taken on the secondary meaning of amatory congress; a young lad from the Parish of Bow might say 'I'm a-goin' upta the ol' Bull and Bush for a bit o' how's-yer-father', meaning he would be going to the pub to find a lady of easy virtue. You are right, though, and I take your point. What do you wish to talk about?"

"Tell me about your boyhood, how you played cricket in sunlit carefree days."

"Cricket? Carefree sunlit days? I did indeed play cricket on the village green, up at school and up at Cambridge, too, and I do love *that* England dearly, it is true. To play a game of cricket, even to watch a game of cricket, to spend all of a lazy sunny summer day just watching cricket, that is a rare delight. Yet even in those happy memories there are dark shadows. I was packed off to Eton, and that damn' school nearly did for me. A brutal place where one is either the bully or the victim, take your choice. Cricket at Eton was *politics*, too, not the simple joy of a game on the village green."

The Captain picked up a biscuit, examined it critically, then ate it.

"My young boyhood was happy, mind you. My mother passed away when I was young, and I only remember her as a kind of a vision, but my nanny, Goosie, was the kindest and most good-humoured soul that ever walked the green earth. My father - 'the Pater', as they made us say at Eton - was a different creature altogether. The mean old bugger spent his entire life obsessing about his damn' estates, so he had nothing to talk about except the price of corn and the villainy of the yokels, and what the grasping old skinflint was thinking every waking minute was how to tighten further the screws on his field-hands and tenants. The money, some of it, went to making me a lawyer, because he wanted a shyster he needn't pay, so that he could make his neighbour's lives more miserable without spending his own money to do it. Eton, Cambridge, the Inns of Court ... and a damn' good lawyer I was, too! I could exonerate the guilty or convict the innocent, as required, and take my fat fee whether justice was served or not. Some cases, though gnawed at me, until it occurred to me that the fine people in their fine clothes were themselves no better than thieves, or indeed pirates. Worse, in fact, for a lusty freebooter wagers his own life, not the lives of others, and does his business honestly with the edge of his cutlass, not with secret whisperings in dark corners and dirty deals in back-rooms. It further occurred to me, after I had broken a cider-jar over my father's head and been disinherited, that piracy may be just as morally corrupt as the practice of the Law, but it is certainly much more fun. So here I am.

"We are pirates, Peter! The Free Brotherhood of the Coasts, for all its many faults, will take any buccaneer into its membership whether black, white, brown, yellow, red, or even," he waggled his beard, "partially green. Even women! And all are equal! To be a pirate is to be more free, more democratical, than even those ancient Greek coves in Athens knew of. We take people's money, and sometimes we have to kill them, but that's a small price to pay for freedom. If you ever go to England, Peter, go as a pirate and be proud of it. They will either hang you at Tyburn or make you Equerry Of The King's Chamberpot, it cannot be foretold which, but if you go as a would-be squire they will put you in a cage and charge gawpers a shilling to look at you, and half-a-crown to poke you with a stick."

"Sylvestre, you have crushed my dreams!" laughed Blue Peter. "Is there indeed a custodian of the royal pisspot?"

"Indeed there is. He is called the Chamberlain of the Stool, if I recollect a'right. It is a position of great influence and power. I dare say the fellow doesn't touch a po these days, that is merely the origin of the title. Such a fellow must have access to all the King's private apartments and all of his private affairs, and so must be loyal and trustworthy."

Captain Greybagges rose to get another bottle of beer from the bucket, and stretched lazily, looking out to sea, unable to resist scanning the horizon. He settled back down again, searching around for his knife to open the beer.

"Tell me of *your* boyhood, Peter, if you will."

Blue Peter took a swallow of beer, wiped his mouth and burped.

"Where I was born there was little distinction between summer and winter. There was the season of the rains, but it was still hot then, so one couldn't call it winter. Time was reckoned in lunar months, but I suppose I was about eight years old when I was given into slavery by my uncle, my mother's elder brother. I was what you would call the *heir apparent*. My father was the chief - the *sachem*, if you will - of the tribe and I was his only son. My mother and my father died, one after the other, and, after a period of mourning of thirteen months, I was to be made chief. My uncle, who was acting chief, *pro tempore*, took me to the sacred grove alone, as was the custom, said the sacred words and cut my cheeks with these marks." Blue Peter indicated the cicatrices on his face. "He rubbed ashes into them, then some fellows came along and he told me to go with them. I thought it was part of the ceremony, so I did."

He drank some beer.

"Good Lord!" said the Captain. "Do you believe that wicked man killed your parents?"

"I'm not sure. He may just have taken advantage of circumstance. He had a son the same age as myself, and alike to me in looks. I believe he may have cut his own son's cheeks, but savagely, to disguise him, and passed him off as me. Those that detected the substitution would pretend they hadn't, since my uncle had been chief for thirteen months and, presumably, had firmly seized the reins of command. I was young, of course, and my recollection is fragmentary, so these are mere suppositions."

"Why, then, did he cut your cheeks?" asked the Captain.

"So that I was unsuspecting of betrayal, and distracted by the pain of the cuts, most likely. Perhaps he was also afraid of the Gods; he had thus done his duty by custom, and had not killed me, other men had then taken me away, and I had gone willingly, so what befell me subsequently would be their evil-doing, not his."

"Men, and women, will often lie, as it is the natural thing to do. I have often observed this, and not only as a brief in the courts, I assure you," said Captain Greybagges. "Yet when a man begins to lie to *himself* each step he takes carries him further down the sloping path to Hell. You must loathe your uncle greatly."

"I do indeed, but that has taught me the futility of hatred. The forest grows quickly, trails and rivers change their course, villages move. I cannot even be sure which barracoon I was taken to, since they are all alike from inside a stockade of logs. There are no maps of the interior of the African continent, nor likely to be. Retracing my steps back to my homeland is impossible now; it is quite literally a lost kingdom. Strangely, when I was a slave I never met a single soul from my own land, or indeed any slave who even knew of my country, so I have not spoken my own tongue since, except to myself. I met some few who spoke *similar* languages, so that we could talk after a fashion, but never my own mother-tongue."

Blue Peter heaved himself up to get a bottle of beer. When he had made himself comfortable again against the tree, with a full glass in his hand, he continued.

"I will not speak of the barracoon, or of the sea-crossing on the slave-ship, as they are foul memories. I was bought by a family in Virginny, who, because of my scars and my size, thought it a fine jest to make me a page, and dress me in a little jacket and knee-britches of pink silk. This was a lucky thing for me, as a house-nigger I was not treated too brutally, and I was encouraged to learn a fine clear English and even to read and write. The plantation owner's younger brother taught me, and gave me some Latin and Greek, too, and some other learning. He was a drunk and a pederast, but I think he had a genuine affection for me. He never molested me, and my times learning under his often-bleary tutelage were some of the happiest I experienced as a slave. The family were great despisers of the English, thinking all Englishmen to be effete, pompous and sly, whilst counting themselves rugged pioneers, despite their life of luxury and idleness. I have few illusions about the English, Sylvestre, but if the likes of Master Chumbley and his vile wife hate them, then they are the fellows for me! The dislike of the English is becoming widespread in the colonies, and it will smoulder into flame one day, I feel sure. Not all Colonials are like the Chumbleys, of course. As you once said, 'the Colonials can be rare plucked-uns when they be a-riled-up', and indeed they can be, but in such a circumstance the Chumbleys would be hiding under their beds a-shivering and a-praying, not getting a-riled-up, the sanctimonious hypocritical sods.

"When I was fourteen I punched the son of the family on the nose, which he richly deserved, and they flogged me and then put me to work in the fields like a beast of burden. To my small surprise the other slaves despised me as a house-nigger, so I had to punch a few of them, too, and got flogged again for damaging the livestock. The years in the fields put muscle on me, so, after the last flogging, I was able to pull the ring-bolt from the wall and knock the overseer unconscious when he came a-calling. I would have dearly loved to have killed him, but that would have led to a larger hue-and-cry, so I took his keys and chained him up with my shackles and gagged him with his own socks. I went to free the other slaves but only one of them was game, a skinny old fellow of the Kroo tribe. The Kroo boast that they've never been slaves or owned slaves, so he had a point to make, I suppose. Strangely, the Chumbley's daughter, a skinny little madam who was always spying upon me, saw me and the Krooman sneaking away, but she only grinned and put her finger to her lips, childishly thinking us upon a mere lark, I suppose. We made our way to the Great Dismal Swamp and joined some other escaped slaves, *cimarroons*, who were living there. It was nearly as damn' *dismal* as slavery, that swamp, so I took off for New Amsterdam. The few glimpses I'd gotten of the ocean on the slave-ship had intrigued me, so I signed on as a sailor. After a couple of voyages before-the-mast, I met Bulbous Bill Bucephalus in a tavern in New Orleans, he was sailing with Jean Lafitte back then, and I became a pirate. So here I am."

"That is an extraordinary tale, Peter," said Captain Sylvestre de Greybagges, "I understand better your detestation of the slave-owners of Virginny. A little suit of pink silk! That is almost satanic in its cruelty!"

Blue Peter threw an apple core at him, and they both laughed, then lay against the trees in silence for a while, gazing at the sea and sipping their glasses of beer.

"It has been truly excellent to sprawl here, eating, drinking and yarning with you on my banyan day," said the Captain at last, "but I fear I must now darken the occasion with serious talk. As the Bard wrote 'I now unclasp a secret book, and, to your quick-conceiving discontent, read you matter deep and dangerous', and it is indeed deep and dangerous, what I have to say, so harken to me now!"

And Blue Peter turned to him, and listened.

Chapter the Fifth,
or The Captain Unclasps a Secret.

"Before I start my grim tale I must explain a couple of things," said Captain Sylvestre de Greybagges, "or you will be confused."

He scratched his belly and drank some beer.

"In your readings, Peter, you may have heard of the theory of Nicolaus Copernicus."

"From his book *De revolutionibus orbium coelestium*, or 'On the Revolutions of the Celestial Spheres'," said Blue Peter, "in which he coyly suggested that the Earth was not the centre of the Universe."

"Indeed, and he was right, and that cove Newton, whom I saw at Cambridge but never spoke to, put the whole thing square by identifying gravity - the force that makes the apple fall and the cannonball curve in its flight - with the force which holds the moons and planets on their courses," said the Captain. "Furthermore, you may have heard of the ideas of the Italian monk Giordano Bruno."

"I was thinking of him only this morning, and how I was not unduly surprised that the Congregation of the Holy Office of the Inquisition tied him to a stake and burned him, by way of a critical appraisal of his work."

"He was right," said the Captain.

"What? That the stars of the welkin are suns alike to our own sun?"

"Yes."

"And that planets may orbit them as our Earth orbits the sun?"

"Yes."

"And that creatures may inhabit those distant planets?"

"Yes."

"And that those creatures may be intelligent aware beings, such as we are?"

"Yes."

"*Ay caramba!* Be you serious? You seem very certain, how can you be sure of that?"

"Because, Peter, I have met some of them," said Captain Sylvestre de Greybagges.

Blue Peter was silent for some time, then he drained his glass of beer in one long swallow. The Captain stood up and looked in the sailcloth bucket.

"The last two beers," he said, handing Blue Peter a bottle. He settled his back against the tree-trunk again. "Now you are thinking that I am bereft of my wits, or else engaged in some kind of egregious spoof, or leg-pull. I am neither insane nor jesting, I assure you. You can see why I have kept this to myself for nearly a year."

Blue Peter poured his beer, a thoughtful expression on his face.

"Pray continue, Sylvestre. I shall reserve judgement for the meantime, although this tale is becoming a little rich to easily swallow."

"When I rowed around the point into Nombre Dios Bay a year ago, dressed all in black, with my face blackened, in a black boat with muffled oars, I believed myself invisible. I was not. As far as those extramundane creatures were concerned I might just as well have been in a Venetian carnival-gondola, strung with coloured paper lanterns, playing a bugle. They have a device to see in the dark. It sees heat instead of light, and our bodies are always warm. So they caught me, Peter, and I was enslaved.

"The *brujo* who spoke to Bill's pal spoke the truth; it was not the Spanish plate fleet, but the Martian saucer fleet. The extramundanes have ships which sail the empty voids between the stars as we sail our ships upon the oceans. They are called 'saucers' because they resemble a saucer if seen from below as they fly by in the air. They do not come from Mars - which is a bleak cold lifeless place of nothing but empty deserts, the air too thin to breathe - but they do use it as a base, as we use the island of Recailles. Thus the Martian saucer fleet."

"What do they look like, these extramundane creatures?" said Blue Peter slowly.

"I did not clap eyes upon the Glaroon at all - it was he who had captured me - He cannot breathe our air, and so resides mostly in a sealed chamber filled with the noxious air of his own home-world. His minions serve him and do his bidding, some human slaves such as I became, some extramundanes of various sorts, some of them slaves, too. One sort are small grey men with slanting black eyes. Another kind is alike to a toad-man, and very strong but not very clever. Another is alike to a lizard with six limbs; the front two being arms, the rearmost legs and the middle two somewhat in between. They are excellent mechanics, those lizard things, as they can work on an engine with four hands, sitting back on their rear legs and their tail. Their speech sounds like the chirm of birdsong, but some of them can mimic our tongues well enough to converse. They are congenial company, too, unlike the little grey buggers, who are so dreich that they could make a conventicle of Methodies seem like a beano in a bawdy-house."

"*Congenial company,* Sylvestre? Six-legged lizards *congenial company*? You stretch my credulity too far!"

"I only speak the truth. They are fond of an alcoholic drink, particularly beer; as spirits are too strong for their heads, unless watered. They enjoy a good yarn, well-told. They like to dance and cavort, although their music sounds strange to our ears. They do love a game of cards and are great gamblers. And great cheats, too! With four arms it is almost too easy for them to finesse a deck, d'you see? Actually, they are more alike to chameleons. They cannot change colour - they are a shade of greeny-blue - but they have those woogly eyes that can point in different directions, if you know what I mean."

The Captain demonstrated 'woogly eyes' by putting fingers in front of his eyes and waggling them around. Blue Peter got to his feet, walked slowly down to the beach, then ran up and down on the sand, shouting 'arrgh!' occasionally. He walked back to the knoll and sat down again against the tree.

"There is no more beer," said the Captain, "but here is rum." He poured a large shot into Blue Peter's glass. Blue Peter took a swallow, and grimaced.

"Captain, if the green of your beard did not tell me *something* strange had happened to you," he said, "I would have already shot you for trying to gull me with such a ludicrous account. I shall call you 'Captain' now as your banyan day must be over; if you have gone mad that is serious; if you speak truly that is surely even worse. Pray continue, but perhaps tell me how it is that you were away from the barky for three hours, yet seem to have been away for much longer, having had the time to socialise with six-legged reptiles?"

"Well, I said that I must explain a *couple* of things, but I got distracted," said the Captain. "The second thing is that time and distance are the same. Some extramundanes, such as the Glaroon, have found the way to travel in the void, in space, but that means also travelling in time, so they have mastered travel both in distance *and* time. From *your* point of view I was away for three hours, but from *my* point of view I was away for about three years. Don't ask me to explain it, as it is not yet completely clear to me, but it has to do with the speed of light not being infinite. It is very quick, but not instantaneous, and that has consequences, apparently. Time is often a fractured mirror, reflecting a bizarre image of reality."

Blue Peter emptied his glass in a single gulp, and refilled it from the rum-bottle.

"Now please explain about your beard, Captain," he said, "and how it was made green."

"It isn't my beard, is how," said the Captain. "Each filament of it is an extramundane creature, especially bred to replace the hairs of my beard. They draw sustenance from my body, and I can feel them as though they are strange nerves. The Glaroon had them put on me, as I was his butler. They are sensitive to certain emanations, and so could be used to call me, or to tell me things over a distance."

"I find that very disturbing. Does it hurt?"

"No. It was agony when they were growing into my face, replacing the hairs at their roots, but they don't hurt now. In fact, I am rather fond of them ... or It. I could not have escaped without the Beard. It talked to the library of the Glaroon's mansion on Mars, so to speak, and I was able to learn enough about saucers to navigate my way back through space and time to Nombre Dios Bay. The sun is setting. We must go back to the barky soon enough. Ask the question which is on your lips."

"The question on the lips of every crewman aboard the *Ark de Triomphe*," said Blue Peter, "and the one asked in the awful poem; 'whether anybody knew where he had buried his pelf'."

"Nowhere," said the Captain, "and yet everywhere. As the treasure came in I converted it to *financial instruments* - banker's draughts, letters of credit, stocks and shares - as fast as I ever could. You may remember that many of the prize cargoes were goods anyway - flour, wine, whale oil, saltpetre, mercury in greased goatskin bags, even a cargo of porcelain plates! - Eddie Teach would have insisted on payment in gold, if he could even be bothered to take and sell such merchandise, and would have taken a discount for so doing. I traded them instead for shares in cargoes-in-transit and the like until I could get the money safely berthed in a bank, or rather in several banks in several countries. I don't like the idea of burying a chest of gold on an island. It seems a little foolish, especially when one can get two-and-a-half percent at Coutts and the stock-market is booming. Don't tell the Free Brotherhood of the Coasts that I said that, mind you!"

"What are you going to do with the money?" Blue Peter said, pouring the last of the rum into his glass.

"The influential extramundanes are a mixed bunch, much like your Colonials, I suppose, Peter. There was one, Great Cthulhu, who is the ugliest bugger I ever did see. Alike to a big scaly daemon with the head of a squid, he is. Tentacles waving about like the Medusa's snakey hair. He was a half-decent old cove in some ways, though. Lent me a book by some mad old Arab, *Abdul al* something-or-other. I have a great dislike of the Glaroon, though, and a grudge, too. I was the Glaroon's butler, which was bearable for the most part, but slave-owners are all alike, d'you see? whether they be Colonials or extramundanes. When the Glaroon had parties, he'd put me out the front to greet the guests - 'Hello, sir! and welcome to the mansion of the Glaroon!' - dressed in a *little blue sailor suit*, and I intend to have my revenge for upon him that!

"I have spent much of the treasure on my plan to avenge myself, but there is plenty left. I have set up a pension fund for the crew, but don't tell anybody yet."

Captain Greybagges stood up, stretched, and started packing the picnic things.

"It is in my mind to tell the crew about the money soon, at a share-out meeting. I think they will be pleased with the arrangements that I have made - if I can get the wooden-headed sods to understand what I have done for them - and will consequently be easily enthused by my plan to punish the Glaroon, about which they need to know nothing just yet, not even that there is a plan. If my plan succeeds there will be more loot, more pelf, more boodle, more *treasure* than even Croesus himself ever dreamed of. Enough to make Morgan's raid on Panama seem mere apple-scrumping. I'll have to tell Izzie and Bill something of this business, too, but I think that must be slowly, as we go, lest they become ... unsettled. I welcome your advice on that; on what, how and how much to tell them and when, but sleep on it first, it's a lot for you to comprehend. Come on, let's go!"

Blue Peter was silent as they loaded the skiff and pushed it into the sea, small waves lapping around their bare feet.

"I'm sorry I've been obliged to tell you all this, Peter - ignorance is bliss, indeed! - but I need your help with this, your *involved* help. And who else could I tell first? I nearly told Bill once or twice, for the navigating has given him a fine head for the arithmetic and the geometry, so the time-and-space stuff might be easier for him. Izzie? He is my oldest shipmate, and before that my articled clerk when I was in chambers, but any notion of six-legged reptiles would drive him straight to the bottom of the nearest rum-bottle. You are the cleverest of us four, Peter, so it had to be you."

The Captain pulled the oars. Blue Peter remained silent for a while. The sun was setting against a mauve sky, its orange light dappling the ocean like a fiery path to the horizon.

"Captain," he said at last, "what are these lizard-creatures called?"

"Why, we called them 'lizards', or 'the lizard people', Peter."

"Do they have a name for themselves?"

"I'm sure they do, but I don't know it. Anyway, I can't do bird impressions."

They clambered up the side of the *Ark de Triomphe* in the quick-growing dark. The pirate crew had lit lanterns, casting yellow pools of light in the purple twilight. Some of the pirates were sprawled on the deck, or sitting on bollards or guns, eating their supper. They muttered 'good evenings' to the Captain and Blue Peter, intent on their beef-stew, bread and beer.

"Arr! *Bon appetit*, shipmates, wi' a curse!" answered the Captain.

The rest of the crew would be below, eating their meals between the cannons in the gundeck messes, on boards hung from the deckheads on ropes. When the wooden bowls were scraped clean with hunks of bread and cleared away greasy packs of cards would appear, and draughts-boards made of canvas squares, and sly rum-flasks would pass from hand to hand. Captain Greybagges could smell the aroma of the stew, the smoke from the cook's charcoal oven, tar, sweat, sawn timber; the frigate's reassuring fragrance. He turned to Blue Peter.

"A toddy, Master Gunner?"

"No, Captain. I find that I am weary, and you've given me much to think about. I shall go to my cottage."

"I shall set sail tomorrow, on the afternoon tide. We shall be away from Recailles for some months, so make arrangements for your horse. Good night, Peter." The Captain went down below to the Great Cabin in the stern.

Blue Peter Ceteshwayoo rode the old Percheron mare up the winding road away from Porte de Recailles, the sky now inky-blue above him, the moon yet to rise. The horse seemed to know its way in the dark, so Blue Peter let it plod, and mused as he rocked gently on its back, looking up at the bright stars. There is Venus, he thought. Are there strange creatures dwelling upon it? Or upon Orion's belt? All this is madness! Yet there is the indisputable fact of the Captain's green beard. His account is not without points of reference, either. There are tales of fellows spirited away to the Land of Faerie, returning years later, no older. There are tales of men and women aging overnight; one day young and hale, the next morning ancient, sere and white-haired, and sometimes babbling. The myths of the Greeks, also, full of monsters, 'tentacles waving about like the Medusa's snakes', as the Captain himself had said. Legends of flying chariots, too, and all kinds of supposedly-mythical beasts; daemons, hobgoblins, ogres, kobolds, fetches, lemures, dragons, wyverns, basilisks, yales, golems, bunyips and bugaboos ... The Captain's teratological narrative provided a possible basis for these fables, an exegesis of their provenance, at least...

The old horse, sensing Blue Peter's unease, skittered sideways a trifle. Blue Peter muttered soothingly and patted its neck.

His account squares with the things he muttered whilst comatose during the flight of the *Ark de Triomphe* from Nombre Dios Bay, thought Blue Peter, but that is no confirmation. If his wits were addled from his experience, as they undoubtedly were, then he may have entered a state of delusion, or fugue, and his memories would be false, experienced as in a dream yet recalled as though real ... I am a pirate, thought Blue Peter, yet I cannot find a curse-word strong enough to express my frustration and dismay with this. My instincts are at odds with my reason. Still worse, my reason is at odds with my reason, and my instincts at war with my instincts. He rode on up the hill in the darkness, towards his cottage, deep in thought, the bright stars twinkling above him.

Captain Sylvestre de Greybagges sat at his desk in the Great Cabin, an oil lamp spilling yellow light onto his ledgers and account-books. The abacus went *click-clack* and his goose-quill pen went *scritch-scratch* as he worked, a tankard of hot punch and a dish of sweet biscuits at his elbow. When he had finished the accounting and the letter-writing that he had interrupted earlier that day he closed the books and locked them away, rubbed his face with his hands, drained the tankard, changed into a black nightshirt and nightcap and went to bed in the hanging bunk, falling instantly into a deep and dreamless sleep.

Blue Peter's slumbers were racked by nightmares. A six-legged reptile with chameleon eyes cheated him at cards. A daemon with the head of a squid danced a quadrille with the Medusa. Saucers, cups, teapots, plates, chafing-dishes, tureens and porringers whizzed around his head, trailing sparks like thrown grenadoes. In the quiet of the small cottage he twisted and turned, sweating and moaning, the woven ropes of his charpoy-bed creaking.

He awoke late the following morning, the sun already high, feeling surprisingly clear-headed. He put sticks on the banked-in fire in the kitchen stove, blew on it carefully, and added charcoal when it sputtered back into flame. He filled a copper kettle from the well in the yard, set it upon the stove, then drew another bucket of cold water and washed, shaving with a Spanish blued-steel razor, a small mirror of polished silver placed upon the well-hoist. The kettle whistled in the cottage kitchen and he made coffee, setting the pot on the side of the stove to brew as he dressed. To his very slight surprise, he found that he had dressed himself for battle; loose red cotton shirt, brown moleskin breeches, a green coat with japanned buttons, a sash of multicoloured silk, grey hose and comfortable well-worn buckled shoes with hob-nailed soles. He found that his decision was made; whatever scheme Captain Greybagges was planning he must support it. If the Captain was right, then he would need all the help he could get, but if the Captain was deluded then only as a confederate, as a close confidante and as a friend would he be able to prevent disaster for the Captain, for himself and for the ship and crew. His way lay clear before him, if not exactly obstacle-free. He drank a mug of coffee, then slid the cutlass with the knuckle-duster grip into his sash, and then the cannon-barrelled horse-pistol and the elegant Kentucky pistol. He packed his things into a rectangular wooden sea-chest and a canvas sack, tied them together with rope and slung them over the horse's hind-quarters. He shuttered and locked the cottage and hid the key in the outhouse, clapped a brown tricorne hat on his head and mounted the old Percheron mare, using the stone horse-trough as a step, and rode away from his cottage without a backward glance.

At a neighbour's farm he stopped and, after a little negotiation and the passing of a silver thaler, obtained an agreement that a weather-eye would be kept upon his cottage and that the Percheron mare would be collected from the yard of

Ye Halfe-Cannonballe tavern and looked after until his return. Blue Peter considered his neighbour a shifty fellow, but reckoned that the generous payment, his size, his profession and a second or so of eye-contact accompanied by a grin of his filed teeth would be sufficient to prevent curiosity about the contents of his dwelling-place or mistreatment of his horse, unless it became apparent that he would not be returning.

"Ay-oop! The Blue Boy cometh!" said Jemmy Ducks, "and he has girded himself for war!" He swung himself from the mainmast top onto the rat-lines by the futtock-shrouds. His friend Jack Nastyface followed through the lubber-hole.

"War? What?" he said, as they clambered down.

"He be wearing the old green coat," said Jemmy Ducks.

"Now you are an authority on gentlemen's attire," said Jack Nastyface. "Why are you yourself such a ragamuffin, then?"

"Green coat he wears so's he don't get powder-burns on his finery," explained Jemmy Ducks, patiently, "thou mutt. 'Tis on the cards that we be sailin' on t'afternoon ebb."

They reached the deck and went below as Blue Peter strode up the gang-plank.

———————

"Now, listen, shipmates!" said Captain Sylvestre de Greybagges in a strong clear voice.

The pirate crew of the *Ark de Triomphe* were assembled in the waist of the frigate, or seated on the convenient lower yard of the mainmast. Captain Greybagges paced the quarterdeck, dressed in his full pirate-captain's rig; black tricorne hat upon a black scarf, black *justaucorps* coat with jet buttons and turned-back cuffs, black breeches, black sea-boots and a thick black leather belt with an assortment of weapons thrust into it. His long grass-green beard was resplendent in the rays of the low sun.

"You may be a-wonderin' why I have dropped anchor here, we havin' only just sailed from port two hours since," the Captain said, "but this anchorage do seem to me to be a fine spot, har-har! It be sheltered. It be quiet. It be a fine spot for a share-out meeting, be it not, shipmates?"

A ripple of interest stirred the buccaneers. Conversations stopped. Jack Nastyface desisted from poking Jemmy Ducks in the ribs. Jemmy Ducks ceased kicking Jack Nastyface in the shins. The cook's head emerged from the starboard companionway, where he could hear and yet watch his pots.

"The rules for a share-out according to the Free Brotherhood of the Coasts sez that it must be in gold, silver, coinage or articles o' rare worth, an' nought else besides," bellowed the Captain, "an' also that oppurtoonity - *reasonable* oppurtoonity - be allowed for the crew to bury their shares on a island or upon a remote shore. I am not going to abide by them rules, curse 'em!"

A rumble of discontent came from the crew. Oaths were muttered.

"You old robber! Trying to do us up very brown!" came a voice from the back of the crew.

"'Pon my soul, Jack Nastyface, I shall do *thyself* up browner than a Manx kipper iffen thou wilst not shut up! Now listen to me, shipmates!" The Captain pounded on the quarterdeck rail with his fist. "This will not be a share-out under the damn' rules, but a share-out it still will be! Listen to me, and you may find yourselves damn' pleased with your portions! Firstly, damn' yez, you must *listen* to how I have arranged things. Iffen it *bain't* be to your likings, then you may scrag me and feed me to the sharks, an' damn' yez all to hell! Wi' a wannion! But firstly yez-all must *listen*!"

He is mad, thought Blue Peter, standing behind Captain Greybagges on the quarterdeck. The crew had not actually been grumbling, as they had already gotten some of the treasure, at least. Now he offers them more, and then takes it away again. Is he stark mad? He stole a glance at Bulbous Bill Bucephalus, who looked impassive. The crew of angry pirates were talking, shouting, jostling. Blue Peter noticed his own gun-crews looking at him, not at the Captain. I must look fully confident, he thought, they must not think that I am not with him in this. He squared his massive shoulders, smiled a small confident smile and fixed his gaze on the Captain's lips. He found that he could not understand what the Captain was saying. The effort of seeming serene set off his own doubts about the Captain, and his inner conflict prevented him from following a single word. You chose your path this morning, he thought, and now your resolution is tested. The hubbub amongst the crew lessened slightly, and Blue Peter caught a snatch of the Captain's speech:

"... the Stock Market bain't be any wise differing from a fish market, which you all do know of. Shut up and *listen*, you cursed lubbers! The one be sellin' shares in ventures an' the other be sellin' fish, but they be the same in their *principles*, look'ee! The price o' fish depends upon the supply an' the supply o' fish depends upon the price, d'yez see? Not many fish, up goes the cost o' a fish supper, har-har! Iffen the price o' fish is high, then more cobles, smacks and busses goes to sea and more fish be caught, an' the price do come down. Shut *up*, yez scurvy dogs! Fish be a commodity, d'yez see? 'Tis the same with shares in ventures, 'cept yez cannot see, smell or touch what yez be buying or selling. O' course, that may seem addled 'til I tells yez that ... "

The crew of furacious matelots were becoming less restive, and hanging onto the Captain's words. Blue Peter felt a slight sense of reprieve. The pirates were no longer jostling and calling out. They were listening, some with expressions of knot-browed concentration and open mouths, it was true, but listening nevertheless. The Captain was still talking:

"... coz I was buying into cargoes-in-transit, d'yez see, I was bettin' on a race that was already run! I am a captain o' buccaneers, so's I knows which cargoes were most likely to get safe to port! So's I was gamblin' the loot, surely enough, but gamblin' with loaded dice! Any of yez think perhaps that I should not have done such a terrible *wicked* thing? Har-har! I did not think yez would! And that's not all, shipmates ..."

The crew were paying attention now, and Captain Greybagges shouted down the companionway:

"Bring it up, Chips!"

The ship's carpenter, Jesus-is-my-saviour Chippendale, and the First Mate, Israel Feet, carried an easel and a chalkboard up onto the quarterdeck and set it by the Captain.

"I must be yez schoolmaster! A *pedagogue*! Har-har! My old black hat shall be my mortar-board, 'pon my soul! Now listen yez to where I hid the treasure, har-har! Yez'll have heard o' banks, shipmates, but here's a few notions about banks that may not have struck yez, look'ee ..."

The Captain spoke on, scrawling diagrams on the chalkboard, tapping them with the chalk to emphasize this or that. The crew were now looking slightly stunned. He is talking for his life, Blue Peter thought, if they think he is doing them down they *will* feed him to the sharks. Why is he risking that? He could have kept them quiet with an occasional handful of *moidores* or *columnarios*, and a few vague promises. That is what Morgan or Teach would have done. Indeed, it is accepted that captains of buccaneers are venal and slippery, that's why they have the crew's respect ... The Captain was scribbling on the chalkboard again:

"Har! *Fungible*! I do loves that word, shipmates!" he tapped the chalk on the board, "for, d'yez sees, *fungible* means *transferrable*, and that do mean that it can go anywhere, like the angel of the Lord that girdled the Earth, hah-har! Consider the fish-market. Iffen yez has a ton o' fish here, then it be the same as a ton o' fish there, providin' all else be equal, so yez don't needs to send a ton of fish if yer can transfer ownership, and then it be *fungible*, d'ye see? Iffen the one ton of fish *there* were old and stinky, then it would not be *fungible*, would it? Not being the same for purposes o' trade, d'yez sees? That be the problem with fish, o' course, it do stink arter a few short days, then it be not *fungible*, it be *olfactible*, har-har-har! But there be things that do not stink arter a few short days. 'Like what?' sez ye. I could say iron, but then iron do rust, not in days, mebbe, but surely with years. Copper? Copper do not rust, so it do stay *fungible*, but it ain't worth a vast amount. Now yez sees where I be headed! Gold! Gold be the most *fungible* of all things. Iffen yer takes an ounce o' gold and puts it in a bank, then yez goes back later an' takes it out again it do not matter if it is not the same ounce of gold, only if it be the same weight and the same fineness, and yez can test gold easily with yer teeth, as yez all knows, or on a touchstone. Ah! Gold! Yez all loves gold, but yez forgets that it is *fungible*, so yez do! A chest o' gold buried on a distant isle has not lost its *value*, but it has lost its *fungibility* as ye cannot spend it. The only way to return the fungibility is to have a *treasure map* - har-har-har, that perked summa yez up! - but that be just a piece o' paper, an' who knows iffen it tells the truth? A note upon a bank, d'yez see, to be *paid* in gold, is better than a treasure map. It still be a piece o' paper, but the gold is more likely to be real. And the chest is not buried on an island, no, shipmates, it is as though that chest o' gold was buried right under yer feet and followed yez around, always right under yer feet, *fungible* d'ye see? Nice and handy when yer needs it, but nicely out of sight when yez do not."

Blue Peter observed that roughly one third of the crew were intent upon the Captain's words, brows furrowed. Another third were paying attention, but looked a little bewildered. The final third seemed to be in a waking coma, their mouths open, their eyes wandering.

"So when I gives each o' yez a letter such as this," Captain Greybagges held up a square of paper, "yez must regard it as a treasure map! And it is a treasure map, for it will take yez to the offices o' the Bank o' International Export - my bank, *your* bank, *our* bank, which we all *owns* - where yez will find two hundred and fifty golden guineas held there in yer very own personal account. Yer very own little treasure chest under yer very own feet at all times. Now what does yez think of that?"

There was a rumble of approval from the crew. A *low* rumble of *qualified* approval, but nevertheless a rumble.

"Now iffen yez is daft when ye does that, yer will draw out the whole nut and get robbed in the first tavern or bawdy-house that yer sees, and my wise words to yez this day will have been wasted. If yez is smart yer will take out enough for a shant and some fun, enough to buy yer missus or yer tart a new dress, enough to put shoes on yer sister's weans, even, but leave the rest under yer feet for the next day, an' the day arter that. That'd be the sharp way, shipmates."

The Captain folded his arms and beamed at them for a few seconds.

"Now, shipmates, I'll be giving yez these papers in the Port o' London, and any of yuz that wishes to shake hands and bid goodbye to the buccaneering life may do so then, an' I will buys yer a drink afore yer goes an' no hard feelin's. Some of yez will wish to sign up for another cruise, an' yer may do that, too, but until then we are finished with freebooting. From now on we are a innocent Dutch armed merchantman, so's we can travel *incognito*, and we will disguise the good old *Ark de Triomphe* tomorrow, whilst in this pleasant anchorage. Then we shall leave, firstly for the port o' Gabes, and then on to London. Now gets yer rations and fills yer bellies, for yez will have heard enough o' my yammerin's, and there is hard work to do on the morrow!"

"Well, they took that better than I thought they would," said Blue Peter quietly. He, Bulbous Bill Bucephalus and Israel Feet were sitting in the wardroom, eating ham-and-egg pie and drinking small beer.

"T'were a fine speech, it were," said Bulbous Bill in his high squeaky voice. "When Cap'n spoke a' compound interest an' leveraging - why! - I ain't never reely thought-a it like that afore, I have'nt. It do make a person ponder..."

"Yer can rip out me liver iffen I follered even the one word, dammee, yer can," said Israel Hands, munching on pie, crumbs spraying. "The Cap'n do speechify nice as kiss-yer-hand, mind yez, and damn me for a lubber, else! An' two hunnert an' fifty guineas be even nicer, har-har!"

"If yer'd bin a-listening," said Bill, "then yer'd know yer be gettin' eight shares. That be two *fahsand* guineas. Same as me an' Peter, you bein' First Mate, an' all."

The First Mate continued chewing for a second, then his face went red and he choked. Blue Peter reached across and slapped him on the back. His huge hand nearly knocked the scrawny First Mate from his chair, and lumps of pork, egg and pastry were expelled from his mouth like buckshot. Blue Peter went to to slap Israel Feet on the back once more, but he raised his hand and shook his head, coughing and spluttering, his thin face red. He recovered somewhat and took a drink of ale.

"Two thousand guineas!" he whispered, the piratical slang leached from his language by sheer surprise, leaving a soft Dorset accent. "Why, that be enough to buy a baronetcy!" He continued coughing.

"Ho-ho! Or a bishop's mitre, belike to ole Lance, eh? D'yuz recall the cully? Archbishop o' York he now be, don't 'ee," chuckled Bulbous Bill, his chins and jowls wobbling.

"You jest!" spluttered Israel Feet.

"No, Izzie, he speaks the truth, perhaps," rumbled Blue Peter, smiling. "Lancelot Blackburne - the *very reverend* Lancelot Blackburne - was the chaplain to a small fleet of privateering ships in the Caribbean, and some say that he himself turned pirate in a discreet way, but I don't know the truth of that. He is, however, presently the Archbishop of York, and there is talk that he bought his mitre from debonair King Charles with looted gold. We met him once or twice down in Jamaica. He can be pleasant company, but he has a wicked sharp tongue when he is in drink. He is a learned cove, too. Fond of quoting Waller."

Blue Peter took a draught of ale to clear his throat, and declaimed:

"Such game, while yet the world was new,
   The mighty Nimrod did pursue;
   What huntsman of our feeble race
   Or dogs dare such a monster chase?"

The last lines reminded Blue Peter of the Captain's tale. *He is chasing a monster*, he thought, *one way or another. Is he sufficiently a mighty Nimrod, though? Another thought struck him; if he is mad, then he is mad like a fox. He bored the crew into acquiescence, and I believe he meant to. He dared them to mutiny, then he stunned them with words, then he gave them a bag of gold, and a bag of gold dependent upon his goodwill, at that. The cleverer members of the crew will be too busy trying to explain the meanings of* negotiable instrument *and* assignat *to the slower crewmen to stir up any discontent. That is what they are doing right now, I am sure.*

"Two thousand guineas! Archbishop o' York, wi' a curse!" muttered Israel Feet, becoming piratical again as he mastered his surprise.

"I got summat that might be just the thing for a night-cap," said Bill, getting up from his settle. While he was away from the wardroom Blue Peter and Israel Feet sat in silence, thinking of two thousand guineas. From the galley came the sound of voices, Bulbous Bill's squeaky tones among them, then the sound of a slap, and a shriek. Bill returned to the wardroom with a tray.

"Cap'n 'as decreed that all shall get at least a single share, even the young 'uns. Jack Nastyface were overcome by the thought o' that gold, got so giddy I had to give him a slap," said Bulbous Bill complacently. "He be alright now, mind." He passed out porcelain mugs. They drank.

"What on earth is this?" said Blue Peter, his eyebrows raised. "I have never tasted the like, yet it is exceedingly good!"

"Denzil got it from one o' his indian pals," said Bill. "Them's little beans. Yer a-roasts 'em, then yer grinds 'em to powder, then yer chucks 'em into boiling water and stirs like buggery. Bit o' sugar. Bit o' cream. It be called *chocolatl*, in the indian lingo."

They sipped from their mugs.

"This has been a day of wonders, it has, an yer may skewer me with a marlinspike, else!" said the First Mate.

The *Ark de Triomphe* cut cleanly through the ocean. The wind was brisk, slightly gusting, on the larboard beam, and the sea was choppy. The frigate was making eight knots on the log, and the sun was shining.

"It itches a trifle, is the only thing," said Captain Sylvestre de Greybagges, pacing the quarter deck.

"Even in the bright day it is impossible to tell," said Blue Peter Ceteshwayoo. "Even where the boot-polish has been rubbed off slightly. The glint of green just looks like a trick of the light." He examined the captain's newly-brown beard critically. "No, it is very convincing. Fine rig, too!"

Captain Greybagges was dressed in the powder-blue uniform of a *kapitein van schip* in the Dutch East India Company, with gold epaulettes and frogging, and a bicorne hat with gilt edging. Blue Peter was wearing the more-sober blue uniform of a *luitenant*, Bulbous Bill the black-and-tan broadcloth of a *bootsman* as he stood at the wheel. The crew were in VOC *matrozenpak* slops, the red and grey *wijde jurk en broek*.

"Where did you obtain such an abundance of apparel?" asked Blue Peter.

"From the *Vereenigde Oost-Indische Compagnie* itself," said the Captain. "Slight seconds and part-worn. Bid on them at auction in Rotterdam, through an agent."

"You speak the language well. I have no Dutch myself."

"I was a year in Den Haag as a lawyer. The Dutch are the great masters of the law. The French think that they are, but they are just Creation's greatest wranglers, which is why they have so many skilled in the arithmetic, the geometry and the algebra. The Dutch realise that the law is the work of men, and so can be challenged and altered, which is how the the *Republiek der Zeven Verenigde Provinciën* - the United Provinces - can function perfectly well without a king. The French have *le Roi Soleil*, who believes that he is king by the grace of God, so there the law is perceived as an illuminating light shining from Louis' bumhole. If anybody challenges the law in France then soldiers are billeted upon them until they recant of their heresy, such a punishment is called a *dragonnade*."

"Because it is alike to having a dragon in one's house, I presume?"

"It may well be, but it is so-named because the soldiers are dragoons."

"They are indeed a rough bunch of fellows, by reputation."

"They are. Louis is not worried about the peasants rebelling - they are too starved to fight - nor the aristocrats - they are too few - but the middle people, the *bourgeois*, could be trouble, the merchants, artisans, tradespeople. If he billeted the common soldiery on such a fellow that would be seen as terrible, and the aristos might think 'will it next be us?'. If he billeted cavalry they would not gleefully hump the fellow's wife and daughters, having a dozen mistresses already, and they would not drink his cellar dry because it would not contain a single bottle of vintage *Montrachet*, probably they would instead contract the fellow to make them a suite of dining-room furniture. So it is the dragoons he sends; the townspeople can pretend they are civilised like the cavalry, and turn their faces away, yet they behave as cruelly as reivers."

"Stupid men will often believe that their spite is cleverness," said Blue Peter.

"Louis is indeed a stupid man. Soon his idiot's pride will bring all Europe to war."

They stood against the taffrail in silence for a while, watching the sails snap and vibrate in the wind, and the red-and-grey-clad foremast jacks in the rigging trimming them.

"Tell me, Captain," said Blue Peter, "when did you buy the Dutch clothes?"

"Oh, about four months ago," said Captain Sylvestre de Greybagges, smiling.

Insane, deluded, or not, thought Blue Peter, his plan has been deeply laid. Where is he taking us, on his monster-chase?

Chapter the Sixth,
or A Close Shave.

"As we are a-pretendin' to be nice peaceable Dutch persons," bellowed Captain Sylvestre de Greybagges, "it behooves yuz to learn yerselves a few words o' the lingo." He tapped the blackboard. "First word, o' course, be 'please', because we are polite Dutch persons, and that word is *alstublieft*, which is short for *als het U belieft*, meanin' 'if it you pleases '. Now you say it ... ***alstublieft***."

The crew, assembled in the waist and in the rigging, mumbled '*alstublieft*' as best they could. There was little wind, and the sails hung, flapping occasionally when a stray cat's-paw of breeze caught them.

"Pay attention, shipmates," bellowed the Captain. "We are in the Gulf of Gabes, an' so we are in the waters o' the corsairs of Barbary, who are a parcel o' nasty buggers, and no mistake. Pirates they may be - and indeed they pays fees to use the ports o' the Spanish main - but they are *not* members o' the Free Brotherhood o' the Coasts, curse 'em, and they would surely take us prize as soon as look at us. Iffen they did that they would sell us all at the slave-market and we'd spend the rest o' our miserable lives pulling the oar of a galley."

The Captain paused for breath, and to run his cold grey eyes over the faces of the buccaneers.

"However, I knows that the admiral o' the Algerine fleet, Suleyman Reis, is actually a Dutchman, name of Salomo de Veenboer!"

There was a mutter of surprise from the crew.

"Strange, ain't it, mateys?" said the Captain, "but it be true. He was taken into slavery himself, but worked his way up through cunning and brutality, an' now he's the *donanma komutani*, which is to say admiral o' the fleet. He has recently squeezed the Dutch East India Company into givin' him much gold to let their ships be, an' some say he do yearn to go home, to the country o' his birth, and wishes to be seen in a favourable light, and so we be pretendin' to be Hollanders to take advantage o' his present benevolence to them. All this'll be for naught if yuz cannot learn yerselves a few words o' the lingo. Think o' the galley-oar iffen yuz finds yer minds wandering, and how many times ye has to pull it every day! Now says it again, you lubbers!"

"***Alstublieft!***" roared the crew.

"The next word is 'thankyou', or 'thank'ee', which is *dank U wel* or *bedankt* ..."

This notion of the Captain's to bludgeon the crew into obedience with words works wondrously well, thought Blue Peter Ceshwayoo, but I pray that he does not over-use it. If he ever intends to give them lectures in the appreciation of water-colours I shall try and stop him. The sun was hot on his neck, and the still air oppressive, the sky a blue bowl from horizon to horizon. The Captain was still bellowing.

" ... the Dutch for 'no' is *nee*, or *neen* in some parts. 'Yes' is *ja*. After me ..."

There was a shout from the mainmast top. Blue Peter was jerked from a reverie about a plump Dutch lady he had once seen in a painting. The look-out at the main-top was pointing.

"Lesson over!" roared the Captain. "Do *any* of yuz lubbers speak any Dutch at all?" A few hands went up. "Yer must stay on deck, then. Enough crew in the rigging to trim sail iffen the wind stiffens, the rest o' yuz below. Cutlasses and guns ready. Cannon loaded and primed, but not run out. And be as quiet as little mice below, d'yuz hear me? As quiet as little mice!"

"Do you intend adopting Lord Mondegreen's stratagem of concealing the crew below decks?" said Blue Peter.

"Well, I do have the advantage that *my* crew will come up when I call them," said the Captain, "but I would rather convince any corsairs that we are a Dutch ship, and so not their prey. Peter, go and attend to your guns, then come back on deck. Your great size and fine uniform may impress them if we parley."

"I have no Dutch, Captain."

"Well then, look shy and mumble. I must go up and see for myself." The Captain strode from the quarterdeck and jumped up onto the ratlines. Blue Peter was briefly obstructed by the ship's carpenter wrestling the blackboard and easel down the companionway before he could get to the gundeck. The gun-crews were already loading and ramming the cannons, the gun-locks were out of their wooden boxes and fixed to the touch-holes, while the rest of the crew armed themselves in silence broken only by muttered curses and the clink of metal.

When Blue Peter returned on deck Captain Greybagges was climbing down from the shrouds.

"It is Algerines, blast 'em. A galley. With no wind we cannot even bring the guns to bear. If I launch a longboat to swing her round, then we don't look much like a peaceable Dutch ship that has its protection paid for. I shall have to brazen it out, Peter, unless a wind comes."

No wind came, and the galley came closer, until Blue Peter could see the massed corsairs on its deck and the glint of the bright sun on their scimitars and breastplates. The oars of the galley moved as one, like the wings of a bird, as it manoevred to approach the frigate from the prow, out of the line of fire of her broadside guns. There is something odd about those Algerines, thought Blue Peter, but I cannot place what it is exactly.

When the galley bumped gently into the becalmed frigate, its low rakish silhouette sliding easily under the bowsprit, corsairs clambered over the forepeak rail and flooded onto the ship. Captain Greybagges, Blue Peter and Bulbous Bill stood on the quarterdeck. An enormous corsair bearing a huge *tulwar* and a ferocious grin led the boarding-party up the steps to the quarterdeck and stood before them. They have no beards, thought Blue Peter, that is what is odd. They have turbans, curved scimitars and baggy pants, but they are all clean-shaven.

"Goed middag, heeren! Hoe ik u kan helpen?" said Captain Greybagges affably.

"Spraak-je '*Scheveningen*!'" commanded the huge corsair, waving his *tulwar* menacingly.

"Wat? *Scheveningen*! Potverdomme! Bent-jou gek?" said the Captain, with surprise.

"Hie zijn en Engelsman!" said a voice, and a pale blue-eyed man stepped from behind the huge corsair.

"Hah! A cursed Englishman!" roared the corsair, waggling the *tulwar*. "Dank U wel, Jan!"

"Ik bent en Nederlander, zeker!" protested the Captain.

"Hah! Nobody but a true Hollander can pronounce the word *Scheveningen* correctly! You are caught, cursed Englishman!" the huge corsair laughed. "Did you think our mighty admiral Suleyman Reis is such a fool? He gives me his own quartermaster," - the blue-eyed man bowed - "to unmask such pitiful impostures. The Dutch East India Company have paid their *tarifa*, but you have not! Now *you* will pay, ho-ho-ho!"

"You speak English remarkably well," said the Captain.

"Hah! You think compliments will make me look upon you more kindly!" sneered the corsair captain. "How little you know! My father had an English slave whom he trusted, and the fellow swore that English schools were the best in the world, and so I was sent up to your cursed Eton College. Five years of hell! Drinking! Brutality! Endless dreary sermons! Foul food! Vile infidel depravities! I have loathed the filthy English ever since. You will find no mercy in me, Englishman!"

"Good Lord!" exclaimed the Captain, "I remember you! You were one of the warts who came up to school in my final year! You fagged for Stinky Bodfish!"

"*Bismallah!* I remember you, too ... Greybagges, that is your name ... you clean-bowled the foul cretin Bodfish out for no runs in the House matches, third ball of his first over, middle stump with a wicked slow bouncer! That will not help you! I laughed at the vile Stinky Bodfish when you did that, and he beat me cruelly with a leather slipper, the infidel fiend!"

"He was always a bully and a sneak, that Stinky Bodfish," said the Captain, shaking his head. "Always creeping around and peaching to the beaks."

"But wait!" said the corsair captain, "the Greybagges chap at school had fair yellow hair, and yet you have a brown beard!"

"Merely part of the imposture," said the Captain. He pulled a black handkerchief from his sleeve and rubbed carefully at his long beard. "There, green, can you see? I am not only the Greybagges who took Bodfish's wicket, I am also Greenbeard the pirate."

"*Bismillah ir-Rahman ir-Rahim!*" said the corsair, lowering his huge *tulwar*, looking at the beard with awe. "This is a sad day! The buccaneering exploits of the fearsome Greenbeard are known even here - even as the name of *Abu Karim Muhammad al-Jamil ibn Nidal ibn Abdulaziz al-Berberi* is known in your neck of the woods, I dare say - and that was indeed a wonderful ball you bowled that day! I remember it now! There was so much spin on it that a little puff of dust went out sideways where it bounced and jinked behind foul Stinky's bat ... so I would dearly love to have swopped tales with you over a glass of *serbet* or two, but my thirty-nine pirates and I have sworn a solemn oath to be the greatest thieves on land or sea until all infidels are driven from ... from ... well, from just about everywhere, actually. It's that kind of oath, it goes on a bit, you know? Until then we will not grow our beards, either. We follow the teachings of our mullah, Ali."

The corsairs parted, and a man stepped forward as if summoned by those words. He was small and wiry-looking, and his orange turban was the size of a prize-winning pumpkin. His shaven chin was as brown as mahogany, his nose was a blade like an eagle's beak and his eyes were as mad and yellow as a chicken's.

"I am Ali!" he spoke in a light musical voice, red light glinted from the large ruby that he wore on his orange turban. "Too many infidels infest the world! We shall sweep the infidels from the seas, and from the lakes, and from the rivers, and from the ... and from all the rest of the places. Thieving is not thieving if it is from infidels! So we are thieves gladly! We have sworn not to grow beards until the task is done! I, Ali the Barber, have sworn an even mightier oath! I have sworn ..."

He brought out an enormous cutthroat razor and opened it. It was as big as a scimitar.

"I have sworn that I shall shave every man who does not shave himself! I have sworn a mighty oath that it shall be so! So take your choice, captain of dogs, shall you shave yourself, or shall I, Ali the Barber, shave you?"

I have a pistol in my belt, thought Blue Peter, but my coat is buttoned over it. Can I wrench my coat open, ripping off the buttons, and get to the pistol before the big fellow splits me in twain with his *tulwar*? The tension in the hot air seemed suddenly to fizz and crackle. Out of the corner of his eye Blue Peter saw Captain Greybagges's green beard, still with a few patches of brown boot-polish upon it, wave slightly and shiver as though stirred by a breeze. Yet there was no breeze, he thought, and the hairs on the back of his neck lifted.

"You should be very careful before making such terrible oaths," said Captain Greybagges evenly. "Oaths which you cannot possibly keep."

"I shall keep this oath! I have sworn so! Your beard will be shaved one way or another!" hissed Ali the Barber, waving the enormous razor from side to side, glints of light sliding along its honed edge.

"That is not what I meant," said the Captain. "You swore that you would shave the beard of every man who did not shave himself, did you not?"

"I did! I, Ali the Barber, swore that! And it shall be so!"

"But who shaves you, Ali the Barber?" said the Captain, smiling reasonably.

"I shave myself, of course, you infidel fool!"

"But your oath, your mighty unbreakable oath, was that you would shave every man who *doesn't* shave himself, so how did you shave yourself without breaking the oath?" said the Captain, still smiling reasonably.

"I, Ali, ..." The mad yellow eyes under the orange turban crossed slightly in thought. The thirty-nine corsairs and the corsair captain looked at each other in consternation.

"That's ... that's nothing but a mere quibble!" shouted Ali at last.

"No, it is not," said the Captain. "You have broken your oath! Your mighty oath is broken and meaningless! You swore that you would shave every man who *did not* shave himself, then you shaved *yourself* and made your mighty oath into a lie!"

"I, Ali, do *not* shave myself. I get my servant to do it! I forgot that!"

"But then," said the Captain, again smiling reasonably, "you *should* have shaved yourself, because you swore to shave every man who did not shave himself, did you not?"

"I, Ali, ..." the yellow eyes were now *very* crossed in frantic thought.

The captain of corsairs was looking down at Ali the Barber appraisingly, his lips pursed and his brow furrowed in thought.

"Captain Greybagges would seem to have the right of this," he said slowly. "Ali, you have misled us, I fear ..."

"Are you sure you would not like a glass of fruit juice, Abu?" asked the Captain. He and the captain of the corsairs were seated comfortably in the Great Cabin, in the shade, by the open stern-windows.

"No, Captain Greybagges," said the big corsair, "a glass of cool beer will be perfect. Anyway, I find I am disillusioned with oaths and pledges just now. Call me Muhammed, if you will. *Abu* is more of a courtesy title, meaning 'father'."

"By all means, Muhammed. Please call me Sylvestre. We are no longer up at Eton, thank God, and need not use our sire-names."

There was a high-pitched shriek from the deck above, followed by a rumble of laughter.

"What are your men doing to the fellow?" asked the Captain, pouring beer carefully into his tilted glass.

"They are shaving his ... his *body hair* with his own razor," said the corsair, leaving the last drops of beer in the bottle so as not to disturb the yeast-lees at the bottom. "Mmm, this is good ale! I haven't drunk its like since I left England. Your fellows are watching, and giving encouragement and advice. When they have had their fun I shall find an oar for him to pull. I dislike being made to look a fool."

"Ali the Barber speaks English very well," said the Captain.

"Winchester College," said the corsair.

"A Wykehamist! Why am I not surprised?" said the Captain.

"Yes, indeed! As some wise cove once said; 'You can always tell a Wykehamist, but you can't tell him anything much'." Muhammed al-Berberi, the captain of corsairs, sipped his beer and smiled the wolfish smile of a Barbary pirate, his teeth white against his sunburned face.

In the gloom of the gundeck Blue Peter was facing a minor mutiny, his gun-crews wished to go on deck and view Ali the Barber's humiliation.

"Gun-crews never see anything! It goes with the job, you know that, you lubbers! There's nothing to see through a gun-port except the side of another ship and clouds of smoke! Anyway, you've seen a fellow getting his nadgers shaved before. We do it to somebody every time we cross the Equator, don't we?"

In the end Blue Peter allowed the youngest gunners and the powder-monkeys to go on deck, but the remaining crew must stow the gun-locks, stopper the touch-holes with spiles and the bores with greased tompions, lash down the guns and sweep and water the deck first. Thorvald Coalbiter, a Dane from the Faeroe Islands, master of the starboard number-three gun *Tordener*, was still aggrieved, as he had wished to see the giant razor. Blue Peter made safe the powder-magazine, locked the copper-sheathed door then took the lantern from its glazed box on the magazine bulkhead and blew it out. He went on deck. The freshly-shaven Ali was being manhandled over the rail into the galley. The corsairs and the pirates were socialising warily, and bartering Ali's clothes and possessions. A corsair was washing suds and hairs from the giant razor in a bucket. He wiped it dry, oiled it and put it in a velvet-lined box. Blue Peter had a thought.

"Ali the Barber will not be needing that anymore, I think," he said to the corsair. The corsair had no English, so Blue Peter repeated it in Swahili, and was answered with a nod. After some negotiation Blue Peter acquired the huge razor for five *gulden* and a bottle of rum, the corsair insisting that the rum was not for drinking, but as liniment for his *baridi yabisi*. Blue Peter had not heard the words before, but the corsair's mimed pain suggested rheumatism. Yes, indeed, thought Blue Peter, liniment to be applied from the inside, but kept a straight face. The corsair stashed the coins in a fold of his sash and the bottle in his baggy shirt.

Blue Peter showed the razor to Thorvald Coalbiter.

"I have never seen one as big as that," said Thorvald wonderingly. "The engraving is very pretty, isn't it?"

The rectangular blade of the razor was as long as Blue Peter's forearm and as wide as his hand. The black-filled etching on the silver-steel blade showed a hunting scene in rolling countryside, the huntsmen and hounds in the middle distance with sly reynard in the foreground. The other side of the blade was etched with a pattern of curlicues and whorls around the words:

William Occam
fine cutlery
Sheffield, England.

"I think it must have been made to go in a shop window," said Blue Peter, "as an advertisement of the cutler's skill. It will make a good keepsake for the Captain, and we can use it for the next line-crossing merriments. Neptune's court will have some fun with it, I feel sure."

Blue Peter folded the blade back into the ebony-and-silver handle and put the razor back in its box.

" and the Pipsqueak, what of that little devil?" asked Captain Greybagges.

"Ho! Billy Pitt! The fellow acquired a taste for old port wine and got gout! Only fifteen and he got gout!" said Muhammed, shaking his head.

"He always was an adventurous little scallywag." The Captain sipped his beer. "Indeed! Pluck of a lion. Crafty as a fox, too. He was forever reading

Demosthenes in Greek, looking for tips. The *Philippics* mainly, as I recall."

There was a knock on the door, and Bulbous Bill entered with the blue-eyed corsair. Bill's meaty hand rested on the Hollander's shoulder in a friendly way, but the corsair looked rattled nonetheless.

"I thought I'd bring *myneer* Janszoon down here, Cap'n. The crew was miffed he tricked you, like, and wished to shave him, too," fluted Bill.

"Sit you down, mister Janszoon! That was indeed a wily ploy! *Scheveningen!*" the Captain chuckled. "A shibboleth, 'pon my word, and I am caught alike to an Ephraimite! Does it indeed work for all who are not Dutch?"

"*Ja, kapitein,* even for Germans, who are by us in speech." The Dutchman grinned uneasily.

"I do love a subtle stratagem!" said the Captain. "Do not quake so! We captains of buccaneers do not bear grudges! We do not have the time for 'em, we be too busy killin' people! Har-har! ... Jake! Bring some Hollands *jenever* for the quartermaster of Suleyman Reis!"

The Dutchman did not look entirely reassured, and downed the gin in one gulp.

"The wind do seem to be stiffening, too, Cap'n," said Bulbous Bill.

"Get the jacks back up the masts, then, Bill," said the Captain.

"In that case I shall go to my ship," said Muhammed al-Berberi, "but I will escort you into the port of Sfax myself, if you will permit me, and please consider my house to be your house for as long as you shall stay."

They went up on deck. Bulbous Bill started shouting orders to the foremast jacks. Jan Janszoon stayed warily close to the corsair captain.

"What do you seek in Sfax, Sylvestre?" the corsair captain asked. "I do not wish to appear inquisitive, but perhaps I may be able to aid you."

"I wish to ransom a fellow from slavery. A Mr Frank Benjamin," the Captain said.

The captain of corsairs nodded, then went to board his galley. The Dutch corsair hung back for a moment.

"The false name of your disguised ship, '*Groot Ombeschaamheid,*' is chosen well, *kapitein.*" The Dutchman smiled, then ran to catch up with Muhammed al-Berberi.

The wind was playful; gusting airs and small calms. The frigate would lead for a time, then the breeze would wane, its sails would flap, and the galley would pull ahead. As the ships passed the crews would shout cat-calls, and Captain Sylvestre de Greybagges and Muhammed al-Berberi exchanged friendly insults from their quarterdecks.

"If it were not for the slaves a galley would be a fine vessel," said the Captain admiringly. "They do indeed resemble a large bird in slow flight, as the ancient Greek coves used to say."

"The Greek triremes of old had hand-picked crews of volunteers," said Blue Peter. "If Thucydides wrote truly, then they could top eleven knots, and keep that up for a whole day and a night. The port of Piraeus to the island of Melos in twenty-four hours."

"I ain't fussed 'bout that Ali the Barber a-pulling on an oar, the tom-fool," piped Bulbous Bill, keeping an eye on the sails.

"Indeed, he was a *klootzak*," chuckled the Captain, "and now he has a shaved *klootzak*, har-har-har!" He saw his friends' incomprehension. "It means both 'idiot' and 'clot-bag' in Dutch, d'you see?"

"Blood and bones! They bain't be funny iffen yez has ta spell 'em out, Cap'n, and damn me for a lubber, else!" said Israel Feet.

"Arr! Izzie, an' thou art a *klootzak*, too! Get yerself about readyin' the barky to anchor, there be a smudge o' land on the horizon."

The pirate frigate *Ark de Triomphe*, masquerading as *VOC schip Groot Ombeschaamheid*, lay at anchor off the port of Sfax. The sun was setting behind the low hills and the first stars twinkled in the deep-blue sky. Captain Greybagges had changed into his customary all-black clothes and wrapped his long green beard in a black scarf, only his face and hands showed clearly in the twilight.

"Hear me, yez lubbers! We be havin' the goodwill of *one* Barbary pirate, mateys, but there be more than one, so I will keeps yuz gussied-up as Dutchmen whilst we be in these waters, and yez shall keep a sharp look-out, too. The Master Gunner has not drawn the charges from the guns, and yez will surely have espyed that we be not in the inner harbour, drawn up at the quay alike to a pie on a window-ledge, so yez can see that I be not a trustin' sort of cully. Yez'll be not missin' much by not goin' ashore, as there be no drink there, which being why they corsairs was so eager to buy your'n. If any little boats comes yuz must point muskets at 'em, not buy dates from 'em. I must go to parley with Muhammed al-Berberi. Keeps yer eyes peeled!"

Captain Greybagges waited while Loomin' Len Lummocks and the crew of bully-boys lowered a keg of beer into the longboat, then clambered down the side of the ship. There was a splash of oars and the longboat rowed away to Sfax. Blue Peter, leaning on the quarterdeck taffrail, watched them go. In the gathering gloom he could just make out the longboat tying up at the harbour wall, the bully-boys passing up the keg, then the darkness became too profound.

The Master Gunner, the sailing-master and the First Mate were sitting at a folding table on the foredeck drinking *chocolatl* and playing Puff-and-Honours with a deck of greasy dog-eared cards when Captain Sylvstre de Greybagges returned. The first bell of the middle watch had just struck, a muffled *bong* as the clapper was muffled with a rag; half past midnight a low whistle from the mainmast look-out told them a boat was approaching, then two whistles told them it was the Captain's longboat. Captain Greybagges joined them at the card-table and unwrapped the black cloth from his green beard. Mumblin' Jake brought him a mug of *chocolatl*. He laced it with a splash of rum and stirred it.

"Jake, gives Len and his bully-boys a mug o' this, and a double tot o' rum, when they has stowed the longboat."

The Captain took off his belt and black coat and rolled up his shirt-sleeves, placing his cutlass and pistols within easy reach.

"Shall I deals yer a hand, Cap'n?" said Bulbous Bill, shuffling the pack.

"Nay, Bill. I shall be for me bunk arter I sits awhile." Captain Greybagges yawned, slapped at a mosquito. "Muhammed al-Berberi is a fine gentleman, but still a slaver at heart, I fear. He wished to purchase the ship's carpenter from me."

"Har-har! Hello, sailor! Wi' a curse!" chuckled Israel Feet.

"No, I do not believe he is of that persuasion, else he could o' gotten Mr Chippendale for a bunch o' flowers an' a shy smile," said the Captain. "He cannot see a pair o' mighty arms an' wide shoulders alike to Chips and not wish to see 'em chained to an oar, is what. To see a man as though he were a horse be a failin', I finds, especially these days. When I were a brief I would have sold him, an' laughed as I spent the money, but a man changes as he do age, he do indeed." The Captain shook his head. "Muhammed is fine company, mind yez, he is fond o' an ale and he has a great love o' cricket, so I cannot find it in my heart to mislike him at all."

"Cricket be damned," said Bulbous Bill, dealing cards. "Did you sees any o' them hareem ladies, wif the baggy pants o' gauze and them curly-toes shoes, Cap'n?"

"Not a one. The only fellas allowed into the hareem be eunuchs, o' course, so's I thought it best not to pry. We was mostly talkin' business, anyways." The Captain drained his mug. "I be for me bunk. Keep look-outs posted, an' check that they be awake. Goodnight to yuz."

Captain Greybagges awoke suddenly, for no reason it seemed, a little before the change to the morning watch. Half-past three, by the *pings* of his repeater, he replaced the Breguet on the night-stand. A sense of unease prevented him from sleeping again. He got out of the hanging bunk, buckled his belt over his black nightshirt, slid two pistols into it then grabbed his cutlass and another pistol. As he went up the companionway he reached down and tapped on Blue Peter's cabin door with the tip of the cutlass.

He padded swiftly up the steps. In the dim glow of the stern-lantern he saw Israel Feet laying face-down on the quarterdeck, a figure in dark clothes crouched over him, preparing to hit him again with a club. Captain Greybagges shot him in the head, and he fell down. Other dark figures swarmed the decks. Captain Greybagges threw down the discharged pistol and ran down the steps from the quarterdeck, roaring, brandishing his cutlass and grappling at his belt for another pistol. Behind him came the sound of bare feet slapping the deck and Blue Peter joined him, armed to the teeth. They both fired pistols into the silent crowd; there was a cry, and also a *clang*, and a ricochetting ball whirred past the Captain's ear. They charged at the dark-clad men, and there was a brief melee, then their opponents seemed to vanish over the side of the ship like rats. The pirate crew of the *Ark de Triomphe* suddenly erupted from hatches carrying lanterns, muskets, pikes and cutlasses.

"Quiet, you lubbers!" roared Captain Greybagges. The crew were quiet.

From the dark there was the faint sploshing of muffled oars. The Captain pointed.

"There! Fire!" he said, raising a pistol. There was a crackle of musketry, and several shouts and a *clang* from the dark.

"Cease fire! They be too far now."

On the quarterdeck Bulbous Bill Bucephalus was crouched over Israel Feet. He carefully turned him onto his side. The First Mate's eyes were shut, and there was a dribble of blood on the deck.

"He breathes. I better get him below," said the sailing-master, "it be too dark to see up here."

He picked the unconscious First Mate up in his arms, and carried him gently, resting on his substantial stomach, down the quarterdeck steps.

"Where is the fellow I shot?" asked the Captain. "I shot him in the head."

"Those fellows were wearing black turbans over steel helmets, I think," said Blue Peter. "You may have only stunned him."

"If I had shot the sod with your long-barrelled Kentucky pistol, Peter, he would be laying there still."

"Indeed, it is a lucky gun." Blue Peter handed the pistol to the Captain and pointed. There was a bright silver gouge deep into the blue'd metal of the lock. "One of those fellows ducked down, and came up at me from below with a rapier. The gun was in my sash, and it struck and caught on the lock-plate."

"A lucky gun, indeed!" said the Captain, turning it in his hands.

"When the fellow lunged he looked up at my face to see my moment of death, the dog, and I saw his blue eyes. It was Jan Janszoom."

The Captain was quiet for a while.

"Jan Janszoom van Haarlem, also known as Murat Reis," he said. "That makes sense. I won Muhammed al-Berberi's goodwill today - or yesterday, rather - but Janszoom will not be well pleased, nor will his master Suleyman Reis. If he wishes to be Salomo de Veenboer once more, and have his morning *jenever* and coffee on Warmoesstraat, then he will not appreciate us wicked buccaneers masquerading as Dutchmen on his patch. It complicates matters. Also, I wish to ransom Frank Benjamin from him. If this little caper had succeeded he would have Mr Benjamin *and* the ransom *and* my ship *and* my crew *and* me as well, to ask politely why I wanted Mr Benjamin in the first instance. I should have seen this coming."

"Should we raise anchor and leave, then?"

The Captain was again lost in thought for a while.

"No. They will not try again. The Barbery corsairs are not a navy, they are pirates alike to us. Admiral of the fleet or not, *myneer* Veenboer cannot antagonise his captains willy-nilly, and Muhammed has had me as a guest in his home - an invited guest, too - so he will lose face by this. If it had succeeded it would be a *fait accompli*, and Muhammed would have been obliged to keep still about it, but it did not succeed, so Veenboer will pretend he knew nothing of it, and will ransom Mr Benjamin tomorrow - sorry, today - as agreed. Poor Mr Benjamin will be roughed-up, I am sure, to find out if he knows why I want him, but he does not know why, so he cannot tell them. The ransom is substantial, though, so they will not do Mr Benjamin any permanent harm, I hope."

"Why *do* you want Mr Benjamin, Captain?" said Blue Peter.

Captain Greybagges winked and tapped his nose with a forefinger.

"I can only answer such questions when I have myself a banyan day, and I shall need one soon enough, I feel. Double the watches until we leave this place. I'm going to try and get another couple of hours of shut-eye. Tomorrow may be a trying day."

Blue Peter slept no more that night, and frankly admired the Captain's ability to do so. Israel Feet was still unconscious, a wound to the back of his head where he had been clubbed, but Bill said he could feel no bones moving in the skull and that both the pupils of his eyes were the same size.

"Where did you learn the surgeon's arts?" Blue Peter asked him.

"Boxing ring," said Bill. "The other three are not so bad. Lumps on their heads like goose-eggs, mind yer. The main-top look-out had come down from the mast, the stupid bugger, to wait for the end o' his watch, so they were all four on deck, and they came over the side real quiet and quick, all dressed in black wif they faces a-blacked-up, and a-clobbered 'em. Lucky the Captain heard something. They musta been wearing black breastplates, too, coz I heard the musket-balls bounce offen 'em, but I didn't see no glim."

"Old Spanish trick," said Blue Peter. "The breastplate is warmed over coals and pitch melted and smeared on to it. It can be done quickly, if a night attack is needed. Unless they were lacquered, of course, but that would make them hot in the sun of the broad day."

The sun of the broad day rose, and Captain Sylvestre de Greybagges awoke. Mumblin' Jake shaved his head, mumbling that maybe he should use that big razor, har-har! Then made coffee as the Captain dressed in black and armed himself.

"How is Izzie?" he asked, when Bulbous Bill and Blue Peter joined him for breakfast.

"Still out cold, but he be a-mutterin' and a-movin' a little. Others just have headaches and lumps, like." Bill attended to his bacon and eggs.

Captain Greybagges finished his plate, spread butter and marmalade on toast and poured himself another mug of coffee.

"Bill, I wishes you to bring the barky closer inshore, now it is daylight, so that Blue Peter's guns can cover the piece of flat ground next to the harbour wall. I will make the exchange there, not bringing the ransom on-shore until they produce Mr Benjamin in reasonable condition. Peter, load grape, chain and musket-balls. If there is any funny business and I am killed - for I have no mind to pull a galley-oar - then you must sweep the ground clear and make your escape as best you can. I hope the threat will be enough, though. When Mr Benjamin will be brought I do not know, but the later the better, as I intend to sail immediately he is aboard, and the closer to dusk that is, the happier I will be. A pursuit, even with galleys, is more trying in the dark, and the wind then will be strong from the shore. When I am ashore you must keep a watch on me with spy-glasses, at least two at all times, but do not neglect to keep a sharp look-out to seaward. Perhaps last night's caper will keep the crew a little more on their toes today. Who came down from the mast early from look-out?"

"Jemmy Ducks, Cap'n," sighed Bill.

"I will have to punish him, you know," said the Captain, "but do not scare him to death before I do that. A lump on the head and the ill-will of the rest of the crew are nearly punishment enough, perhaps, and he is young, so I will not be unduly harsh."

Blue Peter and Bulbous Bill watched the longboat as it went to the harbour wall, Blue Peter peering through a long Dolland spy-glass. Captain Greybagges clambered up onto the quay followed by Loomin' Len and four of the bully-boys. Two stayed in the longboat, cutlasses across their knees and pistols in their hands and their belts. Through the spy-glass Blue Peter could see the Captain clearly, but the field of view was narrow.

"Here comes Muhammed," said Bill.

Blue Peter shifted the spy-glass a trifle.

"*Caramba!* What a beautiful horse!"

Blue Peter watched as Muhammed al-Berberi rode to the Captain on a magnificent black horse. Four mounted corsairs in bright breastplates and white turbans followed him, but he waved them away, swung down from the horse before it had stopped, and strode to the Captain his arms held wide to show he was unarmed. The bully-boys were not impressed and moved to cover Captain Greybagges, but the Captain gestured to them and stepped forward to meet the corsair captain.

"Damn! Here's trouble!" squeaked Bill.

Blue Peter scanned with the spy-glass; a group of corsairs coming onto the open ground. He moved his view back to Muhammed; the corsair captain was shouting and pointing. He looked at the corsair party again; they were spreading out to occupy the ground, some with long matchlock *jezails*, some with scimitars, a squad with pikes were poking them into the scrubby bushes, the mounted corsairs were scouting the edges of the ground.

"I think it is alright, Bill. I think Muhammed is protecting our Captain." Blue Peter felt a sharp sense of relief, but he continued scanning with the spy-glass. He risks his life and pays much gold, thought Blue Peter, to get this fellow, and I do not know why. I have more confidence in him now, but I am still perturbed by his tale of monsters. The Captain slapped Muhammed on the back and clambered back into the longboat, leaving two bully-boys on the quay. The longboat came back to the ship. Captain Greybagges climbed aboard.

"Well!" he said, "I was right. Muhammed was affronted, and intends to prevent further capers. He says that Suleyman Reis smoothly denies all knowledge, and that Mr Benjamin will be brought along presently. He exacted a price, though, for his friendship. He wishes to play a game of cricket, corsairs against pirates, for a wager."

"What is the wager?" asked Blue Peter.

"A ha'penny. One half of an English penny. Peter, would you like to be captain? I feel it would be bad form for me to do it."

"Well, yes, I suppose I could..."

"Excellent! Go and pick another nine men. Volunteers, but I will give each man a sovereign if we win."

A bewildered Blue Peter went below, to find a cricket team.

"Bill, I will have to leave you in charge," said the Captain.

"S'alright Cap'n. I be more of a boxin', wrestlin' and racin' man, meself, like. I do like a bet, yer sees, but cricket be too long to wait for a result."

"The situation seems to have eased somewhat, and Muhammed seems to be my ally, but do still keep a very sharp look-out."

Captain Greybagges went below and came up with his cricket-bag, wearing his old straw hat. The longboat ferried the cricket team ashore in two journeys. Bulbous Bill Bucephalus watched, occasionally peering through the spy-glass, the pirate crew watched from the cross-yards.

What a tedious game cricket is, thought Bulbous Bill, but the lads do look fine in their grey trousers, red shirts and straw hats, and here is Muhammed al-Berberi's team, all in blue with orange turbans, they must be picked from his thirty-nine thieves. He peered through the spy-glass; yes, they are clean-shaven, but some with stubble today. But what is this? Jan Janszoom is with them, the dog! I am surprised he has showed his face. Why! He must be the captain of the corsair team; he and Blue Peter are tossing a coin.

The pirates went to bat, the corsairs spreading out as fielders. The *clack* of bat hitting ball was muted by distance, but still audible. Bill noticed that the noise came almost a second after the impact, and, brows furrowed, calculated an approximation of the velocity of sound; a little over six hundred knots, a prodigious and unimaginable speed. The morning passed. There was one alarm from the maintop when sails were seen on the horizon, but it was just a felucca. In the late morning Bill passed the spy-glass to one of the steersmen and went on a tour of the ship. All was in order, the gun-deck temporarily under the eye of

Torvald Coalbiter, the cannon loaded, primed and laid to cover the ground. Bill returned to the quarterdeck.

On shore the game was at half-time. Muhammed al-Berberi's men had erected a marquee, and the teams were having refreshments. I should have liked to taste them sherbets, thought Bill, they say they are very tasty, especially with the sun high and hot, as it is. He peered through the spy-glass; the Captain and Muhammed were conversing, Captain Greybagges miming a stroke with a cricket-bat.

Play resumed with the corsairs in to bat. The afternoon wore on. Bill did not pay much attention to the game, except when Captain Greybagges was bowling to Muhammed al-Berberi. He ain't a-givin' him no mercy, thought Bill, that 'un were a scorcher, if I ain't mistook. Another sail on the horizon; another felucca with a lateen rig.

There was an outburst of ill-tempered chatter and a few groans from the crew, some sitting on cross-yards, some leaning on the shore-side rails.

"Whassup?" Bill asked a steersman. The pirate gave him a sideways look.

"The corsairs have won, curse 'em!"

Bill continued his watch on the shore. Well, I'll be damned! thought Bill, the dog Janszoon has gone to shake Blue Peter's hand, the tom-fool! Grinning like an ape, he is. Har-har! Blue Peter has crushed his hand! There he goes holding it, Muhammed laughing alike to a drain, the corsairs grinning. Har-har! Who is this arriving? It must be Suleyman Reis. Yes, that would be him, in the big turban. There is a man who drinks far more than is good for him, a nose as red as a beetroot. That must be this Mr Benjamin fellow. He has a black eye, but he still has his scrub-wig and his eye-glasses; they must have taken them off him before they clobbered him. The Captain is coming to the longboat with some of the cricket team.

The longboat came to the ship. The Captain went below with two bully-boys and returned on deck with a small wooden chest. The bully-boys lowered it into the longboat.

"Bill, I shall send back Mr Benjamin and the rest of the team," said the Captain, "and then return myself. Start raising the anchor when I'm on my way back, and we will set to sea straight away."

The longboat splashed away. Captain Greybagges and Muhammed al-Berberi stood on the quay.

"I am grateful for your help and support, Muhammed. I hope this will not bring you trouble from your admiral."

"Maybe, but I do not think it matters. Suleyman Reis or Salomo de Veenboer, he cannot decide which he wants to be, and it weakens him. He also lets his greed outgrow his wits. The treacherous assault on your ship was a mistake; what use is it to have persons to ransom if you cannot be trusted to make the exchange? Pah! You and I are pirates, Sylvestre, so we do bad things sometimes, but we are not bad men, not at heart. Suleyman Reis pretends to be a muslim. His mouth repeats words but he does not listen to what they are saying. He hears '*lâ hawla wa lâ quwwata illâ billâh*' - 'there is no transformation or power except through Allah' - every day, but he still believes that who he is, Dutchman or Barbary corsair, is within his power to choose, and that he has power enough to order the world the way he would like it to be, but he cannot, so his time as admiral may be short."

"What will you do with Ali the Barber?"

"The crew still need a mullah, but first Ali Nasruddin will learn some humility at the oar."

"Will you grow your beard now?"

"Beard, no beard, I don't know. Maybe I shall shave my beard to the bottom of my ears ... so ... and grow a big moustache."

"That might suit you. Perhaps you will start a fashion throughout the whole Ottoman empire! The longboat comes, Muhammed. I must go. Thank you again for your help and your friendship. Oh! I nearly forgot. Here are your winnings."

The Captain solemnly gave Muhammed al-Berberi a ha'penny coin, shook him by the hand and climbed down into the longboat. As the rowers pulled towards the ship Muhammed al-Berberi called after him:

"*Lâ hawla wa lâ quwwata illâ billâh!* Remember that, Sylvestre! There is no transformation or power except through Allah!"

CHAPTER THE SEVENTH,
or A Barrel Of Fun.

"He is suffering from *commotio cerebri*, I should think," said Mr Frank Benjamin, a tall portly man with a gloomy face, made more gloomy by a black eye, and *pince-nez* spectacles upon the end of his large nose.

"That would be the Latin," said Bulbous Bill Bucephalus.

"Yes, it is Latin for 'he has been hit on the head', you see."

"Stop talkin' like I'm not here, ye scurvy hounds!" whispered Israel Feet, his head swathed in a bandage.

"That be the way doctors talk, Izzie," said Bill.

"You bain't be a doctor."

"Yes, but me an' Mr Benjamin are trying to be doctors, so it follers that we must act like doctors, if we are to make you well."

"Iffen yez wishes to help me give me some rum, you lubbers," the First Mate pleaded.

"I'm afraid, Mr Feet, that alcohol is presently forbidden to you," said Frank Benjamin solemnly, "as it is stimulating to the brain, and yours is concussed, or bruised. It would ease the pain for a little, but then a hangover would set in and you would be in agony. Drink plenty of warm tea and try and sleep."

"He should 'ave a draught, perhaps?" pondered Bill.

"It can do no harm to exhibit a little bark and steel," said Frank Benjamin, "but no purgatives of any sort. No rhubarb powder."

Bulbous Bill departed to the galley. Frank Benjamin squatted down next to the bunk.

"Your friend has treated you with skill," he said quietly. "He has cleaned your wound with a cotton swab soaked in clean brine, then he has stitched up your skull as neat as a Jermyn Street bootmaker. The king's own surgeon could not have done better, but he has an enthusiasm for draughts and potions. In your case these will do little good, but no harm either, so I ask you to accept them as tokens of his regard for you, as his wishes for your speedy recovery. I will restrain him if he wishes to dose you too liberally. The pain in your head will lessen in a day or two, and we have no opium, so I must ask you to be patient and endure it. After that your recovery should be progressive, but you will be prone to occasional headaches for a time."

"Arr! How long be a time?" moaned the First Mate.

"Weeks, maybe months, but they will stop eventually."

Captain Sylvestre de Greybagges paced his quarterdeck, dressed in the fine powder-blue uniform of a *kapitein van schip* of the Dutch East India Company, his beard a rich boot-polish brown. The wind was steady and fresh and the pirate frigate *Ark de Triomphe*, disguised as the armed merchantman *Groot Ombeschaamheid*, was making seven knots, spray occasionally flying over the leeward taffrail. The day was fine, the sky blue with a few small puffy clouds, the noonday sun warm rather than hot, now that the ship was sailing northerly, away from Gibraltar and the Pillars of Hercules.

Bulbous Bill and Mr Benjamin joined him on the quarterdeck, discussing the velocity of sound.

"It was indeed astute of you to calculate it so, Mr Bucephalus," said Mr Benjamin, "but I am afraid that you are not the first. That estimable Frenchie Mersenne - *la pére* Mersenne, as I should say - has it in his book *Traité de l'harmonie universelle*, and applies it to a theory of music, the wily old cove."

The Captain had been listening.

"Newton mentions the velocity of sound in his *Principia Mathematica*, but as an ideal to be calculated from the elasticity of the air, not as a quantity to be measured. Yet you are in good company, Bill. The ancient Greek fellows had no cannons, or games of cricket even, did not perceive the tardiness of the report after the flash, and so expressed no opinion on the matter."

"The Greeks, wonderful fellows though they were, are not to be entirely trusted on many subjects," said Mr Benjamin. "There is a fine examination of this in the *Pseudodoxia Epidemica* of Thomas Browne. Are you familiar with the work?"

"Indeed! The *Pseudodoxia Epidemica*, or 'enquiries into very many received tenets and commonly presumed truths'. I am a great admirer of Browne," said the Captain. "The *Pseudodoxia* brushes away old wives' tales as though it were a besom sweeping dry leaves. Some wags call it the *Vulgar Errors*, mistranslating the Latin. I have it in my cabin. A sixth-printing, bound in varnished canvas against the sea airs."

Mr Benjamin expressed a desire to consult the book; his own copy was in his house in Virginia, a treasured volume. Captain Greybagges and Mr Benjamin explored their mutual regard for Sir Thomas Browne. His wit! His elegant language! His extensive learning; did he not have the best library in England? Not the largest, maybe, but surely the most well-chosen!

Bulbous Bill Bucephalus ceased to listen. The ship took his attention for a while, and then they were talking of things of which he knew nothing. What do I know of latitudinarianism or urn-burials? thought Bill, I am pleased I was right about the velocity of sound, even though that Froggie priest thought of it first. He shouted to a foremast jack to tighten that sheet, you lubber! and thought of the First Mate; he sleeps now, and that is good. There is a small chop, but the barky rides it well, so he will not be unduly disturbed even though we are making a good rate. John Spratt is doing well as his stand-in, but he lacks authority over his mess-mates and does not wish to acquire it, for Izzie will recover and then they will be his mess-mates again.

When Bulbous Bill turned around again Captain Greybagges and Frank Benjamin had gone below.

"I remembered the inspiring words of Sir Thomas Browne when I was a prisoner in Barbary," said Mr Benjamin. "He wrote, 'rest not in an ovation, but a triumph over thy passions; chain up the unruly legion of thy breast; behold thy trophies within thee, not without thee: lead thine own captivity captive, and be Cæsar unto thy self', which was good advice at the time."

"I am sorry that Suleyman Reis had you questioned, Mr Benjamin," said Captain Greybagges. "I offered too much for your freedom, in order to save haggling, and that must have stimulated his curiosity. Will you have more wine?"

"Indeed I will, and thank you. The bearded fellow in the big turban was quite insistent, but I had no notion of who you were, let alone why you should wish to purchase my release. I am deeply grateful that I am freed, however, and drinking a glass of this excellent Madeira with you. May I have another of these little pastries? They are very good."

Captain Greybagges passed the plate with a smile.

"You seem lacking in curiosity yourself, Mr Benjamin. Do you not wish to know why I paid that rogue eight hundred guineas in gold for your liberty?"

Frank Benjamin brushed crumbs from his waistcoat, and sipped the sweet wine.

"I feel sure that you will tell me in due course," he said, "but if I were to hazard a guess I would say it was my compressed-air cannon."

Captain Greybagges looked startled.

"A gun worked by mere air? Is such a thing possible?"

"Indeed. Air is reduced in volume by means of a pump, then allowed to expand again in the barrel of a gun, thus discharging a ball in the same fashion as the expanding fire of gunpowder."

"You have constructed such a weapon?"

"Yes, a small model, firing balls the size of peas, but I confess there were problems. The flasks into which the air was compressed exhibited a sad propensity for bursting explosively."

"What advantages does such an engine have?"

"No smoke, and a smaller noise. I am not sure about the noise, though. If an air-cannon could be made with the same power as gunpowder I suspect it would sound just as loud. Such a cannon might be made to repeat-fire reliably and quickly - *Pom! Pom! Pom!* - but that is only a notion, and not yet tested."

Captain Greybagges got up and walked to the stern-windows of the Great Cabin, the slight roll and pitch of the ship unnoticed.

"Why do you think that I would require a compressed-air cannon?"

"Because all men are fascinated by engines of destruction, of course! I said nothing to the corsairs, not even when they beat me, because otherwise I would be there still. I gambled that they would know nothing of it, being in Barbary. However, you, Captain, speak English well and have lately been in the waters of the Americas, so you may have heard a rumour, if some of my friends or workmen in Virginia have been indiscreet. Also, you are no Hollander, yet you masquerade as one, so I might rationally suspect you of representing some foreign power who wishes to acquire my knowledge for the purposes of aggressive war."

"Be at ease, I do not wish to build a compressed-air cannon," said Captain Greybagges, "or to encourage warfare between nations in any way, and I do not act as agent for any potentate or cabal. I find the notion of confining air in flasks very interesting, though. It may solve a problem for me. If you would tell me more of this I should be in your debt, but it is not the reason that I ransomed you. I wish you to tell me your knowledge of lightning-rods."

Blue Peter Ceteshwayoo and Torvald Coalbiter were in the sick-bay, sitting with Israel Feet, to give him tea and biscuits and to distract him from the pain of his head-wound.

"That be a prodigious great razor, an' you may drown me else, wi' a curse," whispered the First Mate.

Blue Peter replaced the enormous razor in its velvet-lined box. He had been recounting the tale of how the Captain had out-thought Ali the Barber, as the First Mate had been below at the time, waiting for the order to lead the armed pirates on deck.

"He be a sharp one, the Cap'n, and you may lay to that, wi' a curse," whispered Israel Feet.

"The beard did not like the razor, I expect," said Torvald Coalbiter, "and it is a lucky beard, a beard with a witch-charm upon it."

"Why do you say that?" said Blue Peter.

"Back in Norðragøta my father's mother is a witch. She talks to whales and she can call the fishes with an iron fry-pan and a piece of coal."

"How the bugger does she do that?" said Israel Feet.

"She bangs the coal on the fry-pan and shouts 'fish! fish! come here you bloody fish!' and the fish usually come. She says it is because they are curious."

"Does she put charms on beards, then?" said Blue Peter.

"No, not that I remember, but she will put charms on most things, if you ask her nicely and give her money. She charmed my boots so they would take me home again, and charmed my knife so that I would not drop it. See? It has the lucky knotted string on its hilt. I tie the lucky string to my wrist when I use the knife. So long as the lucky string is tied to my wrist I will never drop the knife."

Blue Peter and Israel Feet considered this in silence for a while.

"How did you come by your name, Coalbiter?" asked Blue Peter eventually.

"It is from a forebear, a long time ago. My father's father's father, maybe even longer. He had a cousin, a *birsarka*, who was called 'the Foebiter' because he was so mad in battle that he would bite and kick at his enemies even after they were dead.

My ancestor preferred to stay by his own hearth, so his cousin mocked him and called him 'the Coalbiter'. He had the last laugh, though, as the Foebiter and all of his men went away a-viking and were lost at sea, and then my ancestor became the *jarl* and had sons with all their wives."

"And yet you went to sea despite your ancestor's tale?" said Blue Peter.

"The Coalbiter was a great sailor, it is told, and no coward. He was warming himself by his fire when when the weather was too bad to venture to sea, and by his fire when battles were lost, not when they were won. His great power was to know when to sail or to fight and when to sit quietly by his own hearth with his dogs at his feet. Anyway, those *birsarkas* were foolish men. They would eat the fly-mushroom and drink mead before battle until they were in a blind fury, then howl like wolves and tear their shirts off and gash their chests. Very frightening to farm-boys, but not so frightening to seasoned warriors, I think, which is why there are no *birsarkas* left now. The sea is not frightened by howling and chest-beating either, but it respects cunning and a knowledge of its ways. So I am glad to be at sea with the Captain. I think I would be less happy to be at sea with Blackbeard Teach, for he is alike to the Foebiter and mistakes recklessness for fearlessness and madness for cunning."

"Har! You be in the right there, shipmate, wi' a wannion!" said Israel Feet, forgetting to whisper piteously, "but don't be telling Captain Teach that to his face, har-har!"

"Tell me, Torvald," said Blue Peter, "what did the whales say to your grandmother, when she spoke with them?"

"Well, she used to talk to the whales right enough, in the late summer when they would come and sport off the north headland, but I am not sure if they ever said anything to her in reply."

"We must let Izzie sleep some more," said Blue Peter. "Tomorrow, Izzie, you can go on deck and get some fresh air, then you will soon be right as ninepence."

In the Great Cabin Mr Benjamin and Captain Greybagges had discussed lightning-rods and their peculiarities - and was it not true that the excellent Sir Thomas Browne had coined the word *electrick* to describe the mysterious fluid? Was there nothing that his mighty intellect had not mused upon? - and they had drunk most of the bottle of Madeira and eaten all of the pastries. The evening twilight blue'd the tall windows of the stateroom, earlier now as the ship's latitude grew ever more northerly, and Captain Greybagges lit the oil-lamps with a spill from the candle-stub they had been using to light their pipes.

"Of course, Captain," continued Mr Benjamin, "I had the advantage of a mechanical education. My father was a blacksmith and farrier, my uncles on either side a clockmaker and a gunsmith, so I was apprenticed to all three, one could say. Even so, I might still have followed in my father's footsteps and worked a forge if my mother's cousin Nathaniel had not been a printer. He was a fine typesetter, but all thumbs when it came to a mechanism, so as a boy I was often sent to help him work his press. At times he would give me proof-reading to do, and so I learned not only good English but also the rudiments, at least, of Latin and Greek, and German, too, there being a number of Hanoverians in Virginia at that time. The combination of manual skills and book-learning made a productive ground in which new ideas might grow and bloom. I have been lucky in that, and may stake no claim to genius, although I enjoy your generous compliments, Captain!" He raised his glass and sipped a little Madeira.

"You are right about the skills of the hand and eye being as illuminating as any text," said Captain Greybagges. "As captain of a ship I am made aware of this every day. The ship would founder without continual repair, and no book can give the smith or the carpenter his art. When I was a boy I made a little boat to sail on the lake on my father's estate, and there is a great pleasure in taking wood and shaping it, making it into a vessel that draws the wind and cuts the water, a great pleasure indeed. Perhaps one day I shall have the leisure to build another."

"The art of the boatwright is indeed profound. A cabinet-maker feels he is a fine fellow for making an inlaid *vargueño* with a secret drawer, but the boatbuilder's work must survive the battering of the seas, and has not a single straight line anywhere to put a try-square to."

"That is the truth. If you ask a cabinet-maker to make you a more expensive box he will make it of precious woods, inlay it with ivory and put gold handles on it. Ask a boatwright to do the same and *he* will make it more watertight, giving it a barrel-top and curved sides so the planks strain against each other and stay close-fitting as in a carvel-built whaler, thus expending the extra value in its construction and not on mere ornamentation. Mr Chippendale, the ship's carpenter, has such a sailor's chest. I shall show it to you betimes. It is surprisingly light in weight."

"I have seen such a chest. The light weight comes from it resembling more an egg than a box. An egg-shell is made of thin friable stuff, yet when it is complete and whole it will withstand much rough treatment. A cubical egg would be a sadly weak thing."

"And quite painful for the chicken, too!" said the Captain, and they roared with laughter.

"The last of the Madeira, Mr Benjamin?" Captain Greybagges emptied the bottle into their glasses. "The skills of the hands! I suppose that is why I respect our King Charles. I met a Guernsey man once who told me that when the King was exiled to the Channel Islands during Noll Cromwell's time he would sail a cutter from dawn to dusk, just for the joy of it, and that he could easily be master of a ship if he wasn't the king. I admired that, and I also learned that as a young prince he had insisted on being taught smithing and carpentry despite the dogged opposition of the dukes and earls who had been appointed to be his tutors, who thought such things beneath his royal dignity. They say that he is a man who enjoys his pleasures too much to be a good ruler, but I think a king who has willingly worked a forge and a bench, and who loves to sail a jolly-boat, cannot be bad. Many pirates make a pretence of being Jacobites, and toasting *the king across the water* like a parcel of drunken Scotsmen, but I do not. King Charles would maybe hang me if he should catch me, but that does not make him a bad king, merely a monarch whose wily diplomacy would sacrifice a few freebooters if that will give him peace with Spain. If there is war with Spain, then I will miraculously become a buccaneer once more, loyal and true, and not - heaven forfend! - a wicked pirate, and the King would then surely smile upon my depredations, as he has done already with Captain Morgan."

"You freely confess to being a pirate, Captain Greybagges, and yet all my instincts are to trust you," said Mr Benjamin. "Kings, popes and potentates are often constrained by circumstances to act in ways that are morally dubious, as you imply, and yet they are held to be the fount of order and law in this turbulent world. A pirate may be as much a creature of virtue as a king, I find. That man with the beard and turban in Barbary caused me to confront my mortality, to brace myself to face death, imprisonment or slavery with as much courage and dignity as I could muster. A barbarian, indeed, without honour or pity. You are not such a man. You buy my freedom at much risk to yourself, and yet you say that should only earn my goodwill, and that you will pay me for my labours and deliver me safe home to Virginia in the spring. I am honoured by your courtesy and your straightforwardness, and I will gladly accept your offer."

He held out his hand and Captain Sylvestre de Greybagges shook it solemnly.

"I am pleased to have you aboard, Mr Benjamin, as one of my pirate crew. Do please call me Sylvestre, but not on the quarterdeck, as that would breach naval ettiquette."

"Call me Frank. I drink a glass with you!"

They touched glasses and downed the last sips of the sweet Madeira wine.

"Frank, I must take a turn around the deck, as it grows dark. Please do accompany me, for the appetite is stimulated by the fresh salt air, and then please do join my officers and myself for a little supper."

The pirate frigate *Ark de Triomphe*, disguised still as the Dutch merchantman *Groot Ombeschaamheid*, cleaved a white wake thought the darkening sea into the gathering dusk. She had been heading northwest into the Atlantic to avoid lee shores and inquisitive Spaniards, but the wake was heading now northeast towards the Channel, with the prevailing southwesterly winds at her stern. The sailors hauling on the ropes were dressed in the red-and-grey *matrozenpak* slops of the Dutch East India Company, but they were singing in English - many of them in various accents, perhaps - as they hauled:

"Farewell and adieu to you, Spanish ladies!
Farewell and adieu to you, ladies of Spain!
For we've received orders for to sail for old England,
But we hope in a short time to see you again,
We will rant and we'll roar like true British sailors,
We'll rant and we'll roar all on the salt sea.
Until we strike soundings in the channel of old England;
From Ushant to Scilly is thirty-five leagues."

Captain Greybagges awoke at dawn as the tall windows of the Great Cabin let in a cold grey light. The ship was pitching more - a rougher sea - and rolling more - a gusting wind. A splatter of rain rattled against the stern windows. He yawned and swung his legs out of the hanging bunk, slowing its swinging with his feet on the canvas deck-cloth. He put a black coat of thick Duffel cloth on over his nightshirt, fastened its wooden toggles and went up to the quarterdeck. The ship was thumping through a moderate chop, the deck was wet and cold under his bare feet from the spray blown over the leeside taffrail. Two steersmen were at the wheel, under the watchful eye of Bulbous Bill Bucephalus, who wished the Captain a good morning and then indicated upwards with his eyes. The Captain looked up; Mr Benjamin was standing on the lower crossyard of the mizzen mast, facing sternwards into the wind, wearing only his wig, his spectacles and a pair of cotton drawers. He had tied a length of rope around his waist and the mast so that he could spread his arms wide and not fall.

"A very good morning to you, Captain!" he called down, just audible against the buffeting of the rain-filled wind.

"How long has he been up there?" asked the Captain.

"Oh, about half an hour," said Bill.

Captain Greybagges nodded and sighed, and went below. After his head had been shaved by Mumblin' Jake, and he had washed and dressed in his piratical black clothes, he returned to the deck. Mr Benjamin was standing by the pump, waiting for two foremast jacks to rig the handles.

"Taking a seawater bath, Mr Benjamin? It sets a man up for the day! Though I must confess that I prefer to do it in warmer climes."

"I feel it would be a grand thing to do after an air-bath, Captain, if I am not inconveniencing anybody."

"They will tell you quick enough if you are. But what is an 'air-bath', pray?"

"Why, a bath in the air! I have a theory that certain vapourous humours are drawn from the *corpus* by exposure to a brisk breeze, and that clothes tend to insulate one from the roborative effects of fresh air, much as they are necessary for warmth."

"I notice that you have tied your wig and spectacles to your head with cod-line. Surely it would be easier to leave them off?"

"I need my eye-glasses to see, Captain, and keep my wig on that I might retain my dignity. If I may presume to ask you a question in return, why is your beard green?"

"Because I am Greenbeard the pirate, Mr Benjamin. I am not in disguise as Myneer Oplichtenaar, *kapitein van schip*. This is how I normally attire myself."

"Ah! You are indeed a notable buccaneer, Captain Greybagges! Even a landlubber like myself has had report of you."

"The price of such fame is that I must colour my beard with brown boot-polish and, sadly, restrain myself from writing for the broadsheets as I used to do. After your seawater bath there is breakfast in the wardroom, Mr Benjamin. I must attend to some paperwork."

Captain Greybagges turned and addressed the crew in the rigging in a loud carrying voice.

"Listen, you swabs! There looks to be a great storm a-blowing up from aft, damn me iffen there ain't! It will be upon us before dark, so's you keeps the sails in good order betimes, keep a weather eye open and attend to Mr Bucephalus, for iffen yez don't and the storm don't tear out yez guts I surely will, and yez may lay to that, wi' a wannion! The Bay of Biscay is a graveyard for damned lubbers, but not for canny sailormen, so sets yez the sails handsomely, shipmates!"

The pirates had rigged the pump and fitted a stand-pipe. The Captain noted that Mr Benjamin removed his wig and spectacles before standing under the gushing gouts of cold seawater.

There was a knock at the door of the Great Cabin. "Enter, wi' a curse!" shouted Captain Greybagges, lifting his quill from the paper. Mr Benjamin looked around the door, his wig still looking slightly damp.

"Ah, Frank. Come in."

"Captain, Sylvestre, I have a notion to demonstrate to you something of the electric fluid, if there is to be a storm with lightning, but I need the assistance of a carpenter. Is he busy?"

"I do not think so. Tell him I said to do your bidding, unless there is some pressing task which must have his immediate attention."

"Thank you, Sylvestre. I am sorry to have disturbed you."

Captain Greybagges returned to his correspondence and the comforting *scritch-scratch* of the goose-quill on foolscap. I wonder what Mr Benjamin is intending to do, he mused, as he penned a letter of instructions to be sent to a clockmaker in Dublin.

As the Captain wrote letters and dealt with the mundane paperwork of the frigate he was aware that the weather was slowly worsening. The pitch and roll of the ship increased and became more random. He had to keep things stowed in drawers rather than have them slide around the top of his desk, and he spread his feet wider to steady his seat in the chair, in case there should be a sudden lurch. This did not bother him unduly, but he wondered how Mr Benjamin was taking it. If he was working with the ship's carpenter the activity would perhaps keep his mind off any queasiness.

Mumblin' Jake came with the Captain's lunch; a doorstep-thick sandwich of bread, cheese and sliced onion, two boiled eggs, a thick wedge of pork pie with mustard, an apple and a tankard of ale. The Captain kept the tankard in his left hand on the desk's leather top and the basket of food in his lap, and was able to enjoy his repast and continue writing in between mouthfuls despite the movement of the ship. The ship was by no means troubled by the wind and waves, and made agreeable creaking noises as though it were a live creature grunting with the effort of shouldering its way through the green seas. I hope Mr Chippendale has checked the bilges, he thought, and not been distracted by whatever it is Mr Benjamin wants of him.

The storm following the *Ark de Triomphe* worsened as it drew closer. As twilight fell the waves rolled past it one after another, lifting the stern with a lurch, and the wind howled. The foremast-jacks swarmed in the rigging, trimming the canvas to catch the blow yet not burst the gasket-ropes. Some of the pirate crew donned oilskins and boots, but the more-active men on the yards could only wear shirts and pants as heavy-weather gear would hamper their freedom of movement, and freezing cold and wet are better than a fall into the churning sea. They were relieved on a rolling-shift system so they got hot drinks and burgoo below before they became stupid from the cold, and fresher men took their place.

Jemmy Ducks was still in disgrace and was not relieved from his watch at the main foretop crosstrees, although he was well bundled up in several woollen jumpers, an oversize griego and a tarred sou'wester. Jack Nastyface had joined him in his lonely vigil out of friendship, a meaningful gesture when young Jack could have been lollygagging by the warmth of the galley stove with a mug of sweet coffee in his hand. Jemmy Ducks was resentful of his friend's sacrifice at first, it seemed to diminish his punishment, and he was aggrieved at himself for his near-calamitous dereliction of duty, but Jack Nastyface was such a well-meaning fool that soon they were arguing as of old.

"You must have heard him wrong then, you ass!" said Jemmy Ducks. "He probably wanted a barrel of beer, the mad old bugger."

"He did not," insisted Jack. "He *pacifically* asked for an empty barrel. I heard him clear as I hear you now."

This was no guarantee of clarity, as the wind howled around them in their lofty perch, but Jemmy Ducks was partially convinced.

"And three fathoms of cotton cloth, the sort that is dyed for flags," continued Jack Nastyface, "and forty fathoms of codline, and a bar-shot, and some oilcloth, and four pounds of gunpowder, and …"

"And here he comes now!" shouted Jemmy Ducks above the wind's noise, pointing down to the deck. He then felt a twinge of guilt. "I cannot look. I must keep watch on the horizon. Tell me what they are doing." There was not much horizon to watch, as the squall-line crept closer, a mass of angry clouds, dark in the twilight and stitched with flashes of lightning. Jack Nastyface hung over the yard, to better observe the deck.

"Yes, it is Mr Benjamin. He has tied his wig on with string, and it is flapping, hee-hee! The Captain, too, and Mr Chippendale, and the barrel, and a bundle of sticks, or something. They are going forward … onto the forepeak. Mr Benjamin is buggering about with the sticks … aah! It is a kite! A big kite! I used to have a kite when I was a boy ashore, but it is much bigger than that. He has launched the kite into the wind! … It soars! The carpenter is paying out the line, and the kite soars ahead of the barky … the Captain and Mr Benjamin have put the barrel on the rail. Aha! The bar-shot is rigged alike to a keel on the barrel, and something sticks out of the top, alike to a little mast. They are tying the line off to the little spike-mast. The kite flies high now, and almost all the string is paid out."

Jemmy Ducks, in his scan of the obscured horizon, could see the kite as it lofted high towards the cloud, but he tore his eyes from it to continue his watch; if he missed something again the Captain would surely have him flogged, or else the crew would kill him. Jack Nastyface continued, shouting about the keening of the wind.

"The line is all paid out … they have pushed the barrel over the side! The Captain waves to Mr Bucephalus by the wheel."

The *Ark de Triomphe* turned away from the floating barrel. Jack Nastyface hauled himself upright to let a party of foremast-jacks clamber out on the yard. He could see the barrel bobbing amongst the white wave-tops. The kite was towing it perceptibly, such was the strength of the wind.

"By the Saints! The kite pulls the barrel! Take care, Jemmy, the squall is almost upon us!"

"I can see that, you dullard! Look to your own handholds. Watch the barrel! What the devil are they doing? Why throw a barrel into the oggin to get pulled by a kite? It makes little sense."

"The kite is soaring into the cloud-bottoms! I never got my kite to fly so high! Here comes the squall! … Oh!"

From the corner of his eye Jemmy Ducks saw first a white flash, then a red light, and a fraction of a second later heard a 'boom'.

"Oh, crikey!" yelled Jack. "There is a strange thing! I have never seen the like of that! I trow I have not!"

"Seen the like of what, you fathead?"

"Well, that is a wonder! A wonder indeed!"

"What is a wonder, you donkey?"

The squall howled around their ears, and a lightning flash lit the bottoms of the clouds an eerie blue. Jack Nastyface waited to speak until the thunder and the squall had abated.

"A great wonder, indeed! I have never seen the like of that!"

"Of WHAT!" pleaded Jemmy, still keeping his watch as though his life depended on it.

"Har! When the kite went into the bottom of the clouds lightning ran down the string, like a line of white fire, then the barrel blew up, 'boom!' The fire of the levin-bolt must have lit the gunpowder in the barrel! How very extraordinary!" He peered down at the deck. "The Captain congratulates Mr Benjamin, and claps him on the back! He must be a wise old cove to know the nature of lightning, and to guide it into a barrel of powder! I take my hat off to him!"

Captain Sylvestre de Greybagges and his officers were still chuckling from the surprise of the explosion, shaking their heads and going, in their different ways '*zzzzt! BOOM!*', to demonstrate how the barrel had detonated. The Captain sloshed dark rum into Bulbous Bill's *lignum-vitae* beaker, then Israel Feet's tarred leather drinking-jack, then Blue Peter's tumbler of precious diamond-cut Bohemian crystal, then his own chased-silver goblet and finally Frank Benjamin's pewter tankard. He raised his goblet:

"A toast, me hearties! A fulsome toast to Mister Frank Benjamin, the man who has mastered the fire of the lightning-bolt, leading it where he wills, alike to the good farmer who directs water to the parched field through leats and ditches with a turn of his spade! A toast!"

They downed their rum and banged their various drinking-vessels back onto the Captain's desk. The ship rolled with the seas, and rain rattled on the tall transom windows from the following wind, but the Great Cabin of the *Ark de Triomphe* seemed cosy with light from the oil-lamps and the warm fellowship of the pirates. Mr Benjamin grinned modestly and raised his tankard:

"My thanks, friends and shipmates! Captain Greybagges has done me great honour by inviting me to join your illustrious company, and I am glad to have given such pleasure by a modest demonstration of the power of natural philosophy. I return your toast in full measure! To the lusty buccaneers of the good ship *Ark de Triomphe* and to their captain, the illustrious Sylvestre de Greybagges!"

They drank again. Mr Benjamin seated himself, staggering a little from a lurch of the ship. He filled his pipe.

"I must say, though, Captain," he said, "that you may have to repay your excellent carpenter for the reel of fine copper wire which I used to direct the flow of electrick fluid down the kite-string. He was loath to part with it, and I had to invoke your name to ensure his compliance. It is a pricey commodity, that cuprous filament, not valuable for its metal, but for the rare skill required to draw it so hair-like thin, and now most of it is turned to vapour."

"Surely I shall reimburse Mr Chippendale his reel of wire, and another reel of wire of pure gold if I can find such a thing, for his metal thread has shown to me that certain things, certain *plans* of mine, lie within the bounds of the possible, and are not mere pipe-dreams. I am grateful for that, and relieved, and grateful to you, too, Frank."

The Captain refilled their cups once again. Mr Benjamin leaned forward to nod and acknowledge the Captain's compliment, the flickering light of the oil-lamp reflecting on his *pince-nez* spectacles as ovals of yellow.

"This is also an opportune moment for me to add that Mr Benjamin is now a full member of the crew, with all the rights, responsibilities, emoluments and perquisites appertaining to that position, as laid out in the Free Brotherhood o' the Coast's rule-book. Somebody give Mr Benjamin a copy to study at his leisure. Be assured, though, Frank, that I shall not command you to stand a dog-watch as masthead lookout dressed only in your wig and your drawers, har-har!"

There was mirth at this sally, but Mr Benjamin did not seem unduly put out, smilingly slyly and sipping his rum.

"You said as how you might have plans, Cap'n?" said Bulbous Bill Bucephalus carefully.

"Indeed I do, Bill. Indeed I have plans. They are still in a state of vagueness because of their dependence on certain things happening, mind you, so I am unwillin' to discuss them much. Things will be clearer to me after I have settled some business in London."

Up in the mainmast cross-trees Jemmy Ducks and Jack Nastyface wrangled idly about this and that, Jemmy all the time keeping a regular circle-scan of the horizon, or what could be seen of it through the darkness and rain. Occasional flashes of lighting lit the clouds from within and without.

"... yes, I am envious of you, Jack. The crew do not have a down on you. I don't blame them, but it's mortal hard on a fellow to get all these black looks, I can tell you."

"Har! 'Let age, not envy, draw wrinkles on thy cheeks!' The Captain said that earlier to the sailing-master," said Jack, "but I think he was just quoting and didn't mean that Bill had been being envious at all. He said it were by a famous fellow name of Sir Thomas Browne, he ..."

Jack would have said more, but a face appeared over the mast, dimly pale in the cloud-dimmed moonlight.

"Cap'n says you two nippers, you two young gentlemen, are to go the galley, get something hot inside yuz," said the foremast-jack, "and I to take yer place, for my sins."

"Not just yet!" shouted Jemmy Ducks. "Call you down to the steersman! There are white breakers to port side! White breakers less'n two miles to port!"

The foremast-jack turned and hailed the steersman at the wheel in a deep and powerful voice.

Chapter the Eighth,
or The Great Wen.

"**Y**ou did not save the ship, it is true, Jemmy," said Captain Sylvestre de Greybagges. "The sailing-master had already seen the white of the waves upon the rocks – a ship does not depend upon the sight of one pair of eyes alone - but your warning was timely and seamanlike. It has restored your good name among the crew, too. Why do you wish to pay off and go ashore? I am curious."

The Captain sat at his desk in the Great Cabin of the pirate frigate *Ark de Triomphe*, with a tankard of London-brewed ale in his hand.

Jemmy Ducks spoke, after a little thought.

"I am glad to have regained the trust of my messmates, indeed, I am, but I am not, by my own nature, suited to the life of a pirate, Captain. I have been in some brisk engagements, and I believe I have not shown a want of courage?" Jemmy Ducks looked hopefully at the Captain, who nodded his agreement. "And yet I get but little pleasure from being in an action. Not like the others, to whom fighting is like nuts and cake. I am proud to have been a buccaneer, and consider myself fortunate to have served under your command, Captain, but, in all truth, I find I cannot make it my life, so I intend to use my portion of the plunder to seek another path more suited to my nature."

The Captain turned his attention to Jack Nastyface, who was standing next to his friend, staring at him with an expression of amazement upon his long face.

"And you, Jack?" said the Captain. "What is your wish?"

"That poor fellow Jack Nastyface *actually* squirmed," said Captain Greybagges to Blue Peter, while pouring ale for them both. "I have never seen anybody *squirm* before, I think. Not properly. His whole bony frame was twitching. I could see his toes wriggling in his shoes."

Blue Peter grinned and drank some ale.

"All very well for you to snigger, Peter, but I could not laugh. After a while he squeaked 'I wish to remain, Cap'n! I wish to be a buccaneer!' while tears came to his eyes."

"And you accepted?" said Blue Peter, one eyebrow raised.

"Indeed I did. I had planned to let them both pay off, and maybe keep Jemmy Ducks if he insisted, but Jack had chosen the ship and the pirate's life over his best and only friend, and in a moment, too, so I felt that I must allow him the confidence of his own decision. Oddly enough, Jemmy was not much surprised, and shook Jack's hand and wished him well. They are off ashore now, getting themselves drunk."

"And swearing eternal friendship, too, I do not doubt. It is sad, you are right, but I am impressed by Jemmy's decision, and by Jack's, too. I had not thought them so mature in their considerations. How many have you paid off now?"

Captain Greybagges took a swig of ale and consulted the papers on his desk.

"One hundred and sixty-two. Most of them willingly. Old Joshua from the larboard watch did not want to go, but I persuaded him that a turn ashore living in comfort would set him up ready to sail again in the future. I don't think he ever will, mind you. I arranged for him to buy a cottage near his sister in Gravesend, and made him see a surgeon about his bursten belly. He wishes to put his nephews through school, and that too is arranged. Eton would not have them, of course, the stuck-up sods, but Christ's Hospital school at Greyfriars were not so particular. Our Bank of International Export loaned them the money for their chapel roof so I had them recommend the two little thugs to them as souls worth saving. They will have to wear those blue coats and yellow stockings, which will make them more humble, and perhaps the beaks there will thrash some learning into their dirty little heads. One of those brats tried to lift my purse, you know, when I took Old Joshua down to Gravesend."

"That one will grow up to be a minister of the Crown, surely," laughed Blue Peter, "or an archbishop. Speaking of ministers of the Crown, did you see your school-friend Billy Pitt?"

"We had a decent dinner yesterday in Dirty Dick's tavern at Bishop's Gate. He is a shrewd fellow. He has taken on some of the business that other ministers disdain, the kind of work that does not allow for entirely clean hands."

"Intelligencing, you mean?"

"Exactly. He has a relish for it, the bloodthirsty little devil. I was able to assist him by offering our Bank of International Export as a conduit for funds to pay his agents, since we have branches in foreign parts, and he was able to assist me by helping to keep our affairs discreet."

"How so?" said Blue Peter, refilling their tankards. "This is good ale."

"Indeed. Some say the finest ale is from the countryside, but a London brew is hard to beat in my opinion, provided it has not been watered, of course. We are currently still masquerading as the *Groot Ombeschaamheid*, but that vast and well-informed enterprise the Dutch East India Company has surely heard reports by now that they have a ship that they do not have, so to speak. Billy Pitt will be able to confuse the matter a little by feeding them false information. Otherwise, we are well concealed, yet in plain sight. Listen ..."

The noises of the waterfront murmured through the open stern windows. The Pacific Wharf at Rotherhithe was only recently constructed, a fine new quay of timber pilings and planks with a wide apron of rammed gravel behind it, so making a solid wall to shoulder against the weight of the slapping River Thames. It hummed with activity. Stevedores rolled barrels and staggered under the weight of sacks and crates, Waggons and carts came and went, their wheels crunching on the gravel, their drivers cracking whips and roaring imprecations at each other. Persons of importance, by their own estimations or otherwise, clad in broadcloth, fustian, nankeen or silk, topped by powdered wigs and hats limited only by their purses and the fevered imaginations of milliners, came and went in sedan chairs, shays, fiacres, flys, dogcarts, coaches, diligences, carrioles, sulkies and even a solitary four-in-hand, their coachmen returning the costers' curses with enthusiasm and wit, real or imagined. A light breeze carried the scents of spices, tar and sawn timber, the rot-stink of a slaughterhouse, the acrid stench of a tannery, the wet earthy smell of the river. The *Ark de Triomphe* moved gently with the breeze and the slapping of the river-waters, and the oakum dodgers that protected it from the rough-planked quay squeaked and the hempen mooring cables, as thick as a thigh, creaked and groaned sullenly. From the taverns, wine-shops and bawdy-houses that backed the wide quay came occasional shrieks, shouts and gusts of drunken laughter.

"This wharf is new, yet bustling," Captain Greybagges sipped his ale. "This means that our barky will be less noticed and less remarked upon, especially as the wharfage fees are promptly paid and small gratuities distributed to certain persons of influence. The bustle of the wharf covers the *Ark de Triomphe* in distractions. The distance from the City and the recent construction of the wharf reduces the number of watching eyes with established links to interested parties - London's flourishing and resourceful criminal underworld, London's quick-witted and venal merchants, London's many spies and government informers, as if one could tell the difference between those classes, or indeed if one was innocent enough to attempt to make such a distinction - The small bribes ensure that at least some of the watching eyes are on our own payroll, at least in theory ..." Captain Greybagges sighed.

"And the watchers that you had me station up and down the quay in shabby clothes, pretending to be idlers and along-shore men, will tip us off to any untoward interest in us," completed Blue Peter.

"Yes, indeed. Yet we may not remain here too long, Peter, or else some clever soul will wonder why the Dutch East India Company, not known for its prodigality, pays steep daily wharfage fees when there is not much loading or unloading of cargo. We must be away from here in a day, or two at the latest. The crew who are no longer needed are paid off, very handsomely paid off, and happy. They are ashore, but not cast off like an old shoe, and so still feeling part of the pirate brotherhood and not likely to gossip. Some new crewmen, with skills that we shall need, are arriving daily. When the ship's complement is aboard we shall slip away into the sea mists."

"Where did you find these new recruits? They are mostly young, but already have some sea-going skills and discipline."

Captain Sylvestre de Greybagges smiled smugly and drained his tankard.

"All apprentice-boys dream of being pirates, Peter. Being young and full of hot blood, do they not wish to romance Spanish *senoritas*, to fight with cutlasses and to fill their pockets with *reales* and *doubloons* and *moidores*? Of course they do! I had some broadsheets printed, copies of the actual ones but with a notice added in the 'men wanted' part asking for apprentice buccaneers. I had them left in the coffee-houses and pie-shops that apprentice-boys frequent. I harvested a fine crop of young fellows – clerks, mechanics, foundrymen, blacksmiths, whitesmiths, tinsmiths, carpenters, printers – and had them practice swordplay and musketry in secret on evenings and weekends. Those that boasted to their friends, despite strict warnings, I dropped. Those who could keep a silent tongue in their heads I moved on to more training in small sailing boats. Some of them I have used to man our Bank of International Export, here and abroad, some to do other work for me ashore, which you will see the fruits of in due course. Many of them are doing the same jobs that they have always done, but the knowledge that they are now secretly pirates, and a little extra money in their pockets, makes them happy and loyal whereas before they were bored and discontented and hated their masters."

"I am impressed!" said Blue Peter. "Organising their selection and training cannot have been easy."

"Indeed not, especially as I had to do much of it by correspondence. I was lucky in my first recruits, though, and they did a lot of the work once they were properly instructed. The biggest problem was finding places for them to practice the arts of war. There are few halls to rent, and apprentice-boys have a reputation for political trouble-making. In the end I bought some vacant buildings and established them as clubs for playing pall-mall. I thus had control of the meeting-places, and a sporting activity as a cloak for comings and goings at odd hours. Pall-mall has become so popular that the clubs even make a fine profit! Ain't life strange?"

"Is it a game, then? I have not heard of it."

"It is a game played with wooden balls that roll upon a levelled floor of packed earth, struck with long-handled mallets. The Italian for the game is *pallamaglio*, but it's called pall-mall since Londoners talk as though they have a permanent head-cold."

"I have heard the word, but I thought that it was a street of commerce."

"Indeed it is, but the street had no name until a covered alley for pall-mall was built there. I don't know why the cockaignies don't say 'pall-mall street', though, which would make more sense." The Captain shrugged and drank some ale, as though dismissing the foibles of Londoners.

"These apprentices, with their varied skills, are required for your plan for revenge upon the extramundane creature, I assume," said Blue Peter carefully. He had refrained from asking the Captain further questions since their discussion during the banyan day at Porte de Recailles, but the choice of new crewmen with diverse skills had aroused his interest.

"Indeed yes," replied Captain Sylvestre de Greybagges. "I need to make some alterations to the *Ark de Triomphe* in furtherance of my plan, and they are the fellows to do it, with Frank Benjamin as their overseer and tutor. Mostly the metal-workers and mechanics, of course, not the clerks and book-keepers, who shall stay ashore and run our banking business. I have retained about ninety of the original crew – I have specifically chosen those who are not afraid of new things, and who are, so to speak, not overly *superstitious* – and with about fifty new fellows we shall be able to get the work done over the coming winter, if all goes well. That gives us a crew smaller than before, but we shall not need so many fighting men and gun-crews as I intend to take no more prizes as we are well in funds, but we shall need excellent smiths. I have ordered and paid for the things that I shall need for the work well in advance, so they shall be ready in a timely fashion."

"Where will these alterations be done?" asked Blue Peter.

"I have purchased a boatyard, a very suitable boatyard" said the Captain, with a wink that ended further questions.

There was a knock at the door of the Great Cabin.

"Who be it? Damn and blast yer eyes!" roared Captain Greybagges.

"It is … it be … only I, Frank Benjamin," came a voice through the door.

"Come in then, Frank Benjamin, wi' a curse!" roared the Captain.

Mr Benjamin entered, looking slightly unnerved. The Captain smiled and indicated a chair.

"Excuse me, Frank. There are certain formalities to being a captain of buccaneers, and I did not know it was yourself."

Mr Benjamin looked relieved and seated himself. Blue Peter grinned at him, his filed teeth gleaming whitely. He took the jug, poured a tankard and gave it to Mr Benjamin.

"There is nothing finer than a good London brew, Frank, provided it has not been watered, which is to say diluted with a small portion of the river Thames."

"Don't be such an ass, Peter," laughed the Captain. "Tell me Frank, have you been introducing yourself to the new lads?"

"Indeed I have," said Mr Benjamin, sipping the ale, "and they are good fellows. Skilled at their trades. Adroit with their hands. Alert in their minds. Full of the fine intelligent curiosity of the mechanic, although I could not sate that yearning, except to tell them that all would be made clear in time."

"And indeed it will be," said the Captain, "as indeed will your fine intelligent curiosity also be satisfied, Frank."

There was a another knock at the door, and Bulbous Bill and Israel Feet entered without waiting for a response. The First Mate's head still had a bandage around it, but he looked cheerful and pain-free. They helped themselves to ale. Bulbous Bill scowled at the First Mate and went to take the tankard from him.

"Nay, Bill. Mr Feet may surely have a wet of ale if his headaches have diminished. No rum or other spiritous liquors for the present, mind," said Mr Benjamin.

"Thank'ee kindly," said the First Mate. "Please do call me Izzy, since you have joined the ship proper-like." Mr Benjamin nodded in acknowledgement, replying that Izzy must surely call him Frank, as indeed must all of them.

They sipped ale in silence for a while, listening to the noises of the wharf.

"We must away soon. Tomorrow, or the next day at the very latest. Tell me the state of things," said Captain Greybagges.

The Captain's officers made their reports. New sailcloth and cordage had been delivered, said Bill, but new sheaving-blocks, paint and pitch were still awaited. He had been promised them for tomorrow morning for sure. Israel Feet recounted how he had settled in the new crew, allotted them their watches and messes, told the old hands to show them the ropes and warned them to be sober and careful. The old hands who had been allowed ashore to visit families, wives and girlfriends were all now returned, except for two, and they had sent messages. Blue Peter confirmed that powder and shot had been delivered and stowed safely, and that timber and strap-iron had been brought, too, so that the carpenter could make some small but necessary repairs to the gun-carriages. Mr Benjamin confirmed that the carpenter's stock of fine copper wire had be replenished and that certain tools and equipment had been received, or else were expected on the morrow.

"Well, it seems that we shall depart the day after next," said the Captain reflectively. "Upon the morning ebb, with luck, in the afternoon, against the tide, if there are any last-minute hitches. Things are nicely ship-shape, so it may be that I shall go ashore myself and grow my beard a little, and you gentlemen must join me, for your company is welcome, and we have seen but little of London's society."

The others murmured appreciatively.

"Go and check everything once more. The watchers on the wharf must keep a sharp look-out. Tell Loomin' Len and his boys to come to me for their orders."

The officers left the cabin.

"Jake!" roared Captain Greybagges. "Come here, and bring the boot-polish!"

Blue Peter Ceteshwayoo lay in his bunk in his tiny cabin in the *Ark de Triomphe*, but sleep would not come easily, despite the food and drink that he had consumed during the afternoon and the gentle rocking of the ship. I do not like London that much, he thought. It may well be the greatest city of the entire Globe, but I am greatly disappointed with it. Perhaps after all I have read, and all the tales I have heard, my expectations were too high. In the Caribbean it is warm, and here it is cold and the the sun hardly shows its face. The nights of the Port de Recailles are made for talking, for music, for dancing, for drinking, for taking one's ease with friends, but here the cold black nights are uncomfortable and threatening. Everybody must be home before dark because of the fear of footpads and the like, and yet the day ends very early. Even if they stay in their own parlours the penny-pinching sods begrudge the cost of a tallow candle. The very rich can carouse through the midnight hours, of course, but they have coaches to take them home, servants to guard them and many bright lights to illuminate their feastings and shindiggeries, the lamps burning that great new luxury, the oil of whales. The night belongs to the thieves, the burglars and the highwaymen as well as to the wealthy, mused Blue Peter, and I suppose I shouldn't mind that, as I am a pirate and so first cousin to them. The growing of the Captain's beard had started on a strange disquieting note, too, he recalled. Israel Feet had declined to come with them at the very last moment; it would be no great pleasure going out upon the fuddle if he could not drink rum, he had said, and someone should stay with the ship, for Loomin' Len had not the wit to deal with the unexpected. If that great roisterer Izzy was seized by a mood of responsible sobriety, even allowing for his convalescent condition, then what was afoot? Indeed there is a serious and sombre mood aboard the barky, especially so given that a new draught of young crew is settling in, and we are after all a pirate ship and freebooters are rarely so sequacious. The surprising atmosphere of discipline that has prevailed since the greening of the Captain's beard must be partly responsible, thought Blue Peter, but there is something else. Even though the Captain says nothing of his plans and there is little discussion of our destination, there is yet a feeling that we are upon a dangerous enterprise. A voyage into the unknown, one might say, and that will make intelligent men thoughtful, and most of the stupid ones have been paid off and gone ashore to enjoy their shares in the plunderings of the past year.

Mind you, said Blue Peter to himself, the fellow Frank Benjamin was in fine spirits. The coach-ride that took us into the City of London itself would have been a mumpish affair without Frank jesting about yokels losing their hearts to pretty ewes, and hallooing and waving his hat at the country-girls we passed along the road. Once the coach had left the little knot of taverns and warehouses fronting the Pacific Wharf at Rotherhithe they had been rolling through open countryside, rich with fields of crops despite the lateness of the year, the red-brick of the occasional farmhouses standing out against their greenness. That England is what I wished to see, perhaps, mused Blue Peter, the strong bones of Albion. Perhaps it is only London that I don't like. What was it that the wit Sam Johnson called it? 'The Great Wen', that was it. London is not easy to love, despite the fine great dinner we had, and those French wines which were worthy of the well of Hippocrene itself. The Red Cow at Wapping was perhaps a poor choice of tavern, though, being so close to Execution Dock where pirates such as we are hanged, and the tarred corpses of a couple of them hanging from a gibbet almost outside the window of the upstairs room where we dined. Frank Benjamin is a good fellow, thought Blue Peter, as he felt himself falling asleep at last. He was very enthusiastic for the game of pall-mall, there were wooden balls flying everywhere like a cannonade, and none through the hoop. He is an empirical fellow, though, with a passion always to try things out to see what happens, and that is both a curse and a blessing; I must be careful if I ever let him near the guns, for he is sure to ask. Ha! That strutting fool of a bruiser on the door of the Red Cow called me a blackamoor, but Frank snarled at him that he is not as black as your black heart, you whoreson jackanapes, and the bruiser had quailed before the Frank's fiery indignation. Blue Peter smiled, then he started to snore.

Captain Sylvestre de Greybagges awoke at first light with a hangover. He blinked a couple of times, then sat up and swung his legs onto the deck, the painted canvas deck-covering cold to the touch of his feet as he steadied the swinging of the hanging bunk. He rubbed his face and shouted for Mumblin' Jake. Despite his crapulence there were things to do, and he must be about them. Mumblin' Jake came, mumbling curses under his breath, with a cannikin of hot coffee which he thrust into the Captain's hand then went out again, still mumbling. He returned with a bowl of hot water and shaved the Captain's head while he drank the coffee, then, on the Captain's instructions, applied brown boot-polish to his green beard where the previous application had rubbed off on the pillow, mumbling about the hard, the *washerwoman's*, work to get boot-polish out of linen pillowcases, damn yer eyes, yer sod.

The Captain dressed himself carefully, not in his accustomed black, nor in the fine gold-frogged powder-blue uniform of a *kapitein van schip* in the Dutch East India Company, but in an unremarkable buff coat and breeches, grey hose and stout buckled shoes; he had no intention of drawing attention to himself.

While Mumblin' Jake fetched him some breakfast he took out his writing-case and penned one last letter to add to the bundle that he had written the day before. It read:

My dear friend Muhammed,

I trust this missive finds you and your family in good health and prosperity, and that your fine crew of corsairs is in good spirits.

I recently had an excellent lunch with the pipsqueak Billy Pitt, who asked to be remembered to you, and spoke of you with great fondness. He had news of your old chum Stinky Bodfish. An uncle of the fellow's passed away last year and, since he expired without issue, Humbertus de Pfeffel Bodfish is now the Earl of Jobberknowle and possessed of a very considerable fortune. Bodfish has wasted no time in putting his new-found wealth to work. He has purchased a colonelcy in the Royal Bumbleshire Light Horse (known as the 'Never-Show-Fears' because of the brown breeches of the regimental uniform) and has used his presence at Horse Guards Parade and the influence of his inheritance to have himself appointed an attaché to Britain's Consular Mission to the

Kingdom of Naples. He will be taking up this posting in the spring of the New Year, and will in consequence be travelling from the port of Southampton to Napoli aboard the barquentine *Alcibiades*, his voyage commencing shortly after the midwinter festivities of Yuletide. As he will be passing through the Mediterranean Seas I am sure that you will be eager to take the opportunity to meet him again to renew old friendship and to congratulate him on his accession to an Earldom and his acquisition of such a large fortune. I am sorry that I shall not be able to be there for such a joyous reunion of old school-friends!

Please excuse the briefness of this communication, but I have much business to attend to at the present, and but little time for its accomplishment.

Your friend,

Sylvestre de Greybagges

After the last *scritch-scratch* of his quill as he signed his name with a flourish Captain Greybagges sanded the letter, read it through again, smiled to himself and sealed it with the green sealing-wax that he had recently bought. He tucked the letters into an inside pocket of his coat, tucked a small double-barrelled pistol into a waistcoat pocket, clapped a short brown scrub-wig and a brown felt hat upon his bald head and called for Mumblin' Jake to send for two bully-boys.

On the wharf Captain Greybagges found that there were no coaches willing to go to the City; those that were there had all been secured to wait for clients by non-payment of the outward fee and promises of a tip after the return. He was annoyed by this, but returned to the *Ark de Triomphe* and had the longboat launched, with four of the new intake of crew to assist the bully-boys in pulling the oars. As the longboat was pulled against the slackening tide up the river he was glad that he had done so. He never really felt comfortable in a coach – nasty rattling contraptions, unlike a ship or a boat – and the day was pleasant, although cold. After rounding the first bend Captain Greybagges shed his buff coat and took an oar for a while to warm himself, He found his hangover and sour mood lightening to a more equable state of mind, and he chaffed the new crewmen to put them at their ease, the two bully-boys pulling steadily and saying nothing. It took nearly an hour and a half to reach Blackfriars, where he leapt nimbly ashore. The bully-boys followed him, slipping oaken cudgels under their coats. He left the four new crewmen to watch the boat, tossing them a few coins for an ale and a pie each, warning them with a wink to keep a sharp lookout for wicked pirates.

Captain Greybagges sent some letters from a postal agent's office, then went to the representatives of Tristero's secret mail service, a ramshackle shop dealing in second-hand clothes and moth-eaten wigs. The place smelled sourly of old sweat from the piles of apparel, none of which seemed to have been washed, but he found the box marked W.A.S.T.E behind a pile of ragged undergarments and slipped a bundle of sealed and stamped letters into it. The keeper of the shop, a fat slatternly woman in a mob cap and shawl, had no letters for him. He tossed her a silver coin anyway, which she bit, then winked at him lewdly as she hid it in the folds of her gown. The bully-boys waited patiently for him out in the narrow street, but as he was about to walk away he saw a shop nearly opposite. The dusty window was full of bottles on wooden stands. His curiosity made him walk over and peer through the dusty glass. Each of the bottles had a small ship inside it. The Captain felt a pleasurable surprise; how did the little barky get into the bottle through so small a neck? He smiled, as though at a sudden thought, bade the bully-boys to wait, and entered the shop, a bell above the door jangling discordantly.

The shop was filled with bottles of all shapes each containing a tiny ship, and unbottled models of ships of all sizes and types, crammed onto shelves, in glass-fronted counters, hanging from hooks in the the ceiling. A teak model of a pleasure-yacht as large as a kayak, gaff-rigged with red cotton sails, sat on the floor in a cradle of varnished yellow deal. Next to it was a very small ship's cannon with a bore of no more than an inch, perfect in every detail, even to tiny Chatham proof-marks stamped into the brass barrel next to the touch-hole.

"Can I assist you, good sir?" came a deep voice from the rear of the shop.

The Captain walked towards the voice, pausing to admire a beautiful Spanish galleon in a two-gallon rum-jug, its sails of silk stiffened with starch to appear filled with a stiff breeze, the pennons flying from its mastheads almost seeming to wave.

"Come, sir, let me see you!" said the voice.

As the Captain reached the back of the shop he saw a broad black-haired bearded face peering over a counter-top, and the gaping brass mouth of a blunderbuss post-carbine pointing unwaveringly at him. Bright blue eyes regarded him from under bushy black brows. He was about to ask the fellow why he was on his knees, but the bearded head moved along the top of the counter and around the end and he realised that the man was a hunchbacked dwarf, his chin barely higher than the Captain's belt. He had the appearance of a keg on stumpy legs, his arms heavily muscled and covered with tattoos. The gun pointed unwaveringly at the Captain's midriff.

"Come, sir! Can you not speak?" he rumbled.

"My apologies, sir. I am Captain … er … Oplichtenaar. I mean you no harm, I vow!" said the Captain, removing his hat and bowing politely.

"No, perhaps you do not," said the dwarf, lowering the gun, carefully slipping the flint to half-cock before placing it behind the counter, "but one cannot be too careful. There are many wicked thievish characters a-circulating around these opprobrious lanes, rascally cullies – aye, and infandous mollies, too! - alike to pi-dogs around a shambles. Now, how may I be of assistance to you this day?"

"How do you get the ships into such tiny bottles? I confess myself amazed!"

The dwarf put back his head and roared with laughter. "Hah! Maybe you would not steal my purse, but you would surely steal my arts, if you could! As would many curious and grasping knaves! Why only last month the fool of a pie-maker next door drilled a hole through yonder wall hoping to espy me about my labours and to learn my secrets. I squirted vinegar and pepper in his stupid eye with a barber's ear-syringe, then sued him for the cost of repairs to the wall. The lawyer took as his fee a brandy-bottle with a little desk inside, and upon it a wee ink-pot and quill, some papers tied about with pink ribbon and a wig on a stand. The pink ribbon was the very devil, but by chance I found some very wispy French silk knickers, cut thin strips of the fabric, treated them with a special solution and made them flat with a pressing-iron the size of a thimble. "

The Captain joined him in his merriment, until he had to wipe tears from his eyes.

"My heart and liver, sir, but you are a droll fellow! I confess myself very pleased to make your acquaintance!" Captain Greybagges shook his head. "Your ship-models, your *mijnheertjes*, as a Dutchman might say, are not only finely-wrought but also very accurate in their representation of the full-sized article. Am I correct to assume that you have been to sea?"

"I have indeed. I was a ship's carpenter for many a long year. Sailed upon many seas, upon waters grey, white and blue. Across the German Ocean, back and forth until I could tell the longtitude by my sense of smell alone. To the Americas. To far Cathay. Sailed in rotten tubs not fit to be broken up for kindling-wood, and in fine ships with bottoms of copper and gold-leaf upon their transoms and figureheads. Served under some of the greatest captains, and endured servitude under dunces, and tyrants, too – I will not dignify them as captains, nor even as commanders – who had but little claim to be even the basest forms of humanity, more alike to devils." He regarded the Captain steadily from under his bristling brows. "Jebediah Vane was the worst. Couldn't keep his hands off a coin. Couldn't keep his manhood in his britches. Couldn't keep a bottle from his lips. The crew voted him out at the last, and we pleaded for pardon from the governor of Virginia, who obliged us in that for only about half of what we possessed. T'was Vane that gave me the notion for my business, though. He would always be a-mocking me for my size. 'Har-har-har!' he'd say, 'ship's carpenter be yuz? Yuz be such a damn-yer-eyes runt yuz oughta make little ships for sailin' around in the bottoms of bottles, round 'n' round 'til yuz goes aground on the lees, ye swab! Har-bloody-har-har.' When I heard he'd been hanged I am ashamed to say I celebrated, which is how I came across the wispy pink French silk knickers, for I am not a frequenter of such places in the normal course of things, only when I have had one too many."

"Good Lord!" said Captain Greybagges, eyebrows raised. "Do you mean to say that you were once a pirate?"

"No more than you, Captain *Oplichtenaar*, who has two pistols in his weskit pockets, a stiletto in an arm-sheath in his left coat-sleeve and two bully-boys outside big enough to pull a ox-plough." The bearded dwarf managed to look innocent and amused simultaneously. Captain Greybagges regarded him for a second, then burst into laughter again.

"I shall ask you no questions, mind you!" said the dwarfish man, "for your business is yours as my business is mine, and I think you wish to consult me in my professional capacity, not I in yours, and that may be done more companionably over a glass or two of hot rum-grog, surely? Tell your two bruisers to take a drink in the corner ale-house. I will put up the 'back-in-an-hour' sign and nobody will bother us while we yarn awhile."

"A very singular fellow, is Alf Docklefar," said Captain Greybagges, "very singular, indeed."

The remains of a very late supper covered the table in the wardroom of the *Ark de Triomphe*: a ham, with not much ham left upon its bone; the skeletal remains of several roasted chickens; heels of loaves; the crumbs of a Spotted Dick, soaking up the last dribbles of a warm sauce of Muscovy sugar, spices, egg-yolks, cider and rum; rinds of cheeses; a large brown-glazed ale-jug and assorted wine-bottles.

"And here is a very singular bottle for you. One which you may not empty, but wonder instead at how it came to be filled."

Captain Greybagges passed a cloth bundle to Bulbous Bill Bucephalus. The sailing-master unwrapped a clear glass wine-bottle and peered at it.

"It be a tiny ship! A barquentine ... no, a hermaphrodite brig! ... no, more of a brigantine, hmm...."

"Give it here, you lubber, wi' a curse!" said Israel Feet, taking the bottle and pering into it. "It be more of a large poleacre, upon my oath!"

"I thought it more of a balener, though it could be a ballinger. Tis surely not a barque, a bilander or a bergantina, that much is clear," said the Captain, sipping ale, and winking at Blue Peter. "The after-mast being a luffing gaff-rig throws it all into the darkest of confusion, d'you see? And that stun-sail on the topmast royal is ambiguous to say the very least. Alf Docklefar makes 'em."

"That cannot be a stun-sail!" said Bill hotly. "It can only be a sky-scraper try-sail, jury-rigged in the Corsican manner! Given the shape o' the rest o' the riggin', o' course."

"I think the puzzle is not what type of vessel it is," said Blue Peter, who had taken the bottle in turn, "but how the vessel got into the vessel, ho-ho!"

Frank Benjamin took the bottle and studied it.

"Is there some doubt about which type of boat this is?" he said, examining the small model closely, his *pince-nez* spectacles on the end of his nose.

"Mr Docklefar has a prodigious knowledge of ships, and that small facsimile is cunningly wrought so that it cannot be easily categorised or given a name. An amusing enigma for sailors to ponder and dispute over. Why! One could claim the lower gun-ports were really unused oar-holes and it thus could be a dromond or even a galleass!"

"How it is put inside is no mystery," said Mr Benjamin. "One's first thought is that the bottle has been cracked open and then re-joined with a transparent spiritous glue, but even the finest shellac has a slight yellow tinge and there is no sign of that. The ship must necessarily have entered through the neck of the bottle, therefore. I think I can see how that could be done, but I shall forbear to say more. Is Alf Dockelfar the only manufacturer of such trifles?"

"Alf claims to be the originator of the art, but others have followed his example," said the Captain. "A tar can work on such a thing in a berth below decks and keep it in his seamen's chest between-times, alike to scrimshaw work on bones and on walrus-ivory. Many of the bottled argosies in his emporium were made by sailormen. He acts as a sort of pawnbroker for them, gives loans on 'em and buys and sells 'em. There is a demand for them in London, as it sees itself as the great mercantile port of the world. I do not doubt that soon there will be a ship in a bottle in every ale-house, every broker's office and on the mantelpiece of every shipping-clerk. He does make models of ships that ain't in bottles. Shipwrights use miniature representations to show to customers what they will be getting for their money. Toys for the children of the wealthy, too, little toy yachts and jolly-boats to sail on duck-ponds. He sells bits and pieces to the other fellows that make little ships. Little anchors of cast printers-lead, little cannon barrels of brass lathed on a watchmaker's turn, that sort of thing, in all sizes."

"How is it done, then?" said Israel Feet, contemplating the ship in the bottle. "If you knows, Frank, speak plain!"

Frank Benjamin opened his mouth, but Captain Greybagges put up his hand.

"Frank is right to keep his council. Alf Docklefar's art is entertaining for as long as it mystifies, and what is life without a few mysteries? Thus you have a congenial puzzle to charm you as you slip into the arms of Morpheus, Izzy, for now we must all retire. There will be much to do tomorrow." The Captain drained his tankard. "The mystery I shall take with me to my bunk is how the devil Alf Dockelfar knew I had two pistols and a knife concealed about me! Good night to you, gentlemen!"

The next morning Captain Sylvestre de Greybags paced the quarterdeck of the pirate frigate *Ark de Triomphe*, dressed once again as a *kapitein van schip*, his head freshly shaven and his beard freshly boot-polished. The last few deliveries of stores were awaited, and the crew were preparing to set sail. He paced the deck impatiently, accompanied by Mr Benjamin.

"Take my advice, Frank. Wait for your sea-water bath until we are actually at sea. Excuse me – belay that there! Yer damn-yer-eyes lubber! Let me sees yuz usin' a grandma's knot like that again an I'll sees the colour of yer liver, yer swab! 'Pon my oath I will! – Sorry, Frank, these young fellows are eager, but sadly ignorant yet. Where was I? Yes, take your bath when we are in the German Ocean, where the water is contaminated only by the sweat of fish. A bath in Thames river-water could easily be fatal to somebody who is not a cockaignie."

"I've seen the seen the boys swimming off the wharf," said Mr Benjamin, "but I've also seen what floats by at times. You are right, of course. Why are they called cockaignies?"

"London fellows of the lower orders of society who find themselves in Paris - as some must inevitably do - are observed by the Frenchies to be forever complaining about the food. Why, in Lunnon-town there is roast beef! And roast mutton! And roast capons! And beer! The French populace, much oppressed by their evil king and his greedy aristocrats and so existing upon thin gruel and bread made of sawdust, mock such fellows and say that they must come from *cockagne*, the fabled land of the fairies where there are fountains of sparkling wine and where meat-pies grow on trees. The lowlifes of London have adopted this cognomen with pride, and so refer to themselves thus."

"Would your ships-in-bottles fellow describe himself as a cockaignie?"

"I should not think so. He craves a degree of respectability, and to call oneself a cockaignie is rather to proudly deny that one has any repectability at all, or indeed any desire for it. It is mostly the young fellows."

"He cannot be too respectable, not if he can tell that you are carrying concealed weapons."

"Respectability is something to be attained, surely, even when starting from a state of brutish and light-fingered poverty. Since Alf Docklefar's respectability started when he purchased a pardon from the gallows for piracy he may be assumed to have a keen sense of its monetary value. He has a sharp eye, though, and I dare say his past experience has made him alert to possible trouble. The outline of a pistol against the cloth of a waistcoat is easy to spot if you are looking, I suppose, and very difficult if you do not look, as most people do not look at most things."

The Captain and Mr Benjamin talked on about the oddities of perception; examples of legerdemain, the obvious frauds which could ensnare even clever people at times, why mirrors turn one side-to-side but not top-to-bottom. Captain Greybagges would occasionally roar curses and instructions at one of the new crewmen.

Down below in the dark of the gun-deck Blue Peter and Torvald Coalbiter were patiently explaining the loading, aiming and firing of a cannon to a group of apprentice pirates.

"Safety must be your watchword!" said Blue Peter in his deep rumbling voice. The young pirates nodded cautious agreement; his size, his scarred blue-black face and his filed teeth did not seem to invite discussion. "The idea is, you see, to blow the other ship to pieces, not this one. The gun-deck is prepared for action by wetting the planking, by hanging wet sacks over doors, by dowsing all lights that are not behind glass and so on, to prevent any spark from entering the powder-magazine. But you yourselves must be prepared for action, too, so that nothing can go amiss with you. You must learn to do your tasks in the right way, tedious though such rote-learning may seem right now. Any questions?"

"Um, cannot we speak more like pirates, if we want to?" said one of the braver apprentices.

"Indeed you can, and Mr Feet the First Mate will be giving you lessons in

116

the language of the freebooter," said Blue Peter, improvising, "but he is presently slightly indisposed from a blow on the head. In the meantime it's best not to stand upon ceremony, and to speak as we are able, to avoid confusion."

Blue Peter was soon sidetracked into an explanation of the First Mate's wound, an account of the night attack and thereby on to an account of the Captain's defeat of Ali the Barber by the cunning twisting of words. Torvald Coalbiter fetched the giant razor and showed it to the apprentice pirates as proof of the tale. They were duly impressed.

"There is much for you to learn about the profession of buccaneering," said Blue Peter. "It's not all rum and cutlasses and 'Arr! Me hearties!' There's some of that, of course, but this is a modern pirate-ship, run on progressive principles, so we operate in a more disciplined way than some others, like Captain Blackbeard, for example." And I hope that accords with what the Captain is planning, thought Peter, whatever it is.

Torvald Coalbiter took up the lesson in Blue Peter's silence, and repeated his tale about his name, and the virtues of avoiding trouble if there was no profit in it. Some of the apprentice pirates disagreed mildly on philosophical grounds, pointing out that if piracy were too well-organised it would be the same as serving before the mast on a merchant-vessel.

"Why, not at all!" said Coalbiter. "it is the spirit of the thing that counts! And all enterprises require a degree of efficiency or they will not work at all! For example, the modern pirate has to be alert to the possibilities arising from the fast transport of information. He must be, or be beached or hanged, else! Even the beserkers, who I have just disparaged for their stupidity, knew full-well the value of an efficient postal system. My uncle Erik Bloodsausage used to recite a poem to us when we were little, just to remind us of this inescapable fact."

Torvald Coalbiter drew himself up, and declaimed:

"Many years ago, an old Norse berserker,
   told me a stirring tale, a real tear-jerker,
   about how he'd never been a shirker,
   when he was a Scandiwegian postal-worker.

He said the Vikings never sacked a town,
Unless first they'd parcelled it up in paper brown,
sealed with sticky tape well-thumbed down,
and hempen string knotted all around.

Up in the North it was often dark and damp,
but in the temporary sorting-camp,
each parcel was addressed and stamped,
by the yellow light of tallow lamps.

Then the long ships raced under oar and sail,
with mail-sacks stacked right up to the rail,
because they must never ever slow or fail,
nothing stops the Scandiwegian mail!

When the town was posted-off, except the pub,
the postmen would sit down for some grub,
they'd dine on pie-and-chips and syllabub,
then belch and grab themselves a club.

The folks of the town they'd gather up,
then bash each one on the head, just like a seal-pup,
it was hard graft after such a hearty sup,
but those carbs helped to keep their blood-sugars up.

When all the savings accounts were discharged,
they'd go back to the boats to get undisembarged,
and with their purses much enlarged,
they could afford an afternoon snack of bread and marge.

If you ask any Norse postman I betcha most'll,
tell you straight, insist that always our boast'll,
be that in mailing matters, whether ashore or coastal,

there's no one like a beserker for going postal!"

His words being being proven true at that very moment, as a last packet of post was passed to Captain Greybagges even as the mooring-cables were slipped from the bollards. A small group of apprentice-boys went ashore and disappeared into the crowds on the wharf, and the gangplank was drawn up. Hired boats slowly pulled the *Ark de Triomphe* out into the stream, turning her to go south-southeast with the current and tide. Captain Sylvestre de Greybags paid them with coins thrown from the quarterdeck rail and an exchange of friendly insults. Bulbous Bill Bucephalus howled at the men in the rigging and the topsails dropped and unfurled to catch the slight breeze, the convenient easterly breeze. Within ten minutes the *Ark de Triomphe* turned the bend of the river looping back around the Isle of Dogs and was lost from sight.

A horse rode to the edge of the wharf, and its rider dismounted and looked at the empty quay where the *Ark de Triomphe* had been. A tall angular man in a long black cloak and a battered black slouch hat, his lower face hidden by a scarf to ward off the dust of the road, his eyes in the shadow of the hat-brim. He asked a nearby idler to confirm the name of the ship so recently set sail, his voice deep and harsh. The idler acknowledged that the ship had indeed been the *Groot Ombeschaamheid*, a Dutch merchantman out of Rotterdam, then moved away from the stranger as quickly as he could without seeming to hurry, unsettled by the man's abrupt question and angry manner. The man remounted his horse in one agile movement like an experienced cavalry-trooper, swinging a heavy boot over the horse's rump, his black cloak flapping. The horse whickered and pranced sideways a few steps, but the black-clad figure mastered it instantly and swung it round so he could stare once more down the river before he turned the horse and rode away. The idler looked back over his shoulder, and as he did a chance ray of the early sun slid under the brim of the black slouch hat and lit the face of the man.

The idler went into one of the taverns facing onto the wharf and bought a large measure of gin. It must just have been a trick of the light, he told himself as he gulped the gin. Nobody has green eyebrows.

CHAPTER THE NINTH,
or *The Pool of Life.*

"I do not like these birds," said Blue Peter Ceteshwayoo. "They resemble the misbegotten offspring of a vulture and a pelican, and they have a malevolent stare. They look like they ought to have teeth in their beaks." He aimed a kick at one of the birds, which avoided the blow easily with a sideways hop, stared at him malevolently with a yellow eye, croaked 'awk!' then flapped away through the cold drizzling rain towards the river, its orange webbed feet dangling.

"The locals say they are called 'snappers', but they are properly called Liver birds," said Captain Sylvestre de Greybagges. "They are only found around the Liver Pool and nowhere else, so it is a reasonable sort of name. Not a name like 'warriangle' or 'merganser', which are meaningless. A merganser does not 'merganse', does it?"

"The warriangle is the red shrike, also called the butcher-bird, or the worrier, or the throttler," said Frank Benjamin, trudging behind them, trying to keep his cloak wrapped around himself against the wind and rain. "Warriangle is but a corruption of *wurgengel*, which is German for 'destroying angel'. I do not know why they have such a reputation, for they are an attractive bird. Unlike these ugly things." He waved a walking-stick at another Liver bird as it skimmed past on the wind, squawking.

"They sound the same as the damned inhabitants of this God-forsaken place," said Blue Peter, "as though they have a head-cold, like the Londoners but worse. I had thought London to be a cold and miserable place, but I see it now as fairly tropical. I am surprised palm trees do not grow on Tilbury Dock."

The three trudged through the mud. It was unpleasant to be abroad, despite their hats, woollen cloaks and greased sea-boots. A Liver bird hovered above them, its cry mournful and strangely nasal; "Awk! Awk! Awk-la!"

The muddy path of Pool Lane skirted the eponymous pool, and eventually led to the hump-backed Towsend bridge over the stream that emptied into it. They looked back from the bridge at the town of Liver Pool, a cluster of buildings dark in the last of the daylight. The bulk of the Old Castle in the midst of the houses, the church standing out by virtue of its square tower, the grey expanse of the Mersey estuary beyond it occasionally visible through the curtains of cold rain.

They carried on over the bridge.

"The fellows in the tavern seemed cheerful and friendly enough, but strangely menacing," said Mr Benjamin. "I didn't know what to make of them."

"It is their way, it seems," said the Captain. "They distrust strangers, and they are surely not unusual in that, yet must deal with them, and so they attempt to appear both amiable and daunting at one and the same time. In a way it suits my purposes, for they are not overly curious, since they themselves do not welcome scrutiny. I hope my words to them, and my small gifts, will reduce the attempts at burglarising. I do not wish to use stronger measures. Come, we are nearly there, and a glass of rum-grog will cheer us."

Captain Greybagges had purchased a boat-builder's yard on the eastern side of the Liver Pool, away from the town. It had been unused and vacant for several years, almost becoming a ruin, its buildings pillaged by the locals for slate from the roofs and wood. The three squelched down the path at the edge of the Pool in the rain.

In the boatyard there was shelter, warmth and light. Light shining from the windows of the yardmaster's house in the increasing gloom, the gleam of lamps visible from workshops and lean-to sheds. Pirates are sailors nevertheless, and are accustomed to making the best of circumstances, and to the continuous frenzy of repair and cleaning that is life at sea. The residence of the master of the boatyard, empty for years, lacking window-glass, window-frames, doors, floorboards and most of its roof, had stood no chance against the nautical repugnance for disorder, and had been made habitable in two days by a busy fury of pirate work-squads, and made neat and painted in a week, the glossy yellow enamel of the front door a bright gesture of contempt to the unremitting rain. They went gratefully in, but Blue Peter excused himself after gulping a glass of grog and walked around the boatyard on an evening tour of inspection.

A number of wooden huts had been built and the crew had moved ashore. There was light from these huts as the watches were changing. Blue Peter stopped at the huts, talking with the men. A supper of crocks of stew, baskets of bread and jugs of ale was being collected and brought to the huts, each mess going to the kitchen at the house in strict turn, the same as at sea. The men would eat, drink, sing, play at cards and dice, then stow the trestle-tables against the wall and sling their hammocks and sleep the sleep of the just, for the work was unrelenting and hard.

Blue Peter walked on down to the *Ark de Triomphe*. Upon her arrival at the boatyard the frigate had been stripped and emptied as it lay moored at the end of the wooden jetty. The frigate's masts had been unstepped and the guns and ballast unloaded with the aid of a sheer-hulk, a floating contraption of great antiquity. Blue Peter had been surprised by the age of the sheer-hulk; its timbers were a patchwork of scarfings and the overlaps of its clinker planks had been undercut a finger's width by the soft abrasions of flowing water in some long-forgotten past when its hull had actually plowed the seas and not been merely the pontoon for a crane built of old masts and spars. Opinions of the age of the sheer-hulk's hull had varied, but the ship's carpenter had assessed it to be one-and-a-half centuries old at least, maybe two. Blue Peter had found himself strangely impressed by this; who knew that a wooden ship could last that long? The stripped-bare, and much-lightened, hull of the *Ark de Triomphe* had been dragged ashore by the cunning application of rollers and the Spanish windlass and placed on a stollage of wooden baulks in a rectangular pit, where it now sat. The vast labour of digging the pit and dragging the hull ashore into it resembled something, mused Blue Peter, but he couldn't think exactly what. Israelites in the Bible slaving to build pyramids? Did they build pyramids in the Bible? Except that the semi-naked slaves had been slaving in the pouring rain, splattered with freezing brown Mersey mud, not in the hot sun of Egypt on the banks of the sluggish warm Nile. The accomplishment of such a gruelling task had drawn the crew together, though, in a very powerful way. There had been some tensions on the voyage to Liver Pool, the old pirates being short of patience with the apprentice pirates for their lack of seamanship, tending to patronise them by strutting about as they felt men should who had seen bloody actions, while the new pirates had responded in turn by mocking the old pirates for their lack of education and knowledge of things mechanical. The heroic struggle with the hull of the *Ark de Triomphe* had made them work together, work to each other's strengths, so now it was 'the old pirates' and 'the new pirates', and not 'the pirates' and 'the apprentice-boys'.

Blue Peter continued his walk around the boatyard, checking that the pickets were alert. The locals were very thievish and there had been numerous attempts to steal, some of them worryingly ingenious. The Captain was paying regular bribes to the Lennons and the McCartneys, the main criminal gangs of Liver Pool, to prevent or at least limit pilfering, but the lesser affiliated clans, the Starkeys and the

Harrisons, were probably not receiving their fair share of the protection-money and so felt less constrained. The Best gang, having been completely expelled from the Liver Pool underworld to the wilderness of the Wirral, felt no constraint at all, of course, but were relatively powerless to operate on the other gangs' turf. Blue Peter was determined to prevent a violent incident causing trouble, so vigilance was important, and he was thankful for the tolerant attitude of the pirates to the locals; they were only thieves, after all, and so regarded as a nuisance and not a threat, to be given a clout round the ear when apprehended, not shot, disembowelled with a cutlass or crippled in such a way as might lead to ill-will. There must be some contacts with the locals, of course. These were mostly of a carnal nature, whether procured by payment or by simple affection, and remained a potential source of incidents.

Jack Nastyface joined Blue Peter on his tour of the perimeter, falling silently into step with him, cloaked in a cape of tarpaulin against the foul weather. The young man had become quieter, more introspective, since his friend Jemmy Ducks had left the pirate crew, no longer the giddy youth who had skylarked in the rigging with whoops and catcalls. Blue Peter was sure that if he had not checked the sentries then Jack would have done so unprompted even though he had just finished helping the cook prepare the supper.

"Have you heard from Jemmy at all?" he asked as they approached the house.

"He sent a letter by the tubs," replied Jack. "He is investing his loot in a brewery in Southall, he says, and in horses and drays for the deliveries. He thinks that the London taverns will gladly forego brewing beer on their own premises as there is then more space for drinkers and more profit to be made. He always did have a clear head for business. He has bought himself a blue broadcloth coat with gold buttons so that he looks more the man of affairs, and he is courting a dressmaker called Edith. He says that she is 'not entirely pretty, but very jolly', in his own words."

The 'tubs' were cargo vessels purchased by the Captain and crewed by retired pirates. They had delivered the sawn timber and other materials for the repairs to the house and to build the huts for the crew, the warehouses for the *Ark de Triomphe's* guns and other contents, the workshops and the walls of the pit where the frigate now sat on its timber cradle. They had delivered other, more mysterious, cargoes, too, and carried letters for the pirates.

"Jemmy will need a hard head for drink as well as a clear head for business if he wants to be a brewer," said Blue Peter, laughing.

"He has hired a brewer to make the beer," said Jack. "I think he got the notion of a brewery from wanting to have a stable and to work with heavy horses. With a brewery he always has plenty for his horses to deliver, and no need to deal with lordly merchants and gentlemen of business, who are known to be tight-fisted and slow to pay. A tavern landlord always pays for the beer and for the delivery on the nail. Jemmy likes his ale, it is true, but I don't think he will ever be a sot."

They stood in the rain for a moment, the raindrops of the downpour glinting golden from the light from the windows of the house. Faint snatches of song and concertina came from the crew-huts, and occasional noises of hammering from the workshops, audible above the hissing of the rain. The boatyard was functioning well to achieve the Captain's plan. But what is that plan? thought Blue Peter. The crew do not ask, they have complete confidence in him. I wish I could feel the same; did he really tell me tales of extramundane creatures on his banyan day, or was that a crazy dream?

Jack Nastyface bid him farewell with a slightly-sad smile and headed around the back of the house to the kitchen, where there would be pots to wash before Jack's own supper. Blue Peter entered the yellow front door of the house, flapping water from his thick woollen boat-cloak.

In the parlour Captain Greybagges and Mr Benjamin were eating beef stew, washing it down with ale from tarred leather drinking-jacks. Blue Peter called for some to be brought for him, too, and warmed his behind at the fire, holding the tails of his coat aloft and to the sides so they would not be singed by the crackling blaze of logs.

"As you know," he said, "I have always wished for the life of an English country squire, and I have imagined myself warming my arse like this before a fire, and thought it would be a fine thing, but now I have to do it from mere necessity I find that dream strangely sad and misinformed."

Captain Greybagges laughed, Mr Benjamin grinned. A 'new pirate' came in with a bowl of stew and a jack of ale. Blue Peter sat down at the table, tearing a hunk from a loaf, polishing his silver spoon on a napkin, preparing to savour his supper.

"It is unfortunate that your first experience of England should be in winter, Peter," said the Captain, "especially as you have seen only London and this godforsaken place. There are more congenial spots. The climate on the south coast is very pleasant in the summer. Why the port of Southampton even has black Englishmen!"

"Is that indeed true?" exclaimed Mr Benjamin. "Are they escaped slaves? Begging your pardon, Peter! I speak from vulgar curiosity alone." Blue Peter waved his spoon dismissively, his mouth full of the rich stew.

"No, Frank, they are not," said the Captain. "They are Englishmen born and bred. Many of them are fine seamen, and can boast that their grandsires fought with Drake and Hawkins against the great Spanish armada back in the time of Queen Bess. That gives them a better right to be called English than many of the fine lords and ladies, I think. The people of Southampton agree, for they are an easy-going folk and the sea is in their blood. If you doubt me, merely consider that not only blacks but also Jews and even Dutchmen make their homes in Southampton in perfect tranquillity and prosperity."

"The Dutch!" exclaimed Mr Benjamin. "Is not England presently at war with the Dutch? The burghers of Southampton must be tolerant indeed!"

"Do you know, I am not sure if England is at war with the Dutch!" said the Captain, grinning. "There have been so many wars with them, and so many peace-treaties, I lose count! The citizens of Southampton are united in their appetite for trade and commerce, and so regard sailors and merchants with great esteem, no matter what their provenance. A war is unfortunate, it's true, but no reason to scupper a fine deal with Myneer van den Plonk, especially as his warehouse is next to the wharf and the Lord Chancellor is far away in the Palace of Westminster. It is an attitude similar to that of pirates in many ways, and laudable to us, if not to the fellows in Parliament. No, I remember now! England is not at war with the Dutch at this time. Perhaps next week, eh?"

"I have much to learn about being a pirate," Mr Benjamin said. "My mind still tries to apply the laws of logic to the affairs of politics, and to the laws of men, too, which is even more foolish. A pirate has a more pragmatic view, and will not label a man a traitor unless he shall betray his own shipmates or friends. It is perhaps a more human reaction, in the long term. There is a wise fellow, John Locke, who philosophises upon these things, and he suggests that the legal constitution of a nation should be based upon the desires and aspirations of its humblest citizens, for there are many of them, and not upon the prerogatives of its most wealthy and powerful, for they are few."

"Um, it is a wonderful notion," said Captain Greybagges, "but I cannot see the wealthy and powerful being at all enthusiastic for it. They are afraid of the many precisely because they themselves are few."

"The rich will not take easily to the idea, of course," said Mr Benjamin, "but the needs of the many are surprisingly modest. Locke says that every man, no matter how humble, should be guaranteed 'life, liberty and the pursuit of happiness'. If these simple rights were adopted as the basis for a nation's laws then the rich could keep their money, which is the only real basis of power, but only for as long as they infringed nobody else's rights. They might also lose their money if they were improvident, but the laws based on universal rights would prevent them from stooping to desperate measures to retain their fortunes. Such a nation might be very vigorous, being based on fairness, and the wealthy might even benefit disproportionately from its prosperity, rather than be murdered in their beds by a howling mob of starving peasants. It is an idea quite close to the democratical nature of a pirate ship, where everyone has their job, knows their worth and is renumerated accordingly, with debate open to everybody."

"If Mr Locke's philosophising ever gets translated into French then *le Roi Soleil* might find himself punctured by a pitchfork," said Captain Greybagges, "which would not lead to a vigorous nation but to civil war, and I would not wish that upon even the French, much as I despise King Louis."

"Ah! but France is an old nation, so that the King would be killed by a settling of ancient accounts, not by the mere desire for new philosophy of governance. A new nation, with no old scores or grudges, might prove a more fertile garden in which such an idea might grow, might it not?"

"You argue your case very well, Frank," said the Captain, "and I say that as a lawyer. I may also hazard a guess that your 'new nation' is the north American colonies. Am I right?"

"You are, but not at the present moment or under the present circumstances. I don't think I shall live to see it, but the spread of an idea is unstoppable, if it is a good idea, so I suspect that it will be adopted when the right moment comes, when it is a useful idea and not a destructive one." Mr Benjamin drained his ale. "I must bid you adieu. We cast a copper test-piece this afternoon in a mould of sand and china clay, and I wish to observe its rate of cooling, and also to prevent any rogue of an empirical nature from breaking open the mould prematurely through mere impatience or idle curiosity."

Captain Greybagges watched Mr Benjamin leave. Blue Peter finished his stew, cleaning the bowl with a piece of bread, topped up his ale from the jug and selected an apple from the basket in the middle of the table.

"He is a clever fellow, is Frank," said Captain Greybagges, "and he may well be right about Locke's ideas. Mind you, Peter, the Dutch do away with their kings, and yet they seem always to get them back again, but under a different name. The present fellow is called the *stadthouder*, meaning 'place-keeper' or steward, but they are a republic so they cannot decide how much notice to take of him. A democratic utopia such as Frank envisages may be hard to build. I like his notion that such a place would resemble piracy, though! An entire nation of buccaneering entrepreneurs giving not a hoot for anything except freedom and happiness, their eyes always on the far horizon, always on the next gamble! What a thing that would be!"

"I am still cold," said Blue Peter. "I stand by the fire, then eat a tureen of hot stew and drink a stoop or two of strong ale, and yet I am still cold." Blue Peter crunched the apple. The Captain's beard glowed green in the light from the oil lamps. It's funny, thought Blue Peter, but I hardly notice it now. He coloured it brown to go into Liver Pool, but now he has washed it off – the boot-polish makes it itch, he says – and I didn't really notice until the lamp-light caught it. How easily we become accustomed to the bizarre if we see it every day.

"Do you feel the time is right to reveal more of your plans?" said Blue Peter softly, almost without thinking. Captain Sylvestre de Greybagges looked at him with raised eyebrows, then nodded.

"You are cold, Peter," he said. "There are too many freezing draughts in here!" He stood up and kicked the thick rug against the gap at the bottom of the door, and stuffed a napkin into the keyhole. "There, the parlour will warm up a little now," he said loudly, and in a lower voice; "If we talk quietly we cannot be understood from outside the door. I got Izzie to test it by standing outside while I sang 'Spanish Ladies'. We both pretended to be drunk. Well, drunker than we were, anyway. Sailors, pirates or not, are always nosey blighters, I have found." He rummaged in a desk, sat down and beckoned to Blue Peter to draw his chair closer.

"So, Sylvestre, you will enlighten me further? I am agog!" Blue Peter murmured, screeching his chair on the stone-flagged floor as he shuffled it next to the Captain. The Captain opened a bottle of Madeira and poured two glasses.

"Indeed yes, Peter. Perhaps it is overdue. I have discussed some of what I am going to tell you with Bill, but only the algebraical and geometrical aspects, which he will need to understand for navigation. Oh, I am not making much sense! It's difficult to know where to begin. Anyway, the point with Bill is that he knows nothing of the extramundane creatures, but he does have some knowledge of their natural philosophy, which I will now explain to you. Don't mention the extramundanes at all to anybody just yet, is what I mean to say."

Captain Greybagges stared blankly for a moment, composing his thoughts. Blue Peter stayed silent, sipping the sweet wine.

"Time is an awkward thing." The Captain took a sheet of paper from the sheaf he had taken from the desk and dipped a quill. "Imagine a tree. Here is the ground" He drew a line across the paper. "Here is the trunk of the tree." A line up from the first line. "Branches, the trunk divides in two, thus, and again, and again, so. But below ground there are roots." A line drawn down from the ground-line. "Roots that also branch, and again, and again, so. Imagine that the air, light and free, is the future, and that the ground, solid and permanent, is the past. The present is the surface of the ground. The tree represents something with a future and a past - you, me, a ship, a rat, a rock - so that the branching represents the choices that are taken in the future, you see? This choice leads to that, that one to this, and so on. In a similar way for the past; these roots represent the narrowing pattern of choices that lead to the present."

"I see what you mean, I think," said Blue Peter slowly. "They are lines in time, leading from the past into the future through the nexus of the present."

"Well put! The Arab scholars wrote of an *aleph*, where all time and space are coincident, and some necromancers claim that there is one in the pillar of a temple in Jerusalem, and that you can hear it buzzing if you put your ear to the rock. I think that is all hogwash, though, and that the Arab savants really meant the *aleph* to represent the constriction of choices as the future turns into the past, alike to several streams joining to rush through a culvert."

"It is indeed a compelling picture," said Blue Peter thoughtfully.

"However, it is more complicated." The Captain drew another tree next to the first. "It is a forest, not a single tree. If that tree is you, and this tree is me, then if our futures are entwined so are the branches of the trees, and if our pasts are entwined then so are the roots, and so for a hundred, a thousand other trees."

"Ah, yes, that begins to be complicated."

"Not only that, but although you are one man you are made of parts, so the tree could represent only one of your arms, or a finger, or a fingernail, and so on down to the atomies that compose your corporeality. Each atomie with its own tree, its branches and roots entwined with a million others."

"Hmm, that is complicated. A dance of atomies weaving the present like a tapestry."

"Precisely! The next part you will have to take more on trust." Captain Greybagges refilled their glasses.

"Why?"

"Because I don't really understand it myself. The whole notion of atomies was thought up by the old Greek cove Democritus. He thought it unreasonable that something could be divided up infinitely. Cut a piece of string in half, cut the half in half, and so on. He deduced that sooner or later one would encounter an indivisible particle, or atomon, and be able to cut no more."

"That does indeed sound reasonable," said Blue Peter, sipping the Madeira wine.

"Ahh! But that implies a general principle!" said Captain Greybagges. "If matter is granular, then maybe everything else is, too. Time. Distance. Heat. Nothing continuous, but everything doled out as in coinage, with no change from a groat. A groat, or no groat. No half-groats."

"These small increments of time, distance or heat," said Blue Peter, "must be very tiny, or we would notice them. The tick of a clock seems to chop up time, but that is an illusion, time itself seems continuous."

"They are very small, but they have an effect nevertheless." The Captain held up his hand. "No, let me finish. I said I did not understand it fully myself. The granular or grainy nature of everything on a small scale has the effect of making the present a little elastic, or deformable. Since there are no half-groats, then at the moment of reckoning - the present - things must be rounded up or rounded down, and that is a roll of the dice, not a calculation. Imagine the atomies as soldiers running out to the parade-square to form up in ranks; they shuffle into lines, they stand to attention, then break up again and run off for their breakfast. Just before they form up, though, there is a period of pushing and shoving - 'this is my position', 'no, it's mine', 'budge up a bit' and so on - then every soldier finds a place and the parade is perfect. That instant of perfect order is the present, but either side of it there is chaos, and the precise position of each soldier depends partly on chance."

"But that is only one instant in time, surely?"

"Yes, but time itself is grainy, so the flow of time is an endless succession of such moments. There are more atomies than are apparent, too. As in a play on a stage, for example, you see the play, but you don't see the actors waiting in the wings, or the stagehands, yet they are there. If you took a bottle and pumped the air out - like that fellow did in Magbeburg, Otto von Guericke - then inside the bottle is nothing, yet little miniscule atomies pop up in there all the time from out of nowhere just in case they are needed. Pop up, say 'anyone need an atomie? No? Oh, well, I'll be off then,' and disappear again back to the dressing-room, or wherever it is that atomies go when they're not here, or there. The constant but *fleeting* presence of atomies means there is empty space in the bottle's vacuum, but not *nothing*. Think of it as alike to moonlight on a dark and choppy ocean; one sees the white foam, but not the vast dark ocean upon which the foam floats. There is no foam in the empty bottle, but the dark ocean is still there."

"My head hurts, Sylvestre," said Blue Peter, "and this Madeira isn't helping. Have you any brandy?"

Captain Greybagges rose from his armchair, put another log on the fire and rummaged through a chest. He came back with a bottle of brandy, and poured two glasses.

"Your head will only hurt, Peter, if you try and understand it, for common sense does not help very much. Anyways, the effect of it is that the present is slightly plastic or elastic. Given that time and distance are the same thing, too, it is possible to tinker about with time to some extent. The extramundanes, or at least the influential ones like the Glaroon, have discovered how to do this. The lizard people and the little grey buggers have not, so they are as much their victims as us. There are constraints on messing about with time, though. If one went back one hundred years in time - which is quite possible - and murdered one's grandsire, then there would be no consequences when one returned to the present, one would only have created a dead-end time-path, and that would heal itself and disappear. By the same token, if one went a week into the future, found the result of a horse-race and came back to the present and wagered on it then one would surely lose, because one would only have seen a *possible* future, one of many."

"Then there is little point in moving through time, surely?"

"Not entirely. It is still possible to cheat a little bit, if one goes with the natural fall of events. For example, I myself was away on Mars for about three years, but I travelled back in time to the very point at which I left. This was a breach of the laws of time, so to speak, but me being displaced from my normal time-line was a bigger one, so I continue with my existence here and the closed loop in the time-line which I took when I was abducted to Mars is what shall wither away from history, or it would except that it is kept open by my beard, which is in contact with the Glaroon's library."

"I'm not sure I follow that," Blue Peter sipped brandy.

"Nobody could. As I say, common sense is inadequate to deal with these matters. I will give you another example." Captain Greybagges handed him a piece of coal. "Note that this lump of sea-coal has the impression of a leaf in it, where it has been split."

"I see it quite clearly."

"The leaf is several tens of millions of years old, yet it remains recognisable, for not much has happened to disturb it. If one were to travel back in time and collect a leaf and bring it to the present then it would be only slightly wilted because it would be travelling in the rough direction of its own time-line, much as that more-decayed leaf has done, and so not much harm would be done by that. It would not, of itself, create an anachronistic problem."

"Tens of millions of years?"

"Yes. The world is much older than is currently assumed."

"Not an anachronism?"

"Not really. Other leaves have made the journey, you have one in your hand, so what odds does it make if another one does? If one was to take something back in time, then there could be a huge consequence, even if the something was only as insubstantial as a mere idea. Take the secret of gunpowder back in time and give it to the ancient city of Carthage, the Romans lose the Punic wars and the whole of history would be different from then on. It's too much disruption, so it can't happen and won't happen. I travelled back three years, but it was a small anachronism as it restored a timeline, which is a good thing, and it was only three years so the past wasn't properly hardened, and so it did happen, and so here I am."

"How does this affect your plans?"

"Now we get down to it, Peter. The Glaroon, having mastered the laws of time, can travel back and bring things forward, and so it does. Inanimate things are best – objects of marble and bronze, jewellery of diamonds and gold – they can be stolen from the past with ease because they could have been lost or buried and then found again, so no problem with them arriving in the present. The Glaroon, as you may imagine, has a large collection of such things stolen from the past, a collection worth more than all the money in the world's coffers, bank-vaults, exchequers and treasuries put together. Is that not a cheery thought, shipmate? We go to plunder the biggest treasure of all!"

"Um, how do you plan to get to Mars?"

"You will see! But there are other things that the Glaroon steals from the past, thefts that are less easy to forgive, for they are thefts of people, men and women like ourselves. We not only go to take a vast fortune, but also to free the Glaroon's slaves, to liberate his menagerie of humanity. That should make you proud and glad, Peter! Mr Benjamin too, I should think."

"People stolen from the past, you say?" Blue Peter gulped brandy.

"Well, not in person. The principle of minimum disruption still applies, and people are more fragile than bronze statues. The Glaroon instead steals a fragment of a man or a woman – a flake of skin, a hair, even a drop of saliva, I believe – brings it to the present and by some process can recreate the whole corpus and animate it. That of itself it not a particularly wicked thing to do, but the copied people – the artificial identical twins, if you will – do not then have the freedom to make their own time-line, but are kept as slaves in durance vile. Worse than that, their real memories are erased and replaced with artificial memories, so that the Glaroon may converse with Ghenghis Khan if he so wishes. I think the Glaroon does it to ease his boredom, the crushing *ennui* resulting from the millenia of its unmitigated selfishness. The wretched slave is not commander of his own destiny and is not even master of his own soul. Poor Ghenghis! How captivity grates upon his noble warrior's spirit, even though it is not truly his! Yet he is a cheerful fellow, and witty. I shall be pleased to see him again!"

Blue Peter was silent for some moments.

"This Glaroon thing, it has many people such as Ghenghis Kahn?"

"Why, yes! People from the recent past and from antiquity, even from pre-history. There was a fellow there who had supposedly invented the wheel. He was a glum cove, but then the Glaroon would force him to make wheels all the time, copies of his original wheel, so that he could give them as amusing gifts to other influential extramundanes, and that must have been galling. The poor fellow would often curse the day he thought of making a wheel-barrow, and bewail the fact that the mere desire to ease his aching back when taking his melons to market should have caused him such torment. Yet if that tormented slave should end his own life, well, then – abracadabra! – the Glaroon would just make another copy of the poor fellow and carry on. It must be stopped, you see. Also, all the going into the past and shifting things forward does have a cumulative effect, so the history of these regions is currently a little scrambled-up, with broken and stretched time-lines all over the place. There are things happening now that should not happen for years yet, and things that should have happened which haven't. Sooner or later it will mend itself, of course, but that won't be a good thing, not unless the Glaroon has been stopped by then and some repairs made to the time-fabric so that the unravellings and the re-ravellings end up creating a past that's much like it ought to have been. The Glaroon is just amusing himself at the expense of the whole human race – and the races of the lizard people and the little grey buggers, too – and at the expense of the past, which is our past and which should not be used as a play-thing for such as the Glaroon to diddle with ..." Captain Greybagges swallowed some brandy. "... the bastard. It is personal, too. I told you that, Peter."

"What are these creatures, creatures of the the Glaroon's breed? Where do they come from?"

"Creatures such as the Glaroon call themselves the Great Old Ones, or the Great Ancient Ones, but I think that's just pure conceit, alike to a French count who traces his ancestry back to Jesus's cousin Freddy by way of Alaric the Goth. There's no doubt that they are old, very old, but they are still just creatures. It is said that the great turtles can live for centuries, but they are still just turtles, are they not? I don't know much about the Old Ones, really. I don't know where they hale from. I don't know how they reproduce, or if they have emotions as we do. I don't know if they are all the same breed, distantly related or all entirely different, being only similar in their great age. I don't know if they are allied with each other, although I do suspect that they are like the Italian princes of old who would smile courteously while plotting each other's doom, the kind of sly fellows for whom Machiavelli wrote his *Il Principe*, that *vade mecum* of treason and betrayal. I have never seen the Glaroon, never actually clapped eyes on it, but I have seen some of the other ones. They are pretty ugly and weird for the most part, although I did find a very few of them congenial. Great Cthulu was always pleasant to me, and his daughter Lulu has a mischievious impish sense of humour that lightened some moments of my imprisonment."

"Are you not afraid that attacking the Glaroon may earn you the emnity of the others?"

"I must risk that, but I think that they will be secretly amused if I succeed, much as a tyrannical potentate might be delighted by another such being scragged by his peasants, as indeed Louis was mightily pleased when the father of the present King Charles was beheaded, despite his pompous protestations to the contrary."

"Politics would seem to be the same everywhere, even on faraway worlds. I am not sure if that is a very depressing thought or a richly amusing one." Blue Peter shook his head sadly, then drained his brandy.

A pirate knocked on the door, opened it against the dragging rug, and brought them mugs of hot cocoa, which they laced with brandy as a nightcap.

The next morning Blue Peter Ceshwayoo rose early, as was his custom, and shaved and dressed by the light of a candle in the pre-dawn darkness and cold. In London he had purchased long woollen underwear, and he blessed his foresight. He loathed the late rising of the sun in these northern latitudes, but found his pocket-watch oddly reassuring as he wound it and stowed it in his waistcoat pocket; it was light and warm somewhere, the watch proved that, just not here. He ate a bowl of oatmeal burgoo and drank a cup of black coffee in the kitchen, in the hope that it would ease his slight hangover, and went on another tour of the boatyard, wrapped in a boat-cloak against the unceasing rain.

He found Mr Benjamin in his copper-foundry, red-eyed but happy. The castings he had poured the previous afternoon were solidified, he had been breaking open the moulds at intervals throughout the night to obtain knowledge of the cooling, and was satisfied, he said, clambering out of the smoking casting-pit, peering through his *pince-nez* spectacles as he scribbled in a note-book. Now he was ready to cast some proper pieces, not test-specimens, and he was quietly eager.

"Go and get some sleep, Frank," Blue Peter said kindly. "Your men can finish up here."

Copper ingots were stacked in the foundry ready for the crucible, and laid on the stone floor against the wall were dozens of rods of copper the thickness of a pencil and four paces long, tied together in bundles with split-withies. When did they come? he thought. No wonder we have burglars What are they for? The foundry was wonderfully warm, but Blue Peter continued his tour in the dark and the cold rain.

At the edge of the dry-dock pit he stopped and watched the work on the *Ark de Triomphe*. Four pirates, supervised by Israel Hands, were carrying a long forged-iron plate into the stripped shell of the hull by the light of oil-lamps. All rotten timbers – and a wooden ship always has some – had been cut out and new timber scarfed-in, and the whole hull re-caulked. Now these long plates were being bolted to sandwich the keel-timbers and create an iron spine. Blue Peter had no idea why.

He paced on in the darkness, considering the implications of fornication and heaps of copper on his anti-pilfering strategies. The sky would not even begin to lighten until the repeater-watch snug in his pocket struck nine, but then he should have breakfast in the warm parlour. A Liver bird somewhere in the dark went 'awk!'

———

During the winter months the work continued on the *Ark de Triomphe*. The iron backbone was completed and curved iron members and angled plates were added to lock it to the wooden ribs of the hull. Three flat iron plates were bolted like tables onto the backbone deep inside the hull; one for'ard, one aft and a larger one in the middle. The outside of the wooden hull was covered in tarred canvas then sheathed in a gleaming jacket of thin copper sheet nailed to the planks with copper nails. The thin copper rods in the foundry were bent into wiggled shapes and brazed together with sleeved junctions, the sleeves cast by Mr Benjamin in his foundry. The fitting of the copper rods into the hull recesses was brutally difficult work. In some places the rods had to be threaded through restrictions, each foot of the rod being bent to pass then straightened to continue - bend-and-straighten, bend-and-straighten - and only those with the most powerful hands and arms could do it, so Blue Peter, Bulbous Bill and Loomin' Len and his bully-boys were recruited to assist in the work. Blue Peter had painful memories of struggling with the unwilling rods, and of taking a break, massaging his aching fingers with tears in his eyes, then returning below decks to do another stint. The work was made more difficult as the rods were wrapped in three layers of tarred linen ribbon and tight-bound with hemp cord, so too much force or abrasion and the covering would tear and everything must start again. The strong-arm crew cursed those copper rods, especially as none of them knew what they were for, and yet Captain Greybagges and Mr Benjamin were very particular as to how they should be laid out and connected.

In the end it was done, but while it was ongoing Blue Peter and Bulbous Bill had lost focus on discipline in the crew, and there was a tragic consequence. Two young pirates had argued over a local girl, and one had stabbed the other. At a drumhead court, convened according to the strict rules of the Free Brotherhood o' the Coasts, the guilty pirate had nearly been sentenced to hang, but doubts remained over whether he had intended to kill his friend and so he was sentenced to be expelled and cast ashore. He went from the boatyard white-faced after being quietly warned by Captain Greybagges of the consequences of unguarded speech. The crew felt that being marooned for ever in Liver Pool would be punishment enough.

The 'tubs' came and went, delivering boxes and crates of various sizes, and other mysterious objects, including a number of what appeared to be large bottles made of gun-bronze. Blue Peter had given up trying to make sense of it. Even the Captain and Mr Benjamin were overwhelmed at times, Mr Benjamin wishing plaintively for an apparatus to duplicate drawings. No such thing existed, but several local girls and women were brought in to act as secretaries and copyists. For once the pirates' romantic urges proved beneficial, for the former apprentice-boys had been discreetly industrious and very ingenious in finding young women who could read and write, disguising their carnal intentions as yearnings for cultured conversation, and these social contacts had proved very useful.

One morning trenches were dug to the Mersey to flood the pit. As the water rose the hull of the *Ark de Triomphe* creaked histrionically, until it finally floated free and swam again. The baulks of timber of the cradle bobbed up and were snagged with long boat-hooks and pulled to the sides, lest the turbulent currents flooding into the pit hurl them against the bright copper sides of the reborn ship. When the level in the pit reached that of the river the wedges were knocked out of the wooden wall at the end until it floated free and was pulled away, the remaining earth-banks collapsing into the water. The *Ark de Triomphe* was drawn out of the now-flooded dry-dock by the whaler, the bully-boys at the oars red-faced with exertion despite assistance from ropes ashore. The *Ark de Triomphe's* hull, light-loaded and high in the water, bobbed and danced like a mettlesome horse being led from its stall, but it was moored at the jetty before the tide turned to the ebb, to everyone's relief. By a pleasant coincidence the endless rain eased and a watery sun appeared through the clouds as the last of the mooring hawsers, the quarter-steady, was looped around its bollard. Captain Greybagges made a short but stirring speech from the quarterdeck rail and ordered a double ration of rum, the pirate crew gave three cheers, and some chaffering cat-calls, and then set to work again.

Over the next weeks the pirates worked steadily to refit the frigate. The iron skeleton inside the hull had added weight, but ballast was still needed. Lead ingots were used instead of rocks. The crew were amazed and impressed by the sheer profligacy of this; even the king's own flagship did not have a ballast of pig-lead! The ancient sheer-hulk was warped over and the *Ark de Triomphe's* masts re-stepped. The tops and cross-yards were swayed up and the frigate re-rigged with new cables, ropes, stays, halliards and rat-lines. The pirates swarmed over the upperworks singing pulley-hauly shanties and joyfully shouting to each other as the *Ark de Triomphe* slowly took its sea-going shape once again.

Blue Peter watched her take shape, frequently pausing on his rounds just to observe her being clothed, put in harness for war. Her shape to a yokel landsman's eyes merely meant that she was a ship, yet to a sailor's eyes she was a predator, a predator as lairy as a wolf, but to a pirate's eyes she was lovely. Her hull was long and lean and low, the foredeck and the quarterdeck barely shoulder-height above the waist-deck – much, much, lower than a frigate of the Royal Navy - the easier to board another boat from, the true mark of a pirate-ship. Yet after the rebuild the low deck was no longer an obvious modification, the decks hacked level more-or-less in haste. Now she looked as though she had been built that way from the keel up, and, more than that, she was a pirate-ship made for piracy with no constraint of expense, and she looked it. Blue Peter was minded of a leopardess. She had always had a wiggle of her stern when tacking, just like the twitch of that animal's hindquarters when she jinked to cut off her prey, and now that little quirk seemed so fitting that it was eerie. The *Ark de Triomphe* was a dangerous lady, a *femme fatale*.

Blue Peter, as Master Gunner, had overseen the mounting of her new guns, whose black snouts now protruded from her gun-ports. The latest cast-steel eighteen-pounders from the Carron Company, none finer, equipped her single lower gun-deck, with twenty-four-pounder iron carronades on her upper decks. He would miss the short bronze Portugese thirty-two-pounders from the foredeck, though; he had been fond of those old smashers. As each new gun-barrel was dragged to the frigate on a sledge the crews had stopped to introduce it to its predecessor, laid on timbers in a shed, to splash them both with rum and 'marry' them so that the new gun would carry the same name as the old one. Sailors are superstitious, and pirates perhaps even more so.

The only thing that looked odd about the *Ark de Triomphe* was the small platform mounted between the foremast and the mainmast on a diagonal spar, at about one-half of the mainmast's height. Blue Peter had no idea what it was for, but his fingers still ached from the fitting of the five thin copper rods that ran to it, the last of the copper rods to be installed, he hoped. The *Ark de Triomphe* is not just a leopardess, he thought, there is more; she has bones of iron now, and yet more, her claws are guns of steel, and, yet more again, her nerves are copper rods made to carry lightning. What is he making here? What kind of beast has he built as his steed for his monster-hunt? And Blue Peter Ceteshwayoo was suddenly cold, and very afraid.

Although it was still freezing cold, there were faint signs, if not of Spring then of the imminent arrival of Spring, and the low sun was occasionally shining apologetically through the scudding clouds. As Blue Peter stood on the bank looking at the frigate's mysterious platform a Liver bird settled on it, flapping its wings whop-whop before folding-up like an old umbrella. In the brief calm between gusts of breeze Blue Peter heard its call, "awk! awk-la! AWK!"

CHAPTER THE TENTH,
or The Captain Calls For A Boucan

The Broadmeadow estuary lay calm and dark under a moonless night sky, and the small Irish village of Malahide showed no lights. The pirate frigate *Ark de Triomphe* lay at anchor, low and black. The ship and the longboat that was shuttling to-and-fro from the shore should have been invisible in the gloom, but the wide estuary was full of small skiffs with bright lanterns on poles.

"I have heard of the cunning Orientals using birds to catch fish, but I never thought to see such a thing ten miles from Dublin," said Captain Sylvestre de Greybagges.

"They are cormorants, it seems. Avian creatures that are accustomed to dive beneath the waters in search of their piscine prey," said Blue Peter Ceteshwayoo. "The fisherman ties a leather thong around the bird's neck, the poor creature cannot swallow the fish and so must bring it back to its master. The lantern's light attracts the fish."

Captain Greybagges looked at him quizzically.

"I asked the fellows down there on the beach," said Blue Peter, pointing. "There seemed to be little point in being stand-offish when we are already exposed in plain sight by their lights. Fishing with birds is a source of extra money for the farming people around here, they said. Fishing with birds, and collecting seaweed."

"Seaweed?"

"A particular kind of seaweed. They told me it is dried, shredded and sold to be used for padding coffins, as it absorbs the stink of a corpse. The departed relative is displayed in the family parlour for the wake, which is an overnight vigil of drunken remembrance. The sad occasion is thus rendered less dolorous by the exsiccative properties of the bier of kelp, so the grieving kin may then enjoy the roborative properties of the beer of barley...."

Captain Greybagges eyed him in silence. Blue Peter looked abashed, and then continued.

"The fishermen may have been making sport of me, of course, as I am but a poor heathen blackamoor, but I doubt it, as they were otherwise quite amiable and polite. Well, they were after I gave them a sip of rum."

"Seaweed to line coffins? I suppose I have heard of stranger things." Captain

Greybagges strode back to the road above the beach. The boat had returned and pirates were carrying small wooden boxes to it from a coach and a cart. The horses snorted and stamped their hooves, their breath swirling in ghostly clouds in the glow from the coach-lamps.

"How many more, you swabs?" growled the Captain.

"One more trip, Cap'n," said Torvald Coalbiter, carrying a wooden box on his shoulder.

"Don't say it!" said the Captain, turning to Blue Peter. "Not until we are safely back at sea. Don't tempt the fates." Blue Peter looked abashed again.

There was a confused outbreak of shouting from the sea. Ghastly piratical oaths answered by curses in Gaelic and the squawking of cormorants; the longboat had nearly rammed a fisherman's skiff.

"I shall say it, now that we are safely back at sea. Everything went well!" Blue Peter grinned and poured rum for himself and the Captain.

"I am not usually a superstitious man," said the Captain, "but these mechanisms are vital to my plans. I feared that such delicate engines might be easily broken, or that an attempt might be made to steal them away to ransom them. Now they are stowed aboard the barky I can feel easier."

"The ride from Dublin certainly will have attracted attention," said Blue Peter. "A cart, a coach and an armed escort of pirates mounted on old nags and mules. I'm surprised the children of Dublin didn't follow us, thinking that the circus had come to town."

"I wish I could have arranged things more efficiently, Peter, but with time pressing I could not. A more clandestine meeting with the clockmakers and a diversion when the boxes were moved would have been better, but instead I just had to load the boxes, go as fast as we could and trust that any wicked rapparees or mosstroopers would be without the time to prepare an ambush. I wasn't going to meet all the clockmakers at the same time and place, either, but I again had no choice. The clockmakers, thus introduced, would discuss the engines and so, in turn, so the gossips of Dublin would certainly have had word of a valuable cargo in transit."

"The clockmakers were a congenial parcel of rogues, though," said Blue Peter, sipping rum from his crystal goblet.

"Indeed, and that is a problem, for they will continue to talk among themselves now, being intrigued by the mechanical devices that I ordered from them, and I do not wish my business to be discussed or bruited abroad by wagging tongues."

"I am intrigued, too," said Blue Peter, "but I am not a clockmaker, so I will remain mystified, I suppose."

There was a knock at the door of the Great Cabin and Jack Nastyface entered, followed by Mr Benjamin carefully carrying a square box. The box was rectangular, as long as a forearm, half that in width and height and made of unvarnished pinewood, with a rope handle at each end, and a number scorched onto its top and sides with a hot iron

"I thought you might like to see an example what you have purchased at such expense, Captain," said Mr Benjamin, placing the box on the table. There was another knock and Bulbous Bill Bucephalus and Israel Feet entered. Mr Benjamin took a small jemmy-bar from a pocket and levered off the top of the box, nails screeching in the wood, while Blue Peter poured shots of rum for everybody.

"No touching! No poking with fingers! Don't spill any damned rum on it, either!" spoke Mr Benjamin sternly, then reached into the box and lifted out a complex mechanism of brass and steel, of cogs and gearwheels. It sat on the table, the machined metal coruscating in the lamplight. The Captain and his officers looked at it in silent wonderment for a while. Jack Nastyface kept quiet and hoped nobody would notice him.

"Why, they are fine craftsmen, these Dublin clockmakers!" said Mr Benjamin at last. "These are not your mere cork-and-nail men!"

"Cork-and-nail men?" asked the Captain with a raised eyebrow.

"Irish travelling tinkers who will attempt to mend clocks. They will hold a piece of drilled sheet-brass with a nail stuck into a bottle-cork, the better to file it into a cog-wheel. Some of them have surprising skill for unlettered oafs, it is true, but the workmanship shown here is of a different order entirely." Mr Benjamin smiled down at the brass clockwork machine.

"What does it do?" asked Bill, frowning.

"It multiplies numbers, or rather *quantities*," said Mr Benjamin. "See, the shaft *here* is rotated to represent one value, this shaft *here* the other value and the resulting multiplicand is the rotation of this shaft *here*. The powerful spring *here* provides the energizing power to drive the mechanism, which is re-wound by this little shaft *here*."

"What be these?" said Israel Feet, reaching out with a finger.

"Don't touch!" snarled Mr Benjamin. "Sorry, Izzy, but these mechanisms are quite gracile, and frangible if mishandled. Those ivory discs are for fine adjustments."

"It is quite beautiful, I have never seen its like!" said Jack Nastyface.

"What be you a-doing in here, Jack?" growled the Captain. Jack Nastyface blushed to the roots of his hair.

"I … I helped Mr Benjamin to carry it in," he gulped.

The Captain regarded him with a baleful eye.

"Curiosity killed the cat, Jack. Go and tell the cook to bring us some snacks, and as a punishment for your nosiness you must pass it around the crew that I nearly ran Izzy through with a cutlass for merely breathing on this engine, and that I will surely keel-haul any fool who touches any one of these mechanisms with even the nail of a little finger. Only Mr Benjamin is allowed to fiddle with them."

Jack departed, closing the door behind him. Mr Benjamin carefully replaced the gleaming brass engine back into its box.

"They are all there, Captain. Nine multipliers, nine adders of the Gaussian pattern, nine differential integrators, plus the regulators, the connecting shafts and all the other bits and pieces. Each component in triplicate to give two spares against breakages. One hundred and forty-seven boxes."

"Once we are returned to Liver Pool and moored, how long to install them in the barky, Frank? The deciheptaxial mechanism we discussed?"

Mr Benjamin scowled. "Two weeks, maybe three if there's a problem."

"Make it two, if you can, Frank!" said Captain Greybagges, before sipping rum from his chased-silver goblet.

The *Ark de Triomphe* ploughed eastwards under full sail through the dark Irish Sea, under a sky bright with stars.

The *Ark de Triomphe* lay moored once again to the Liver Pool boatyard jetty, her masts and decks busy as pirates attended to any small problems that the short trip to Ireland had shaken out. Mr Benjamin and his team – mostly young pirates, but with a cabinet-maker and a whitesmith from the ranks of the old pirates – were installing the Captain's mechanisms in a large locker below the quarterdeck, next to the steering-tackle under the ship's wheel. They all seemed strangely cheerful, thought Blue Peter, and he wondered if it was the simple joy of such precise and exacting work. Whatever the cause, their chatter and the noise of the necessary carpentry had driven Captain Sylvestre de Greybagges out from the refuge of his Great Cabin ashore to the front parlour of the boatyard house, where Blue Peter found him writing letters – *scritch, scratch* – and drinking coffee.

"I believe I have solved the problem of the Dublin clockmakers!" said the Captain, as Blue Peter sat down. "Will you have some coffee? A biscuit?"

"Indeed, yes. Are you sure that the clockmakers *are* a problem?"

"Well, a potential problem. People talk, and skilled tradesmen gossip more than fishwives, and the mechanisms I ordered from them are unusual and mysterious. They would not be the fine artisans whom they undoubtedly are if their curiosity was not whetted to a degree by the mere fact that they are in ignorance of even the purposes for which I require the devices."

"You are right, of course," said Blue Peter. "I have only just been remarking upon how happy Frank and his boys are presently. Mechanical enthusiasts in their earthly heaven! They are filing and scraping and hammering, each bearing a spanner like a field-marshal's baton! Muttering with each other over great sheets of engineer's drawings, and probably bursting into song every ten seconds!"

"Indeed they were," said the Captain wearily, rubbing his face, "when I tried to do my correspondence in the Great Cabin, and yet I had no desire to constrain their keen spirits, their *animae*, so I came here."

"And yet you have denied the clockmakers that pleasure! The pleasure of assembling the machines that they have built into a functioning whatever-it-is. Their *amour propre* of cogs, gears and pinions will remain unrequited and unconsummated!" chuckled Blue Peter. "How they must loathe you! A love-struck Romeo would not hate you even one-half as much if you had shot his virgin Juliette before his very eyes with a blunderbuss loaded with tin-tacks! Surely they are conspiring with your foulest enemies even as we speak!"

The Captain laughed, and went to hurl a biscuit at Blue Peter's head, but dunked it in his coffee instead. "Maybe they would, but I have found a distraction, a will o' the wisp that will divert them for a while to a place where they can do me no harm by their egregious rumour-mongering."

"Where is this magic kingdom of faerie, then, where clockmakers may be spirited away?"

"Switzerland."

"I have heard of the place, but I know little of it, except that it is not magical."

"Ah! The land itself is not magical, but my imagination makes it so for Irish clockmakers!"

"You are obviously pleased with your cunning. Do be so good as to explain."

"Then harken. Switzerland is a country of much cold, much snow, much poverty and much misery. So poor, in fact, that its main export is mercenary soldiers. The average Swisser is a very good gallowglass, it is true. They come from a land where even a casual stroll to church may involve more vertical movement than horizontal, where the mountains have all kinds of traps for the unwary - avalanches of snow, howling blizzards that last for weeks, even the dreaded *tatzelwurm*, a snow-white dragon that has near as many legs as a centipede, the better to grip the ice - and where food and comfort are always in short supply. The Swissers are tough because they have to be to reach manhood. Why! Even the Pope himself has Swiss mercenaries to guard his person and his treasures, and he is not a fellow to stint himself, or so I am told. There would not seem to be much to interest me, or indeed anybody, in such a barren land, but it occurred to me that it was just the place for a bank. It is poor country surrounded by almost-impassable mountains, peopled by stubborn warriors. So it is a land of very little interest to a conqueror looking for rich pickings. It is not a nation grown rich and grown soft, so who would wish to invade such a place? But a nation that has no attraction for a Tamerlane is a place of wonderful peacefulness and stability of government, and so it is an ideal spot for a bank."

"Does not the presence of a bank reverse your logic?" said Blue Peter. "When there is a bank there is money to steal, surely."

"Ah! A bank is a temptation to a band of thieves, and to pirates, of course, but not to an invader. An invader needs bread, beef and beer for his troops, fodder for his horses, clothes, boots, weapons, all kinds of useful plunder and booty. Any banks that he may chance upon in the course of his campaigning are just the cherry on the cake. A chest of gold is nice to put by for his retirement, but it will not feed his men if there is no food to buy. On the other hand an entire nation, even one so wretched as Switzerland, is too big for a mere band of ruffians to subdue … You smile, Peter! I know you think of bloody Captain Morgan! But Panama proves that I am right! Panama thought itself very grand, but it was only a rich town, not a nation with a nation's resources, and so it was vulnerable to a band of ruffians."

"I concede that your logic does seem sound," said Blue Peter, pouring more coffee, "but how does this concern your Irish clockmakers?"

"I opened a branch of our Bank of International Export in Geneva, and while I was organising it one of my correspondents there informed me that Switzerland was so poor that they made their clocks of wood! Not of brass and steel, but of wood! I pointed out to the Irish clockmakers that a country that could make clocks of wood was surely not short of ingenious fellows, and that pocket-watches require very little metal but much skilled labour, and that an enterprise to manufacture pocket-watches there would have low labour costs and a central position in Europe. In quite a short time Switzerland could come to completely dominate the business of pocket-watch manufacture, all it would require was a few skilled horologists and an investor to fund the project through its early stages while the labour-force was trained and premises and tools acquired."

"Do you actually believe this?"

"Of course not! It verges upon the ridiculous – although it is true about the wooden clocks, which gave me the idea - but the Irish clockmakers were impressed by the sums of money I was prepared to invest and so have set off to Geneva to look things over. I am sure they think that I am a great tom-fool with more money than sense, but a pleasant journey across Europe with all expenses paid is hard to resist, especially as they need not take their wives as it is business. They will be gone for months in foreign lands where little English is spoken, and busy with making at least a token appraisal of the possibility of watchmaking in the rocky valleys of Switzerland, so that any chance of my plans becoming known is minimised. I have set it up by mail, and this letter confirms that the Irish clockmakers left Dublin two days ago on a fast and seaworthy barque, bound for France."

"It is a shame that the poor fellows will be on a wild-goose chase," said Blue Peter, smiling.

"I am sure that ..." Captain Greybagges picked up the letter and perused it,

"…Mister R. O'Lecks, Mister O'Meeger, Mister Jago L. Coulter and Mister Pat Philip will have such a pleasant European tour to Geneva and back – the food and wines of France! The gay nightlife of Paris! The splendour of the mountains of the Alps! - that it is possible that they may not even think once of the large-scale manufacture of pocket-watches."

"I am sure that you are right, but I cannot believe that anybody could comprehend what you are planning from examining the clockwork devices," said Blue Peter. "After all, Mr Benjamin doesn't know what you are doing, and he is building it. What is a 'deciheptaxial mechanism' anyway? It's not as if it is something that one can buy in an ironmonger's shop."

"I fear that other interested parties may be trying to trace me by now, those who may be able to deduce my plans from the design of these devices. A deciheptaxial mechanism is a mechanism that calculates in three and a half variables, although I admit that it is a clumsy description." The Captain winked and grinned at Blue Peter. "All will become clear in time, my friend, and in a fairly short time now, so your patience will not be stretched too badly."

Blue Peter left the Captain calling for more coffee, whistling happily and sharpening his goose-quill to continue his letter-writing.

That night Blue Peter slept in his small cabin in the *Ark do Triomphe*. He had become accustomed to the sea from his years within wooden walls and now found the land somehow too stable and solid, its quiescence too obliging to be entirely trustworthy. Spring storms far away in the Irish Sea sent waves rolling into the mouth of the River Mersey sending diminishing ripples up as far as the boatyard jetty, and the very gentle rocking of the frigate soothed him, the faint rhythmic creaking of the ship's timbers a lullaby to his sailor's ears as he lay snug in his bunk, wrapped in a thick blanket that was wonderfully dry and smelled of lavender.

Blue Peter became aware that he was dreaming. He found himself to be laying at his ease under the sparse shade of a baobab tree, his back against its rough trunk and the African plains in front of him stretching away into the heat-haze before reaching the invisible horizon. The brown grassland had a scattering of bushes and the occasional noble baobab tall against the blue sky. A few gnus wandered in the middle distance. He felt a deep sense of peace and, simultaneously, a great homesickness. He sighed. Slowly he became aware that he was being observed. He turned to his left, and a leopardess was sitting almost within reach of his hand, watching him with yellow eyes, her tail swishing. Blue Peter did not feel alarmed. The leopardess yawned, and he noticed that her teeth were polished steel like cutlass blades and the claws that flashed briefly from her paws were cannon-barrels.

"Hello," said the leopardess.

"You are the ship, the *Ark de Triomphe*," said Blue Peter. "Hello."

"I am the ship as you imagined me to be. You also imagined me as a wolf." The leopardess changed into a grey wolf, but the yellow eyes stayed the same. "You thought I was 'as lairy as a wolf'. It's an odd word 'lairy', isn't it?"

"I believe it is Irish," said Blue Peter, "meaning 'afraid', but in the positive sense of 'alert, watchful and cautious' rather than in the negative sense of 'cowardly'. It is not derogatory."

"What a pedant you are! Since you are so learned perhaps I should present myself as Nike, since my figurehead is Winged Victory arrayed with a rainbow." The wolf changed into a rather handsome woman with the wings of a giant eagle, dressed in a white Doric *chiton* belted with a wide *zoster*. "Or perhaps all three." She changed into a chimera with the head of a woman with a wolf's mane of grey hair, a feline, but still human, body with yellow dark-spotted fur and the multicoloured wings of a parrot.

"I find that rather disturbing."

She laughed and turned once more into a leopardess. "I rather like being a leopardess," she said, "it's the wiggle of my bum when I run, just as you thought." She twitched her hindquarters playfully from side to side, her tail swishing.

Blue Peter laughed, and they sat in companionable silence for a while.

"It's been a long time since I've been in Africa, and it's been even longer since I talked with my tribe's old sorcerer, but I seem to remember that a visitation in a dream usually comes to impart a message. Do you have a message for me, Nike the leopardess?"

"Trust your heart."

"Is that all? Trust my heart?"

"Yes, of course it is. Your logic and your reason should tell you that the Captain has gone completely insane - his wits have flown and he is off on a mad hunt for monsters! - but your heart, your instincts if you prefer, tell you that he is sincere, and that he seems to know what he is doing, so you take your part in his plan and follow the path of your fate. If you followed your reason you would not avoid your fate, for nobody can, but you might have a more tedious and unpleasant time, as you would be swimming against the tide of events."

"Have you also given encouragement and advice to Captain Greybagges."

"This is *your* dream, and I am *your* imagining of how the soul of the ship would appear. How could I talk to the Captain?"

"I shall trust in my heart, then, and hope that the ship's spirit appears to him in his dreams in a form that is as congenial as you."

"For your gallantry I shall reward you with more good advice. Trust your heart!"

"Once again? Trust my heart?"

"Certainly! Trust your heart. You hold in yourself a belief that in a time to come there is a great love waiting for you, so you try to keep yourself in a fit state to welcome her when she arrives. You are a great ruffian and a pirate, and you are a frightening sight with your pointed teeth and the cicatrices on your cheeks, but you try to keep to certain standards, to exercise good taste and restraint in your actions. You try not to be a beast, even though you are indeed a pirate and could behave as a beast quite easily. The alternative is, of course, giving up your belief in your future, in your destiny, and so giving up your humanity in the anger of your disappointment, and then your true love may come to you at last, but spurn you for being a beastly knave. Trust your heart."

"Umm," said Blue Peter Ceteshwayoo.

"The sun is setting. I must go." The leopardess stood, grinned at him, the low sun glinting red on her steel cutlass teeth, and loped away. Blue Peter watched her until she vanished into the tall grass with a last twitch of her hindquarters.

Blue Peter awoke briefly and shook his head groggily. The African plains? he thought, that's odd, I grew up in the forest. The thick woollen blanket that he had warmed and dried in the kitchen oven with sprigs of lavender between the folds was very hot around him. Hot, he thought, yes, Africa, hot. He wriggled and pulled the blanket looser, rolled over and went back to sleep, a faint smile on his lips.

Blue Peter awoke before dawn. On deck it was dark except for the faint glimmer of a lantern in the waist. He took a dousing under the pump, one of the pirates on watch working the pump-handle for him, singing a lilting song in an incomprehensible west-country dialect to the rhythm of his pumping, Blue Peter hearing the singing in snatches between the gushes of river water over his head and shoulders. He dressed in his cabin, regretfully fingering the sleeve of an embroidered blue-satin coat before donning brown broadcloth; Liver Pool was not Porte de Recailles and it would not do to be too obviously a buccaneer. The sun was just starting its rise as he strode along the jetty, and he turned back and gazed at the *Ark de Triomphe*, low, sleek and dark in the blue dawn gloom, her masts, yards and rigging a black tracery against the grey sky. He walked on. I am still dreaming, he thought, the figurehead did not wink at me, it is made of painted wood and the light is too bad to see clearly anyway.

In the kitchen of the boatyard house there was coffee and oatmeal burgoo with brown sugar and yellow cream. Blue Peter ate at the dining-room table, hearing the tramp of feet outside the door and muttered salutations and insults as pirates came to the kitchen to collect tubs of burgoo and cans of coffee for their messes' breakfasts. It had started raining again so he put on a boat-cloak and clapped on a wide-brimmed hat before going on a morning inspection of the boatyard.

Now that the work on the *Ark de Triomphe* was coming to an end the pirates were clearing the boatyard and some of the wooden huts had been dismantled as the pirates moved back aboard. Captain Greybagges had decided to keep the boatyard, which would be staffed by retired pirates and suitable candidates from Liver Pool. Blue Peter found this an encouraging development, as it showed that the Captain's plans did not include a suicide mission. Trust your heart, Blue Peter thought, I suppose I must do just that. It's good advice, even if it did come from a shape-shifting leopardess in a peculiar dream.

Mr Benjamin was standing naked on top of the foundry building, his arms spread and his face tilted upwards to the rain.

"Good morning, Frank," called Blue Peter. "Don't get washed away."

"And a fine morning it is! The wind and the water are a sovereign tonic, you should try it, Peter!"

"I had a bath under the pump earlier. That was cold enough and wet enough for me."

Blue Peter plodded back to the boatyard house for a second breakfast, thinking about his work for the day. The new cannons were installed in the gun-decks and he was almost satisfied with their carriages, but he wanted to reinforce the eye-bolts on the recoiling-tackles. Torvald Coalbiter had a notion to increase the width of the forward gun-ports so that the two forwardmost cannons could be slewed if required to be more useful in a chase. Blue Peter wasn't sure about this, but Torvald made a good case. He would have to make a decision this afternoon, as the carpentry would take at least three days and time was beginning to press.

In fact widening the two ports took two days, but reinforcing the eye-bolts took longer than planned. The ship and crew were now very close to being ready for the oceans. A contingent of retired pirates had arrived in the tubs to work in the boatyard, and the boatyard's affairs were in a fit state for the Captain to hand over day-to-day control to Mavis O'Bacon, the chief of the women in the drawing section. He had worried about this, but none of the retired pirates could manage a business, excellent hands though they were at carpentry, caulking and rigging. Handing control to any of the men of Liver Pool would be to invite them to strip the boatyard to its bare bones, for that was the way their minds worked; they would the loot the boatyard even though more profit could be made by operating is as an honest venture. The widow O'Bacon, though, would defend the boatyard because she would be running it herself and opportunities like that did not come often to womenfolk, so she had every reason to wish it to prosper and to continue. She was a red-haired dragon with a fiery temper and a tongue that could lash like a bull-whip, too, so she stood a reasonable chance of keeping the workforce in a state of productive fear. All the drawing-section women would be staying on, too, and the widow O'Bacon was their acknowledged queen, so any attempts at peculation by the Liver Pool men would face daunting opposition.

Captain Sylvestre de Greybagges sat in his Great Cabin enjoying the return of peace now that Mr Benjamin and his boys had finished installing the deciheptaxial mechanism. Mr Benjamin was testing and adjusting it now, but that was a comparatively quiet labour, carried out in hushed whispers with only the occasional tap of a hammer, the squeak of a screw being tightened, to be heard through the oak of the cabin door. The Captain sipped coffee and wrote letters with a new goose quill and fine black ox-gall ink, *scritch-scratch*.

Jack Nastyface, Torvald Coalbiter and a Yorkshireman called Jake Thackeray were sitting on the maintop cross-trees, smoking pipes, yarning and taking their ease. Jack had seemingly grown two inches taller and put on muscle with the labours of the winter, labours which he had not minded for the hard work had eased the loneliness he felt from the departure of his great friend Jemmy Ducks. He had lately been assisting Torvald on the gun-deck, and had made himself so useful that he had been given Jake as an assistant to take over some of his kitchen duties. Jake Thackeray was a tall, skinny youth with a long gloomy face, hooded eyes and a down-turned mouth. His lugubrious mien concealed a sharp wit, and he was known for composing comical songs lampooning his shipmates, a talent that was greatly valued 'tween decks. He was supposed to be a cabinet-maker, but he had little skill with wood and preferred kitchen duties, even being so confident as to question Bulbous Bill Bucephalus's sacred recipe for hot chilli, feeling that it had insufficient garlic. He was lucky that Bill was not very agile in the rigging, and so he had eluded chastisement for this blasphemy. Torvald Coalbiter, being a gunner and not a foremast-jack, was not entirely at ease perched in the cross-trees, but an invitation to a morning smoke had to be accepted out of courtesy to a shipmate.

"So, even Mr Benjamin don't know what the clockworks are for?" said Jake.

"The Captain does, though," said Jack, "and that's good enough for me."

"He told Blue Peter that it would become clear soonish," said Torvald.

"He is a deep old file, our Captain," said Jake, "and no mistake on that, but I am still curious, thou knows."

"When we had the run-in with the corsairs down off the coast o' Barbary he saw off that mad bugger Ali the Barber just by twisting words around," said Torvald. "I think he often sees further than most men, but to explain himself would take too long, so he doesn't bother."

They had been watching one of the tubs manoeuvring in the sluggish slack-water river to come alongside the *Ark de Triomphe* where she lay at the jetty, and now it did with a slight bump, and a burst of shouting and curses as pirates put bumpers between the hulls and tied-off the ropes.

"And what be this now?" said Jake, peering down.

"It looks like the top half of a big barrel," said Jack, examining the cargo on the deck of the tub, "with iron shackles on its head."

"More alike to an upturned bucket for a giant. They are going to lift it onto the barky," said Torvald, seeing pirates laying down wooden slabs on the frigate's deck for the huge half-barrel to rest upon. "Here is yet another mystery for you to ponder, young Jake. Let's get down, they'll want to rig the steadying-tackles from up here and we will be in their way."

Torvald Coalbiter crawled carefully through the lubber's hole and climbed slowly down the rat-lines; the younger men slid down the back-stay.

The giant upturned bucket was settled between the foremast and mainmast, lashed down with ropes to iron staples in the deck, and covered in a black tarpaulin. The crew were mystified, and wrangled a little over what it might be, The enigmatic nature of the large piece of coopering only added to a sense of expectation; it seemed they were off on an adventure, the meanings of such things would be revealed in time, and the crew were eager to get to sea, wherever it was that the ship was headed.

Of all the pirates, Bulbous Bill Bucephalus had the clearest perception of what the deciheptaxial mechanism was for, even though he wouldn't like to try to spell the word. Through the study of navigation he had acquired a good knowledge of mathematics and an excellent grasp of spherical geometry, that bane of midshipmen. Through the study of navigation he had also acquired a good knowledge of astronomy and an excellent understanding of the motions of the planets as they sail on their orbits through the heavens. These two separate, but related, subjects were suggesting possibilities to him. Three and one-half variables is also three and one-half axes of a graph or, looked at another way, three and one-half dimensions. Could the one-half dimension be ...? No, he shook his head, it was daft enough to be right, but he could not be sure. He would think about it some more, perhaps after supper. He had no opinion of the bucket on the foredeck, except in that it would raise the centre-of-gravity of the frigate just a whisker, as it had heavy cast-iron weights around its lower rim, he had noticed.

Israel Feet did not have any perception of what the deciheptaxial mechanism was for, nor did he have any idea what the purpose of the upturned bucket was, what he did have was a headache. The headaches were coming less often and with diminishing severity, but the hoisting, levering and lashing-down a vast great thing of oak staves and iron hoops and iron this-and-that was a sure way to get a head-splitter. After supper he would ask Mr Benjamin for a small piece of opium, and sling his hammock in a quiet corner and sleep.

Blue Peter had put aside the mysteries of mechanisms and giant buckets as mere codicils to the larger mystery of Captain Greybagges's plan, which would unfold whether he worried about it or not. Another enigma intrigued him, though; could ships have souls? He posited this question to the Captain, Bill and Mr Benjamin over the remains of their supper seated at the table in the Great Cabin, telling them of the leopardess in the dream, but not of her message.

"I have not had a dream such as yours," said the Captain, "but then I hardly ever dream, or remember dreams, which is much the same thing. Ships do seem to have a spirit, or why else would we put a figurehead on them."

"Ha! The figurehead is there because most sailors cannot read. That is, for the same reason that inns have signs," said Mr Benjamin. "If both ships and taverns were not so readily identified the average matelot would not be able to find his way between them, and then international trade, the navies of the world and even - I hesitate to say it! – piracy itself would wither away and die of despondency!" He poured himself some rum, and winked at them over his eyeglasses.

"You are right, Frank, which is why I have arranged for a *boucan* upon the day afore we leave," said the Captain. "Oxen, sheep and pigs to be roasted over coals. Barrels of ale and cider, and some port wine and rum-grog for later. Let us kick up our heels before we get about our business, grow our beards a little. I think that ships do have a sort of a spirit, though, if not the sort of full-blown immortal soul that a theologist would give his approval to."

"The French fellow, René Descartes, would say not," avowed Mr Benjamin with a mock-serious expression, "rather he would say that *mentality* is a non-physical substance, from which he deduces the doctrine of duality. He says 'I think, therefore I am' and he would say 'the ship cannot think, therefore it aren't'. I feel he may have a point there, although he confesses himself to be puzzled by insects, being unable to decide whether they think or merely act in the fashion of a machine, without will or consciousness."

"That be true," said Bill. "It be in his book *The Passions Of The Soul*, which I has in my sea-chest."

"Ho-ho! Did you purchase it under the misapprehension that it was salacious, Bill?" laughed Blue Peter.

"I did a deal wiv a book-seller when we was in London, for all the books he had by Descartes, an got 'em a good price, too. All I knew was that he were a mathematician, like. I haven't read much o' it, but I remember the bit about insects." Bill selected an apple and munched it, a glint of amusement in his piggy eyes.

"Why did you want to read Descartes' mathematical musings?" asked Mr Benjamin, looking taken aback.

"He has some notions about this and that. Summa them very canny. His ideas of *ordination*, fr'instance, might lead me to say that three and one-half quantities is three and one-half dimensions, which is length, breadth, width and the half-dimension of time."

The Captain stared at him, mouth slightly open.

"Why is time a half of a dimension?" said Blue Peter, not noticing the Captain's surprise.

"Because it only goes in one direction. The other three can go back-and-forth, so to speak," said Bill.

"I confess myself humbled, Bill," said the Captain. "I was sure that nobody would spot that, I even dubbed the thing 'deciheptaxial', smugly content that the name was obscure enough for safety."

"I would not have smoked it iffen I had not just been reading *Mon-sewer* Descartes, Cap'n, so I was fortunate there."

"Well, all of you, please do not breathe a word of these notions outside this cabin for now," said Captain Greybagges earnestly. "We only have another few days here, and then we are away. All will become clear, I hope, and trying to explain now is, well, too difficult. It's easier if you just bear with me for now. Here! I have an amusement for you!"

The Captain got up and lifted a square wooden box onto the table.

"I ordered this in London, and it was delivered today."

He took away the box lid and lifted out a spherical glass bottle the size of a pumpkin.

"Alf Docklefar made it for me. It is our frigate *Ark de Triomphe* in miniature."

The Captain moved the oil lamp close to the round bottle and his three officers leaned forward to peer inside.

It was indeed the frigate *Ark de Triomphe*, the length of a hand-span and beautifully modelled. The black hull ploughed a choppy sea of blue-tinted plaster set in the bottom of the bottle, with whitecaps painted on the crests of the waves. The sails were made of fine silk stiffened with glue-size so that they appeared as if full-drawn by a stiff breeze, the little black skull-and-bones flag flying at the masthead was of stiffened silk, too, as though frozen mid-flap. Every stay, halliard, ratline, hawser and cable was represented in its correct place by silken threads and cords. The tiny muzzles of the cannons peeked from the open gun-ports,

There was silence for several minutes as they examined the ship in its round bottle, broken by the occasional quiet slurp as rum was sipped.

"Goats and monkeys!" said Mr Benjamin at last. "That is indeed a fine maquette of this noble vessel! Perfect in every visible detail! That Docklefar fellow is an artist, in his way."

"Well, not perfect in every detail," said Blue Peter.

"Surely yuz jests!" said Bill.

"Look carefully," said Blue Peter, "those front gun-ports are far too narrow. I know that for a certainty, for we have just spent the past week widening them."

The days went by quickly as the tempo of work increased towards the day of departure. The tubs came and went, delivering cargoes both mundane and strange; reels of copper wire of different gauges; thirty barrels of sauerkraut; ten sausage-shaped bottles made of cast gun-bronze, each as long as a cannon; forty-two barrels of salted herrings; a device similar to an iron fire-pump, but exquisitely made of polished brass and steel; hogsheads of wine, casks of ale, kegs of rum; ten rifled muskets (a source of much wonder) with their bullet-moulds and tools; sailcloth, canvas, rope, cable and cordage; a portable blacksmith's forge; rectangular slabs of glossy-black pitch and kegs of turpentine from the pine-forests of the Baltic; tinplate cans of fine castor-bean oil in several grades of viscosity (for "lubrication, not purgation", as Mr Benjamin assured Israel Feet); fifteen boxes of soap and a hemp sack full of scrubbing brushes; a surveyor's theodolite with its tripod; two tons of cheese, the truckles wrapped in straw....

Alarms and panics occurred, as some necessary action or essential article was nearly overlooked, but these became fewer, and those pirates responsible for ensuring readiness started to lose their haunted looks, although they were often found staring glassy-eyed at nothing, their lips moving silently as they ticked-off mental check-lists. Captain Sylvestre de Greybagges oversaw the organisation of this chaos from the Great Cabin, consulting ledgers, rosters, inventories and charts piled all over his desk and scattered on the floor around his chair. The cabin-door was wedged open, as people were coming and going all the time. He wrote letters, and pirates were despatched with bundles of them to deliver to the post-coaches and mail-boats. Occasionally he shouted for Mumblin' Jake to bring him more coffee.

"We casts off tomorrow, shipmates" roared Captain Greybagges. "We be a-leavin' on the evening tide!"

The crew of buccaneers cheered, waving their hats like madmen.

"We be a-sailin' off on a voyage to far lands, me hearty lads, on a very great venture indeed. We sails to strange seas and unknown shores, it be true, but success be assured, since I has laid me plans deep, and I has laid them well! I be keeping me plans under me hat, for now, because you swabs be a bunch of old ladies for the chatterin' and the gossipin', and, as the old pirate motto do say, 'three may keep a secret ... if two o' they be dead', har-har!"

Blue Peter stood on the quarterdeck behind the Captain and watched the crew, the buccaneers standing packed into the waist or sitting on yards and cross-trees in the rigging. It was no longer easy to tell which were the old pirates and which the new pirates. They were hanging on the Captain's words, even though he was not telling them much. But then, thought Blue Peter, I know more than any of them and I don't know what he's up to either. I suppose the crew are trusting their hearts, just as I am. Captain Greybagges was dressed as a prosperous merchant skipper, in a fine blue broadcloth coat with gold buttons, and his beard was boot-polished a rich brown. Blue Peter had donned his embroidered blue-silk coat, a white ruffled shirt and dove-grey breeches tucked into polished boots, for there seemed little point in being too restrained in dress on the last day, and there was to be a party. The Captain was still speaking:

".... an' Captain Morgan, Captain Bloody Morgan, *bloody* Captain Bloody Morgan, he do think himself to be cock o' the walk because he and his rag-bag rag-tag ragamuffins took the great port city o' Panama, but that will seem like mere apple-scrumpin' when our tale is told!"

The crew cheered again, louder and longer, tramping their feet on the deck. The Captain raised his hands and they quieted.

"Now, listen yuz swabs! Today we shall have ourselves a *boucan*, and yuz can already smell the meat a-roasting over the fires. Today we grows our beards a little, and has an ale or two! But, me lads, let us have no strife or squabbling! Summa the people from the town are a-coming, so I wants yuz on yer best partyin' behaviour. Don't yuz be tryin' to sweet-talk their womenfolk ..." Laughter from the pirates. "... no, not even if they gives yuz a wink! Don't yuz be drinking yerselves mad or dead, neither, and no scrapping, unless it be the boxin' in the ring that Bill is a-fixin' up. Surely yuz shall enjoy yerselves, but no shennigans! for tomorrow we sails to meet with fortune, becuz we be gentlemen o' fortune, boys, and I tells yuz *that we shall meet with great good fortune indeed!* Now off with you, me cheery lads!"

Somebody called "three cheers for the Cap'n!" and the pirates hip-hip-hoorayed three times, then took themselves to the boatyard for the food, drink and entertainments, filing off the frigate in a surprisingly orderly fashion, with a quiet hubbub of high spirits.

Captain Sylvestre de Greybagges, Blue Peter Ceteshwayoo, Israel Feet and Mr Benjamin took a glass of wine and a biscuit in the Great Cabin before joining the party in the boatyard. Bulbous Bill Bucephalus was already down there, rigging a boxing-ring and arranging the bouts so that the less-skilled combatants would fight first.

"That was a fine rousing speech, Cap'n," said Mr Benjamin, "and this is capital wine!"

"Thank you, Frank! I had to tell them something to raise their spirits afore we go. It's difficult though. I was thinking that it's a bit like wooden clocks. I had Mumblin' Jake open a bottle of the Margaux, as it is an occasion. It is an excellent vintage, fifteen years in the bottle."

"Wooden clocks again? said Blue Peter. "They are surely a great inspiration to you!"

"Ah, but hear me out! Your Swisser makes a wooden clock. That's clever, thinks you, I should like to make a wooden clock myself, so you asks a Swisser to write up an account, call it, say *How To Make Traditional Swiss Wooden Clocks*. You read it, and it is most enlightening, and you wish to put it in your library, but where in your library do you put it? Do you put it on the shelf reserved for books on carpentry? Or on the shelf for books on clockmaking? Or on the shelf for books on Switzerland? Or on the shelf for books on traditions? It is not obvious, and so the book may not be easily found when you wish to find it again!"

"I can indeed follow you thus far," said Blue Peter, sipping wine.

"But think! The memory – my memory, your memory, anybody's memory – is much alike to a library. Many of the notions which I would have to impart to explain my plans are the same as the Swiss clockmaking book. It is difficult to categorise them, and if I tried to explain my plans to the crew they would be confused and not enlightened because those slippery notions would not fit comfortably on this shelf of their memory or that shelf of their memory, let alone whether the notions themselves would be understood."

"That is an intriguing way of considering the condition of incomprehensibility," said Mr Benjamin. "The memory imagined as a library, and the mind, or pneuma, as its librarian. Rational thought thus dependent on the system which joins the two. Fascinating!"

"Librarians are indeed much under-valued, in the general way of things," said Captain Greybagges. "I confess that I would not have achieved very much at all, were it not for a … for librarians."

"Wooden clocks, by the bones o' Davy!" said Israel Feet. "That be a marvel, or yuz may fry me in dripping, else, wi' a curse! Damm'ee!" He emptied his glass in a gulp.

The First Mate was practicing his pirate patois, the others guessed, for he would be master-of-ceremonies at some of the entertainments, and the pirate's lingo had been at a low ebb of late, as the influence of the educated new pirates was felt, despite the enthusiasm of the young men for speaking it.

"Come, gentlemen!" said Captain Greybagges, with a sudden smile. "Let us be away to the revels! Izzy shall be our Lord of Misrule, and with luck it may not rain too much! Come, I wishes to grow me beard, I does! Wi' a curse I does, damn' yuz eyes!"

Captain Greybagges strode out of the Great Cabin, shouting to Mumblin' Jake that he may come to the *boucan* once he had washed the glasses and locked the Captain's pantry. His officers followed.

Blue Peter was the last to leave the Great Cabin, as he was savouring the last of his glass of vintage French wine. The Captain is very good at deflecting any curiosity about his plans, he thought, bamboozling Mr Benjamin with the problems of libraries, dazzling the crew with promises of riches and fame. Blue Peter noticed that the carpenter had fixed the ship-in-a-bottle on a special shelf on the cabin bulkhead, and it was brightly lit by the weak sunlight through the tall stern windows. He took a moment to examine it in daylight, rather than the yellow glow of a lamp. It was a beautiful model, quite surprising in its tiny details; there was a seagull on the foremast topgallant yard, barely the size of a flea, and a wash-tub by the hatchway to the galley. Blue Peter noticed the incongruous diagonal yard with a little platform that had been fitted to the *Ark de Triomphe* between the foremast and the mainmast. It was partially obscured by the sails and rigging, but he saw that there was something on the little platform. It was a tiny golden sphere, the size of a small bead. How odd. thought Blue Peter, the little platform of the real frigate has nothing upon it. Even more odd, the bright golden orb appeared to be at the exact centre of the spherical glass bottle. That is strange. He scratched his head. There seemed to be only two human figures upon the model's deck, a dark figure and a pale figure upon the quarterdeck. The figures were very tiny, so he could make out no more.

Blue Peter recalled that there was a magnifying-glass in the drawer of the Captain's desk. Through the lens the model frigate was even more exquisite. The tiny wash-tub by the galley hatch was visibly made of separate wooden staves barely the size of splinters. The two figures on the quarterdeck swam into focus in the glass. They were very small and lacked detail, the faces just dots of pink paint, but so cleverly wrought that the dark figure was quite recognizable as the Captain, with a black *justaucorps* coat, black tricorne hat, clad entirely in black except for his long green beard. The pale figure that stood close to the Captain was a tall slender woman with black hair, dressed in a white Greek *chiton* belted at the waist with a wide *zoster*. From far away Blue Peter heard a faint roar; the first boxing-bout of the *boucan* had just ended.

CHAPTER THE ELEVENTH,
or Blue Peter Trusts His Heart.

The pirate frigate *Ark de Triomphe* thumped through the Atlantic rollers on a freezing-cold grey spring morning, the strong wind full of sleety rain. The dawn sky was light behind the frigate, yet dark with the promise of more dirty weather to the west where her bowsprit pointed. She bears it handsomely well, thought Blue Peter, standing in greased sea-boots on the quarterdeck, wrapped in a boatcloak and hatted with a tarred sou'wester. A wave topped the leeward rail and washed across the deck, foaming against the giant upturned bucket lashed-down on the foredeck, then knocked over a pirate in the frigate's waist. The rebuilt pirate-ship's freeboard had been made low for ease of boarding a prize, but perhaps a little too low for the north Atlantic in the blustery spring. Bulbous Bill Bucephalus stepped forward from the wheel, which was held by two experienced steersmen with a bully-boy for added weight, and shouted down at the unfortunate pirate.

"Moors yerself with a safety-line, yer damn-yer-eyes lubber! If yuz goes over the side we shall not turn back for yuz! 'Pon my oath we shall not!"

The pirate, one of the new recruits from the port of London, rolled helplessly in the scuppers until another grabbed his arm and hauled him upright, water draining from under his griego, where a mischievious water slosh had filled it, rolling from his bare feet to his head as he lay on the deck.

"Arrgh! Take him below to dry off. He's no use frozen!" and, in a much louder voice, "Pay some mind, yer swabs! Old Neptune he be playful today! Har-har!"

Blue Peter had noticed that the new pirates seemed slightly stunned by the unremitting violence of the seas in mid-ocean, although in truth the *Ark de Triomphe* was romping through the waves as playfully as a seal, just occasionally sliding beneath a wave-crest in an insouciant fashion. It is a good thing, really, thought Blue Peter, they will realise that the ship has no desire to founder and their fright will then subside, for every sailor must master his fear of the sea. But then, he thought, Bill's words are a concealed rebuke to me, for I am not tied down yet he has a stout length of rope around his great belly attached to a cleat by the binnacle, and the steersmen are lashed to the wheel-stanchion in a seamanlike fashion. I have no wish to be roped, so I will go below.

Why do I not wish to be roped? he thought, as he clumped down the steps to the waist, water dripping from his sou'wester. Is it because we approach the North American Colonies, and the remembrance of slavery rises within me? Are memories linked to places by some invisible bond, some *genius loci*, so that the coast of Virginia stirs recollections of old pains, old humiliations, even though it lies hundreds of miles yet to the west? Even though it is not visible to my eyes? The very thought of being tied then seems offensive, being freighted with suggestions of bondage, despite it being an entirely reasonable and necessary precaution.

Mr Benjamin and an assistant were working on the demiheptaxial mechanism in its locker underneath the ship's wheel, talking in low voices. The locker was now almost filled with brass and steel shafts, cams and gear-wheels, all glinting in the yellow glim from a lantern and the wan rays from a skylight. The ropes from the wheel came vertically down through the quarterdeck above, through the rear of the locker and down into the tiller-room below, from where the ship could be steered if the wheel was carried away by a cannon-ball, and where strong men could be stationed to haul on relieving-tackles to ease the load on the steersmen, and would be if the seas got any rougher. Mr Benjamin and his assistant had just connected an indicator to the mechanism showing the position of the ship's rudder, a blue-steel arrow on a brass quadrant graduated in degrees. As the steersmen turned the frigate to ride the waves the steering-ropes went up and down creaking, and the blue-steel arrow swung slightly from on side to the other and back again. Mr Benjamin regarded it with a happy smile, and reached out to buff the brass quadrant with a rag.

"This is but a mere gee-gaw," said Mr Benjamin, "but is it not pleasing? The mechanism itself detects the movement of the ship with the little lead weights in the little box there…" Blue Peter peered into the locker. There was indeed a small cabinet with glass panes, inside he could see a number of spindly levers with balls of grey lead on their ends. As the boat moved under his feet the little levers waggled and glittering brass escapements whirled, faint clickings and whirrings came from deeper inside the mechanism. "This indicator of the rudder's position is a frippery, a mere curlicue I have added to this wonderful engine, so I that may more easily perceive if there is a discrepancy between the rudder's movement and the heading given by the mechanism. A crude measure, but a useful one, *and they are in complete agreement!*"

Mr Benjamin's jowled face beamed his satisfaction, his eyes shining behind his *pince-nez* spectacles. His assistant, a young pirate, a gangly youth who had been apprenticed to a clockmaker in Clerkenwell, grinned happily, nodding and repeating *"in complete agreement!"* several times. Blue Peter noted that both of them had acquired very steady sea-legs. They both shifted their bodies easily as the frigate pitched and rolled, and kept a firm grip against any sudden lurch with at least one hand.

Blue Peter squeezed past them, stepping over Mr Benjamin's canvas tool-bag, and knocked on the door to the Great Cabin. Captain Sylvestre de Greybagges was at his desk writing in a ledger, dressed all in black, his beard seeming to glow a wan grass-green in the pale easterly light from the tall stern-windows. He shouted for Mumblin' Jake to bring coffee. Blue Peter sat down.

"Tell me, Captain," he said, "who designed the demiheptaxial mechanism?"

"Why do you ask?" the Captain smiled.

"It was not Frank. The joy which I saw in his eyes just now was admiration, not the pride of a creator, and anyway he has been too busy with other things, and before that enslaved in Barbary."

"The devices of which it is composed are familiar to clockmakers, and their principles may be found in a library, if one knows where to look. It is the work of many minds, but Frank has brought all the pieces together into a complete whole, so you grant him but little credit for his labours. I fear that I cannot tell you anything more."

"I know, I know," said Blue Peter, "I must wait and all will become clear in time." He sighed.

Mumblin' Jake came with the coffee and a dish of sweet cakes on a tray.

"To change the subject, Captain," said Blue Peter, his mouth full of cake, "can we not raid the slave-masters of Virginia? You once told me that you had no objection if the time was right, and we are headed there with in the finest pirate-frigate ever to sail the seas, and with a crew who have not seen action for a while, and a good half of them who have never seen action at all. It might be useful experience for the new pirates and an encouragement to the old hands. These are very good cakes!"

"That young fellow Thackeray makes 'em. Cookie is quite jealous. A raid on Virginny? Umm, it's not a bad idea – you are right that the crew could do with some action to sort them out, and the young fellows are eager to show their mettle - but we are on a tight schedule, and I don't wish to draw any attention to ourselves. We must call at Norfolk, where I have some business, and that will surely set enough tongues wagging up and down the coast, so I must say nay. I appreciate your feelings in the matter, Peter, but I don't think it can be done at this time. I must stick to my plans."

Blue Peter felt obscurely thwarted by this. He ached to do some damage to Master Chumbley and his odious fat wife, or any other slave-owner, and he could almost feel the heat as he imagined their white mansion burning, could almost hear the crackle of the flames and their screams as they burned in their canopied feather-beds. I had forgotten how much I loathe them, he thought. He sipped his coffee glumly.

Blue Peter wished to argue the point further, but it seemed useless when the Captain's mind was made up. Instead he turned the conversation to discussing the romantic attachments that the crew had made during the past winter in Liver Pool. The necessity for arranging payments to common-law wives and pregnant girlfriends had given them a tedious extra burden before leaving the port, yet it had to be done to maintain goodwill and discretion. The two buccaneers were tired from the stormy passage across the Atlantic, and they got into the kind of argument that only old friends can have, where the issue remains unclear and where the participants end up attacking their own original propositions.

"Why then did you not yourself take a mistress in Liver Pool?" asked Blue Peter Ceteshwayoo, in some irritation.

"Well," said Captain Sylvestre de Greybagges, rubbing his eyes tiredly, "I didn't have the time. Always busy, you know."

"What poppycock! The red-haired widow, overseer of the copyists' room, Mavis O'Bacon, she would have warmed your bed, massaged your back and made you possets, too. She looked at you the way a cat looks at a dish of cod-scraps."

"I don't know. I was aware of her ... interest. I think it's because I have been obsessed with time these past months. Every man hates time, and tries to ignore its flow, thinking each day is a repetition of the last with a few trivial changes, and it is not. That is the secret of peasants, you know. Although poor and hard-driven they see the flow of time clearly through the rise and fall of the seasons, and so realise the arcs of their destinies. The rich, by contrast, can insulate themselves from even noticing time, dividing it with clocks and calendars and account-books until they feel it is under their control, and so they are unpleasantly surprised when they grow old, and are outraged when death approaches, whereas the old peasant is sanguine as he goes to meet his maker. Once one starts to think about time, to take the long view, brief *amours* lose some of their savour. One is always then thinking 'what next? shall we marry and have children?' and if the answer is 'no' then it all seems a little sad and futile. But then I could ask you the same question, Peter. You could have ensured that half the next generation of Liver Pool scallywags were large and brown. The boys would have been impressive oafs, I'm sure, but I would have pitied the girls if they favoured you in looks."

They glowered at each other, then burst out laughing. Captain Greybagges refilled their coffee-mugs, taking care not to spill any as the Atlantic combers made the frigate roll and pitch.

"I do know what you mean about time," said Blue Peter, eating another cake, "and that there should be some purpose to one's rogerings, too. I did find the ladies of Liver Pool alluring - they have sharp tongues and even the humblest of them has a queenly gaze - but there are enough bastards in this sad vale of tears, and I would like your monster-hunt to be over before I consider domesticity."

"My 'monster-hunt'?" Captain Greybagges looked surprised. "I had not thought of it quite like that."

"By what other name could one particularise those creatures, the *extramundanes* that you described in your tale to me?"

"I suppose you are right, but I like the lizard people, and cannot think of them as *monsters*. A few men and women that I have encountered have been far more monstrous. Some of them fair of face, witty, elegant and charming in their manner, too."

"I cannot argue with that, Captain, for I have met similar human monsters, although they are quite rare, thankfully."

"We are both pirates, Peter, and so perhaps less inclined than others to judge by mere appearance, but still we can be deceived. Did you ever meet that mad cavalier Prince Rupert of the Rhine? He was a-buccaneering around the Carib seas before the King was restored. He had a little poodle-dog called 'Boyo'."

"I don't believe that I ever did, Captain, why do you ask?"

"Well, the first time that I came across the fellow was in the Dry Tortugas, in the old *Ponce de Leon* tavern. I was sitting drinking rum-and-water in a civilised way when in came Prince Rupert. Without a word of warning the sod thrust a globule of glass under my nose and tweaked it – the glass globule, that is, not my nose – and it exploded like a bomb! My eyes were full of splinters of glass! I had to bathe them in salt water! That good fellow Izzie had to get some of them out with the wetted corner of a kerchief. I feared I might be blinded, and the cursed hound laughed like a drain! Prince Rupert, that is, not his little dog Boyo. If I could have seen anything at all I would have shot him or run him through without a second thought, but my eyes were full of tears and glass. Yet when I got to know him better I found that he was a congenial sort of cove. The glass-bomb was an invention of his, and he had been merely over-enthusiastic in the pride of his discovery and over-eager to demonstrate natural philosophy, and not the depraved lover of cruelty that he seemed at that first meeting."

"How did the glass-bomb function? Was it filled with gunpowder?"

"Not at all, Peter. If one heats a rod of glass until it melts like pitch, then allows the molten glass to drip into a bucket of water, each drop is instantly solidified, but the outside hardens first, squeezing the interior, so that forces are frozen in the solid glass. When one snaps off the tail of the globule it precipitates the whole into shattering quite energetically, *bang!* Prince Rupert is presently much caressed by London's society for his learning – he has invented a new method for printing pictures, you know - and the glass-bombs are called 'Prince Rupert's drops', so his name shall be written in the pages of history for an invention of no use whatsoever, except to fill unfortunate souls' eyes with glass-splinters, and not for his failed siege of Liver Pool."

"He laid siege to Liver Pool? Whatever for?"

"It was in the war 'twixt King Charlie's cavaliers and Noll Cromwell's round-heads, and nobody seems to have had much notion of what they were about in those times. The people of Liver Pool remembered him well, and his little dog, too, which they said had the evil eye, although how a poodle-dog may possess the evil eye is beyond my imagining, I must say, even though it was a horrid little mutt, always trying to roger one's leg, you know? The Liver Pool ruffians said that he lifted the siege because they stole most of his supplies while his army was camped outside the town, which I can well believe."

"Does this tale of Prince Rupert have a moral? or indeed an ending?" said

Blue Peter, selecting another cake.

"Well, I suppose I was musing upon the nature of monsters, and that although Prince Rupert seemed like a monster at our first encounter he wasn't, really. There is the Liver Pool connection, too, which brought him to mind." The Captain took the last cake.

"I suspect that you are attempting to divert me from my ploy to trick you into revealing something more of your plan, Captain."

"Well, Peter, I think I was going to say that a monster – which is to say a *monster of evil*, and not just a poor sad malformed thing such as a kitten with two heads – is defined by a lack of interest in the welfare of other beings. Such a person is so utterly focussed upon their own selfhood that they incapable of the normal human attributes of sympathy, generosity, magnaminity and so on. In fact, they may exult in defying the vestiges of their conscience, if indeed they have one, and so relish cruelty."

"We pirates are generally regarded as monsters, surely, Captain? Those were very good cakes, and now there are none."

Captain Greybagges shouted for Mumblin' Jake to bring more cakes. Mumblin' Jake put his head around the door and mumbled that there were no more cakes, an' damn yer eyes yer greedy bastards. He took the coffee pot to refill.

"Pirates may be monsters, Peter, of course they may. Alf Docklefar, who made the *Ark de Triomphe* ship-in-a-bottle over there, has sailed with most of them, to judge by his yarns. But when exactly is one a pirate, and thus a criminal, and not a privateer, and so a legal entity plying a legal trade? That is not clear at all. The Treaty of Tordesillas in 1494, sanctioned by the Pope himself, gave everything west of the Cape Verde Islands to the Spaniards and everything east to the Portugese, and yet was that not itself a great act of piracy? Most of those lands were already inhabited by folks who would not know the Pope from a coster-monger, after all. The other countries of Europe regarded the treaty with derision, of course. Francis the First, who was king of the French, roared with laughter when he heard of it, and asked to be shown the clause in Adam's will that made such a bequest legal. As a lawyer, I do applaud him for that! He was a fine fellow, was Francis, a very learned king. He made Guillame Budé master of his library at Fontainebleau, which shows great judgement of character as well as an appreciation of the importance of librarians. So, was Drake a pirate? The

Dons say that he was, of course they do, and the English say that he was a hero, of course they do. Since then the situation has become even more confused. The meridian has been moved three hundred and seventy leagues westwards, so as not to discommode the Portugese, and a further *understanding* among the European nations means that any *incident* west of that cannot be regarded as legal grounds for a war, which is how bloody Captain Bloody Morgan could besiege and sack Panama and be made Governor of Jamaica, and why the Spanish have to grin and bear it as best they can. In the seas and lands west of the mid-Atlantic meridian it must be assumed that European laws are only honoured in the breach, and that therefore the only law that needs to be considered is 'might is right'. Under such a legal regime the label of *pirate* becomes meaningless. I rest my case."

Mumblin' Jake came with the refilled coffee-pot and a plate of biscuits, mumbling curses. Blue Peter poured coffee and took a biscuit.

"I am desolated to find that I am not a pirate," he said, dunking the biscuit and eating it in one mouthful.

"And neither are you a monster, Peter, but if certain parties were to apprehend you they would hang you nonetheless. Now I am diverted from the point I wished to make, which is that I am not a monster, but that my monster-hunt compels me to behave as one. I cannot tell my officers or my crew what I am about, but must instead strut about like a tyrant insisting my orders be obeyed even if they seem not to make much sense, and yet there is no other way. Leave me one biscuit at least, Peter, you greedy sod!"

Blue Peter pushed the plate towards the Captain, but a lurch of the frigate propelled it further and the Captain caught it as it slid off the desk.

"Well caught, sir!" said Blue Peter, clapping. Captain Greybagges ate the biscuit.

"However, Peter, I may vouchsafe you a little of my schemings. Our next port o' call is St John's in Newfoundland. A cold and miserable place, but we shall only water and provision there before heading south to Virginny."

The mention of Virginia reminded Blue Peter of his thwarted desire to commit arson upon white mansions, which put him in an ill humour. I am tired, he thought, we all are from the hammering of the seas, and the cold, and the need for standing watch after watch. He made his leave to the Captain and retired to his cabin for a couple of hours sleep. The ship seems to enjoy these high Atlantic seas more than the crew, he thought, as he tied himself into his bunk. *I think of her as a wolf at first, then as a leopardess, and now as a seal. There is something very alive, very animal, about a good ship, even though a ship is conceived by the mind of man, not God, and made of wood, not flesh. Perhaps she will come to me again as I slumber.* But Blue Peter had no hypnogogic visitation, only a dreamless restorative nap, rocked by the frigate's pitching, lullabied by the gentle creaking of its timbers, until woken at midday by the eight bells of the end of the forenoon watch. Dinner was a broth of barley, dried peas and salt-pork, with bread, not hard-tack, as there was still flour this early in their voyage. Blue Peter ate his in the officer's mess-room, which was a little larger after the frigate's rebuild, and now tastefully panelled in light oak. Israel Feet joined him at the table in fine high spirits, drops of spray still glittering in the locks of hair that stuck out from under his head-scarf. The officer's mess-room of the *Ark de Triomphe* was not like that of a ship of the Royal Navy, and pirates on various errands came in and out without ceremony. They seemed in fine spirits, too. *I was right,* thought Blue Peter, *the rough weather and cold high seas have given the crew faith in the vessel, and now they are exhilarated by its romping progress through the waves.* He drank some coffee, and wondered if any more cakes had been baked yet.

The *Ark de Triomphe*, sailing due-westerly under topsails alone, slipped slowly into the Hampton Roads from Chesapeake Bay, leaving a white wake on the choppy grey-green water, trailing a small flock of optimistic seagulls.

"Starboard on my mark, mateys," Bulbous Bill Bucephalus told the steersmen, and, stepping forward, roared "Goin' about to port! Be ready to brace up!" to the foremast-jacks, then to the waisters; "Lead-swingers to the chains! Ready the longboat, you lubbers, har-har!"

The breeze on-shore was light but steady, and the *Ark de Triomphe's* wake curved smoothly from due west to due south as she turned into the wide mouth of the Elizabeth River. The pirate on the port fore-chain started swinging the seven-pound lead weight on its line, at first back and forth, then around like a sling in an accelerating circle before releasing the coiled line to hurl the hand-lead far ahead of the slow-moving vessel. After a moment the second pirate on the starboard fore-chain started swinging his lead, timing the cast so that the depth-soundings would come alternately as the hand-leads sank to the bottom and were pulled in and cast again.

"Take her past Half Moone Island," said Captain Greybagges, pointing into the distance, "and then we'll anchor south of Town Point. The harbour-master will be assured of our goodwill when a little gold is pressed into his sweaty palm, I'm sure, and the Half Moone fort will keep us safe from any impudent Dutch privateers who may be sniffing about the coast. They can exchange broadsides with the fort, should they come up-river, whilst we may make wagers on them, sitting comfy, sipping rum and eating hot chestnuts."

The lead-swingers called; "No bottom!" and; "Six and a half! Six and a half and sand!" and; "Five and some! Five and some and gravel! Brown gravel and shells!" The hand-leads had hollows in their bases filled with tallow, to which the silt would adhere as they thumped onto the river-bottom. As the soundings grew shallower and the bottom more gravelly an anchor was prepared for dropping, swinging free from its cathead, and the longboat was launched to kedge the ship if required. After a normal ration of skinned knuckles, pulled muscles and curse-words the frigate swung in the slow river current, its anchor securely bedded in the gravelly river-floor, and its sails furled into swags on the yards.

The frigate's last port of call, St John's in Newfoundland, had indeed been a cold and miserable place, but they had not tarried there. Two days to replenish water and food, for the Captain to despatch and receive some letters and for a few small repairs to be made, occasioned by the battering of the Atlantic. The widened forward gun-ports which Torvald Coalbiter had suggested had needed to be reinforced, as they now took more of the weight of each wave, and the high seas had shaken the hinge-bolts loose. There had been a great surfeit of fresh fish in St John's, though, and the crew of the *Ark de Triomphe* had gorged themselves on fillets of cod fried in batter for breakfast, dinner and tea. Captain Greybagges had allowed four parties of six to go ashore, each accompanied by a bully-boy to ensure discipline. He felt that this would prevent the remainder of the crew from feeling aggrieved at having to stay aboard, and indeed the shore-parties duly reported back that St John's was a cold dirty slum of a hole of a place which smelled overpoweringly of whale-oil and rotting fish, that the ale was alike to horse-piddle, that the pies were made of whale-meat and that the only entertainment to be found was a toothless old bugger with a guitar who sang songs in French, although Jake Thackeray said that the song about the gorilla was very funny and that he was going to translate it. The crew were not unduly surprised that Jake spoke French, as he was a very good pastry-cook. Captain Greybagges had impressed upon the shore-parties the need for discretion, and had provided each party with a different yarn to spin to the townspeople about the frigate's destination: they were collecting Mayan princesses from Mexico for the hareem of the Ottoman Sultan in Constantinople; they were on a diplomatic mission for the king of Sweden; they were carrying a letter from the prophet Sabbatti Zevi to the Emperor of Cathay, or perhaps to Prester John; they were going to navigate a nor-westerly passage to the Orient. The *Ark de Triomphe* had departed St John's on a morning tide in a fall of swirling snow, leaving a certain bemusement in her wake, and had sailed east out into the Atlantic. She then curved south and west back towards the north Americas, encountering an iceberg along the way, a magnificent blue-green ice-castle which they had fired upon for target-practice with the new rifled muskets, the guns wonderfully accurate even at three hundred paces. They had seen no other ships until they were close to New Amsterdam, and then only mast-tops on the horizon, glimpsed through the haze. The frigate sailed on south-south-west, occasionally heading south-by-west or southwest-by-south to keep a generous margin of sea-room from the coast, to drop anchor in the river by the town of Norfolk, Virginia, on a calm and sunny forenoon.

"It is indeed a fine day, Captain, but why are we here?" said Blue Peter.

"We are here because I must meet with a Dutchman. A Dutchman who possesses something that may be useful to me," said Captain Greybagges, snapping his telescope shut after surveying the foreshore and the river. "A Dutchman who is not yet here."

"How long shall us wait upon him then, Cap'n?" said Bill, standing at the rail eating a large wedge of cold sea-pie.

"I would wish that he were here now, but I may allow him one week, and no more."

"Should we not then bow-and-stern her with the second anchor, Cap'n? In case the wind blows up, or rain swells the river?"

"Um, yes, if we are to be here for a week then I suppose so, but keep the second anchor nipped and close-by, so we don't lose both of 'em if she drags, and drop a couple of light kedges, too, to keep her from swinging should the wind veer."

Captain Greybagges, Blue Peter and Mr Benjamin sat at their ease at the table in the Great Cabin. Through the open stern-windows they could hear the splashing, grunting and cursing of the longboat crew.

"Those little anchors, they are called *kedges*, then?" said Mr Benjamin, peering out the stern-windows.

"Indeed, yes," said the Captain, "to distinguish them from their larger cousins. Some call them 'fisherman's anchors', because they are pretty much the same as those of a lugger or a herring-buss."

"A lugger? Would that be a vessel that lugs things about?" said Mr Benjamin.

"Well, yes and no," said the Captain, grinning. "A lugger may indeed lug a cargo from hither to yon, but that is not the origin of its name."

"Satisfy my curiosity, Captain, I beg you! I find myself a-thirst for nautical lore these days! Being aboard this grand frigate has enthused my spirits for things maritime, and whetted my desire to be a sailor, or to at least pass for one when quaffing ale in a dockside tavern. What is a lugger, and why is it so-named?"

"That is a question, indeed it is, Frank. A question that requires a full and detailed answer. You mention the quaffing of ale in dockside taverns, too, so let us combine these two activities, and grow our beards a little! I shall need to disguise mine first, of course, so as not to cause tredidation in the local inhabitants ... Jake! Jake, you lazy swab! Bring the boot-polish!"

The clapboard tavern could not be considered to be on a dockside, but rather faced a beach of stones and river-mud, with boats in various stages of decrepitude hauled up onto it, and fishing-nets hung on poles for repair. The tavern's name was *Wahunsunacock's Mantle*. The inn-sign represented the famous mantle with a wooden board in the shape of a deerskin cloak, the figures of a man and two deer painted upon it, the white paint applied it in a pattern of dots to mimic the tiny shells with which the actual cloak had been embroidered. It was warm in the front parlour of the tavern, with a fire of logs in a brick hearth, and there was a pleasant aroma of baking bread and roasting coffee-beans.

Captain Sylvestre de Greybagges had visited the harbour-master, finding him in the day-cabin of the harbour pratique-boat drinking tea and eating a meat-pie for his lunch. The harbour-master was a beefy ginger-haired man with sharp grey eyes and a bluff honest countenance, but he was not immune to the power of a clinking handful of Spanish *reales d'or* and the Captain was able to conclude his business with him amiably and expeditiously: The Dutchman whom the Captain sought was not there, but he had left word for the Captain that he would return in ten days hence. The Captain would be kept informed of any undue interest in the *Ark de Triomphe* or its doings. There were no privateers or naval vessels currently in the vicinity, and would the Captain join him in a glass of rum? The Captain would, and a cigar, too, as he had not before smoked one from Virginia. He parted with the harbour-master on excellent terms and joined the others in the tavern, where his conversation with Frank Benjamin had continued almost as though without interruption.

"… so you see, Frank, every lugger has a lug-sail, but not every boat with a lug-sail is a lugger, if you follow me." Captain Greybagges sipped his hot rum-and-water.

"There are so many variations upon the theme of a large tub with a sail affixed to it," said Mr Benjamin. " I now see the wit of that ship-in-a-bottle. The one whose precise classification confused you all so. Perhaps each ship in unique unto itself."

"Arrrgh!," spake Captain Sylvestre de Greybagges, "it be incontravertibibble that ay craft o' ay sea-goin' nature do have a soul! Begging the pardon of any preachy lubbers who may object themselves upon grounds 'o blasphemy, it must be clear to any right-thinkin' buccaneer that a ship o' the seas has an immortal soul! Much like a man - an' damn yer eyes iffen it ain't the truth! — a ship has a soul!" Captain Greybagges leaned forward, shut one eye conspiratorily and lowered his voice. "…. although I must confess that my opinion about riverboats remains uncertain!"

There was a moment of pause, then a rumble of appreciative laughter.

"Arrgh! Curse all bumboats an' damn wherries too! Wi' a wannion!" squeaked Bill, the tone of his voice sent even higher by hot rum-grog.

"There is substance to my joshing," said the Captain in a less-piratical voice, "for there are indeed many variations upon a wooden tub with a mast, so many that they resemble the varieties of animals. Is a zebra a horse? Or do its stripes make it necessarily a relative of the tiger? Its preferences - to run in herds, to eat grass, to kick its enemies with its hind legs – must lead one to believe that it is a horse and not a tiger, and so it must have a *pneuma* or spirit, some kind of a soul which predisposes it to a horse-like behaviour, and not to a solitary life of carnivorous predation. Is each sailing vessel equipped thus? Do some ships huddle together in fleets because they are predisposed to do so by their nature, like horses? Do other ships plough a more solitary wake, maybe even a more savage one, because their souls ache to prowl the seas in lonely freedom, as does the tiger in his jungle?"

The Captain would have spoken more, but he was interrupted by a polite "ahem!" from a man sitting in an armchair by the fire.

"Excuse my horning-in, sir!" he said, arising from the depths of the winged armchair which had concealed him, "but I guess and calculate that riverboats are surely possessed of souls! Souls that love to wander! Mischievious and sprightly souls! Powerful souls full of great determination! I have voyaged through these lands on rivers wide and narrow, in boats great and little, and I speak from experience. Excuse me again! I am remiss! I am Richard Bonhomme, trader, horse-coper, arkwright and *voyageur!*"

The small portly man puffed out his chest like a bantam-cock, swept off his battered hat and bowed, tottering slightly.

"Why, no slight taken!" said the Captain. "It be a free discussion. Be pleased to join us and sit at our table." He called for more drinks.

"… the birch-bark canoe is decried by mariners, but it is a … a paragon of the nautical virtues!" Richard Bonhomme took a gulp of grog. "The cunning Wampanoag or Pequot indian can make a small one in a matter of days, but it will carry him for a thousand leagues or more. All he needs is birch-bark, split-pine laths, vines for stitching and pine-sap for caulking, all of which can be gotten in the forest. You may think such a craft simple to make, but I would wager that your ship's carpenter could not make one in less than a month, and it would not then stay afloat for one single day. It is an art. Canoes can be made over ten paces long, too, to carry three tons of cargo and ten men! The big canoes take longer to make, and need careful handling, but no other boat will take the trappers deep into the interior where the beavers, martens and lynxes roam, for often the canoe must be carried over *les portages*, and a wooden boat would be too heavy. I have built many such canoes, and made many such journeys. Each canoe is different, too, so they must have souls, it stands to reason!"

The Captain, Blue Peter and Mr Benjamin listened carefully, but Israel Feet and Bulbous Bill were playing cards in a tipsy fashion, only lending half an ear.

"Mr Bonhomme," said Mr Benjamin slowly, "I am Frank Benjamin, and I believe that you are my cousin!"

Mr Bonhomme stared at him, round-eyed with surprise, then nodded slowly.

"Frank Benjamin! Of course I have heard tell of you! The famed mechanician and printer of books and pamphlets! How pleased I am to meet you at last, cousin!"

"And I you, Mr Bonhomme. Please do call me Frank! I heard through the gossipings of my family's womenfolk that you are become prosperous through horse-trading, which says much for your wit and cunning!"

"It is true, Frank," Mr Bonhomme simpered, "I have been blessed with some good fortune, but I must be modest and say that I was lucky to be amongst the first of the *voyageurs*, and so able to make a goodly profit before the whole business of trapping fur was stolen away, stolen away by powerful companies, companies with deep pockets for the bribing of government clerks, curse them all! I was lucky, too, to be among that company of freedom-loving men and women, whose home was the woods, and whose eyes were always upon the unreachable horizon! Alas! Those that remain are now no more than mere employees, slaves to the whims of stock-holders in London and Paris. I, too, would have stayed a *voyageur*, for I love the woods and the rivers, but my back and legs were getting no younger, and carrying a pack over the muddy trail of a *portage* was no longer such an easy stroll. Still, I was blessed there, too, for I put my money into horse trading just as the demand for horses and mules grew great here in Virginny, and then into breeding-studs, stables and livery, too, so I have not done so badly. I still dream of the woods, though, and the rough companionship I knew there. I even miss my indian friends, for they are savages, it is true, but they have a wild nobility that we civilised peoples have not had since the times of the warriors of the ancient legends. Some of them do, anyway! You are of my family, cousin Frank, so please call me Richard. You fellows, too, as we meet so congenially, and talk of the souls of boats like philosophers. I salute you all!"

Mr Bonhomme raised his glass of grog and emptied, the buccaneers followed suit and banged their glasses down on the table.

"Captain Greybagges ...." said Mr Benjamin, in a tentative voice.

"Sylvestre, if you please, in these cordial circumstances," said the Captain, refilling his glass from the jug.

"Sylvestre, meeting my cousin Richard for the first time is a pleasant surprise, yet it reminds me that I have a mother, six brothers, ten sisters, a wife, a son and a daughter, none of whom have I seen for over a year. This Dutchman of yours will not arrive for a week, so might I have a leave of absence, a furlough, for three days, to visit them? You know that I will return and not 'jump ship', as you matelots say."

"You are fortunate that that you ask me this now, while I am in drink and thus full of good cheer," said the Captain. "You are vital to our company in this enterprise, yet I am inclined to allow you this, provided you will return. How far is your family home? How debatable are the roads you must travel? The malice of an indian brave or the greed of a footpad might delay you, or worse, and then our success will be put in doubt, despite the good work that you have done in schooling your assistants."

"Upon horseback it is but half a day, ..." said Mr Benjamin.

"And I shall provide the horse!" cried Mr Bonhomme. "And I shall accompany my cousin Frank, with two of my men, stout fellows and not shy! We shall bring Frank back to you even if we have to carry him on a shutter, if he shall be the worse for drink, ho-ho!"

"Why, then it is difficult for me to refuse, Frank," said the Captain slowly, not looking entirely content.

"Upon my honour, Captain!" said Mr Bonhomme, placing his hand on his chest, "I shall ensure my cousin's timely return! We could start now, and so be back the sooner! We will arrive in Boston after dark, 'tis true, but the last four leagues are on a straight path through open pasture, and there is the twilight until the moon rises. Come cousin! On with your hat! Let us away!"

Captain Greybagges put on a stern expression, then nodded.

"I mislike enterprises conceived in grog," he said, "but if your two stout fellows are sober and your horses obedient, Richard, then maybe you will arrive approximately in one piece. Go now, Frank, before I change my mind."

Mr Benjamin struggled to his feet, trying to put on his hat and finish his grog at the same time.

"Thank you, Captain! ... Sylvestre!" he gasped, putting his glass on the table.

"Do you have enough money in your purse? Are you sure? Then get on your way as quick as you can, lest nightfall catch you on the road. Do please pass my kindest regards to your mother and family." The Captain waved them away, with a brief smile.

The two hurried from the inn. The First Mate and the sailing master appeared not to have noticed, intent upon their cards. Bulbous Bill discarded a two of diamonds, took the top card from the deck, examined it, smiled, his fat jowls dimpling, and laid his hand down on the table-top.

"Har-har! A forced *quinola* an' so the *espagnolette!* Your goose be cooked, Izzy! Har-har!"

"Bloody *Rovescinio*! I curses the cursed game! I do swear that you be making up the rules as we plays, Bill! 'Pon my oath I does! Where is Frank and the little fat cully?"

Captain Greybagges sighed and shook his head sadly. Blue Peter stood up.

"Captain, I will follow after Frank and his cousin," he said. "If Mr Bonhomme's horses are overly boisterous, or if his stout fellows are as inebriated as he is himself, I shall persuade them to wait upon the morning. Otherwise I shall make sure that they are expeditiously away on their travels."

He put on his hat and strode from the inn. Captain Greybagges sighed again, gestured to the innkeeper for another jug of grog, and turned back to the table.

"*Rovescinio* you say? By my bones! That be a game fit only for Venetian *zoccoli*, prancing nincompoops and French dressmakers! Deal me in, Bill, and I shall skin you both."

They played several hands, Bulbous Bill winning all of them. Loomin' Len came and asked if the crew could go ashore, as their tasks were done.

"Of course!" said the Captain. "This is a fair haven for we jolly pirates. There is but little chance of any surprises, so long as we pays our way, respects the local customs and the indians don't go on the war-path, har-har! Look-outs to be posted and watches to be kept, mind! You know the drill with the crew. Parties of six only, bully-boys to stay sober, no trollops on board. Sails need be mended and trunnions be slushed on the morning, remember, so no man to get himself paralytical, and no fighting."

Loomin' Len made to leave.

"Oh, and see if'n you can't find Peter. It ain't like him to go wanderin' off, specially when we shall be havin' ourselves some afternoon tea. And cakes, too, if I am not mistaken." The Captain sniffed the aroma of baking from the inn's kitchen, sipped his grog, now cold, and picked up his cards. After some deliberation he discarded two and took two from the pack. The game continued.

Loomin' Len came back into the inn, followed by several pirates. They doffed their knitted caps, mumbled greetings to the Captain and sat at the table by the fire. Loomin' Len came to the Captain, bent down and whispered:

"He's hired a hoss, Cap'n, an' he's rode orf. The ostler said he didn't say where he's going, but he didn't foller after Mr Benjamin and his pal. Says he spurred the hoss an' rode orf like he was on a wager, coat tails a-flying."

Captain Greybagges hand stopped halfway through carrying his glass to his lips. He sat perfectly still for several seconds, then placed the glass back on the table.

"Izzy, Bill, come let us get some air," he said softly, standing and putting on his black tricorn hat.

The First Mate and the sailing master hurried after the Captain, who was almost running. They were a unsteady on their feet from the afternoon of rum-grog, but they caught up to him as he entered the stable-yard of Mr Bonhomme. With a few terse questions the Captain confirmed what Loomin' Len had told him. He tore off his hat and nearly threw it onto the ground with anger, but mastered himself and put it carefully back upon his shaven head, breathing heavily.

"Damn the man!" he hissed. "Damn me for a dunderhead, too! I come ashore and forget myself, drinking and playing cards like any empty-headed jolly sailor on a toot! I have a little time waiting for a damn Dutchman, I think! We are safe-berthed! I may relax and grow my beard a little! What a tomfool I am!"

"Where is he away, then, Cap'n?" said Israel Feet, exchanging a puzzled glance with Bill.

"He is gone to burn down his former master's house. I did not realise the depth of his feelings about the things he endured as a slave. He is a proud man, and he means to have his vengeance if he can. We must stop him." The Captain turned and shouted to the ostler, who was pitch-forking hay into a manger; "You! Fellow! We must have three horses and we must have them now! Here is gold!"

Captain Greybagges led them out of Jamestown at a sedate walk, telling his two friends that they must not give any indication of hurry, but when he came to the road that Blue Peter had taken he spurred the horse, snapped the reins and galloped, snarling 'gid-yap! gid-yap!" at the startled nag. Israel Feet followed him on a lean gelding, almost keeping up despite his lack of horsemanship, and Bulbous Bill Bucephalus trailed after, his wobbling bulk bouncing on a large and good-natured mare, a good-natured mare which, despite its complaisance, ignored his squeaked exhortations and trotted with no sense of urgency. A small boy with ragged trousers and a fishing-pole over his shoulder stared open-mouthed with surprise as the trio rode past him into the deepening twilight.

Blue Peter, many miles ahead, lay along his horse's neck and growled words of encouragement to it as it hurtled along the muddy road. The horse's flanks were lathered with sweat and slather foamed from its lips. Clods of earth kicked up by its flying hooves fell back to the ground seconds after it had passed and become invisible in the gloom. Through Blue Peter's mind ran the phrase *trust your heart, trust your heart, trust your heart,* like a mantra. His emotions roiled and swirled like a hurricane, but at the hurricane's eye, at his heart, there was a calm filled with the cold thirst for vengeance.

CHAPTER THE TWELFTH,
or *The Summoning of Satan.*

"Cap'n, we be lost," said Bulbous Bill Bucephalus, "and it be as black as pitch."

"I have faith in Izzy," said Captain Greybagges, " for he is an excellent scout. He used to track down witnesses and absconders for me when he was my clerk, when I was a lawyer and buccaneered with wig and pen."

"The Ratcliffe highway on the kinchin lay an' the rookeries o' St Giles, that were his nursery, Cap'n,. He can find 'is way around most o' Lunnon by pure instinct, even in a pea-soup fog. These woods here-abouts be colonial woods, which, begging your pardon, do not even smell like proper woods, not being like Epping Forest at all."

"No, Bill, it is not. Epping Forest stinks of corpses, it being very convenient for garrotters and suchlike, those who cannot dump their victims into the Fleet river because of other pressing business. These woods are quite fragrant, although dark to be sure."

The path under the canopy of the trees was indeed dark, but not pitch-black. There was a bright moon, but the sky had clouded over and the moonlight came only in occasional beams through gaps in the overcast. One of these moonbeams revealed Israel Feet and his horse walking carefully back up the path. He and his mount were both ectomorphic, and haloed in the moonlight they made a sinister sight.

"I looked and I beheld a pale horse! Its rider was named Death, and Hell was following close behind him!" Captain Greybagges cried, still fuddled from the afternoon's drinking, theatrically waving an arm.

"By my liver and lights, Cap'n! Be thee less lusty an' blaring!" hissed Israel Feet, gesturing for quiet.

"My apologies, Izzy, but you gave me a turn, popping up like that, and your damned horse is rather pale. The verse in Revelations says *chlôros*, which is Greek for 'pale green', I think, and your nag does look a little sickly in this gloomy light …" The Captain spoke in an undertone and looked abashed.

"I cannot find Peter's trail anymore, curse it, so it may 'appen as we took a wrong turn," said Israel Feet, in an aggrieved tone, "but the horse be not to blame, anyhow, so there be no need to call it green and sickly."

"No, indeed, and you are not to blame, either," said the Captain soothingly. "These clouds over the moon are the only culprits, blast 'em."

"We 'ave lost Peter's trail, an' we be lost our own selves, an' it be dark," said Bulbous Bill. "Mayhap we should seek shelter for the night, Cap'n, since we be adrift wi'out a chart."

"I hate to admit such a thing, Bill, but you are right," said the Captain.

"There be a light up ahead, Cap'n" said the First Mate. "A sort o' dim glow offen the path. That be why I come back direckly."

There was a 'squeak-pop' noise, followed by a 'glug-glug' noise, then Bulbous Bill handed the rum bottle to Captain Greybagges, who glug-glugged then passed it to Israel Feet. Then the three, without a word, walked their horses slowly up the path by the intermittent light of the moon.

"There be a signpost here-abouts," whispered the First Mate eventually. They stopped, a horse whickering discontentedly, and dismounted, clumsy and cursing softly in the black-velvet darkness. The moon came out for an instant.

"Arr! There it be!" The First Mate pointed. The signpost stood at a crossroads, wan in a shaft of the pale moonlight. "There be a field just here. We can moor these horses, an goes on a foot."

Their mounts tethered in a shipshape fashion, they proceeded up the path like blind men, stepping high and carefully, waving their arms in front of themselves, bumping into each other, stopping once or twice to sip on Bill's rum-bottle. The occasional stray beam of moonlight gave them a vague idea of the path between the trees. One of the stray beams illuminated the signpost as they passed.

"The signpost be sayin' there be a town two mile away, Cap'n" said the First Mate. "Mayhap we should ride there. Start lookin' for Peter again at daybreak. Rested, like."

The Captain stopped. "That is a pleasant idea, but we do not know yet what devilment Peter has conjured up in these parts, and we are his friends and we are pirates. It may be for the best if we do not draw attention to ourselves. What town was it, anyway?"

"The signpost said 'Salem', Cap'n. 'Salem two mile' it said."

"Well, in that case we are still lost, for that is not a place that I have ever heard of. Let us investigate your 'light in the trees'. It may be woodsmen or travellers, and we may share the warmth of their fire until dawn at the cost of sharing Bill's rum, for I am sure he has another bottle or two."

"What if it be injuns?" said Bill, offering the bottle. The Captain took a reflective sip.

"I am sure indians are fine fellows, and are as partial as any other men to a nip o' rum on a cold dark night. They shall see that we are armed, too, which will surely make them at least pretend to be friendly. But first let us find out whose fire it is, shipmates, then we may decide what we shall do." The Captain passed the rum bottle to Israel Feet, and strode off down the path, cursing in an undertone as he stumbled over a pothole.

"As you said, Izzy, the light of a fire deep in the bosky grove, ho-ho! That is cheering, for it is growing chill," Captain Greybagges said softly. The three buccaneers walked into the woods in single file, treading carefully. No twigs snapped under their boots. Israel Feet took the lead, Captain Greybagges next. Bulbous Bill Bucephalus followed. His bulk made passage through the undergrowth a slow business, but he made no sound. The fire-glow through the trees became brighter as they crept towards it. At last the First Mate stopped, crouched down and peered through the leaves. He stayed still for a while, then gestured for the others to come. Captain Greybagges dropped to his knees and edged next to the First Mate, Bill lowered himself to his belly and wriggled forwards on the other side, the branches rustling slightly.

"I thought it be best you be a-seein' this for yerselves, belike," whispered the First Mate, and the three looked through the leaves.

Three women dressed only in their undergarments stood around a small fire of logs. A cauldron was suspended from a tripod above the flames, steaming and bubbling. One of the women, a tall slim figure with a mop of black curls, was reading aloud from a book:

"........ *rua yed sith suh vig neveh ni si za thre ni nud eeb liw eyth muck modngik eyth main eyth eeb dwohlah nevah ni tra chioo retharf rua!*" She paused and looked around. "Hmm, nothing. Nothing at all. This is plainly tedious."

"Are you sure you're chanting the right piece, dear?" said the very fat woman in a sour tone of voice.

"Of course I am! It's the Lord's Prayer backwards. I may not be pronouncing it correct, but how do you pronounce gibberish correct, tell me that?"

"I tole yah we should be nekkid," said the third, a small skinny black woman, "an' we prolly shoulda kilt summat. Summat instead o' that chook, I means. Summat bigger, mebbe a dog. Chooks get kilt alla time. It don't mean much, killin' a chook, f'it did debbil be appearin' in kitchens all over d'place."

"Well, we've done most exactly what it says in your stupid cousin's book," said the tall woman, "excepting the naked business. *Sky-clad*, or whatever it said."

"I was sure that wouldn't be necessary," said the fat woman. "It seems in poor taste, and we aren't wearing very much except our stays and smalls anyway. Try another incantation, please, dear."

The tall woman gave her a withering glance and riffled through the pages of the book.

In the bushes the three pirates stared open-mouthed. The First Mate nudged the Captain and passed him the rum-bottle. The Captain took a swallow and passed it to Bill, without taking his eyes from the women.

"Alright, let's try this one then … *in girum imus nocte et consumimur igni!*" the tall woman paused, looked around. "No, nothing with that one either."

"Perhaps you have to say it backwards?" said the fat woman. The tall woman gave her an amused look, shaking her head slightly.

"What it mean?" said the small black woman.

"It means 'we spin in the darkness and are consumed by fire'. It's Latin. Oh, here's a good one …" the tall woman drew herself up and spoke in a commanding voice. "Emperor Lucifer, prince and master of the rebel spirits, I implore you to abandon your dwelling, in whatever part of the world it should be, and come and speak to me. I command and entreat you by the authority of the great living God, the Father, the Son and the Holy Spirit, to come noiselessly and without giving off any offensive scents, to answer me in a loud and intelligible voice, article by article, everything that I ask you, otherwise you will be obliged by the power of the great Adonay, Elohim, Ariel, Jehovah, Tagla and Mathon, and all of the other superior spirits who will compel you against your will. Come! Come! Submiritillor Lucifuge, or go and be eternally tormented by the power of the blasting rod!" She waved a twig. The three women stood in silence, looking around hopefully.

"Ain't nuffin comin'," said the small black woman sadly, "an' I'da liked to see that ole debbil, wit his hooves an' horns an' such. We could eat the chook. It must be boiled to soup b'now."

In the bushes Israel Feet cast a glance sideways at Captain Greybagges; he had a look of boyish mischievousness on his face, his lips drawn back in a grin. The Captain suddenly stood up and pushed through the leaves into the clearing. The women stared at him open-mouthed, the fat woman gave a small shriek.

"Ladies! You have summoned Lucifer, and here he is!" he said cheerfully.

"You doan look like no debbil to me," said the small black woman after a pause. "You looks like you some kinda ole sailorman or summat."

Captain Greybagges swept off his black tricorne hat and bowed deeply. He gave the hat to Israel Feet, who was emerging from the bushes behind him, then took off his black *justaucorps* coat and threw it to one side, then, fixing the ladies with the gaze of his gray eyes and grinning, he pulled his black shirt over his head and threw it aside too.

"Behold, ladies!" he cried. He turned his back to them and spread his arms wide. The three women gasped as by the light of the fire they saw the great tattoo on his broad back, the tattoo of Satan sitting upon his dark throne, shaded by his black bat's wings, staring down upon the Earth. "Behold, dear ladies, here is Lucifer!"

Behind him Bulbous Bill Bucephalus struggled cursing from the undergrowth, clutching the rum-bottle to his chest.

Captain Sylvestre de Greybagges awakened slowly as the first rays of the rising sun fell upon his face. He felt thirsty and hungover, but a comfortable feeling of satiated lust pervaded his being. He could smell the fragrance of the woods; the earthy smell of the grass; the clean scent of the pines. He could feel the silk lining of his coat against his chest, the heavy coat that was a blanket over his naked torso, and he could feel the roughness of the springy turf against his back, the dry forest-meadow that had been his bed for that night. He luxuriated in the warmth for a while, even though his lower legs and feet were chilled. Finally he yawned deeply and stretched his arms above his head. He noticed the absence of a slim female body beside him and opened his eyes. Stern faces looked down at him. He was surrounded by men, colonials in their grubby patched tan coats and breeches, several of them pointing muskets.

"I pronounce this Court of Oyer and Terminer to be in session!" the fat man at the lectern banged his gavel on the wood, his wig wobbling on his head. "Magistrate Algernon Chumbley presiding," he added, then pounded his gavel again, although nobody was speaking except him. "We are here to try a witch! An evil witch! An abomination in the sight of God and a disgrace to the eyes of God-fearing men! Let the proceedings begin! Bring forth the accused!"

Strong arms thrust Captain Greybagges forward before the bench, and the spectators in the small courtroom muttered and hissed.

"Silence!" roared Magistrate Chumbley, pounding his gavel again. He addressed Captain Greybagges; "You, who have given your name as John Smith, are hereby accused of having made unlawful covenant with the Devil, of having been complicit with the Devil, of having afflicted persons or persons with witchcraft, and, in short, of being a witch. How do you plead, you scoundrel?"

"If it pleases your eminence," lisped the Captain through split lips, "a witch is surely a woman by definition, and I am not a woman, so I cannot be a witch. I plead my innocence of these ridiculous and unsubstantiated charges!"

"Don't bandy words with me, you dog!" roared the Magistrate. "Whether you are a woman, a man or a eunuch you have surely engaged in witchcraft and consorted with Satan, and that makes you a witch, damn you!"

Captain Greybagges went to reply, but a stout man, one of his captors, stepped up to the bench and whispered in the Magistrate's ear.

"What?" grumbled the Magistrate. "Is that so? Show me!" the stout man handed him a book, pointing to a page. "Ah! Well, it says here in the Reverend Cotton Mather's exegesis of witchery that a male witch is called a *warlock*. Ha! Only a vile person engaged in the black arts would be cognisant of such a fine distinction! Are you then a *warlock*, you knave!"

"The Reverend Cotton Mather himself is aware of the difference, surely. Is he therefore a practicioner of witchcraft?" said the Captain. The crowd tittered its appreciation. "I repeat, I am innocent of these trumped-up and nonsensical accusations!"

"Damn you, you insolent hound! The Reverend Mather is a cousin of my own wife. It is his book, *The Wonders of the Invisible World*, that has opened our eyes to the evil that lurks in our midst! How dare you impugn him with your … your … impugnings! Shut up, you rabble!" Magistrate Chumbley pounded his gavel savagely until the audience ceased sniggering.

"Any fool may write a book, your magnificence," said the Captain reasonably, "but that does not make its contents true. I go further; I am not a witch, or a warlock, and there is no such thing as witchcraft! There is only the babblings of poor deluded souls, and the tales of old wives tattling gossip around the well!"

"You blackguard! Your serpent's tongue will not save you! The book of my wife's cousin is a work of great learning, and a fine example of the most modern philosophical thinking!" Magistrate Chumbley brandished the book at Captain Greybagges as though he wished to ram it down his throat. The Captain noticed, with surprise, that the book appeared to be the same one that his partner of the night before had been reciting from over the cauldron, not merely the same edition but exactly the same volume, with identical scuffs and stains on its calfskin binding. The realisation made him smile, then wince as his split lips stretched.

"You whoreson villain!" screamed Magistrate Chumbley, his face purpling. "How dare you smirk in my court!"

"I merely try to ease my lips, your vastness, which have been bruised by the fists and boots of your beadles…" said the Captain soothingly. A mumble went through the crowd, revealing that the beadles were perhaps not well-liked in the town.

"And how right they were to chastise you thus, since you now insult their esteemed elder brother, for here are Linen Mather and Grogram Mather, officers of this court!" The two burly men nodded to the Captain, smiling grimly.

"The Reverend Cotton Mather may well be esteemed by his brothers and by his relatives by marriage," said the Captain, "but one book does not make a fact, but merely an opinion expressed upon a printed page, that much must be obvious, surely, your worshipfulness?"

"You curséd miscreant! Some wise cove once said 'Satan's greatest triumph was to convince men that he does not exist' and that *must be obvious, surely*, or there would be no evil in the world! All learned men agree upon the reality of sorcery!" Magistrate Chumbley scabbled among the papers on the lectern. "Aha! Listen to this, you viper!" He read from another book; "'How so many learned heads should so far forget their metaphysicks, and destroy the ladder and scale of creatures, as to question the existence of spirits. For my part, I have ever believed, and do now know, that there are witches!' So you see, the great savant Sir Thomas Brown is also of the opinion that witchcraft is not mere tittle-tattle by old wives! How say you now, you slubberdegullion?"

"I stand second to no man in my admiration of the excellent Thomas Brown!" said the Captain stoutly, "and yet even he is not an infallible paragon of veracity in all things, because no man can be! I note that you quote his comments upon the Bury St Edmunds witch trial from *Religio Medici*, which is a most estimable book, and yet he also says in that work, and I quote from memory: 'I have often admired the mystical way of Pythagoras and the secret magicke of numbers.' By your way of thinking that would also cause the good Sir Thomas Brown to be suspected of being a witch!" The spectators laughed and clapped at this sally, and the Captain turned to them and winked. "*Religio Medici*, meaning 'the religion of the doctors'. A book which the *infallible* Pope himself has banned as wicked!"

"You can twist and turn, you slippery rogue, but we have ways of finding the truth!" shouted Magistrate Chumbley. "Bring me the witch cake!"

Grogram Mather scuttled from the chamber and returned with a soggy-looking pudding upon a wooden trencher. "Here it is, Magistrate Chumbley!"

"This smells ... odd, Grogram. Did you follow the instructions I gave you?"

"Indeed, Magistrate Chumbley, but we had the greatest difficulty getting the dog to piddle into a bucket. It is not in their nature to do so."

"You fool! Can you do nothing a-right! The witch cake is to be made from rye meal and the urine of the witch's *victims* and then *fed* to the dog, not the other way about!"

"But we could find none who would admit to being afflicted by the witch's sorceries, Magistrate, so we thought it must be that way!"

Magistrate Chumbley covered his face with his hands and groaned. The spectators howled with laughter.

"*We could find none who would admit to being afflicted by the witch's sorceries!*" repeated Captain Greybagges, turning to the spectators and shaking his head sadly.

"You have tested the patience of this court too far, you scurvy rapscallion!"

shouted Magistrate Chumbley. "We shall discover the truth! Then we shall find you guilty! Then we shall hang you like a dog, you dog! Bring the stones and the board! We shall resort to *peine forte et dure*, as is required by the law!"

"That torture has been banned by act of Parliament these twenty years past!" shouted Captain Greybagges as the beadles grabbed him.

"We care but little in these parts for the vaporings of weaklings who sit upon velvet cushions!" snarled Magistrate Chumbley. "Here in Salem we follow the law of God! Take off his shirt!"

The beadles ripped Captain Greybagges's black shirt from his back. There was a gasp from the spectators, then a mutter of admiration. "Nice tattoo!" someone called out.

"Your guilt is writ upon your own skin, you sorcerous ... you sorcerous ... you sorcerous ... scamp!" crowed Magistrate Chumbley.

"You fat fool! That was a costly shirt! If every sailor with a tattoo was to be tried as a witch there wouldn't be enough of them left to crew a jolly-boat!" cried the Captain.

"Throw him down!" roared Magistrate Chumbley. The beadles grappled with the Captain. He was a large and powerful man, and might have prevailed, but his wrists were tied before him, and they tripped him, and lay him on the wooden floor, one sitting upon his legs. "Arrgh! I've got a splinter!" the Captain shouted.

"Hah! You won't notice that in a minute, I promise you!" snarled Magistrate Chumbley. "Pile on the stones!"

The beadles put the wooden board upon the Captain's chest and loaded the stones – great slabs of granite – upon the board. They stood back, and watched as his face turned slowly purple. The courtroom was silent, all that could be heard was the Captain's laboured wheezing gasps as he strained against the crushing weight forcing the breath from his lungs.

The door was flung open with a crash, and a striking figure stood in the doorway. It was a man of unusual height, a tall angular man in a long black cloak and a battered black slouch hat, his eyes hidden in the shadow of the hat-brim. His big dusty square-toed boots clumped loudly on the wooden floor as he strode into the chamber.

"What? In the name of all that's sacred!" he growled in a harsh deep voice.

He shouldered the beadles roughly aside, reached down, and with a huge hand, the knuckles the size of walnuts, he hurled the board and the granite slabs from Captain Greybagges's chest with a clatter. The Captain took a vast gulping breath, and another, and struggled to sit up. The tall man helped him with an arm around his shoulders. He turned to the bench;

"You tomfools! This is an honest seaman and no sorcerer or witch! What species of preposterous hare-brained caper is this?"

"He is a witch!" Magistrate Chumbley insisted querulously, his eyes flickering nervously round the courtroom for support.

"And you, Master Chumbley, are a jackass!" The tall man, squatted down by Captain Greybagges, who was wheezing and coughing, his eyes red and watering.

"Are you alright, Sylvestre?" the tall man murmured.

"John ... Smith ..." whispered Captain Greybagges to him, in between gulps of air. The tall man winked a clear blue eye at the Captain and helped him to his feet and onto a courtroom settle, roughly shoving aside several spectators who were not quick enough to move from it.

"I know this man ... John Smith ... of old!" thundered the tall man. "He is a stout-hearted mariner, and a God-fearing man! This is disgraceful clownish monkey-trick!"

He untied the rope from the Captain's bound wrists. A plump man with a cheerful red face and a stained apron appeared in the courtroom doorway, a look of bovine surprise on his face, and a wooden tray piled with tarred-leather jacks in his hands. The tall man spotted him, grabbed a jack − "my thanks, innkeeper!" − and gently placed it in the Captain's hands. The Captain waited until his wheezings lessened, then gratefully took a sip of the ale. The tall man patted him on the shoulder and turned to the bench.

"You are an imbecile, Master Chumbley! Witch-finding is not work for the ignorant! If this fine man had been in truth a warlock, and not an honest sailor, why! he could have ensorcelled you and glamoured you such that you would have imagined your own fat fingers to be pork sausages, and you would have bitten them off one by one and eaten them, smacking your lips with relish as you did so! I repeat; witch-finding is a task for those who know the ways and wiles of witches, not for fat bumpkins like yourself!"

"He has a great tattoo of the Devil himself upon his back ..." muttered

Magistrate Chumbley sullenly.

"And examine it it closely!" cried the tall man. The spectators clustered to look at the Captain's back as he sat hunched upon the settle. "There is Lucifer gazing down upon the Earth *with an expression of the profoundest disgust upon his face*! He knows the evil that men do, and even *he* is perturbed by it! That is hardly the sentiment of a witch! And everybody knows that rough sailors oft-times have tattoos in, shall we say, dubious taste!" The spectators chuckled. "That is hardly a reason to try to crush him to death by piling great heavy stones upon him!" The tall man looked around and saw the innkeeper, his tray now empty, his ale distributed among the crowd and their coins in the pocket of his apron. "Landlord! have you a room for the night, so this poor abused fellow may recover himself? I shall stay, too." The innkeeper nodded nervously, and slipped out of the door.

"Now where is poor Mr Smith's coat, and his purse and possessions?" called out the tall man. The beadles rushed to obey, their delving into their pockets making it obvious to the crowd that they had divided the Captain's money and valuables amongst themselves.

"Why, here is a fine thing!" cried the tall man. "The very officers of this trumpery court are thieves! For shame! For shame!" The crowd echoed him, shouting "For shame, you dogs! For shame!" with apparent keen enjoyment. The beadles' faces burned red and they kept their eyes cast down as they restored the Captain's things to him and helped him into his coat.

" Master Chumbley!" said the tall man, pointing his finger at the dumb-struck magistrate. "It seems to me that your devotion to your religion is far less than your devotion to causing pain to your fellow men! You freely torment and mistreat your slaves, and wish to torment and mistreat free men, too, if you may find the least excuse! God watches us all, and we will all stand before Him in our time and be judged! Mend your ways ere it is too late!" Then the tall man stepped forward, knocked away the magistrate's wig with a slap of his hand, and up-ended the trencher of soggy witch-cake on the revealed bald pate. "There, you jackass!"

And with that he escorted Captain Greybagges from the courtroom, supporting him tenderly with an arm at his waist and a hand at his elbow. The crowd gave an appreciative cheer, but whether it was for the tall man's performance or for his righteousness was not entirely clear.

Captain Greybagges chewed on a chicken leg, then shifted uncomfortably. "I have a splinter in my arse from that damned courtroom floor," he explained. He and the tall man were sitting at a table in an upper room of the inn. The picked-clean bones of the roast fowl lay on a pewter platter between them, and a basket of bread. The Captain tossed the chicken bone onto the platter, squeaked the cork out of the rum bottle and refilled their glasses.

"Master Chumbley is an odious man, Sol, and I have met a few choice bastards in my time," continued the Captain. "One wonders how they get to be that way."

"Well, owning slaves is destructive of a man's soul, surely, Sylvestre, and should to be abolished on that basis alone. It weakens the spirit of these colonials, who are sturdy pioneers for the most part, and in many ways very admirable fellows. I do not ignore the effects of slavery on the enslaved, of course, but to discourse upon their hardships attracts only puzzlement and derision in these parts, such as might arise from objecting to the flogging of mules or the gelding of harness-bulls."

"Slavery is indeed a factor, Sol, but I have encountered plenty of vile men who have never owned slaves, not even indentured labourers in tied cottages, who are, after all, slaves in all but name. I suspect that it is rather a failure of perception."

"How so?" The tall man cleaned his platter with a hunk of bread and pushed it aside with a satisfied belch.

"Well, Sol, imagine a competition to find the fastest of two horses. One might race them together around a course to see which arrived first at the finish, or one might set them off around the course one-by-one and time each horse with one of these new pocket-watches, the ones with a little dial to count the seconds, such as this fine Breguet *Perpétuelle* which I nearly lost today." The Captain produced the watch from his coat pocket. "Using the watch one makes reference to a standard of absolute measurement, but in the case of the horse-race the competition is relative, for one horse is compared directly to the other and the actual time taken is not known, so in the horse-race there is a temptation to cheat. One jockey may strike the other in the face with his crop, or lean his horse into the other at a corner, or some other unsportsmanlike caper. It seems to me that happiness is an *absolute* quantity – the Hindoo holy man, they say, posesses only a loincloth and a begging-bowl, and yet knows great rapture from his solitary meditations upon the nature of the sublime - yet many people mistake happiness for a *relative* quantity, believing that if they can make those around them unhappy then they will be all the more happy by contrast, much as the cheating jockey imagines his horse to be the faster, despite having stooped to wicked underhanded tricks to win his race."

The tall man sipped his rum, a thoughtful expression upon his long face. "You may have an insight there, Sylvestre. Master Chumbley is a very stupid man, and all the more stupid because none around him may tell him that he is, except his fat wife, and he pays little attention to her, I'm sure. This witch-finding obsession of his, for an example. He knows nothing about it except for the idiotic opinions of his wife's cousin, and yet he fancies himself a great warrior against ghoulies and ghosties and tommy-knockers and things that go 'bump' in the night. I have told him before to leave it to experts like me, but he hasn't taken much notice, apparently."

"How did you become a witch-finder, Sol?"

"Well, as you know, I used to be something of a coffee-house wheeler-dealer."

"Yes, indeed. Specialising in stocks made of horse-feathers, shares in companies that were incorporated to mine the Moon for green cheese. Getting you off those charges took all my arts as a lawyer."

"I think this day I have repaid you with interest, Sylvestre!"

"Yes, you have, and I thank you." The Captain raised his glass in salute.

"Anyway, I felt it might be wise to avoid my usual haunts for a time, so I took a passage here to the colonies. There was little opportunity for selling stocks, for the *bedriegers* of New Amsterdam had the market sewn up tight, catching gullible fools by chalking the prices of their worthless investments up on the wall down by the waterfront. Then there was an outbreak of ghostly manifestations down in Yonkers, accompanied by all sorts of horripilation and collywobbles, so I set myself up as an exorcist! With the last of my money I bought myself a big black bible, a brass hand-bell and a candlestick of German-silver, and set about casting out demons, haints and *grafschenderen* wherever somebody would pay me. It was all great fun, I must say, and I used to put on a good show, rolling my eyes and thundering blood-curdling stuff in Latin, mostly quotations from Caesar's *Commentaries* which I remembered from school. Gave 'em their money's worth, you may be sure. Then there was the witch-panic down here, and I was so well known by that time that they sent for me in person!"

"You, Solomon, are incorrigible! Have you no shame at all!" laughed Captain

Greybagges.

"You may mock me, Sylvestre, but I did a necessary job. The people of these parts were in a mortal terror, imagining spells and sorcery lurking in every nook and cranny, and I calmed their fears and brought peace and tranquillity back to the land. Not only that, I was able to save a number of harmless old ladies from being burned at the stake by the likes of Master Chumbley, poor white-haired old darlings whose only fault was to have sold love-potions - flasks of sugar-water and pepper mostly - to keep a little food on their tables and a few sticks of firewood in their grates. I am sure that the good Lord will view my activities in a kindly light when the Day of Judgement do come."

"I am sure that you are a great benefactor to all mankind," said Captain Greybagges with a grin.

"There is more," said the tall man quietly. "When I heard reports of monsters lurking in the pine-barrens, I went a-hunting them, light-heartedly thinking I would do a little rough shooting and return with a hair-raising yarn or two, but I *did* find monsters! Monsters resembling giant man-like toads! Luckily I had gone equipped to hunt ducks, with a kind of a long-barrelled great arquebus mounted like a bow-chaser on a shallow-draught punt. It fired about a half-pound of small bird-shot, and it discouraged the toad-men quite efficiently, taking down a swathe of pine-saplings, too, and I was able to escape by paddling furiously through the swampy creeks as fast as I was ever able. At which point things became more serious."

The Captain had ceased grinning now, and he nodded to indicate that the tall man should continue.

"I returned to the pine-barrens several times, hunting the toad-men, and winged several of them, but they are fearful hard to kill. I was intent on trying to get a skin or a head for a trophy to prove the truth of my tale, and I did not realise that I had become the hunted, and I was caught."

The Captain held the tall man's gaze. "Little grey men with big black eyes," he said slowly. The tall man nodded, then dipped his finger in his glass of rum and rubbed his eyebrow. He leaned forward into the candle-light and Captain Greybagges could see that the hair of the eyebrow was green. He suddenly looked afraid and went to rise from his seat.

"No, Sylvestre!" said the tall man. "*She* sent me here! *She* sent me here to watch your back!"

Captain Greybagges rubbed his face with his hands, exhaling noisily. "For a moment …" he said.

"It nearly was that way. You are not missed yet, but there is a vague suspicion of something awry. They manufactured a copy of me, a copy with a scrambled soul, and sent him to make enquiries among men. I was to be fed to the toad-men, but she somehow had me smuggled onto the transport as well as my copy, and I dogged his steps all the way here. Maybe I would not have found you by myself, for I am a swindler and a liar, not a human bloodhound, as they had made him. He was easy to follow, though, as all I had to ask was 'has my twin brother been this way?' My twin lies in a shallow grave two miles from here. It gave me a very strange feeling to murder myself and bury my own corpse at midnight, but not a *guilty* feeling at all." He smiled a grim and unsettling smile, and took a gulp of rum. "He was surprisingly easy to kill. In making him so completely their creature they had erased much of his human cunning and suspicion. Fortunately for me, I must say, for I am no assassin either."

"How is she?" asked Captain Greybagges earnestly.

"She is well, but she urges you not to delay any more than you must."

"Why does my beard not detect your eyebrows? I would have thought that it would."

"She has somehow arranged that such things are muffled, confused. The little grey men are afraid to tell *him* about that, and hope to find out what is wrong before they have to admit their failure, for then his wrath may be awesome. There is still some contact, as you will know, but it is sporadic. They will not notice the demise of their creature, my twin, as I am here in his place and, with luck and the muffling, they will not detect the difference. But tell me, why are *you* here in Salem?"

Captain Greybagges explained about Blue Peter, concluding; "I was surprised to see Master Chumbley. I would have expected to find him, his house and his whole household as smoking ashes. I fear for my friend, and wonder what has befallen him since he has not been seen here, but now I must press on without him. Need we anticipate any repercussions from Master Chumbley?"

"I think not. He is cowed and uncertain now, and I have warned him not to meddle, so he will do nothing tonight. Tomorrow is another matter. He may recover his courage with the morning's light, and seek to do you harm for his humiliation at my hands. His is stupid, and vindictive in the way of stupid men when thwarted, so we must leave early tomorrow, before dawn. I have had your horse brought here to the stables. I will wake you. Sleep now for a while and refresh your spirits. I will keep a watch at the window this night, with my pistol ready to my hand. Keep your own pistols and cutlass by your cot, just in case."

As the sky lightened with the first flush of dawn Captain Greybagges and tall man came to the signpost at the cross roads. The Captain had pointed out the forest clearing where the witches' sabbath had occurred as they passed it, causing the tall man much amusement.

"It has been a great pleasure to meet you again, Sol," said the Captain. "You have saved me from the odious Chumbley and from an extramundane copy of yourself, too. I'm glad that I kept you out of the chokey that time, and I forgive you for not paying me my fees for that service." The tall man laughed. "It's also been pleasant to talk to someone who has shared my experiences of the extramundanes," continued the Captain. "It is a burden not to be able to talk about it, for fear of being thought stark-mad … but I must *not* tell you any more, especially of my plans."

"Because of my green eyebrows?"

"Yes. You say that I am still not missed by *him*, or by the little grey buggers, and that you will be mistaken for your manufactured twin in their present confusion, but if they should manage to break through the muffling of their communications they may be able to hear some of your thoughts, so I must tell you nothing, and so we must part company. I would gladly invite you to come along with me, Sol, but I cannot. What will you do now?"

"I will continue with the witch-finding. I find that I have discovered my true vocation, and somebody must prevent Master Chumbley and his ilk from murdering all the harmless old women in these colonies in the name of their malevolent and un-Christian conception of God. I used to swindle people and laugh at their pain and loss, but in many ways that was worse than being a highwayman or a footpad. A man looks so wretched after he has been rooked, for then he must blame his own stupidity and greed, and cannot see himself merely as a victim of bad luck. I may tell a few tall tales these days, it's true, but there *are* monsters and ghouls loose in the land. So many in the pine-barrens, in fact, that they must be up to something wicked there, and who will stop them if not I? People respect me, too, and I must say I like that! Why, some scribbler even penned a ghastly piece of doggerel in my honour!" The tall man struck a pose and declaimed as follows:

"Solomon Pole's Homecoming!

The ravens croaked on London's Tower , soot stained the cold wind black,
The bitter rain fell in slanting sheets when Solomon Pole came back,
An ancient lurking street-hawker sold him an ancient mutton pie,
And when he bit into its rancid meat a tear came to his eye.

Street-urchins followed him, wagering whether he would finish that meal,
When he swallowed it to the very last crumb they knew he was a man of steel,
He trod a tavern's sawdusted floor and bought a pint of bitter ale,
And drank it down to the very last drop, even though it was flat and stale.

'There once sat Spring-heeled Jack, on that very tavern stool,
'He had an idiot's leer and cross-ed eyes, but he was nobody's fool,
'The Bow-Street Runners came for him, well I remember that day,
'He spotted them despite his squint, and so he bravely ran away.'

'Where is Bess?' said Solomon Pole, 'she still owes me thirty bob.'
'The landlord barred her years ago, for she would never shut her gob.'
The soot-black wind battered at the panes and Solomon shook his head,
'She always had that mouth on her,' Solomon sadly said.

'I once knew a Pearly Queen in the street that is called Lime,
'She had a face just like a leather bag and eyes as old as time,
'She was only twenty years old, but she'd drunk a lot of gin,
'She used to beg just around the corner, rattling a rusty tin.'

'And I have seen a vampire mouse in a city made of cheese….."

"Stop! Stop!" cried the Captain, wiping tears of laughter from his eyes. "That was a poem in your *honour*, you say?"

"Well, Sylvestre," said Solomon Pole, "the scribbler's ode contained a number of egregious errors of fact! He said my birthplace was some horrid little fishing-village in the West Country, and that I had sailed with Hawkins and Grenville, which would make me the oldest man alive and not the clean-limbed laughing lad whom you see before you. It was a humourless glum piece of work, too. He even got my name wrong, the hound! So I composed my own version. Ain't it grand?"

"It is, Sol, it is! I must go now, friend, for time presses greatly upon me!"

"Go! I will delay and misdirect any pursuit by Chumbley's men. May your path be always downhill, and may the good Lord crown your endeavours with success! Adieu, Sylvestre de Greybagges!"

They shook hands, the Captain's large hand almost lost in the grasp of the tall man's huge knobbly fingers, and they parted there at the crossroads.

Captain Greybagges spurred his horse along the dusty road back to Jamestown, trying to make as much speed as possible without tiring his mount. His horse was eager, the air was crisp on his face, the day bright with a few clouds in a blue sky, but he felt no joy and his worries oppressed him terribly. Extramundane creatures 'up to something' in the nearby wilderness, Solomon Pole had said, but he could not spare the time to ponder upon that. He had lost his master gunner, and perhaps his sailing-master and First Mate as well, for he had not seen Bulbous Bill Bucephalus or Israel Feet since the night of the witches. That was a catastrophe, and he cursed himself for going ashore and drinking in the tavern called *Wahunsunacock's Mantle*. When he had learned that the Dutchman whom he sought was not yet there he should have gone back out to sea, or he should have anchored in a quiet cove away from the temptations of civilisation, even such poor temptations as Jamestown had to offer. Frank Benjamin would not then have thought of taking shore-leave, and Blue Peter would have seen no opportunity to vent his long-nursed rage upon his erstwhile owner. Captain Greybagges cursed himself again. I relaxed my vigilance, he thought, and firstly I relaxed my vigilance upon myself, and all else that followed grew from that base dereliction. I shall probably find the remainder of my crew laid ashore as drunk as Davy's sow, and my ship boarded and stolen away by sneering French privateers.

Beset by these dismal speculations he galloped around a bend in the road and let the horse have its head as the road straightened. Ahead in the distance he could see another traveller on a horse. As he came closer he could see the hunched rider was enveloped in a loose brown cloak and a big wide-brimmed floppy hat, so he resembled a large sack of turnips. He pulled his horse to the right to gallop past the slow-moving traveller on the narrow lane, as he did so he caught a glimpse of a dark eye peering at him from under the brim of the hat, and felt an immediate surge of recognition.

"Peter!" he roared in delight, pulling on the reins hard so that his horse whinnied and bucked. The face of Blue Peter peered at him from under the hat, with an oddly rueful grin. Captain Greybagges trotted back and turned his horse to ride alongside, feeling a contradictory whirl of emotions; joy, irritation, relief, anger.

"Peter, you bloody … you! … you! … vexacious nincompoop! You great insufferable jackanapes! How immensely pleased I am to see you! Why! I wish to embrace you and punch you on the nose at one and the same time! I am near lost for words! … 'Pon my life, I cannot … Good Lord! Do you have someone else with you inside that great tent of a cloak?"

The folds of the cloak parted, and a face peered out. A very pretty face, pink and heart-shaped, with large wide-set blue eyes and full red lips. There was a look of slight apprehension on the delicate features, but the blue eyes regarded him with an intelligent directness, and the coral-lipped mouth had a determined set to it.

"Captain, allow me to introduce Miss Miriam Andromeda Chumbley. My dear, this is Captain Sylvestre de Greybagges, commander of the ship, and my friend."

Captain Greybagges swept off his black tricorne hat and bowed his head; "Miss Chumbley, your servant!" He was then too taken aback to say more. Miss Chumbley pushed aside the folds and emerged from under the cloak, revealing a mass of blonde hair in sausage-curls, tied with blue ribbons of silk.

"Captain Greybagges, I am so pleased to meet you! My Peter speaks of you with such great regard, and with such fond affection!"

Miss Chumbley smiled at him, revealing small white teeth, perfect and even.

The smile held genuine warmth, her eyes crinkled with pleasure, but deep in those blue depths there was a palpable sense of dispassionate assessment, as though she was measuring him and recording everything for later analysis. This made the Captain uncharacteristically diffident, and he glanced at Blue Peter, whose face had the stunned expression of a man who has just been struck smartly on the head with a belaying-pin, and whose knees are on the point of buckling under him. There was a shout from back down the lane, which saved the Captain from giggling impolitely.

"Why, look! It is Izzy!" the Captain cried. "Excuse me, dear lady, I must take his report! Peter, pray continue! We will catch up with you presently." ·

Captain Greybagges galloped back, the First Mate galloping towards him on his skeletal steed, waving his arm.

"Arrr! There you be, Cap'n! I bin keepin' watch on that Salem place from them woods, but I didn't see yuz leave there. Saw the tall bugger arguing with the fat bugger an' his mates at the crossroads, an' I guessed yer musta scarpered, belike. Bill, he went orf back to ship to get a shore-party to come for yez. We should meet him on his way a-comin' 'ere, I do reckon. Skin me wi' a soupspoon, else!"

"What happened to you on that morning, Izzy?"

"The women cleared orf in the night sometime. Did'n sees 'em go. Me and Bill wuz having a dump in the woods that mornin', wi' our britches round our ankles and thick heads, too. Heard a commotion, belike, then saw 'em takin' yuz away. There wuz too many of 'em for us to stop 'em, and we figured yer weren't doing nuffin wrong, cept sleeping in the woods, so yer'd be back soon enough. When yer wasn't back by midday we crep around a bit, sees what's up. Well, I did, 'cos Bill ain't zackly built for creepin', so he watched the road. Didn't see anyfing until that tall feller took yer t'the tavern, then I saw yer did'n have no shirt on and yer looked a bit banged about, like. So Bill went orf ta get help. I stayed ta keep a watch. Have yer seen hide nor hair o' Peter?"

"That's him up ahead on the horse, Izzy."

"Nah! Reely? Woz he bin up ta?" The First Mate went to spur his horse to catch up with Blue Peter, but the Captain put a hand on his arm.

"Hold up a minute, Izzy, me old cock! He has a young lady with him."

"Naah! Yer jests, yer does! The sly old dog! Scuttle me bathtub with a pickaxe if that ain't rare!"

"Ah, Izzy! Before you go a-haring off I must caution you to be discreet, to be careful what you say."

"Discreet? What about?"

"Well, Izzy," said Captain Sylvestre de Greybagges, with a broad grin forming on his face, "the, ah, large lady that you were pleasuring in the woods the night before last, if you recall?"

"I does, Cap'n, I does! Hur-hur-hur!"

"I do believe that she is the young lady's mother."

CHAPTER THE THIRTEENTH,
or The Return To Nombre Dios Bay.

Captain Greybagges stood on the stony beach of the Elizabeth River. The *Ark de Triomphe* rode in the sluggish flow anchored bow-and-stern, with steadying kedges port-and-starboard the bows in a seamanlike fashion. The longboat which had brought him ashore was tying up by its side, the oarsmen climbing the cleat-ladder to the gangway hatch. Captain Greybagges shook the drips from his manhood, stowed it back in his breeches and buttoned up. A distant muted cheer came from the pirate frigate.

"Arr! Damn yer eyes, yer lubbers! Yer cap'n must piddle, same as all o' yuz, curse yuz! Get on wi' yer work, yer slackers! I sees a man neglectful o' his duties, I'll have his backbone for a walking-stick! Wi' a wannion, by my green beard, I will!" Captain Greybagges roared, scowling. The pirates returned to their tasks with a good-humoured mutter. In truth, he was not displeased with them. During the two days he had been absent in Salem the crew had not given in to the temptations of the flesh and had remained sober. Not entirely sober, he was sure, as a wealth of circumstantial evidence suggested that the crew had entered into commercial dealings with the good citizens of Jamestown; empty bottles incompetently concealed from sight, the cook simmering a vast cauldron of beef stew, *fresh* beef and not salt-horse. Nevertheless, at no time had the ship been left unguarded it seemed, nor had any inebriated foolishness drawn attention to the ship

"I do believe that you did that a-purpose!" said Mr Benjamin. "Widdle in the river to attract their attention, then shout at them, to remind them that you are the captain and that you are back."

"And to keep them hard at it," said the Captain. "Time presses upon me now. I like your choice of name, by the way."

The crew were once again disguising the pirate frigate as a Dutch trader. Canvas strips taut above the ship's rails raised the height of her hull in profile, so that her silhouette against the sea or sky would be plump and complacent, not rakishly low and lean. Painted canvas tacked over the carved and gold-leafed '*Ark de Triomphe*' on her prow and transom now gave a name more appropriate to a ship of the *Vereenigde Oost-Indische Compagnie*, sailing out of Amsterdam. The crew were once again wearing the red-and-grey *matrozenpak* jacket and wide trousers of the VOC. The people of Jamestown courteously gave them little heed, except for a handful of idlers, who were easily frightened away from the beach by the stratagem of offering them paid work.

"A pirate captain must not have too much dignity, Frank," said the Captain, "although he does have need of much authority."

They walked up the beach, gravel crunching under their boots.

"There are many tricks and dodges to the management of men," said Mr Benjamin, "and many tricks and dodges to most things, I find. I have a mind to publish a sort of a journal, where such wrinkles may be presented in a humorous way."

"Do you yet have a name in mind for this journal, Frank?"

"Well, maybe something like 'Humble Harry's Handbook'. That might serve, giving the impression of a farmer's almanac for those who lack a farm."

"Um, how about 'Mean Michael's Manual?"

"Or 'Grudging George's Guidebook'?"

"Hah! How about 'Earnest Edward's Ephemeris'?"

"Damn you! … Ah! … 'Vulgar Vincent's Vade Mecum', top that, if you can!"

"I confess myself bested, Frank."

"Well, perhaps alliteration is not a good thing for the title of such a tract, smacking as it does of excessive cleverness. My intention is to attract readers among the common people, not repel them by exercising my wit in an ostentatious and pompous fashion."

The two arrived at the *Wahunsunacock's Mantle* tavern. They sat a a table in the window, drinking strong coffee and eating flat cakes made with cracked oats, pork-dripping and molasses.

"These are surprisingly good," said Mr Benjamin, taking another. "I suspect that they contain too much sustenance for a mere snack. They are to keep body and soul together when travelling the woods, or voyaging the rivers, as in Richard Bonhomme's tales."

"You may be right, Frank. The cook here says they should not be eaten when freshly baked, for they improve by being kept for a day or so. The bacon-fat may then soak into the hard oats, you see, making the cakes softer in texture and less oleaginous."

"When will your Dutchman come?"

"Before noon, I hope. I have had word from him. A game of cards while we wait, perhaps?"

"As long as we shall not play that accursed Puff-and-Honours, Sylvestre, for it is an uncouth game suitable only for low types in thieves' rookeries."

"I see that Izzy and Bill have lightened your purse, Frank. Shall we play whist, then, like civilised old gentlemen?"

The Captain dealt the cards, and took another oatcake.

The Dutchman departed, his purse made heavier by a number of clinking gold *reales d'or*, and Captain Greybagges surveyed his purchase; four women from an island far away in the Pacific. They had black hair tied tightly back, slanted black eyes and jolly round faces, and were dressed in the jacket and trousers of common sailors. Their clothes were far cleaner than a common sailor's, however, the canvas scrubbed to an almost bleached whiteness. Their small feet wore sandals of leather and woven hemp.

The eldest woman was seemingly in her thirties, although it was difficult to guess their precise ages as the pale-brown skin of their faces was unmarked by wrinkles or laugh-lines. She spoke passable Dutch, despite pronouncing 'r' as 'l', and the Captain conversed with her easily as they walked to the riverside. Mr Benjamin said little, although he appeared fascinated by them. The Captain reassured the eldest woman that he undertook to return them to their homeland when they had finished their work for him, and that they would be well rewarded in either gold or silver, as they wished. The eldest woman regarded him with shrewd eyes, then nodded her agreement and turned and spoke to her companions in an incomprehensible jabber. They replied in high fluting voices. The elder woman informed the Captain that the Dutchman was a vile grease-rag and a clot-bag and that they were all glad to be rid of him at last. He had attempted several times to have his way with the youngest of them when he was drunk, but that she had dissuaded him from such impertinence by kicking him in the balls, which had made his blue eyes, his most unnatural and devilish blue eyes, bulge out of his head in an agreeably comical fashion. The Captain replied graciously that although he had grey eyes and that many of his crew had blue eyes they were not devils and that he would see that the women were treated with respect at all times. Furthermore, he said the women were now temporary members of the crew, but part of the crew nonetheless, and that any such disrespect would be against the laws of his ship and swiftly punished by common agreement. The eldest woman conveyed this to the others in a rattling burst of their language, and they all nodded solemnly in unison.

The longboat ran aground on the beach. Captain Greybagges stepped forward to assist the four women into the boat, but they smilingly dodged him and hopped over the gunwales with the spryness of seasoned sailors, only the eldest accepting a helping hand from Loomin' Len in the bows, solely from queenly courtesy, apparently, as she was as nimble as the others. The Captain and Mr Benjamin followed, Mr Benjamin requiring a discreet heft from the huge hand of Loomin' Len on his coat-collar, the river sloshing around his boots as the longboat slid backwards into the stream.

As the longboat pulled towards the *Ark de Triomphe* Captain Greybagges heard a female voice shouting, its tone jagged with anger. The Captain glanced at the oarsmen; they looked stolidly to their front and gave no sign they heard anything. He turned to Mr Benjamin and raised an eyebrow.

"Um, it sounds like Miss Chumbley, perhaps?" said Mr Benjamin. "Oh, but she has a fine grasp of the vernacular! Who would have thought a young lady would know such words? ... Good Lord! Now she curses in Dutch, too! What does '*zwakzinnige*' mean?"

"A mentally-deficient person, or moron," said the Captain. The longboat bumped against the side of the frigate. The eldest of the island women seemed to be suppressing a smile, but it was difficult to tell as her unlined brown face was impassive. Captain Greybagges stepped from the longboat and hauled himself up the tumblehome of the frigate's side by the cleat-ladder.

Miss Chumbley stood upon the quarterdeck, a small plump package of fury shaking her fist at the sky, her face as red as fire and her blonde sausage-curls quivering like brass springs. Captain Greybagges looked up and saw Blue Peter high up the mizzenmast, squatting on the topsail yard crosstrees, looking glum and agitated. Miss Chumbley took in a deep breath to continue shouting, but the Captain cleared his throat noisily.

"Ahem! Good morning, Miss Chumbley! I am happy to see you in such fine spirits ..."

Miss Chumbley turned to him, and for an instant he thought that she would abuse him, too, as her blue eyes glowed with sparkling blue anger, but the eyes crossed slightly as caution took hold, and she breathed out slowly, lowering her fists.

"Captain Greybagges, I must apologise. I am behaving improperly."

She said the words easily, but the Captain still faintly heard her teeth gritting. She does not like to apologise, he thought, but is practised in doing so.

"No matter, Miss Chumbley. You are not yet used to our ways by ship and by sea, and did not know that the quarterdeck is out-of-bounds even when the captain is not aboard. Also, I must have my Master Gunner back on deck, as there is but little for him to do up there in the rigging. I trust that your … ah … disagreement may be discontinued until a more appropriate time?"

"Yes, Captain," said Miss Chumbley, with surprising meekness but with her winsome smile holding a hint of clenched teeth. A happy thought came to the Captain.

"Miss Chumbley. You speak Dutch well."

"*Ik praat en beetje, Kapitan.*"

"As you are now a member of the crew I may perhaps presume to give you some work to do, may I not?"

Miss Chumbley nodded warily. The Captain turned around to find the four island women standing behind him.

"These ladies are now also part of the crew, yet they speak no English. However, the chief of them speaks Dutch. Will you minister to their needs for me? See the First Mate, Mr Feet, and the ship's carpenter, Mr Chippendale, and get them to rig a private cabin where five hammocks may be slung, and see them settled comfortably there. That will create a women's quarters. You may bunk there if you wish, and shall report to me upon any impudence or attempted lewdnesses by the crew, such as may be occasioned by conceitedness, the boldness of drink or linguistic misapprehensions."

"Yes, I will do that, Captain," said Miss Chumbley, after a moment's consideration. Captain Greybagges smiled and gestured for her to lead the island women from the quarterdeck. They filed down the companionway to the waist. Once they were clear Mr Benjamin came up the companionway steps, still red in the face from clambering up from the longboat.

"I am impressed, Captain," said Mr Benjamin. "You turn an advantage from the most unpromising circumstances."

"Thank'ee, Frank, but I can claim no cunning plan. One thing does puzzle me, though …" Mr Benjamin raised an eyebrow. "… and that is why the crew did not behave as though they were at a boxing-booth and encourage Miss Chumbley with catcalling and applause. They were silent"

"Perhaps they were afraid to attract her attention and so attract the lash of her tongue to themselves," said Mr Benjamin.

"Perhaps we wuz listening too appreciatively, like, bein' attentive to hear if she would not repeat herself, har-har!" said Bulbous Bill, who had come up the companionway ladder as they talked.

Blue Peter swung himself down onto the quarterdeck from the mizzen ratlines, a sheepish look upon his face.

"Well, gentlemen, now we are all present. Let us then prepare for sea, for the tide goes on the ebb in two hours, and I wish to be at the mouth of the Elizabeth River by then, setting a course out of Chesapeake Bay."

The sun shone down on Nombre Dios Bay, a brassy glare that glinted hotly from the small ripples of the water, the fading remains of the waves of the Caribbean Sea which entered the north-facing mouth of the nearly-circular bay. The frigate *Ark de Triomphe* lay at anchor off the beach on the western side of the bay. The beach itself was a-bustle with determined activity, groups of pirates labouring in the hot sun, the lighter-skinned members of the crew wearing straw hats and shirts to ward off its harsh rays, the darker-skinned stripped to the waist and gleaming with sweat. The *thunk* of axes could be heard from the jungle inland. A party of at least a score of pirates emerged onto the beach carrying an entire tree-trunk on their shoulders, their slow synchronised shuffling steps resembling the movements of a centipede's legs.

"The raft will be finished by this time tomorrow, Captain, no later," said Mr Benjamin, wiping sweat from his face with a large linen handkerchief. Captain

Greybagges nodded. "We shall need kedges placed further out in the bay," continued Mr Benjamin, "for the raft is heavy and the frigate may drag her anchors when we use the capstan to haul it off the beach."

"Yes, that would be wise," said the Captain. He walked to the seaward side of the quarterdeck. The longboat was in the centre of the bay, and the island women were diving from it, almost naked except for a skimpy breechclout. They stayed underwater for a surprising length of time, but seemed perfectly happy when they re-surfaced, laughing and chattering and not at all short of breath. The Captain watched them through a telescope; the bully-boys manning the longboat's oars had prim expressions upon their faces, and averted their gaze from the women's breasts, which made the Captain smile briefly.

"They resemble seals, do they not?" said Mr Benjamin, his eyes glittering lecherously behind his *pince-nez* spectacles.

"A little," conceded Captain Greybagges, snapping the telescope shut.

"It is their *muscularity*, and the sleek covering of fat which softens the female outline, whether they be divers or not."

"Do not lust, Frank!" laughed the Captain, "or you may get a knee in your cobblers, as their Dutchman did, who was also surprised by their *muscularity*."

"Cobblers?" said Mr Benjamin.

"No, it is perfectly true," said the Captain. After a pause he took pity on Mr Benjamin. "The word 'cobblers' means 'testicles' in the rhyming language of the London Cockaignies. 'Cobbler's awls' rhyming with 'balls', and also meaning 'nonsense', in some contexts."

"Oh, I see," said Mr Benjamin, looking hot and irritated.

"Frank, it is very hot. Will you not shed that thick broadcloth coat and your wig? Your face is as red as a beetroot."

"I feel it would be undignified," said Mr Benjamin.

"Undignified is better than an apoplexy, Frank, and you were taking your air-bath this morning wearing not much more than the island ladies. Anyway, I must ask you to oversee the unshipping of the tub, and that may require you to be energetic. A cotton shirt and a straw hat to keep off the sun would be appropriate dress, and not in the least undignified in this terrible heat."

The Captain's words were spoken kindly, but did not admit argument. Mr Benjamin removed his heavy buff coat with little grace, and went to direct the pirates working around the huge upturned wooden bucket stowed upon the deck.

The Captain stayed on the quarterdeck, dressed himself only in a black shirt, black knee-britches with no hose or shoes and his frayed cricketer's straw hat. His green beard seemed to glow luminously when the bright sun caught it. He felt happy, despite Mr Benjamin's mumpishness, which he forgave, as heat often makes lighter-skinned people ill-humoured. The work was going well here in the bay, proceeding entirely to plan. To his surprise, the presence of women on the frigate had caused no trouble on the voyage here from Jamestown. The island women had been accepted by the crew even before they had demonstrated their special talents for swimming and diving. The oldest of the island women was particularly respected as she was a forthright and cheerful soul, and fierce in her care of the younger women. Miss Chumbley was well-regarded, too, for her fearlessness and for her awesomely foul language when badly irked. She took her job as chaperone, translator and fixer for the island women very seriously, too, and was at present, sitting cross-legged on the foredeck in sailor's canvas jacket and pants, gutting, filletting and scaling fish, for when they took their noonday break. The island women's love of raw fish was a source of amusement to the crew, but Bulbous Bill Bucephalus had tried it and declared it excellent, especially soused in vinegar with a little cold boiled rice as the island women preferred it. But then, thought Captain Greybagges, is there any foodstuff that Bill did not like? Probably not.

The *Ark de Triomphe* had mysteriously acquired a cat during its stay in Jamestown, a lean black creature with yellow eyes, and it now stalked across the deck planking. Captain Greybagges squatted down and stroked it.

"You have my permission to be on the quarterdeck, pussycat, even though you have not asked politely, as is required by maritime custom even aboard pirate ships," he said. The cat rolled onto its back and playfully batted at his hand. This cat, thought Captain Greybagges, is the only member of the crew who does not know the cause of the friction between Blue Peter Ceteshwayoo and his lady-love Miss Miriam Andromeda Chumbley, there being few secrets aboard a frigate, even though no one speaks of it.

"She will not allow him his full rights as her man," he murmured to the cat, "even though she yearns for him too, as she fears to bear a bastard into this world of tears. There, pussycat, now you know."

The cat seemed offended that it hadn't been told before, and stalked away to the shoreside rail where it curled up in the shadow by a cannon. Captain Greybagges stood up, a thoughtful expression on his face. Perhaps there is a solution, he thought, I shall go to the town of Nombre de Dios this evening.

There was a shout from the bay, a roar of 'halloo!" from the mighty lungs of Loomin' Len Lummocks. Captain Greybagges hurried to the rail. Loomin' Len was waving frantically, standing up in the longboat, a broad grin upon his normally-impassive features. When he saw the Captain at the quarterdeck rail he cupped his hands to his mouth and roared:

"They have found it, Cap'n! They have found it!" Captain Greybagges felt such a wave of relief flood through him that his knees weakened slightly and he gripped the rail to steady himself. The eldest island woman pulled herself into the longboat with a single smooth movement, stood next to Loomin' Len and waved to the Captain, grinning.

"Ha! Fine work, me hearties! Magnificent work, ladies!" roared the Captain across the water. "Get a marker-buoy tied to it quick as can be. Ha! Grand work!"

"They be putting the marker-line upon it now, Cap'n! It is found, and shall not be lost!" roared back Loomin' Len.

Captain Sylvestre de Greybagges could not help himself in his joy, and danced a hornpipe on the quarterdeck, his bare feet slapping on the planks. He became aware of a murmur and noticed the pirates in the rigging and upon the sheerlegs above the huge upturned wooden bucket looking down at him in surprise.

"Har-har!" he roared up at them, "no treasure this, my lads, no treasure in our hands yet, but now we has the keys to unlock a great fortune, har-har! A very great fortune indeed, har-har! We shall have ourselves a few drinks tonight to celebrate, I does assure you all! But time still presses upon us, so back to your work with a will, you lazy swabs. Back to yer work now, me lads, but yer has my permission to dream o' gold, to dream o' gold just a little whilst yez labours! Har-har!"

And Captain Sylvestre de Greybagges continued dancing upon his quarterdeck, emitting an occasional 'whoop!' or "har-har!" or "whee!" of pure joy, his long green beard waving as he pranced.

Captain Greybagges sat at his desk in the Great cabin of the *Ark de Triomphe*. The tall stern windows were wide open to catch any breeze, and the cheerful babble of the crew on the deck above enjoying the celebration was audible above the gurgling of the small wavelets on the hull. The purple twilight was deepening to black night outside, and the yellow light of an oil-lamp spilled onto the desk, illuminating the papers of the Captain's correspondence shuffled into a pile on the leather desktop, and gleaming on the glossy calfskin covers of his account-ledgers. He poured a glass of rum for Blue Peter.

"Oh, good Lord, Captain! It is far too blasted hot for rum. Is there no beer?"

"I would send Jake for some, but the dreadful old wretch has already drunk his fill and passed out in the pantry. Bear with me Peter, for I must broach a delicate subject with you before the others join us."

Blue Peter raised his eyebrows.

"Um, Peter, are you intending to marry Miss Chumbley? Make an honest woman of her, ho-ho!"

"Nothing would give me greater pleasure, Sylvestre, but there is not a parson within three hundred miles of here."

"Aah! but there is a priest in Nombre de Dios town! I sounded him out earlier this evening. At first he stoutly refused even to countenance marrying non-Catholics, but after I presented him with a bottle of rum, a box of treacle biscuits and a couple of silver dollars he conceded that it might be morally preferable to prevent the sin of fornication than to be stiff-necked about Popish rules. In fact, after a glass or two of rum he swore that his conscience would be deeply troubled if he did not perform the marriage service. He is willing not only to officiate at the wedding but also to sign a marriage certificate and enter the wedding into his books. I, as Captain, would also put it into the ship's log, of course. I am certain that such a wedding would be legal and binding – and here I speak as a lawyer, of course - although the authorities in England or the Colonies may require it to be officially recorded in their records at the earliest opportunity for the purposes of inheritance and taxation, it being regarded as an anomalous procedure under common law."

"Pirates do not pay taxes, Captain," said Blue Peter, scowling.

"Come now, Peter, I am trying to help, and actually we do pay taxes. The Bank of International Export – *your* bank, *my* bank, *our* bank – is punctilious in that regard, both for itself as an incorporation and for all its stock-holders. I make sure of that, since it is but a small amount to pay for the gloss of respectability, and to avoid unnecessary and bothersome inquiries from the powers-that-be."

"I am sorry. You are right. I shall ask Miriam if a Catholic priest is acceptable to her," said Blue Peter after a pause for thought, "and thank you, Captain, for taking the trouble."

"No trouble at all, I assure you. If I may risk giving you another piece of advice, Peter, propose the marriage to her upon your bended knee, no matter how foolish you feel – in fact, the greater fool you look the better she will like it, for women do love a man the more if he shall be prepared to make himself appear undignified to win them – and try to look worried, as though you are not entirely certain that she will accept you. Give her a ring, too, when she accepts, which I am sure she will. Gold, but not too gaudy. That is the latest fashion among the idle rich in France, or so my informants tell me. A 'ring of engagement' it is called. A token that you have plighted you troth, posted the banns, that sort of thing."

Peter scowled at the Captain again, his filed teeth and tribal scars making him look particularly irascible, but grudgingly nodded his agreement.

There was a knock at the door. "Come in!" said the Captain. Bulbous Bill Bucephalus, Israel Feet and Mr Benjamin entered, grinning happily. Mr Benjamin was carrying a large glass pitcher on a tray with five glasses, the glass pitcher was making a tinkling noise.

"Hee-hee! Here is a great miracle, Captain! A great miracle for your delectation!" said Mr Benjamin. With ceremony he placed the tray on the desk and poured the purple liquid. It tinkled into the five glasses. He handed the first glass to the Captain, still grinning like an ape.

"Upon my life! It is as cold as ice! Why, it has ice in it!" Captain Greybagges drank. "By the bones of Davy Jones! That is extraordinary! And extraordinarily good, too! Where the devil did you find ice in this heat, Frank!"

Blue Peter had his glass and was sipping at it, his eyebrows nearly on the top of his head with amazement. The three arrivals observed his and the Captain's surprise with great satisfaction.

"I made the ice, Captain," said Mr Benjamin. "Is it not wonderful? Hee-hee!"

"It is indeed! I confess myself almost beyond words!"

"I had the big air-pump brought up from the hold, as you had asked, and got it set up upon the deck and had the six bully-boys work the handles. The bronze bottles get mightily hot as they are pumped up. I had noticed this phenomenon before in my experiments with the compressed-air cannon, so I had them placed in a tub of sea-water as they were filled, so that the heat would not weaken the metal, and the water did indeed become very warm. Then I had an idea, I thought, 'why, if they become hot when they are pumped up, will they therefore become cold when they are emptied?' So I put one of the pumped-up bronze bottles – one of the little ones the size of a quart flagon - into a bucket of fresh water and opened the cock so the air whistled out slowly, and it became so cold that it turned the bucketful of water to solid ice in a matter of moments! In this heat the next thing to do was obvious! In a trice Bill here came up with a recipe for an ice-cold punch – water, wine, sugar, lemon juice and rum – and there you are! Is it not the best thing in this heat? The very best damned thing you have ever tasted?"

"In truth it is, Frank! And a very good omen indeed on this auspicious day…" said Captain Greybagges. "Let us go on deck, now it is a little cooler. I don't feel entirely easy with the crew using the air-pump to freeze water without your supervision. One of them will surely have the notion to tie down the pressure-relief valve, thinking that will make for even colder ice, and one of those little bronze bottles could explode with the force of a grenado. Anyway, the crew will surely celebrate all night if we do not give them a broad hint by retiring with ostentatious yawns at midnight, or shortly thereafter. There is much still to do, and tomorrow will be another busy day."

Captain Greybagges, Bulbous Bill Bucephalus, Israel Feet and Mr Benjamin sat at a folding table on the quarterdeck, playing hands of penny-a-point whist by the light of a lantern, although the full moon's brightness gave nearly enough light as it hung in the star-packed black-velvet sky. The *honk-wheeze, honk-wheeze, honk-wheeze* noise of the air-pump came from the foredeck, where eight of the younger pirates were trying to beat the time that the six bully-boys had taken to fill a bronze bottle, standing four to each side, working the long handles of the rocking frame up-and-down up-and-down until the pressure-relief valve hissed. Torvald Coalbiter was referee, counting the seconds with the Captain's pocket-watch. There were over two hundred crew, and each wanted a mug of beer or sugared rum-grog with a lump of ice in it, so it was well to make a game of the labour needed to make the ice.

"Tell me, Captain, if I may make so bold," said Mr Benjamin, laying down the trey of trumps, "what are we celebrating? What lies down there on the bottom of the bay?"

"Ah! be you patient, Frank! With a little ordinary luck, touch wood …" the Captain reached out to tap the quarterdeck rail, "… we shall raise it up in the next couple of days and then you shall see it with your own eyes." He put down the five of trumps, then grimaced as Bill laid the ten upon it to take the hand.

Captain Greybagges had noticed Blue Peter and Miss Chumbley slipping quietly below earlier, and now he saw them coming back on deck in the waist of the frigate. Miss Chumbley was holding Blue Peter's hand but released it reluctantly as they came up from the companionway. By the light of the moon the Captain saw the gleam of a thin gold band upon her other hand, her left hand. He smiled.

"Are you not afraid that we will be disturbed in these operations, Captain?" said Mr Benjamin. "By the Spanish, for instance?"

"I do hope not, but Peter is keeping the guns loaded and their crews alert in shifts just in case. We may thank that fine fellow Francis Drake for the quiet of this bay, you know. Nombre de Dios used to be a prosperous town, but it lacks natural defences, so Drake raided it several times with impunity, the last time taking the legendary 'Spanish silver train', which was the mule-train that brought the silver bars to this bay for transport back across the Atlantic to Bilbao. After that loss the Dons moved their centre of operations east to Portobello which is indeed a 'beautiful port' with strong defences – and abandoned this place to the jungle. The old priest here has no church, for it was burned down, and must perform his weekly mass under a shade tree in the square. The little town survives, just, upon fishing and a little logging. The few remaining citizens have no reason to annoy us, and every reason to keep us sweet, for they are as fond of a few coins as anybody else. If any of the townspeople think they may get a reward for informing the authorities that we are here they will first have to take a long walk, and a then long wait cooling their heels until the *gobernador* of Portobello will condescend to hear them, and then the Dons will react in their usual leisurely fashion, and we shall be long gone by then. I am mainly worried that other pirates may come here by chance and feel that we have something worth fighting for, since we are taking such pains in the getting of it. Pirates mostly come here to take on water or make repairs, though, so it's unlikely that will be seriously challenged."

A concertina and a fiddle struck up a sprightly jig on the foredeck, although the two musicians seemed to be playing from entirely unrelated music-sheets.

"Let us have another couple of hands of whist so that I may wreak my revenge upon Bill, then we must encourage the crew to go to their hammocks, for an early start will avoid at least some of the day's heat." The Captain dealt the cards. The *honk-wheeze, honk-wheeze* of the air-pump came again from the foredeck. "They are much taken with the pump and the ice it makes," murmured Captain Greybagges to his officers, "but I feel sure that they will loathe and detest the very sight of it before much time has passed."

By the time the sun rose over the jungle on the eastern side of the bay - the squawking of the monkey-birds echoing in the cool air to greet the dawn - the big raft had been dragged off the beach with hawsers and capstan and it and the *Ark de Triomphe* had been manoeuvred by kedging and sweep-oars out to the marker buoy, a yard-long piece of timber painted bright red bobbing in the ripples of the bay. Before mid-morning the huge upturned wooden tub had been raised off the deck by the sheer-legs, blocks-and-tackles and much labour at the ropes, accompanied by traditional pulley-hauly chants. The tub was swung out over the side of the frigate – the canvas strips that had disguised the ship's outline as a plump Dutch merchantman had been stripped away, the starboard rail dismantled and the timbers stacked tidily on the quarterdeck – and lowered gently into the water.

"Are the brave ladies completely sure that they understand the use of the bronze bottles? And the signals to be tugged on the message-line?" Captain Greybagges asked Miss Chumbley earnestly.

"I believe they are, Cap'n," said Miss Chumbley, who seemed to be trying to adopt a nautical way of speech. Captain Greybagges noticed that the elder island woman was nodding too, and that one of the younger island women touched the bronze bottle hanging from her waist when he said 'bronze bottle'. They are absorbing the English language a little, he thought, and that is a good thing in these circumstances, for I am sure that their own tongue does not have words for 'air-pump', 'fathom' or 'shackle'.

"Then let us proceed," he said, in a crisp and confident voice.

"Aye-aye, Cap'n!" said Miss Chumbley, stopping herself from saluting him with an obvious effort.

The island women and Miss Chumbley went down the ship's side into the longboat. The huge upturned wooden tub had sunk beneath the surface and was now barely discernable deep in the slightly-turbid water, its supporting ropes taut and creaking.

"Tell me again, Captain, how this will work," said Mr Benjamin at the Captain's shoulder.

"The tub descends to a fathom above the bottom of the bay. The ladies swim down to it. Inside it is a bubble of air, much squeezed by the water's force. The ladies enter the tub from below and open the taps of the bronze bottles, adding to the air. They tie the empty bottles to a line and send them back up, and a full bottle is lowered to them. With the tub full of air they have a refuge to breath whilst under the water. The air will become stale, but they will know because the candle that they shall light in there will grow dim and flicker, then they signal for more bottles of air. From the tub they can swim out and attach the cables to ... the *prize*. Then we shall raise it up."

"Could they not have worked just from the longboat, swimming down and back up again?"

"That would slow their work. The cables will have to be wormed under the ... *object* ... through the sand of the ocean-floor and that may take some digging and ingenuity. To work from the surface would take a month, maybe longer. The less time we spend here the better I shall like it."

"You do not wish to name it, whatever it is, do you, Captain?" smiled Mr Benjamin.

"I feel it would be unlucky to put a name to it just yet, although that is but foolish superstition, I know. It is not to torment you, Frank, although I admit I get a childish pleasure from keeping it a surprise."

The tub-support ropes stopped descending, and the pulley-hauly crews tied off the ends to bollards, double-knotting them. Israel Feet checked the ropes, then gave a thumbs-up. Captain Greybagges waved to the longboat and the island women rolled backwards over the gunwales and slipped beneath the sea. Captain Greybagges and Mr Benjamin watched them from the quarterdeck. From the foredeck came the never-ceasing *honk-wheeze, honk-wheeze, honk-wheeze* of the air-pump filling bronze bottles.

It took the island women three days to complete the underwater work. The crew were very impressed by their skill and determination, making their appreciation plain by small gestures of kindness when the women boarded the frigate exhausted from several hours on the ocean's floor. Miss Chumbley lost her temper several times when too many pirates crowded round the women as they were going to their cabin for raw fish, hot tea and a lie-down, and again astounded even the old pirates by her fine grasp of the technicalities of personal abuse. The air-pump never stopped its *honk-wheeze, honk-wheeze* during that time, and the Captain's prediction was proved correct as the crew started to regard it as an instrument of torture.

In the early morning of the fourth day the lifting began. The huge wooden tub had been raised already and placed on the deck. The lifting cable was reeved through the block on the sheerlegs, then through other blocks lashed to samson-posts until it came to the capstan, where sweating grunting pirates heaved, two to each capstan-bar. Extra force was applied by nipping ropes to the cable from blocks-and-tackles to the mainmast. At first the object would not move, and the winching only made the frigate heel over slowly. Captain Greybagges and Israel Feet were considering how to take a hawser from the mainmast cross-trees to an anchor off the port side to oppose the list when the frigate slowly rolled back upright again, swashing and lurching gently.

"It was stuck in the sand of the bay," breathed the Captain thankfully. "It is not too heavy."

"The thing be damned heavy enough, Cap'n," said Israel Feet. "Squash me toes with a caulking-mallet if it ain't!" He indicated the masts, which still tilted noticeably to the loaded starboard side.

The lifting continued without a break. The pirates on the capstan and the blocks-and-tackles were relieved by fresh teams every half-hour. Captain Greybagges himself took a shift, as did his officers, so that all should share the brutal labour.

In the late afternoon a pale disk began to be visible through the water, its diameter about eight paces. The chatter of the crew died away until only the grunting and loud breathing of the labourers was heard. When the object started to come clear of the water idle pirates moved to the starboard rail to see.

"Stop, you lubbers!" shouted Bulbous Bill in his high-pitched voice. "Go you to the port rail, or the barky shall tilt the more! You will get to see it in time, sure enough!"

Finally the object hung clear of the water. A lenticular metal vessel with a round hole in its top two paces across with jagged shards of glass around the edges of the hole. The metal of the vessel, where it was not obscured by fronds of seaweed and other marine growths, had a dull matte surface with a slight blue-green colour to its silvery metallic shine. The bully-boys manning the longboat towed the raft of tree-trunks underneath the strange vessel, and the capstan was backed and the blocks-and-tackles were loosed to lower it gently down. The lifting teams relaxed, breathing heavily, spitting on their blistered palms.

"Har-har, me jolly buccaneers! You may look now, and satisfies yer curiosity!" roared the Captain. "Sees you what kind of little fishy we have landed ourselves today, har-har!"

The pirates eagerly went to look, those that were not busy securing the raft and its load, but there was little talk, only a bemused hush. The island women only took a brief glance, as they had already seen it underwater. Miss Chumbley shoved herself through the press of pirates to the rail, not disdaining to use a judicious elbow-jab or kick. She stared at the strange vessel with narrowed eyes and pursed lips, lost in thought.

"It is one of the extramundane saucer-craft that you told me about, is it not, Captain?" said Blue Peter in a low voice.

Captain Sylvestre de Greybagges did not answer, but smiled a small smile and nodded.

CHAPTER THE FOURTEENTH,
or Two Wonders.

Jack Nastyface and Jake Thackeray sat on the mizzenmast mainsail cross-trees, legs dangling twenty feet above the deck. Below them the pirate crew dispersed and went about their tasks. After a short while the air-pumps re-started their endless *honk-wheeze, honk-wheeze, honk-wheeze* on the foredeck behind and below them. The first air-pump had been joined by a second which had been brought up from the hold, an even more devilish air-pump, a high-pressure air-pump that packed yet more air into the large bronze bottles, the ones the size of cannons, after they had been part-filled by the first air-pump. It was an air-pump that would act fairly to break the back and spirit of any man. Any man who was not a stout buccaneer, of course.

"He does speak well, doesn't he?" said Jake.

"*Old Soapy Syl the Shyster*," muttered Jack, under his breath.

"What?" said Jake.

"That's what the old pirates call him sometimes, the ones who were with him before London. You didn't hear that from me and don't you ever call him that. Not ever. I'm not allowed to call him that, really, as I was only Jack Nastyface back then, even though I was there," said Jack Nastyface.

"But you are still Jack Nastyface, are you not?"

"I am, but if this were a ship of the Royal Navy I would not be, and you would be Jack Nastyface instead. It is the customary name for the cook's assistant."

"Ah, but then why were you Jack Nastyface to begin with, this ship not being a Navy vessel?"

"Some of the old pirates were deserters from the Navy, so they just followed the custom notwithstanding, but many of them retired ashore at London and fellows like you joined us, and so I am stuck with Jack Nastyface for all time, I suppose."

They sat in silence for a moment.

"What is a 'shyster'?" said Jake.

"A lawyer," said Jack.

"And that is a bad thing?"

"Certainly. A lawyer is a man of far less honour than a pirate, which is why you must not repeat what I just told you, and already regret telling you."

"The Cap'n was a lawyer, then?"

"Yes, so they say. A man with a silver tongue, an artful tongue which was at the service of any who could pay his fee."

"And the Cap'n was good at the lawyering?"

"Oh, Lord, Jake! You have just heard him, have you not? He says 'I will tell you all, so that you may have faith in me, my fellow buccaneers!' and then he tells us nothing at all, but everyone is happy and feels that he has opened his heart to them."

"He said were are to voyage far, farther than any freebooters have ever gone before, and that we will win a great fortune. He has hinted at this before, and indeed it do seem likely, as he has spent gold like a nabob and we have nothing yet to show for it, not even one prize, which irks the older fellows greatly. Some of them guess that we are off to plunder the Great Cham of Tartary, some reckon it to be the treasure of Prester John, others aver it must be the emperor of far Cathay and yet others speak of the legends of a land even further to the east, where the sun do rise. What say you, Jack?"

"I do not know, but that … device down there," Jack indicated the object on the raft by the side of the *Ark de Triomphe*, "that piques my curiosity, and not in a way that brings me comfort. It has an unnatural look to it. The things that come from the distant east - the porcelain vases, the bronze urns, the painted fans and screens and such – they look foreign enough, surely, but not as strange as that. I look at it and I feel uneasy in my heart."

The two young pirates stared down at the object. Pirates were cleaning the seaweed and barnacles from it, and the strange blue-green-tinted metal of the vessel gleamed in the early-morning light.

"Jack, do you not trust the Cap'n, then?" said Jake slowly, in an undertone.

"As sure as God is my witness, I do trust him, and would willingly risk my life and the salvation of my soul for him, for he has ever shown me the greatest kindness and forbearance, especially when I first came aboard this barky and was no more than a giddy boy, and I owe my good fortune to him entire, but I wish I knew more of his mind and of his plans."

"Blue Peter knows something of those, I say, for he is oft-times inward and thoughtful, and yet he follows the Cap'n without question. All the others, young pirates and old, keep to their own counsel with patience, too, and do not much discuss what they may only hazard guesses at."

"Ah, you are right! Of course you are right! He always comes up trumps in the end, and we are all the richer for his cunning. I regret speaking now, for it may bring ill luck." Jack Nastyface crossed himself furtively and knocked with his knuckles on the brine-pickled pitch-pine timber of the mast. "Do please forget I spoke at all, and say nothing to the others, Jake! Not to anybody!"

"Assuredly, Jack! Speak of what, pray? Ho-ho! Come on, let's to work! There are pots waiting for me to scrub, and you must knot, splice, serve and parcel until your fingers ache, and then take your turn at the cursed air-pumps, too, even if you know not the reason why!"

Jake Thackeray swung himself through the lubber's hole and climbed down the ratlines. Jack Nastyface disdained to follow him and slid down the back-stay to the deck hand-over-hand in a seamanlike manner.

On the raft by the frigate's side the seaweed and marine growth had been scraped from the metal vessel. It resembled two huge shallow dishes joined rim-to-rim.

"A Greek *discus*, that is what it brings to mind," said Mr Benjamin to Loomin' Len Lummocks. "Where is the saw?"

One of Len's bully-boys brought forth a saw. It resembled a shipwright's whipsaw, which is longer than a man is tall, with wooden handles at each end for two men to cut planks from a dressed tree-trunk in a sawpit. However, instead of steel teeth the edge of this saw was set with gemstones along its length. They gleamed with rainbow colours in the sunlight.

"A king's ransom of diamonds!" Mr Benjamin shook his head ruefully. "But they shall work for us and not decorate a lady's breast, which is surely the first time such sparklers have been useful instead of merely ornamental. Set to lads! Use the *lignum-vitae* blocks to hold it steady until it bites a groove, and you!" He pointed to a young pirate, once apprenticed to a millwright, who held a tin kettle. "Dribble the oil on slowly, in a thin stream."

Two bully-boys took up the saw and placed it against the blocks of hard wood held on the convex surface of the strange object by two more bully-boys. The young pirate poured a thread of olive oil onto the blade and the saw was pulled back-and-forth in a smooth continuous action. After a quarter of an hour Mr Benjamin told the sawing bully-boys to change places with the bully-boys holding the saw's position with the blocks. He examined the metal surface while the sawing was halted, squinting through his *pince-nez* spectacles with furrowed brows.

"Bless me! … sorry! … *Avast, shipmates, har-har!* … The saw is biting! This will be slow work, for this strange metal is prodigious hard, but you shall prevail! With a will, my lads! With a will!"

Captain Greybagges watched from the quarterdeck rail, his face tense. When he heard Mr Benjamin's words he looked relieved. He shouted encouragement to the bully-boys sawing at the vessel, the glittering saw-blade moving rhythmically and relentlessly, and halloo'd to the pirates at the air-pumps as well, then went below.

In the Great Cabin the rasping rhythm of the diamond-toothed saw could be faintly heard through the open stern windows, *ssssss-ssssss-ssssss-ssssss*, faster than the laboured *honk-wheeze* of the two air-pumps, as well as the normal shouts, bangs and clatters of a fighting ship at anchor. Captain Sylvestre de Greybagges listened to the odd syncopation of the noises. Mumblin' Jake brought a tray with a pot of coffee, a jug of water with lemon slices and ice, cups, glasses and a plate of biscuits. Blue Peter Ceteshwayoo entered as Mumblin' Jake left, mumbling. He was dressed in a work-rig of an old cotton shirt and knee-britches, his calves and feet bare. He brought with him the sharp musk-tang of fresh sweat.

"You have been at the air-pump, Peter, if I may hazard a guess." The Captain poured him coffee, but Blue Peter first took a glass of iced water and drained it in a draught, wiping his mouth with a soft "ahhh!" of pleasure.

"Indeed I have. It is best if we all share in these tedious labours, Captain. I wished to take a turn at the bejewelled saw, too, as it is the most costly saw in the entire world, but Frank waved me away. I think he does not wish Len and his boys to be put off their stroke."

"I suppose it *is* a little like rowing, Peter, even though Frank isn't calling 'pull-pull-pull' as the cox used to do when I was at Cambridge and training on the Cam for the annual race against Oxford, our deadly rivals in rowing as well as learning. The cox used to ride a horse, trotting along the towpath, shouting at us through a speaking-trumpet, the ass."

Mr Benjamin joined them, dressed nearly as casually as Blue Peter, but with silk hose and stout buckled shoes. His round face beamed with satisfaction, and his eyes twinkled behind his *pince-nez* spectacles.

"Ha-ha! Coffee and biscuits! Very welcome!" He poured himself a black coffee and took a handful of biscuits.

"Does the cutting proceed well, Frank?"

"It does, Cap'n, it does. Len and his boys have got the feel of it now. How hard they must bear down on the saw, how much oil to drip, how often to stop and clear the swarf, which is the little slivers of cut metal, they can clog the teeth. They are doing so well I felt that I could leave them for a short while." He popped another biscuit in his mouth and slurped some coffee.

"How long before the first cut is completed, Frank?" said the Captain, suddenly serious.

Mr Benjamin stared at the ceiling, one eye shut. "Twelve hours, more or less, Cap'n."

"Hmm, then we must work through the night, I'm afraid, Frank. Time presses on me!"

"That will need lamps to light the cutting work. It cannot be done just by feel."

"Peter, can you get a tent rigged over the raft? I do not want to show even a glim of light which may be seen from the sea."

"That does not present any difficulties, Captain. There is sailcloth, and it can be painted black. Surely a screen around would be sufficient? A *blindée*, as the French would say? The men will need air in this heat, even at night."

"Excellent! Yes, do that before twilight. Can you cope with that, Frank?"

"Surely, Captain. There are other strong men in the crew, and the bully-boys will need sleep. If the strong men are paired on the saw with one of Len's boys in daylight they will learn how to do it, and we will be able to continue through the night, I suppose."

"Are there any problems that you can foresee, either of you?"

"I am worried about the saw, Cap'n," said Mr Benjamin, "a couple of the diamond teeth have shattered, and I fear that more will do the same, and as there are less teeth, there is more force upon those that remain, and we must make four cuts to open the … discus and gain access to its interior. Will the saw last long enough?"

"There are another seven diamond saws in the hold, Frank. I thought it best to be over-prepared. We cannot stop to go to the Antwerp diamond-bourse for more, after all."

Mr Benjamin and Blue Peter digested this news in silence.

"Come, gentlemen, I could not advertise that we had a fortune in diamonds in the hold! The crew are loyal, and every one a rich man already, but the temptation to creep down and jimmy a few sparklers out would have been too much for some, I'm sure, even though they are very small diamonds."

"Eight diamond saws, Captain?" said Blue Peter wonderingly. "They must have cost enough to make King Croesus curse!"

"Well, Peter, as I said, they are quite small diamonds, mostly of a poor yellowish colour, and not cut into many facets as are diamonds for jewellery, so I got them at a very good price!"

"Good gracious! Even so …" said Mr Benjamin, shaking his head. "In that case I think we may have the *discus* vessel opened in about forty-eight hours, two days at most, if we saw continuously night and day without respite."

Mr Benjamin stood up and clamped his hat back on his head, bid them good-day and left to continue supervising the cutting.

"Sylvestre," said Blue Peter in a low voice, "this is the extramundane craft in which you made your escape, is it not?"

"Ah, Peter! You have a quick and intuitive mind!" smiled Captain Greybagges. "Indeed it is! I was inexperienced in handling such things - a regular landlubber! - and I hit the waters of the bay moving at a great speed. I was lucky to keep my body and soul intact, but the craft was badly wrecked, the glass cupola upon its top smashed, and it sank like a stone." He poured himself more coffee and took another biscuit. "Let us finish our coffee, then perhaps do a turn upon those blasted air-pumps to encourage the others!"

It took forty-two hours to saw four cuts in the hull of the extramundane craft, creating a square hole. Mr Benjamin and Loomin' Len ceremoniously made the final strokes of the diamond saw and the last connecting finger of blue-green-tinted metal parted with an audible *clink* in the early hours of the second day, shortly after the ship's bell rang the beginning of the first dog-watch. In the yellow glow of the whale-oil lamps two bully-boys lifted out the sawn section, expressing muttered surprise at how light it was, despite being as thick as a hatch-batten. A quiet spatter of applause came from the rail of the *Ark de Triomphe*, where most of the day-watch and the waisters had joined the night-watch to witness the feat.

Captain Greybagges clambered down onto the raft. He bowed a mock formal bow to Mr Benjamin, took the proffered lantern and was the first to peer into the dark inside of the lenticular extramundane craft. He was grinning broadly. He handed the lantern back to Mr Benjamin, who peered inside and grinned when he withdrew his head from the aperture.

"Not a trace of water or damp, Captain! And no obvious sign of damage. We are blessed with good fortune!"

The bully-boys hissed and muttered, outraged that Mr Benjamin should speak thus and attract bad luck.

"Quick, Frank! Knock your knuckles on the side of the ship! Hard as you can! Now whistle and turn round three times widdershins!" He took Mr Benjamin's shoulders and spun him round anticlockwise. "Ah, there, Frank! Any ill turns of fate that may have been brought by your words are averted by our seamanlike wisdom and prompt action!" He winked at Mr Benjamin and continued in a lower voice. "You know what to do now, Frank. Carry on!"

Captain Greybagges climbed back up the side of the frigate with the aid of a dangling rope and addressed the assembled pirates.

"Mr Benjamin spoke without thinking, but he is right! Things are looking very fine and ship-shape! You are all curious as to what this strange metal sea-shell contains, but there is no treasure in there, nor any gold or jewels. BUT!" and he spoke in a loud commanding voice, "in there are some devices which we will need, which I expected to find, which will enable us to do some great things! You will see them as Mr Benjamin and his lads bring them into the ship, so you *will* see them and do not need to sneak onto the raft to get a peek, but they do not look like much, I tell you, just some metal boxes and drums. Do NOT get in Mr Benjamin's way! Do NOT be foolish from mere curiosity! Do NOT touch these things! If you do you will be like an ape in a powder-magazine *with a tinder-box!* Let Mr Benjamin and his lads do their work, and I promise you that in the next weeks you will see some sights that will astound you. Wonders that shall amaze and delight you! Just you be patient awhile! NOW you day-watch fellows and you waisters must go to your hammocks and sleep, for there is more hard work to be done upon the dawn, which is close upon us. Hard work, yes indeed, and plenty of it, but labour handsomely, my fine buccaneers, and we shall have a little jollity before we leaves this bay. We shall have a *boucan*! Two oxen, three hogs and three sheep are coming to be roasted for your pleasure. Mr Bucephalus! Mr First Mate! Give these stout pirates a double ration of rum, so they may sleep as sound as babies! And the same for the dog-watches when they stands down."

The pirates went to their hammocks, accompanied by a low mutter of talk, leaving just the night-watch on deck, and Mr Benjamin, his skilled men and Len and the bully-boys on the raft in the dim glow of the lamps.

The first device was brought out from the strange seashell in the mid-morning, and indeed it did not look like much; a lead-grey cylinder with some flanges, bumps and hollows on its smooth surface. Mr Benjamin, his eyes now red from lack of sleep, and his small team of apprentices-turned-pirates – a watchmaker, a scientific-instrument maker, two millwrights, a coppersmith and a maker of brass trumpets and horns – clustered around as two of Loomin' Len's bully-boys hefted the grey cylinder through the square hole and placed it on a wooden stollage. A block-and-tackle lifted it onto the deck and then it was carried below into the bowels of the ship. Another identical grey cylinder followed three hours later, and then another, and then another. Whispered reports flew round the frigate:

"They have bolted it to the flat plate on the iron keel, under the foremast! The larboard plate!" – *"Mr Benjamin dropped a wrench on his foot and howled in anger and cursed most foully!"* – *"Now there are two of them bolted to the for'ard keel!"* – *"The watchmaker has had a finger crushed under the bottom of one when it slipped, but he has wrapped a silk kerchief around it and he works on! His finger, of course, you lubber, the kerchief went around his finger!"* – *"Now two of them are bolted to the aft keel, side-by-side!"* – *"They are joining all four of them to the copper bars, working to a secret plan of squiggles on a square of paper! No, nobody knows why! I said it was a secret plan, didn't I, have you got ears of sailcloth?"*

At dusk Captain Greybagges told Mr Benjamin to stop and rest, for he, his skilled team and the bully-boys has now been working without respite and sustained only snatched snacks for two-and-a-half days. Then he *ordered* them to stop, for they were unwilling to obey and would have defied him. After a hot meal and a pint of iced rum-grog they fell asleep where they sat or stood, still mumbling that they could carry on, surely they could, and friends carried them gently to their berths, removed their shoes and tip-toed away. Miss Chumbley and the leader of the island women tended to the clockmaker's finger as he slept, cleaning the wound with warm water and vinegar, bandaging it with cotton cloth and splinting the finger with a thin strip of rawhide, sufficient to restrict movement but not so stiff as to cause discomfort. The watchmaker muttered between his snores, but did not awake.

Jack Nastyface and Jake Thackeray sat on the mizzenmast mainsail cross-trees, which had become their accustomed spot for a yarn and a smoke, eating a handful of Jake's biscuits, watching the sun lift itself over the horizon. The air was still cool, but the brassy rising sun foretold a hot morning, which in Nombre Dios bay was no surprise.

"Look! There goes Mr Benjamin and his mechanics," said Jake.

"And eager as foxhounds! Mr Benjamin has not even taken his air-bath!" said Jack. "But see, he gives his wig and spectacles to Len and douses his head under the seawater pump. And he goes straight for the raft, his hair still wet! What wonders will he bring out from the scallop-shell today?"

"Another fascinating grey lump of something-or-other, no doubt. What were those things?"

"The Cap'n knows, and maybe Mr B and his mechanics, but nobody else does, although they do not let that inhibit them from making guesses. Let us be about our business, Jake, for those mechanical fellows have shamed us all, and any slacking today will be much remarked, and not in a kindly way." Jack slid down the backstay, and Jake climbed carefully through the lubber's hole and down the ratlines. Pirates in the rigging called out "har-har, you old woman!" but he ignored their comments with the unshakable dignity of the one who holds the serving-ladle at mealtimes.

The next wonder to emerge from the 'scallop-shell' was not a grey cylinder, but a vaguely spherical object with flat faces, also grey, but a darker blue-grey. It was manhandled through the square aperture in the extramundane craft's hull with great difficulty, for it was almost too big to fit and seemed to be very heavy. Whispers went from mouth to ear round the crew:

"*Mr Benjamin called it a dodecahedron! No, I don't know what that is!*" – "*It is stuck in the starboard companionway!*" – "*Mr Chippendale has been called! He has cut away the bulkheads, and now it moves again!*" – "*Mr B says there must be no more squashed fingers, so Chips is cutting a hole in the 'tween-deck planking!*" – "*Bulbous Bill and Izzy are rigging a hoist, with a tackle suspended from the main-deck hanging knees!*" – "*It sits on the large plate in the middle of the keel, upon the centreline!*" – "*They are clamping it with bolts!*" – "*The copper bars are being attached to it! Mr B calls for tallow mixed with powdered copper! No, I don't know why!*" – "*It is in place! Mr B praises Len's boys for their muscles and Chips, Bill and Izzy for the ingenious tackle-work!*" – "*Now Mr B calls a break for food and water!*"

Mr Benjamin and his team ate beef stew, tearing off hunks of bread to sop up the juices, drinking draughts of iced water, sitting on tool-chests and kegs in the waist of the frigate. The cook collected the plates, and Jake Thackeray brought them coffee and cakes on a tray. They lit pipes and sat at ease. Mr Benjamin took paper diagrams from a battered leather case and passed them around, listening to comments and questions. The members of the crew who contrived to walk nonchalantly past reported that the papers were as incomprehensible as Chinese - lines and squares, symbols, squiggles, hieroglyphs and runes – but that they were discussing them earnestly, and that the talk that was overheard made no more sense than the papers.

Captain Greybagges came up from the Great Cabin and joined them, accepting a cup of coffee and a slice of honey-glazed lardy-cake.

"Fine work, Mr Benjamin, and you fellows, too!" said the Captain. "I assume that there is only the one more thing to be retrieved?"

"Well, that and a few little odds and ends," said Mr Benjamin thoughtfully, lifting his wig to scratch the top of his head.

"It is already getting a little late in the day, and you have worked as hard as Trojans. Do it tomorrow, for it may be delicate work, and you will need to be rested. There is the fitting of the new instruments to the binnacle to be done, which is not such heavy labour, as Mr Chippendale will do the necessary carpentry. Under your supervision, of course."

"Aye-aye, Cap'n!" said Mr Benjamin with a nod and a smile. "That is a sensible plan. The connexions to the demiheptaxial mechanism are mostly already in place, thanks to Sid here," he indicated the watchmaker with a nod, "so the work on the binnacle will go quickly."

"And how is your hand today, Sid?" enquired the Captain.

"Painful, but bearable, begging your pardon, Cap'n. Luckily it is the left hand." He raised the hand in question, the bandage now stained with black grease and smears of the tallow and copper-dust mixture, which was as bright as sign-writers' gold paint in the low sun.

"Make sure you get that bandage changed and the wound cleaned by Miss Chumbley when you finish your work this evening, Sid. You are a pirate - a stout-hearted buccaneer, indeed! - but you are too young yet for a hook!" said the Captain.

The next morning Jack Nastyface and Jake Thackeray, on their accustomed perch on the mizzenmast mainsail cross-trees, noted that Mr Benjamin once again missed his air-bath, merely sousing his head under the seawater pump before climbing down to the raft and wriggling into the 'scallop-shell', followed by his men. Just after the ship's bell rang the end of the forenoon watch, as pirates started to line up to have wooden kids filled with stew from the galley for the gun-deck messes, Loomin' Len's bully-boys carried a new object from the interior of the extramundane craft. A golden sphere, roughly the same diameter as a rum-keg. It gleamed a molten yellow in the bright sun, and the waiting mess-chiefs gasped in wonder.

The auriferous globe, tied with padded ropes onto a wooden dolly cushioned with rags, was block-and-tackled up to the deck with exquisite care, Mr Benjamin clucking protectively around it like a mother hen. It was then hoisted, again with the most diligent attention, to its platform, the platform on a diagonal strut between the foremast and the mainmast that had been fixed in Liver Pool. Mr Benjamin ascended the mainmast to the platform, moving slowly, assisted with great solicitude by the First Mate and two of his 'foremast jacks, who placed Mr Benjamin's feet on the ratlines and yards for him as he climbed, despite his growled protests.

The queue for lunch slowed as the pirates observed the performance above them, their faces tilted to the sky, and the cook roared at them to hurry up, you dogs, until he gave up and came out from his galley to join them watching silently, as no whispered reports were needed this time.

Mr Benjamin and his team attached the golden sphere to the platform with bolts, and joined the thin copper bars to it with clamps smeared with the tallow-and-copper-dust mixture. It took them the first quarter of the afternoon watch, and was performed without mishap, except that Sid the watchmaker, rendered clumsy by his gashed and broken finger, dropped a wrench, which hit the deck with a solid bang, gouging the planks but hitting no one. Mr Benjamin opened his mouth to rebuke him, but stopped himself and gave him a small smile instead. The golden sphere was then shrouded in a tarred-canvas cover, and Mr Benjamin and his men climbed carefully down. The pirates gave them an appreciative cheer as they stepped onto to the deck. The queue for lunch re-formed and Jake Thackeray filled their kids with salt-horse-and-pease stew, informing them cheerfully that he had kept it warm, but that he had some cold stew if there were any *old women* who might prefer it that way.

Mr Benjamin went to the Great Cabin to report to the Captain. Blue Peter was already there, examining the small model of the *Ark de Triomphe* in its spherical glass bottle on its shelf.

"Ah, Frank!" said Captain Greybagges cheerfully. "Excellent work! We must not tempt the fates by any display of egregious *hubris*, but I do not think they will begrudge us a well-earned glass of brandy and a sense of smug satisfaction! Here, let me help you to a glass…"

Mr Benjamin took his brandy, a generous slug in a crystal tumbler, and raised it:

"Aye-aye, Cap'n! To success in your endeavours!" he cried, adding to himself in an undertone, "*whatever they may be…*"

"Indeed, yes," said Blue Peter. "I will drink to that!" He caught Mr Benjamin's eye and nodded towards the ship-in-a-bottle. Mr Benjamin stood beside him and regarded the model of the *Ark de Triomphe*.

"Oh, my!" he said after a pause. "You have laid your plans deeply, Cap'n. Very deeply indeed. I had not noticed that little gold bead on the model before. The close fit of the dodecahedron and the grey-cylinder things to their positions on the iron keel-pieces greatly impressed me, but it seems that you have anticipated this in much greater detail than I could have imagined."

"I hope it gives you confidence, Frank," said Captain Greybagges carefully. "I have demanded a lot of trust from everybody, and everybody has generously granted me that trust, for which you and the entire crew have my deepest gratitude. You have questions, though, they clamour in your thoughts, I can see it upon your face. All I can still say is that...."

"...everything will become clear in time!" said Blue Peter and Mr Benjamin, almost in complete unison. Captain Greybagges barked with laughter.

"Never has a captain of pirates had a better crew!" grinned the Captain. "I raise my glass to you!" He took a swallow of brandy. "We are not yet finished, though, the game is not yet won. I honour and value your patience with me and my annoying secretiveness, but you will understand my reasons before all is done. Come, sit down, the pair of you, and tell me how things progress. You first, Frank."

"The components from the *discus* – or the *scallop-shell*, as the crew are calling it – have been transferred to this frigate. Some small things are yet to be removed, but Sid and the other fellows are doing that as we speak. The fitting of the instruments and the little brass thingummijigs to the extended binnacle is now done, and they are connected to the demiheptaxial mechanism, except for a final look to see that all is well. A few bolts to tighten, a few joints and bearings to be greased, that sort of thing. All complete before lunchtime tomorrow, at the latest."

"Peter?"

"The cannon have been modified as you required, their flintlocks replaced by the new firing devices. Torvald Coalbiter is not entirely happy, of course, as he does not really understand the electrical fluid or how it can ignite gunpowder, even though he saw the barrel exploded by lightning that time, but he is doing what he is told. He, too, has faith in your schemes, Captain. He is in awe of your green beard. He believes it to be magical, you see, like his grandmother, who was a witch, he says."

"I am a man of reason, a lover of natural philosophy," said Mr Benjamin slowly, "but I am beginning to think something like that myself..." He raised a hand to forestall an answer. "But I certainly agree with your pirate crew. They are curious, of course, but they are intrigued. They will go with you to the ends of the Earth, and not ask questions now, I think, because they don't wish to spoil the surprise. Let's be about our work."

Two Wonders

Mr Benjamin left the Great Cabin. Blue Peter murmured "*to the ends of the earth, Captain?*" with a wry grin, revealing his pointed filed teeth, and left too, shutting the door gently behind him.

Captain Sylvestre de Greybagges stood upon his quarterdeck, dressed in his full pirate-captain's rig of black pants tucked into black spit-shined sea-boots, black shirt, black *justaucorps* coat and a black tricorne hat. In his belt was a cutlass and two pistols, and his green beard seemed almost to glow emerald when it caught the midday sun. He felt a mixture of satisfaction, hope and pride as he surveyed his ship, the frigate *Ark de Triomphe*. All the necessary work had now been done, even to small details. The canvas screens that had disguised the frigate's low predatory silhouette had not been re-mounted, but a broad band of a yellowish buff had been painted along the hull at the level of the gun-ports to make her more resemble a merchant ship to the casual eye. The canvas name-plates covering the frigate's real name on the stern and on sides of the bow had been replaced with better ones of thin wood, the false identity lettered bravely in characters of shining copper, for one of the young pirates, once the apprentice of a paint-maker, had compounded a metallic lacquer from a little of the copper dust, perhaps inspired by the shining smears on Mr Benjamin's waistcoat and Sid's bandage.

Blue Peter came onto the quarterdeck, attired in a sky-blue coat with gold buttons, a white silk shirt, pale-grey breeches, white hose and shoes with gold buckles. A multi-coloured silk sash around his waist held a short cutlass with a brass knuckle-duster hilt and the long-barrelled Kentucky pistol. His huge hands glittered and flashed with gemstone rings.

"Peter, do you not find the *nom-de-guerre* of this frigate oddly apposite?" said the Captain. "Mr Benjamin thought of it."

Blue Peter leaned over the stern-rail to read the inscription upside-down.

"I am not sure, but I am glad it amuses you, Captain. They will not let me see Miriam. Those island women barred the way to her cabin, and would not move an inch, even though I showed my teeth and growled."

"It is the custom. You would have brought bad luck upon yourself, Peter," laughed the Captain, "and the island women know that you are not a brute, even if you look like one, har-har!"

Captain Greybagges leaned over the stern-rail to admire the new name-board once more. The former paint-maker's apprentice was using up the last of the copper paint to add highlights to the carved curlicues around the stern windows.

"Good work, Albert!" said the Captain. "Very tasteful, I find it!"

"Why, thank'ee Cap'n! Us slab-boys do know a thing or two, har-har!"

Blue Peter and the Captain walked to the ship's wheel, the binnacle in front of it now much enlarged to hold panels of levers and a number of dials with engraved brass faces and blued-steel hands. A complicated device of brass and steel was mounted in the centre of the new binnacle, protected by a glass bell-jar.

"What is that, Captain?" Blue Peter pointed to the device. "It resembles the bastard love-child of an armilliary sphere, an orrery and an astrolabe."

"Ah-ha! You are not so very far from the truth, Peter. It is called a *torquetum*, although it is more complex than the instrument from which it gets its name."

Blue Peter nodded, but asked no further questions. I am committed to this venture, he thought, for good or ill, and there are no answers that will change that. During the night he had dreamt a confused dream, in which the leopardess with cutlass-teeth and cannon-claws had visited him again. He remembered an amicable and rambling discussion, but could recall no details of what was said. They had walked together in the African bush, then rested together in the shade of a baobab tree. As part of a friendly tussle, as one may have with a playful feline, the leopardess had climbed on top of him and sat on his chest. He had awoken at that moment, feeling short of breath, to find two yellow eyes staring down at him in the dark. He had twitched with shock, for dreams should not become real, and then the ship's cat had jumped from his chest with a hiss. Blue Peter had shook his head to banish the shards of dream. The black cat, on the floor of his cabin, had looked him in the eyes, made a *rrowwll!* noise, then slid through the ajar door. He had left his bunk and followed it, feeling foolish. The black cat paced slowly, its tail twitching from side to side, not looking back, then darted up the companionway. Blue Peter had followed it up the steps, and stopped with just his head above the level of the planking. Captain Greybagges stood on the quarterdeck, wearing his black nightshirt, his bare feet a couple of paces from Blue Peter's face. The Captain stood quite still, staring up at the night sky, a velvet blue-black sky full of bright stars. Blue Peter noticed, with an eerie feeling, that the green beard was moving as though in a slight breeze. There was no wind that Blue Peter could detect, but the green beard waved nonetheless, small ripples rolling from the Captain's chin down to the ends of the whiskers. Of the ship's black cat there was no sign. Blue Peter stepped backwards down the companionway ladder, carefully and soundlessly, and returned to his bunk, where he fell immediately into a deep and dreamless slumber.

In the light of the day Blue Peter was not sure whether he really had been led by a pussycat to observe the Captain communing with the stars, or whether it was a mere continuation of the dream of the African savanna. He felt that it was a good omen either way, although he was not sure why.

He was brought from his reverie by Mr Benjamin, Bulbous Bill Bucephalus and Israel Feet clumping up the steps to the quarterdeck, talking loudly and cheerfully. They were all dressed in their best clothes: Mr Benjamin looking a little hot in a fine buff coat, waistcoat and breeches and a new wig, with a sword with a fine maroon-leather scabbard and baldric, his eyes sparkling merrily behind his *pince-nez* spectacles; the First Mate and the sailing-master in the traditional pirate uniform of dark fustian knee-britches and weskit, colourful kerchiefs on their heads, knotted at the back with the corners hanging down, bright sashes around their waists with a tasteful collection of weapons tucked into them, only so much hardware as was appropriate for a party among friends.

Captain Sylvestre de Greybagges rubbed his hands together, grinning gleefully.

"Har-har! Me hearties! Bill, Izzy, are the look-outs and their reliefs assigned and instructed? Are they content with the recompense for their forbearance and for missing a little of the grog and the dancing?"

"Aye-aye, Cap'n! They are, and they are!" they cried back, touching their forelocks.

"Then let us take ourselves ashore and get this *boucan* started, for I has a powerful desire to grow my beard just a little!"

The old priest's hair was grey, his chin whiskery, his eyes red and his cassock worn and patched, but he asked Blue Peter the question in a firm and resonant voice:

"*Pee-tar, vis accípere Miri-aam, hic praeséntem in tuam legítiman uxórem juxta ritum sanctae matris Ecclésiae?*"

Blue Peter answered "Volo!"

The old priest turned to Miss Miriam Andromeda Chumbley, and asked:

"*Miri-aam, vis accípere Pee-tar., hic praeséntem in tuum legítimun maritum juxta ritum sanctae matris Ecclésiae?*"

In a loud voice, trembling a little from nerves, Miss Chumbley answered "Volo!"

The priest then blessed them with the sign of the cross, as he said:

"*Ego conjúngo vos in matrimónium. In nominee Patris, et Fílii, et Spíritus Sancti. Amen!*"

"He says that you are now man and wife!" whispered Captain Greybagges, who was giving away the bride, at her request. "Pass him the ring, Izzy!"

"Bill's got it, ain't he?" replied the First Mate, and there was a brief *sotto-voce* argument between the two before the ring – a gold band with a rose-pink diamond – was found in the First Mate's waistcoat pocket and placed on the bride's finger. Captain Greybagges was ready to say "you may now kiss the bride!" but Blue Peter forestalled him by lifting the new Mrs Ceteshwayoo off her feet and kissing her lovingly, passionately and lingeringly. The pirates roared their approval, cheering repeatedly, cheering so deafeningly that the monkey-birds flapped from their perches in the surrounding jungle and circled overhead, squawking loudly as though adding their approval, too.

Blue Peter thanked the priest in bad Spanish, and slipped a *reale d'or* into his hand as he shook it.

The bride threw her bouquet over her shoulder. The eldest of the island women caught it, and looked at it in surprise.

"Oh, dear!" said Bulbous Bill, wiping away a tear. "Do they not look lovely together, Cap'n!"

It is true, thought Captain Greybagges, they look wonderful. The bride's wedding-dress is not white, but the island women and the old tars have done a magnificent job. You would not guess it was made from cut-up signal flags. It looks very colourful and flattering. A white gown would have looked a little pale and anaemic next to Blue Peter in his finery, but instead she out-shines him like a firework display. A prancing Froggie dressmaker from Paris itself could not have

stitched her a better one from the silks of Cathay. And the island women have
done her proud, too! They look just right as bridesmaids, all in those nice boxy
dresses with the wide sleeves – *kimonos*, did they call 'em? – even with those sticks
in their piled-up hair, alike to knitting-needles in balls of wool.

Blue Peter and his bride were walking among the crowding pirates, Blue Peter
accepting handshakes and good wishes and Miriam offering her cheek for good-
luck kisses. Captain Greybagges looked around and caught the eye of the cook
and raised an eyebrow. The cook, attending to the barbecue, a white chef's hat
jammed on his head, nodded happily and waved a huge carving-knife.

"Ladies and gentlemen!" roared the Captain, clapping his hands. "The
victuals are ready! Let the *boucan* begin!"

Somebody pushed a tankard of iced rum-punch into his hand, and was
gone before he could turn and thank them. He sipped it, and smacked his lips
appreciatively. Behind him a violin struck up a sprightly jig. A concertina joined it,
followed by a fife and a drum catching the tune and embroidering upon it, and a
small ripple of applause and catcalls, ironic but cheerful, told him that somebody
had started dancing.

"Curse and damn it!" snarled Captain Greybagges. "Why must the damned-
and-blasted breeze be so bloody contrary? On this of all days, too!"

The wind, light and steady, had been on-shore since dawn, keeping the pirate
frigate *Ark de Triomphe* trapped in the almost-circular Nombre Dios Bay. Everything
had now been done that could be done. The last action had been at midday; the
sinking of the emptied husk of the 'scallop-shell' to the bottom of the bay once
again, and the towing of the raft to the shore for the local people to use as they
wished. The ship was ready, the crew were ready – despite more than a few sore
heads from the previous night's *boucan* – and the Captain was certainly ready, yet
the wind defied them all. The *Ark de Triomphe* swung by a single anchor, her bow
pointed toward the open sea, her sails hanging loosely on the yards waiting to
catch the puff of wind which would push her out of the bay and away from land.

As the Captain stomped grumpily up and down the quarterdeck, Blue Peter
tried to compose his features into a stern expression. He had already done so
many times that day, but at even the tiniest distraction – a seagull crying overhead,

a sudden squawking of the monkey-birds in the distant jungle, a laugh from some foremast-jack in the rigging – his face would instantly rearrange itself into a look of the most fatuous and idiotic happiness.

The night before at sunset when he and his new bride had attempted to slip away from the *boucan* to his cabin on the frigate they were waylaid before he could launch the skiff from the beach. Torvald Coalbiter and a party of gunners had respectfully asked the couple to accompany them, as they had a small wedding-present they wished to present, begging your pardons *most* kindly. It would have been churlish to refuse, so he and the newly-minted Mrs Miriam Ceteshwayoo had grudgingly gone with them. Torvald Coalbiter had led them along a narrow jungle-path, until they had come to a clearing where there was, to Blue Peter's amazement, a cottage in the Spanish style. "It was the Spanish governor's, until the town was abandoned," explained Coalbiter. "Me and the lads found it when we was out a-hunting for the jungle-fowl, and we've cleaned it up for you both as best we could." The gunners had indeed 'cleaned it up'; the thick undergrowth had been hacked back, the *stucco* walls whitewashed and the roof repaired with split-wood shingles, all with thorough-going nautical efficiency. Torvald Coalbiter had ceremoniously ushered them in through the yellow-painted front door. The rooms were lit with oil-lamps and the waxed parquet floors gleamed in their glow. A mahogany dresser held covered dishes of food "for you and the lady to partake of a late supper, if you wish" and a dining-table had settings for two places with silver cutlery, crystal glasses and a bottle of champagne in a bucket of ice (the ordinary wooden bucket had been ruthlessly scrubbed and waxed like the floor, its iron hoops polished, and would not have shamed the Palace of Versailles). While an enchanted Miriam had admired the *décor*, distracted by the vases of fresh flowers and the thin white canvas swagged over the windows, Torvald Coalbiter opened a door of oiled oak and indicated the bedroom. Through the doorway Blue Peter saw an imposing canopied four-poster bed, with clean white sheets tucked in and turned down with geometrical precision. Torvald Coalbiter whispered discreetly: "The side-chamber has a wash-stand and the heads, which is alike to a throne. You must lift the seat to find the pot, and there is another pot in the little cupboard. We gunners shall keep watch outside so nothing shall disturb you and your lady." And then he and the gunners had removed themselves, vanishing almost magically, silently closing the front door behind them.

Alone in the cottage, Blue Peter and Miriam had regarded each other with serious expressions, until Blue Peter grinned and pulled back a chair: "Will you be seated for the feast, my lady?" he had said, with mock servile unctuousness. Miriam had grinned back at him, curtsied and settled herself on the chair as he slid it forward. "Will you now take a glass of champagne with me, gracious lady?" he had whispered in her ear, before kissing her neck gently.

"Peter, you seem to be a-practicing for a gurning contest, such as village yokels do when they make faces through a horse-collar to see who can look the silliest." Captain Greybagges drew a hand over his face. "Oh, sod it! I do apologize! I am strung tighter than a fiddle-string! I wish to get away from here. I am *gravid* with eagerness! I am *with child* with impatience for us to be on our way! I do apologise for my unpleasantness of speech, Peter, sincerely I do!"

"There'll be a seaward wind after sunset, you may lay to that Cap'n," said Bulbous Bill Bucephalus, who was by the wheel with Mr Benjamin, explaining the parts of the new binnacle to two of the old pirates and two of the new pirates; the old chief steersmen and two trainees.

Captain Greybagges went to answer, but a cry from the maintop look-out interrupted him; "A sail, Cap'n! A sail! A sail to east-by-nor'-east! *A sail!*"

The Captain stood stock-still for a moment, then called down to the waist:

"First Mate! Go you up the mainmast and have a butchers! Here, take my spy-glass, and don't drop the damn thing!"

Israel Feet took the Dolland telescope in its leather case and slung the strap over his shoulder then went up the rigging as agile as a monkey. Captain Greybagges drummed his fingers on the larboard rail, frowning as he stared at the horizon through the mouth of the bay.

"What does 'a butchers' mean, Captain?" said Blue Peter, to ease the tension on the quarterdeck.

"It is the cockaignie rhyming-slang, Peter. 'Butcher's hook' rhymes with 'look', and long use has shortened it, and the desire to be even more opaque, of course, because it is thieves' cant." The Captain gave Blue Peter a bleak smile.

"Cap'n!" the First Mate's voice came down from the maintop. "'Tain't no fat merchantman, I do lay to that! The sails and rig has themselves a rakish swagger to my eyes, paste me like bloater if I speaks untrue!"

"Keep the glass upon it, Izzy!" roared the Captain at the maintop, and in a lower voice; "Peter, Bill, Frank, we will prepare for action, if you please. Peter, guns loaded and primed, both sides, but not yet run out, deck guns loaded, too, but no hostile signs to show, the crews to lie flat besides the carronades to stay out of sight, if they must. Bill, two men with axes ready to cut the anchor-cable on my word - *only upon my word*, mark you! - and the longboat, with the strongest oarsmen as crew, ready on deck to launch and tow us if need be. Mr Benjamin, ready the sickbay for casualties, if you would be so good. To work, gentlemen!"

Any cheerfulness that remained from the previous night's festivities evaporated and was replaced by a sense of impending danger. The crew, even the stupidest, could see that the *Ark de Triomphe* was in a perilous position if the approaching ship was hostile. Caught in an enclosing bay, penned in by a mischievous breeze from the sea, the frigate's options were limited and she was vulnerable to a determined foe.

"This is what I had hoped would not happen," muttered the Captain. "I knew that if we were here too long some tittle-tattle of our presence would spread, and I thought I had judged things aright, so that we would be gone before anybody came a-sniffing around. Even if no rumour reached the wrong ears there was still the element of chance. Some ship coming here to take on water, or just to anchor overnight, or for whatever reason. Damn!" He roared up to the maintop;

"Izzy! What see you?"

"I think she be a freebooter, Cap'n! She be low over the decks, and the crew be many! She be a-headin' direct toward this bay!"

"Good news, maybe, or bad, depending upon her master," mused the Captain to Bulbous Bill. "Mind you, if it be ..."

The Captain nodded to himself, as though coming to a decision.

"Bill, belay the longboat. Tell the men to re-stow it and send the oarsmen back to their positions. Pray call Mr Benjamin to the quarterdeck, at his earliest convenience."

Israel Feet called reports down as the ship approached. She was indeed a pirate-ship, beyond all doubt, heavily manned and preparing for a fight, although taking some precautions to conceal her intentions. The First Mate's experienced pirate's eyes, aided by the spy-glass, saw through the impostures with ease, although a merchant captain might have been fooled easily enough, his own fervent wish for a trouble-free voyage helping him to delude himself.

The pirate-ship was nearly to the entrance of the bay and easily visible from the level of the deck, so Captain Greybagges called the First Mate down from the maintop, told him to arm the crew ready for an engagement, and reclaimed his telescope. He peered through it at the approaching vessel.

"Ah, damn it!" he hissed. "It is Morgan! *Bloody* Captain *bloody* Bloody Morgan, curse the jumped-up Welsh midget! He means us no good, my friends, I am sure!"

Captain Greybagges slammed the telescope shut, and turned to the binnacle.

"Bill, Frank, I had intended to try this out at sea, where we would be alone from horizon to horizon, so that I would not reveal my hand, but my hand is now forced by that odious little Welsh jackanapes, so I shall take that risk! Frank, take your two best men and go below. Close the main shunt from the dodecahedron to connect the electrical fluid. Lock it in place, so it shall not work loose, then cover it again immediately with the wooden case. Wear the thick horsehide gloves at all times, except when removing and replacing the case! Then return back here as quick as you may, in case I need you to fix something. Bill, we have discussed the *theory* of this enough times, but now we must see to the *practice*! Follow my orders to the letter, if you please!"

Captain Greybagges stood next to the binnacle, quivering with impatience. Morgan's ship entered the mouth of Nombre Dios Bay.

"He is an excellent seaman, is Morgan, for all that he is a jumped-up fool! See how he has positioned himself so that he has enough way on his barky to lay it alongside us, even though the on-shore breeze will lessen in the loom of the land! Oh, what a treacherous dog! Now that he is Governor of Jamaica I believe he means to please his new master, King Charles, by sending him our heads!"

Mr Benjamin came huffing-and-puffing back onto the quarterdeck with his two assistants; Sid the watchmaker had a leather sheath over his wounded finger, tied around his wrist with a thong. He and the other, a millwright from Sheffield, looked apprehensive, but nevertheless agog with excitement.

Captain Greybagges stepped forward to the front of the quarterdeck and grasped the rail.

"My friends! Lusty buccaneers! Harken to me well!" he roared. "I promised you wonders, and now you shall see one! Take hold of something so you shall not fall, especially you jacks in the rigging! Take hold *now*, and keep a-hold!"

The Captain turned back to Bulbous Bill Bucephalus at the binnacle.

"Bill, move the lever marked 'X-ENGAGE' down until it locks! Good! Steersmen at the wheel, be ready for my orders! Bill, move the lever marked 'X-FORCE' – *slowly! gently!* – upwards, but only until the dial reads *one* on the scale!"

The sailing master obeyed, and with a slight but distinct lurch the *Ark de Triomphe* started to move forwards. *Started to move forwards against the wind!* There was a shriek from the rigging, but no thud of a body hitting the deck. Several of the pirate crew on the deck staggered and fell over, despite their sea-legs.

"I told you lubbers to hang on!" roared the Captain. "Now cut the anchor-cable! Don't just stand there with your bloody mouths open, you fools! Cut the bloody cable *now*!"

There was the *thunk!* of axes as the two hefty pirates on the foredeck roused themselves from their amazement and attacked the cable. The cable parted just as the frigate's slow forward movement started to bring it taut. It fell into the sea, the splash audible in the stunned silence.

"Don't bloody stand there, you lubbers! Don't think! Get about your work now! Do your *appointed tasks* now, or, so help me, *I shall shoot you dead* while you stand *with your bloody mouths open gawping like bloody moon-calves! Now go!*"

Captain Sylvestre de Greybagges drew a pistol from his belt, fired it in the air, threw the discharged pistol to the deck and drew another one to reinforce his threat. The crew ran to their positions, a mutter of oaths and expletives breaking the stunned silence.

The *Ark de Triomphe* moved slowly forward against the wind, against all nautical principles and against all reason. Morgan's vessel had now come into the bay, heading straight for the *Ark de Triomphe*.

"Steersmen! Twenty points to port, *now!*" roared Captain Greybagges. The steersmen obeyed, their eyes wide and their mouths still open from shock and surprise.

"Bill, move up the X-FORCE lever until the dial shows two!"

The *Ark de Triomphe* increased speed in complete defiance of the wind and curved to port, cutting a wake, its sails flapping uselessly, driven back against the masts by the light contrary breeze and the frigate's forward motion. Morgan's vessel came on, slowing now that the wind was lessening in the shadow of the land.

Captain Greybagges jumped down from the quarterdeck into the waist and bellowed down the companionway; "Peter! Roll out the starboard guns! Be ready to fire, to fire as they bear, but do not fire unless upon my express order! Do you hear me?" A faint acknowledgement echoed up from the gun-deck. "Repeat what I said!" Blue Peter repeated the Captain's exact words. "Good! Stand ready upon my word!" The Captain ran back up to the quarterdeck. There was a *thump-thump-thump-thump* as the gun-ports opened, and a rumble as the guns rolled out.

"Bill, reduce the X-FORCE back to one! Steersmen, now to starboard, thirty points! Quick as you can!"

Captain Greybagges stood breathing heavily, making an obvious strong effort of will to compose himself.

"Bill, steersmen, we are going to cross Morgan's stern now, and if the little sod makes one move - *just one bloody move!* – I shall rake him, and be damned to him! Steersmen, straighten her up now, and be prepared to go port-thirty upon my command."

The *Ark de Triomphe* curved around Morgan's ship and across its stern. Captain Sylvestre de Greybagges stood at the starboard quarterdeck rail, noting Blue Peter at the foot of the companionway steps, waiting ready to relay the order to fire to the gun-deck. There was an almost complete silence. Captain Greybagges swept off his black tricorne hat in an elegant gesture.

"Why, Captain Morgan, my compliments! I suggest that if you are prepared to lower yourself so far as to go a-hunting of your old friends – *your old shipmates, who never did you any harm!* – then you should at least find yourself a seaworthy vessel! One that can sail in these capricious coastal breezes. A good day to you!"

He made an elegant bow, one leg forward, sweeping his hat across his chest. The *Ark de Triomphe* slid past the stern of Morgan's ship, its sails flapping. He replaced his hat and turned to the steersmen.

"Port thirty, if you please, straighten her up, then out the bay-mouth to the sea. Bill, take her back up to two on the dial, so that we may get expeditiously away from here."

The *Ark de Triomphe* slid through the bay-mouth and into the open sea, beginning to pitch a little as it hit the ocean waves. Sylvestre de Greybagges started to laugh, and laughed and laughed until tears rolled down his cheeks.

"Oh, my! Oh, my! That was good! *Bloody* Captain *bloody* Bloody Morgan stood there in his fine plum-coloured coat with his jaw on his chest and his eyes popped out of his head like organ-stops! He was so close I could almost have reached across and tweaked his long nose! He could not have been more stunned if I had hit him on the head with a caulking-mallet! He was so utterly dumbfounded that I expect when he recovers his wits he will babble like an idiot, poop his britches and then fall over in a swoon! Oh, dear me! Oh, dearie, dearie me!"

"They have run aground," said Bulbous Bill, looking astern from the aft rail with the Captain's telescope.

"Let me see!" The Captain grabbed the spy-glass, looked and burst into another attack of mirth, slapping his thigh. "Oh, dearie me! It just gets better! They must have stood there as still as marble statues, their mouths agape, until their barky hit the beach!"

The *Ark de Triomphe* slid through the sea, now once again under the power of her sails alone, with a fair wind at her starboard quarter. The sea was quiet, merely rippled, and above her the sky was blue with a scattering of clouds, the sun lowering itself down to the horizon behind them as dusk approached, its light giving the white sails a rosy glow.

"I heard your words to Morgan, Captain," said Blue Peter, "but I would give a bagful of gold to have seen his face!"

"It was comical, Peter! I have not seen anything so damned amusing in a very long time," Captain Greybagges grinned a wolfish grin, "and then he ran aground, too!"

"Why did you not give me the order to fire? He had come for us – for you, who once sailed with him! – with malice in his heart, and greedy for more honours from the King, even though he is as rich as several Pharoahs already."

"Well, Peter, that might perhaps have made him a martyr; 'Brave, loyal, *honest* Captain Morgan murdered by the vile *treacherous* pirate Captain Greenbeard!' the broadsheets would have thundered! 'We must scour the oceans and destroy this

wicked highwayman of the high seas! England can ask for no less!' but now it
will be rather 'That wily rogue Greenbeard outsails and out-manoeuvres wooden-
headed Captain *Tom Fool* Morgan, even showing mercy and allowing him to keep
his miserable life, and then diddles him into running his own ship up onto the
beach, the clumsy idiot!' Which is much better in the long run of things, you
must confess. And I did not wish to cause great slaughter to his crew, who are not
really to blame for Morgan's ambitions, after all, even though they sail under his
command."

"Um. Even so…" said Blue Peter, looking doubtful.

"Oh, Lord! You gunners are a bloodthirsty lot, aren't you? I know that a
raking is the supreme challenge for a master gunner, but have you ever raked a
ship yourself?"

"Well, no…"

"I haven't, either, and I would if I had to, but *only* if there was no possible
alternative, for it is not something that should be done lightly. I conversed once
with an old Navy captain who had managed that feat. He had taken his ship
across his enemy's stern, each one of his guns firing as it bore, each one of those
thirty-two-pound cannon-balls smashing through the stern windows and ripping
through the whole length of the ship – *boom! boom! boom! boom!* – and he said that as
they drew away from the enemy ship she lay stricken in the water like dead animal,
with blood pouring in great gouts from all her gun-ports, alike to water gushing
from broken guttering in a rain-squall. He said that all his crew started muttering
prayers for their poor enemies when they saw that, some of them crying, and
they were men hardened by many a sea-battle. He said he had never forgotten
the sight and never would, and that he prayed every night for forgiveness, and lit
candles for the souls of the dead every Sunday without fail, and still sometimes he
would dream evil dreams and awake weeping for what he had done. Don't wish
that upon yourself, Peter! Especially for such a dunce as Morgan! Even though he
was ready to fire upon us, for I saw the red glow of his gunners' linstocks through
his gun-ports as we crossed his wake. That is so typical of Morgan! He is such a
skinflint that he has not got flint-locks for his cannon, rich though he is."

"I was not eavesdropping," said Mr Benjamin, standing up suddenly from
behind the binnacle, holding a spanner, grease smudges on his face and hands,
"but I agree with the Captain … *Cap'n* … sorry, I still struggle with naval

nomenclature."

"Oh, you gave me a start!" said Captain Greybagges. "I hadn't seen you lurking there!"

"I was checking the orientation of the shafts and greasing the elbows of the rods. Everything is as it should be."

"You have examined the main shunt, I presume? No sign of sparking? No excessive heating? No charring of the wooden parts?"

"We looked at it first, Cap'n. It was just as it was when we covered it."

"I am relieved at that, Frank. Please tell me there was *something* wrong *somewhere*, otherwise I might feel that the fates are mocking us."

"The port-side connexion to the gun-deck had loosened – probably by the flexing of the hull – but it is duplicated on the starboard side, with a cross-over, so no harm could have come from it. We have tightened it, and put in an s-bend to allow it more freedom, so the natural working of the ship's timbers puts no further strain upon it."

"Aah! You ease my mind, Frank! There was something amiss! The Muslims regard perfection as unlucky, and always put a small error in even their most flawless silk carpets and alabaster *arabesques*. I understand their caution!"

"As to what you were saying to Peter, Cap'n," continued Mr Benjamin, "it seems to me that by not blowing Morgan to kingdom come you have also not drawn attention to yourself, and that you may not do that because you have now a ship that moves in complete disregard of the wind and tide. I think I mentioned to you before that my idea for an air-powered cannon drew all kinds of unwelcome attention to me. Men are fascinated by engines of death, after all. I confess that I do understand Peter's enthusiasm. Indeed, the temptation to develop the air-weapon was not inspired by the fame, the friendship of the powerful or the wealth that it may have brought to me, but rather by the sheer fascination of building an engine of such power and then *using* it. We are creatures full of curiosity, and nothing tempts us so much as a cannon primed and ready to fire! The *possibilities* intrigue us! "*As swift as a pellet out of a gunne When fyre is in the powder runne,*" said the sage Chaucer. Things other than guns can fire the imagination by their possibilities. I am amazed still by what you have done— *a ship that moves in defiance of the winds!* – and I see that such a wonder would be regarded with acquisitive eyes by many, because of the *possibilities*. A nation possessing such power would dominate the globe! To advertise the existence of a self-propelled ship would have been foolish. As things are, Morgan's account, if he is so indiscreet as to give one, will arouse howls of mocking laughter, the attempt of a beaten man to explain his dismal failure by an improbable tale. Yet I still sympathize with Peter's disappointment! How fine it must be to fire a perfect broadside, and bring a loathed foe – callous and overbearing in his pride and arrogance! - to well-deserved ruin in an instant!"

"Well, Frank, Peter may well have his chance to perform a perfect broadside before too long, and you will be there to witness it, I promise you. A self-propelled ship is indeed a wonder, yet now I will show you another wonder! Night approaches, and we are alone in an empty ocean. Even the sea-gulls have abandoned us. There are no curious eyes to witness us, and no wagging tongues to spread rumours. Where are Bill and Izzy?"

Captain Sylvestre de Greybagges paced the quarterdeck while the two were called.

"I am as nervous as a cat!" said the Captain to Blue Peter. The ship's cat chose that moment to swagger across the quarterdeck and curl up next to the rail, exhibiting no nervousness at all.

"Ah, Izzy! Please get the jacks to furl all sails, and then bring all of them, even the look-outs, down on deck."

"Aye-aye, Cap'n!" said the First Mate.

"Bill, please engage X-FORCE and take it slowly to two."

"Aye-aye, Cap'n!"

"Bill, you have an understanding of the other levers now?"

"I does, Cap'n. The force levers be the *directions*, and the little levers below them on the board are the *rotations* about them directions. The one below X being *roll*, the one below Y being *pitch* and the one below Z being *yaw*. I has that firmly in mind, Cap'n."

The sails were now furled on the yards and the crew were all on deck, looking expectant but puzzled. The *Ark de Triomphe* still cut through the sea, driven now by the mysterious X-FORCE alone.

"Well, no point in delaying!" said Captain Greybagges. "Bill, engage the Z-FORCE and then, on my word, take it slowly up to five ... *UP SHIP!*"

Bulbous Bill Bucephalus moved the Z-FORCE lever carefully and precisely, and the pirate frigate *Ark de Triomphe*, her hull creaking just a little, lifted slowly out of the sea and rose majestically up towards the clouds.

———————

Captain William Schovelle sat in his cabin, humming a tune. His account-books and bills of lading lay before him on his desk, in the light from a lantern. A good cargo: Dutch crockery (very nice blue-and-white glazed earthenware; he would keep a service for his wife, and maybe one for her dim-witted brother, too, if he felt generous); French wine (although one of the damn' barrels had sprung, wine lost and some of the crew now had secret caches of claret, caught in hats and pannikins as the leaking barrel was brought on deck for repair); English cotton cloth in bright patterns and woollen cloth in plain dark sober shades: some pewter; some brassware; Sheffield-made steel blades for sickles and scythes, and a ballast of pig-iron. A good cargo to land in the American colonies, and his strategy of going further to the south in the crossing had proved itself. A less-experienced master would not sail at the lower latitudes of the trade winds and risk becoming becalmed, but Captain Schovelle would run *that* risk for the reduced risk of piracy. The winds had been light and had veered and backed quite remarkably at times, but his ship had not once lain hove-to in a dead calm, her sails flapping. And the ocean had been empty, nobody this far south. He was feeling, truth be told, a little smug.

Captain Schovelle poured himself a glass of rum, and he was just in the process of lighting a clay pipe with a taper lit from the lantern when there was a discreet knocking at the door of his cabin.

"Enter!" he commanded, in a voice made deep by years of bellowing orders into the teeth of gales full of rain, sleet, snow, hailstones and the occasional cannon-ball.

"Why, Tack! Come in my lad!"

He was fond of his nephew, Caractacus Todd, who, despite being the son of his wife's wooden-headed brother Theobald, was indeed as sharp as a tack. The young man seemed distressed.

"You seem distressed, young man. What ails thee?"

Tack's mouth opened and closed several times, then:

"Uncle Bill, I saw something strange," he whispered. "Just now. Nobody else saw it"

"What did you see, then?"

"I find it difficult to speak of it. I fear you will laugh at me, or think that I have lost my reason."

"Tack, you are fourteen years old, but you are a sailor, and so you will have to take a scare once in a while. Here, take this rum, sip it and sit for a moment to collect your wits before you tell me."

The young man sat and sipped the rum.

"When I was your age, or not much older," said Captain Schovelle, "I was on an old leaky barque, sailing off the coast of Newfoundland. In the dog-watches I used to trail a fishing-line from the taffrail, for I am as fond of cod and taters as the next man. One night I was pulling in a fish when something snatched it off the line, I felt the line go taut and snap. Looking down, by the light of a gibbous moon, I saw a monster that had come up from the deep. It had the tentacles of an octopus, a beak - alike to a parrot's but much larger - and round eyes the size of dinner-plates. I saw it quite clearly, and it was very ugly and very real and its tentacles waved at me until I jumped backwards half across the deck. I went and looked over the taffrail again and it had gone. I told the ship's master, and he called me a liar and a rogue. He was not a bad man, either. I have never met anyone else who has seen such a creature, but I have heard old tales and legends that speak of monsters like that. I saw it, you see, and I know what I saw. Sometimes we sailors see things that are best not spoken of by land. Sometimes we see things that even other sailors will not believe. Now tell me what you saw. I will not mock you, I swear."

"I saw a ship, Uncle Bill, and she was flying in the sky. At first, by the light of the moon, I only saw something flitting through the clouds, and I thought it strange, and then it passed almost overhead."

"Um, was this ship the right way up? I have heard of mirages such as are said to occur in the deserts - *fata morgana* some calls 'em - but they are oft-times upside down, as they are but a mere reflection, an image made of light."

"No, Uncle, it was no image. She seemed to be pushing through the clouds, and they swirling around her as water does. She was three-masted. A frigate, I think. Black with a yellowish band along her side. She moved in complete silence, except for a faint sighing noise, *honk-wheeze, honk-wheeze, honk-wheeze.* I looked with the spy-glass, and she had all her sails furled. I could see men on the deck, all clad in red and grey slops as are worn by the crews of the Dutch company. As she passed I could even see her name writ large in gilded script upon her stern. It said '*De Fliegende Hollander*'. I can spell the letters for you, if you wish, for I am no great hand at the speech of foreigners."

"'*The Flying Dutchman*' … that is … um … best not to speak of this to another soul, my boy, for this is a very strange thing, a very strange thing indeed. Have another glass of rum."

CHAPTER THE FIFTEENTH,
or The Voyage to Baart'tzuum.

There could be no doubt about it; Captain Sylvestre de Greybagges was facing a mutiny.

"We will not go ashore! You shall not turn us ashore!" said Mrs Miriam Ceshwayoo, *neé* Chumbley, small but nevertheless daunting, in a low but very determined voice. "You show us your wonderful flying ship, talk of the fabulous kingdoms far away that you shall visit, the great treasure that you will win there, and then you want to dump us all in bloody Porte de Recailles for the mere fact that we are women? I shall *not* accept that, and neither will these ladies!"

The island women nodded in agreement, looking as grim as their inscrutable faces would allow.

"I am surprised that you did not barricade yourselves in your cabin," said Captain Greybagges, trying to gain time to think.

"Do you think we are stupid, because we are women? The walls … sorry, the *bulkheads* … are held in place by wooden dowels and wedges! All the cabins are! Even your own cabin is the same, so it may be knocked-down at need and used as a gun-deck for stern-chasers. Mr Chippendale would have removed the bulkheads in a trice, leaving us holding just the door. Then we would have looked so pathetic that all you *men* would have *laughed at us* and *put us on the beach* feeling *oh-so-smug* that you were doing the right thing, you pigs! If you are going to throw us off your boat then you must do it so that all the crew may see, and see what an ass you are! … Captain."

Blue Peter stood behind the women, looking guilty.

"Please, Miriam, my dear!" he said.

"I hope this … um … *contretemps* was not your idea, Peter," said the Captain.

"I only told her that I was pleased she would be safe in my … in *our* … cottage, away from any battles or hardships, and what a wonderful time we would have when I returned."

Most of the crew had now stopped what they were doing, and were watching with alert and amused interest. Captain Greybagges thought quickly.

"Dear ladies …"

"Don't you *dear ladies* us, you old tyrant!"

"A tyrant I am not. A captain of buccaneers can only command with the full consent of his crew, and there are no floggings or keel-haulings aboard my ship. I shall put the matter to a vote at once."

Captain Greybagges called out to the crew working on deck:

"Shipmates! I calls yuz to an informal vote under the rules of the Free Brotherhood o' the Coasts! Shall these female members of the crew be left behind in Porte de Recailles, so that they shall not be harmed, whatever may befall us? If yuz thinks they should then ye shouts 'aye'! If yuz thinks they should not, as they are pirates of our company, despite they being of the fair and female gender, then ye shouts 'nay'! How votes yuz all?"

There was a loud confused roar of shouts of 'aye' and 'nay', mixed with catcalls and oaths.

"As yer Cap'n, I does then declare that the *nays* has it! The *dear ladies* shall stay on board an' share our hardships and tribulations, share our plunder and treasure and share our exploits and adventures, too! Are yuz satisfied that the vote be lawful under the rules?"

There was another confused roar, this time mostly of 'aye-aye, Cap'n'.

"Well then, dear ladies, you shall stay, and Porte de Recailles will be duller for your absence. Are you now satisfied that your rights have been upheld, as is fair and just?"

"You are undoubtedly planning to trick us! This is just to keep us quiet until we get into port, *then* you'll put us ashore, you *lawyer*!"

"What? Shall we not go into Porte de Recailles? Shall we not have a last carouse in Ye *Halfe Cannonballe*? Shall we not let the old pirates see their girlfriends and wives and children?"

There was a roar, not confused at all, of 'nays', and shouts of "Come on! Let's get on with it!" and "Anchors aweigh, me hearties!" and similar sentiments.

"Oh, sod!" muttered Captain Greybagges. "I forgot that they were all still listening. I shouldn't have mentioned the wives and girlfriends, either." He raised his hands, then addressed the crew again; "Alright! Alright! Then we shall go *now*, upon this very instant. But only *if* there are sufficient stores, and *if* the air-bottles are all filled, for then I have no objections."

There was a prolonged burst of applause and cheering. Mr Benjamin whispered that the air-bottles were charged to maximum pressure, Cap'n, all of them, even the two which had leaky taps, which we have ground-in with jeweller's rouge and re-packed the stoppers with fine cotton and grease, d'you see? Then Jake Thackeray was pushed up to the quarterdeck steps to swear that there was plenty of food and water stowed, enough for three months, at least, Cap'n. The crew's enthusiasm for an instant departure was palpable. Again Captain Greybagges raised his hands for silence:

"It is agreed, then, shipmates!" he spoke in a commanding tone, "we shall start our *cruise* upon this very moment. First we must make ready! Belay the course for Porte de Recailles, steersmen, and take her away from the wind! … First mate, all the sails furled, if you please, and all the jacks down on deck! … Bill, engage the forward force as the sails are furled, one or two on the dial, just to keep some sea-way upon her … Mr Benjamin, please bring the telescope up from the hold, and the alidade and the transit circle, too, … Peter, are the guns unloaded, plugged and lashed? The powder-magazine swept, locked and secured? Excellent! … Everybody else, have you no work to do? There be things to be done still! Look there on the foredeck, the bottles are all filled now, so the air-pumps can be dismantled and stowed …"

There was a brief ironical cheer for the demise of the hated air-pumps and the crew went about their tasks with an excited mutter. The mutinous women dispersed, the new Mrs Ceteshwayoo giving Blue Peter a shrewd glance over her shoulder. After a moment the waist and the foredeck became a scene of activity; pirates pulling on ropes, flemishing cables, tightening braces and catting the bowsed anchors, the rigging full of men wrestling with the heavy canvas sails, their sheets snapping in the wind. The quarterdeck was empty except for the Captain and the master gunner.

"I had not actually given any thought to whether the ladies might come or stay, Peter. Well, not your beloved lady wife, anyway. I did have a vague plan to take the island women back to their island, but I had not decided anything. The landfall at Porte de Recailles was just to pick up post and get some more rum, as the *boucan* depleted the supplies somewhat. Why did you tell your spitfire of a spouse that you were going to leave her behind, you ass?"

"Because I am an ass, too stupid to be hired as a village idiot," said Blue Peter. "I had thought she would be pleased by my concern for her safety and comfort. Am I to be the first of your crew that shall be flogged and keel-hauled, Captain?"

"You escape by the skin of your teeth. I had no idea the crew were so eager for the off. Since they are champing at the bit, I shall not disappoint them."

"The things they have seen – first a ship that ignores the wind and tides, then a ship that floats in the sky and sails amongst the clouds – have whetted their appetites for wonders, especially after a prolonged period when they all suspected that you were as mad as two squirrels in a hat-box, but didn't care as long as they were paid with shovelfuls of gold coins. Now their confidence in you is unshakable, and they are agog to see what you will do next."

"Well, then I shall not keep them waiting. Ah, Frank!"

Mr Benjamin came onto the quarterdeck with a crew of his men, all carrying boxes. One box contained a tripod, which was quickly assembled and fixed to the planking with screws. Another long box held an astronomer's telescope, a fat brass tube with an eyepiece jutting out of its side, which was mounted on the tripod. More boxes produced two smaller tripods and the transit circle and the alidade, which were also assembled and screwed down to the deck-planks.

"My quarterdeck is becoming a little *cluttered*," said Captain Greybagges, eyeing the brass instruments, "but there is no helping that. Where is Izzy? Ah, there you are! Please be so good as to remove the cover from the … um … golden globe up there."

The First Mate sprang to obey, with an "aye-aye, Cap'n". The *Ark de Triomphe* now had the wind at her stern, and was driven sluggishly into the swell by just the windage of the bare masts and by the 'two on the dial'. The Captain strode impatiently up and down the quarterdeck, avoiding Mr Benjamin and his assistants as they fiddled with the telescope and the other instruments. Israel Feet climbed down from the mast, the rolled canvas cover over his shoulder. The golden globe gleamed on its platform between the masts.

"Well now, me hearty buccaneers!" roared Captain Greybagges, "here be another miracle for you! Bill, engage the bubble!"

Bulbous Bill Bucephalus moved a lever on a panel of the binnacle, and there was a strange *ooom-pop!* noise. The crew looked about, but there was nothing much to see, except a barely-discernable flickering glow of purple light around the globe. More noticeable was the sudden cessation of all wind over the decks and of all the noise of the sea. Blue Peter, to his surprise, saw a seagull apparently collide with nothing and flap away. The ship seemed to be surrounded by a very faint gauzy curtain, barely perceptible except where it met the sea, where spray was blown against it, glittering.

"Bill, now take us up above the clouds, if you please!"

The *Ark de Triomphe* rose slowly from the sea, straight upwards. As the ship passed through the clouds the billowing whiteness was held back by an invisible barrier, the ship at the centre of a sphere of clear air in the enveloping luminous white fog. The crew, quiet until then, gave an 'ooh!' of appreciation, for it was a strangely pretty sight.

"Har-har!" bellowed Captain Greybagges to the crew, "now we be surrounded by a bubble of protection, d'yuz sees? An invisible bottle, as you might say."

The *Ark de Triomphe* continued to rise until the enclosing nimbus became tinted a rosy pink, and then the ship broke free from the clouds and lifted above them. The cloud-deck lay beneath the ship, stretching from horizon to horizon, the cloud-tops rolling slowly like strange waves, casting off occasional rags and wisps of vapour to twist and whirl in playful breezes. The sun was now low in a darkening deep-blue sky. Its warm rays infused the clouds below the ship with a fiery glow of orange and red hues, some scraps of cloud still miraculously as white as snow, tumbling in the drifting blue shadows cast by the fluffy towers and mountains of their larger brethren, The crew was utterly silent for over a minute, then broke out into a joyous hubbub of 'oohs', 'aahs', curses, oaths and shouts.

"Hold her steady here, Bill!" said the Captain. "Let's enjoy the view for a while, until the sun is set."

"Oh, my! Oh, my!" whispered Mr Benjamin. "It makes perfect sense, of course. This is what clouds look like from above. Down below the clouds are grey and drizzle rains upon our heads, but up here there are no clouds above, because they are below, so the sun is forever shining. If I had ever asked myself 'what do clouds look like from above?' I am sure I would have imagined, *conceived*, something similar, because it makes perfect sense that they should look like this, but I could not have imagined how lovely they look. Oh, my! Oh, my!"

The crew had clustered at the rails, excitedly talking and pointing at the glory of the sunlit clouds as the dusk deepened and shades of red and purple washed away the yellow and orange.

"Er, Captain," said Blue Peter, "have you noticed that we have lifted a large piece of the ocean up with us?"

"Of course, Peter!" said Captain Greybagges, joining him at the rail and looking down. "The bubble of protection is perfectly spherical and goes under the ship. The seawater is caught inside it. We truly resemble the ship-in-a-bottle now, except that the sea is real sea, and not plaster of Paris tinted blue with paint. It is not just a fanciful whim, either. The salt water will absorb certain noxious gases, gases which we exhale as we breathe, and so prevent them from accumulating to poisonous levels."

"I see that you have given this some small thought, Captain!" said Blue Peter. "I am sorry that I ever doubted you."

"You concealed your doubts very well, Peter, and for that I thank you most heartily, for without your support and *apparent* belief I would not have been able to get this far in my plans."

Captain Sylvestre de Greybagges and Blue Peter Ceteshwayoo watched the sun slowly disappear below the horizon, the clouds below losing their purple tints until they were grey, an odd grey that seemed clean and washed, like the grey of an old but well-loved white cotton shirt. The stern-lanterns were lit, casting their yellow light over the quarterdeck where Mr Benjamin and his assistants tinkered with the brass telescope and surveying instruments. There was an eerie, but not unpleasant, silence because of the protective bubble, broken only by the clink of spanners and the squeak of screwdrivers. Bulbous Bill Bucephalus stood by the binnacle, occasionally checking a dial, touching a lever gently, his broad jowly face pensive in the gloom.

Captain Greybagges sent a message to the cook to start serving the crew their supper. He and Blue Peter took a snack of apples, bread, cheese and small beer while leaning against the rail. Mr Benjamin and his men shared in the basket and the jug that Jake Thackeray had brought, but kept working while they ate. The sky darkened as dusk slid into black night.

Mr Benjamin finally pronounced the telescope and instruments to be correctly aligned and ready for use.

"Bill, Frank, take the sightings and adjust the demiheptaxial mechanism to accord with them," said the Captain. "Do please check each other's readings and repeat them three times, for we can afford no errors! They may be difficult to correct once we are … er … *under way,* so to speak. How long do you believe that will take you?"

"An hour. Maybe a little longer, Captain … Cap'n," said Mr Benjamin, wiping grease from his hands with a rag.

"Um … one-half of a dog-watch … please do carry on, Frank, Bill," said Captain Greybagges. He turned and strode to the stern rail of the quarterdeck and looked out at the moonlit cloud-tops. Blue Peter joined him. They stood in silence for a while, watching the clouds billow and roll underneath, an occasional wisp marking the invisible boundary of the 'bubble' as it slid around it.

"Your deep-laid plan seem to be coming to fruition, Sylvestre, but I sense that you are apprehensive," said Blue Peter in a low voice.

"I am not sure that the crew will like what is going to happen next, even though they have become accustomed to seeing wonders. It may be *unsettling.*"

"They are all brave men, Cap'n … even the women," said Blue Peter.

"True, but some things are too *unsettling* even for brave souls to witness without feelings of disquietude. I think that even you, Peter, will be a little daunted, and you are perhaps the bravest of us all. So stiffen up your sinews, summon up the blood, old friend! I need you to look resolute and unafraid at my side, for the crew will first look to me, but then they will look to you."

"I will do my best, Cap'n. I think that I shall discard this Dutch uniform, since we are unlikely to be hailed by inquisitive naval vessels, floating as we are above the clouds, and I find it easier to be courageous as a declared pirate, rather than as a fraudulent officer of the *Vereenigde Oost-Indische Compagnie*." Blue Peter stumbled over the Dutch pronunciation, and laughed.

"Yes, you are right! Disguise no longer has any purpose. Let us be pirates, stout-hearted gentlemen of fortune, unafraid and unashamed!" Captain Sylevestre de Greybagges stood back from the rail, slapped the light-blue sleeve of his VOC uniform with disdain and headed for his cabin, calling for Mumblin' Jake.

A little later, Captain Greybagges - his head freshly shaved by Mumblin' Jake, dressed entirely in black from his sea-boots to his tricorne hat, a pistol and a cutlass in his belt and his green beard washed, combed and almost glowing - returned to the quarterdeck. Mr Benjamin and Bulbous Bill had finished their observations, calculations and tinkerings with the demiheptaxial mechanism. Israel Feet confirmed that everything aboard the *Ark de Triomphe* was shipshape and stowed. The crew were in the waist and on the foredeck, idling and talking. There was an air of expectation as sharp as the electric stillness before a storm. Blue Peter came onto the quarterdeck, resplendent in a yellow satin coat, white trousers tucked into tan Hessian boots with tassels, a silk sash around his waist carrying his short knuckleduster cutlass and Kentucky pistol and his huge hands a-sparkle with multicoloured gemstone rings.

Captain Sylevestre de Greybagges nodded to him, cleared his throat loudly, then spoke.

"Gentlemen o' fortune! An' ladies o' fortune, too, har-har! We shall now be a-casting-off on *the greatest pirate raid in all o' history!* When we are done wi' it, and a-counting our treasure, then *bloody* Captain Bloody Morgan's raid on Panama will seem alike to pinchin' apples offen a costermonger's cart, it shall! You shall see great wonders, an' you shall see sights that would turn honest men's bowels to water! But yuz are pirates, buccaneers an' freebooters, stalwart an' brave, an' I knows that I can lay to that, wi' a wannion! Keep yer nerves steady, an we shall all become rich as nabobs, that I do swear! Richer that nabobs! Richer even than that ole King Croesus o' legend!"

Captain Greybagges turned to Bulbous Bill Bucephalous and raised an eyebrow.

"Be you ready, Bill?"

"Aye-aye, Cap'n!"

"Then point her at the stars!"

Bulbous Bill worked the levers on the binnacle. The frigate *Ark de Triomphe* pitched up slowly until her bowsprit pointed to the sky. Several of the crew staggered involuntarily as the horizon of moonlit clouds rotated, although no force was felt inside the bubble. Mumblin' Jake fell over, mumbling loud curses, but nobody laughed.

"As you can see, shipmates," spoke the Captain, "inside this bubble o' protection we are alike to a separate world, not even under the influence of Doctor Newton's universal laws o' gravity. We be safe inside, shipmates. Whatever be on the outside cannot harm us! Mark that well, me hearties!"

Captain Greybagges turned again to Bulbous Bill, who checked the dials on the binnacle and nodded.

"Now, shipmates, we shall be away on our cruise, and we do most truly cast off!"

Captain Greybagges waved his hand to Bulbous Bill, who moved the levers on the binnacle. The pale clouds below began to move away from the frigate *Ark de Triomphe*.

"As you now see, shipmates, the clouds seem to move away from us, but actually we is a-moving away from *them*! We do not feel the movement because we are safe inside the bubble o' protection! Remember that; *we be safe within the bubble o' protection!*"

Captain Greybagges nudged Blue Peter, whose mouth was open. Blue Peter closed his mouth and tried to look serious, as though he had expected such a thing to happen. In truth, I should have expected it, he thought, for it should have been apparent to me that the Captain is heading for the planet Mars, but even though he has confided much to me, and I have already seen great wonders, yet it did not seem reasonable to expect any such thing.

"Increase the X-FORCE smoothly to ten, Bill," said Captain Greybagges quietly.

The pale clouds fell away from the stern of the *Ark de Triomphe* faster and faster.

"Har-har, shipmates! Now yuz all can see that the world is truly a globe! A globe, alike to the one in me own cabin below!"

A murmur, almost of anguish, came from the crew.

"Be yuz all of strong heart, shipmates! Remember we be within the bubble o' protection, so nothing may cause us harm!"

Captain Greybagges stood and watched the disc of the Earth slowly diminish behind the frigate. The crew were completely silent and awe-struck.

"Now we shall go even more swiftly, shipmates! We need not tarry in such a well-found ship as this!" roared the Captain to the crew, then in a lower voice, "Bill take the X-FORCE gently to the maximum! Frank, do you now go and check the connecting bars! See that they are not becoming too hot, if you please!"

Mr Benjamin tore his wide eyes from the sight of planet Earth dwindling behind them and went down the companion-steps, swaying slightly as if drunk.

"Har-har, me hearties! We have now passed the point o' greatest peril ... for we have not crashed ourselves into the poor old Moon! Har-har-har! Pardon me little jest!"

The Captain's words seemed to break a spell for the crew, for they broke into loud talk, with many a profane exclamation and heartfelt curse.

"Be ye not a-feared, shipmates!" roared the Captain over the hubbub. "We be safe within the bubble o' protection! Yuz have seen the highest seas, blue waters that could daunt any stout heart! Yuz have fought in many a battle where a cannon-ball could have sent yuz to hell in a moment! Yuz have sailed the oceans of the world! None o' that cast you down, so why be a-feared when you are safe as mother's milk, when no wave or storm do threaten yuz? Especially when we sails to find wealth beyond measure an' fame beyond the poor imaginings of landlubbers. Yuz be sailors of the starry voids now, pirates of the skies, and yuz will have tales to tell! Be cheery! You there, Jake Thackeray! Strike up a song now! A song to stiffen the brave hearts of stout buccaneers!"

Jake Thackeray was pushed forward and encouraged to stand upon a barrel. He looked lost for a moment then smiled and launched himself into song, a song that the crew knew well, and roared out in harmony:

"What's that stuff with the awful smell?
That sticks when it's flung?
What's brown and rings like a bell?
DUNG! DUNG! DUNG! DUNG! DUNG!

When you tread in it you can tell!
For to your feet it's clung!
What's brown and rings like a bell?
DUNG! DUNG! DUNG! DUNG! DUNG!

We're neck-deep in it, you knew it well,
long before this song was sung!
What's brown and rings like a bell?
DUNG! DUNG! DUNG! DUNG! DUNG!

What's that stuff with the awful smell?
That sticks when it's flung?
What's brown and rings like a bell?
DUNG! DUNG! DUNG! DUNG! DUNG!"

"Jake Thackeray, I shall personally bury *you* in dung iffen you cannot think of a more encouraging song!" shouted Captain Greybagges over the laughter of the crew, but he was grinning. The song, and the moment of humorous relief, seemed to have taken away the crews' apprehensions.

Jake Thackeray thought for a moment, then struck a pose, and sang again:

"There was a jolly old sailorman upon the Rotterdam docks!
Where the merchants do their business to the chimin' of the clocks!
For I tell 'ee that no sailor be a-sleepin' when opportunity knocks!

He was a-flogging parrots and apes on Rotterdam docks!

259

To bewigg-ed burghers and bishops in their frocks!
Because a sailor ain't a-sleepin' when opportunity knocks!

He's going to sell 'em wonders an' stuff their guilders in his socks!
Then he'll drink himself shit-faced an' go off and catch the pox!
Because a sailor ain't a-sleepin' when opportunity knocks!

In Africkee the parrots flap around in squawking flocks!
An' he'd catch 'em with his net an' keep 'em in a box!
Because a sailor ain't a-sleepin' when opportunity knocks!

He's going to sell 'em parrots, an' stuff their guilders in his socks!
Then he'll drink himself shit-faced and go off an' catch the pox!
Because a sailor ain't a-sleepin' when opportunity knocks!

He'd knock the apes out of the trees by throwing little rocks!
Then to the beach he'd drag them by their little monkey cocks!
Because a sailor ain't a-sleepin' when opportunity knocks!

He's going to sell 'em monkeys, an' stuff their guilders in his socks!
Then he'll drink himself shit-faced and go off and catch the pox!
Because a sailor ain't a-sleepin' when opportunity knocks!

With a cargo of apes and parrots he's got his trading stocks!
And he'll fill in the nooks with leopards an' springboks!
Because a sailor ain't a-sleepin' when opportunity knocks!

He's going to sail back to Holland and stuff guilders in his socks!
Then he'll drink himself shit-faced and go off and catch the pox!
Because a sailor ain't a-sleepin' when opportunity knocks!

So now he's a-flogging parrots and apes on Rotterdam docks!
To bewigg-ed burghers and bishops in their frocks!
Because a sailor ain't a-sleepin' when opportunity knocks!

He's going to sell 'em apes and parrots an' stuff their guilders in his socks!
Then he'll drink himself shit-faced and go off and catch the pox!
Because a sailor ain't a-sleepin' when opportunity knocks!"

The pirate crew sang lustily, and with good heart, as planet Earth receded behind the frigate *Ark de Triomphe* until it was no more than a star among the other stars in the velvet black of the sky.

"Well, that went as well as it could have done, I suppose," said Captain Greybagges, then took a large swallow of rum.

"It is not every day that a fellow may see his home world disappearing behind him into the night sky, so I would have to say it went *very* well. Very well, indeed. It was a sight that both afrighted the wits out of me and enthralled me at the same time, and I am not sure that I will ever feel quite the same when I gaze at a sky full of stars," said Mr Benjamin. Then he too took a large gulp of rum. The door of the Great Cabin creaked open and Blue Peter and Bulbous Bill came in.

"As you can hear, the crew are still a-roistering," said Blue Peter. The crew could be heard singing, accompanied by a wheezy concertina, a badly-tuned fiddle and some sort of squeaky flute. "I told Izzy to let 'em have rum and beer with their supper, and I set the bully-boys to watch 'em, so that they don't drink too much." He and Bill sat down at the table and helped themselves to rum.

"How long will it be before we ... drop anchor again?" asked Blue Peter.

"The journey will take about three weeks," said Captain Greybagges, "but it will seem to us to take only ten days or so."

Blue Peter raised his eyebrows in surprise.

"The flow of time is apparently reduced by travel at high velocities," said Mr Benjamin. Bulbous Bill nodded sagely, and said, "To a cully a-watchin' us through a strong spy-glass it would take three weeks by his timepiece, but by *our* timepieces it will be less. *An' both of us will be right*, which is a thing I find most wondrous, 'pon my soul I do! The Captain showed me an' Frank how the figuring of it be done, but I be none the wiser for the figuring of it, I will lay to that!"

"I had the way of it explained to me," said Captain Greybagges, "but it is mysterious to me also, for I am no great natural philosopher. I doubt if even Doctor Newton himself could make sense of it, but it is so."

"The numbers astound me!" said Mr Benjamin. "The planet Mars is presently a little more than *thirty-two million sea miles* from our Earth, or about twelve and one-half million leagues. That is, I am told, the closest that the two bodies do ever approach each other in their endless circumgyrations around the sun, which is convenient for us. Such distances are meaningless to my poor mind, though, so I am trying not to think of them. Best if they remain merely figures to be writ on a piece of paper, or clicked into the dials of the demiheptaxial mechanism, which seems to understand them far better than I!" Mr Benjamin took another gulp of rum, his *pince-nez* spectacles gleaming in the lamp-light.

Blue Peter made as if to speak, then thought better of it and stayed silent. The four of them all stayed silent, sipping their rum, each lost in their own thoughts.

———————————

Although the frigate *Ark de Triomphe* was travelling at a great speed, and indeed accelerating at a great rate, it seemed to be hanging in the empty void of space in its enclosing 'bubble o' protection'. This gave the days that followed a dreamlike quality, the passing of time only measured out by the bell that rang to change the watches. The pirate crew ate well, imbibed rum and beer (under the watchful eyes of the bully-boys), gambled at card-games or crown-and-anchor, sang and danced (to an impromptu band, under the direction of Jake Thackeray, when he wasn't baking pastries and cakes in the galley's electrical oven) and took their ease. Jack Nastyface and Jake Thackeray still met at the mainmast cross-trees to smoke their pipes, but confined their conversation to mere commonplaces, for, like the rest of the crew, they found it easier to ignore the circumstances of the voyage than to acknowledge them by discussion. At regular intervals Mr Benjamin and his assistants would open a cylinder of compressed air (with a loud "bang!"

and a penetrating "hissssss'), then bring a keg of slaked-lime up from the hold and empty it over the side into the pool of sea water in which the *Ark de Triomphe* was apparently floating. Despite this, the air inside the bubble became quite bad-smelling, but this was the only real hardship, and easily borne by the crew, most of whom had, after all, been born and raised in the filth and stink of London.

If Miriam was not sharing Blue Peter's narrow bunk the ship's cat would often climb in, burrowing under his arm or laying at his feet, but its purring warmth was companionable in the dark of his cabin. Sometimes he would have half-remembered dreams, dreams in which the leopardess with cutlass-teeth and cannon-claws appeared to him again, with the wings of an eagle rising from her shoulders.

Every six hours Bulbous Bill Bucephalus took sightings of the stars with the telescope and alidade, comparing his readings and calculations with the dials of the demiheptaxial mechanism. On the second watch of the fifth day of their voyage he informed the Captain that the frigate had reached the mid-point of their course, and would now be reducing its speed to approach to the planet Mars. Captain Greybagges called the crew together and spoke to them in a somber and serious manner, with his blackboard once again set up on the quarterdeck. He announced that after that evening there would be no more drinking, except for a mug of ale with their supper ("boo!" muttered the crew, but with good humour) and he began to instruct them in the duties that they must perform when they arrived at their destination. The rifled muskets were brought out, cleaned, oiled and checked. Cutlasses and boarding-axes were sharpened. Squads of pirates were drilled over and over in their appointed tasks, with charts to study and written lists to memorise, so that every man should know his part in the coming action. The red disc of the planet Mars was now apparent ahead of them, and it was growing in size in the black sky.

Mars now loomed large in front of the frigate *Ark de Triomphe*. The red planet was no longer a blurred circle, it was now a rust-coloured sphere showing surface features; smudgy dark patches, meandering valleys, the pock-marks of craters and white frost at its polar regions. The crew kept glancing incredulously at it while they went about their tasks. There was a growing air of tension on the frigate as Mars grew larger in front of the bowsprit.

"Soon the inhabitants of Mars will realise we are here," said Captain Greybagges. "Then things will become interesting quite quickly."

"The guns and crews are ready," said Blue Peter. "The guns are loaded single-shotted and primed, but the main switch for the electrical fluid is not closed, to avoid mishaps. I have set Torvald Coalbiter to stand by it, as a precaution."

"The squad of marksmen are ready, too" said Israel Feet. "The rifled muskets loaded and half-cocked, two to each shooter, with two assistants to load for each. They are well-drilled and know what they are to do. I have set Jack Nastyface over them. He is much changed from the giddy fool that he once was, and will not let us down, I lay to that … '*wi a wannion!*'" The last words added as the first mate recalled his piratical nature.

"There be no signs of anything yet, Cap'n," said a pirate - formerly a Lincolnshire poacher, chosen for his sharp eyes – who squinted through the large tripod-mounted telescope at Mars, moving it slightly this-way-and-that as he scanned the surface of the planet. Another hawk-eyed pirate grunted agreement from the for'ard quarterdeck rail, upon which he had rested the Captain's Dolland spyglass.

Bulbous Bill Bucephalus said nothing, concentrating on manipulating the levers on the binnacle. Mr Benjamin and his assistants leant or squatted against the stern rail, leather bags of tools in front of them, in case any last-minute adjustments or repairs were necessary.

Time passed. Nobody said anything, the only noises were the "pop-hiss" of a cylinder of air being opened and the creak of the deck-planking and hanging-knees as each slight change of course put a stress on the hull.

"Aye-oop, Cap'n!" the Lincolnshire poacher called, his eye fixed to the large telescope. "Somethin's a-moving! Two *things* a-moving! By the small mountain, going down and to starboard!"

"Got 'em!" confirmed the pirate with the Dolland spyglass. "Two dark things! Glinting now with the sun. Picking up speed to the starboard and down!"

"Good work! Keep your eyes on 'em! Don't lose the buggers!" roared Captain

Greybagges, and, even louder to the whole crew, "The buggers be a-coming now! Remember your orders an' we shall have 'em presently! Steady, lads, steady!" and in a lower voice to Blue Peter, "Do you go below now and take command of your guns, Peter, and be ready upon my mark!" And, under his breath, "By all that be holy, grant me good fortune this day ..."

Time passed. The only voices were the two pirates watching through telescopes, reporting the movements of the two 'things' as they approached, until they went out of sight under the hull.

"Peter! Hold yourself ready! You too, Bill! On my mark!" ordered Captain Greybagges in a firm voice.

The two 'things' slid up from below into view, one on either side of the frigate, and revealed themselves to be long sausage-shaped objects of a dull metallic green, with irregular patches here and there of shining gold and silver. They were perhaps twice the length of the frigate. They had odd lumps and sharp projections on their surfaces, and dark circles which appeared to be port-holes. They slowly moved closer to the sides of the *Ark de Triomphe*, as though to bracket her between them.

"Bill, reduce the bubble's strength ... NOW! ... Peter! Both broadsides ... NOW!"

There was a stunning concussion as the frigate unleashed full broadsides from both port and starboard, and the 'bubble o' protection' was instantly filled with sulphurous smoke.

"Bill! Bring the bubble back up to full strength! Peter! Reload! Quick as you can, but wait upon my order! You, down there in the waist! Spray with the fire-hoses! Pump now! Pump NOW! Pump, you swabs, har-har-har!"

The spray of seawater from the fire-hoses slowly doused and cleared the eye-stinging brimstone-stinking smoke from inside the bubble. Outside the bubble the two alien craft were rolling away and falling down towards Mars, great rents and holes in their metallic-green hulls, shedding fragments and spinning shards of wreckage, spewing out streamers of gas and gouts of liquid which bloomed eerily into glittering clouds of crystals in the vacuum of space.

"Har-har! Take that you little grey buggers!" roared Captain Sylvestre de Greybagges. "Not so bloody clever now, are yuz, ye swabs! Har-har-har!"

"Good lord!" said Mr Benjamin, his ears ringing from the cannon-blast in the confining bubble. "How did the cannon-balls go through the bubble?"

"Har-har!" chortled the Captain. "They just pop through, iffen the bubble be at its weakest! Har-har-har! Those war-vessels o' the little grey buggers be impervious to death-rays, heat-beams, quantum disruptors and all that sort o' clever stuff, but they cannot withstand a good honest broadside o' iron cannon-balls! Har-har-har-har!" Captain Greybagges tried to compose himself, but he was dancing a jig of joy, a hornpipe of happiness. "T'were a *calculated* risk, but I have pulled it off! Har-har-har! I knew they would a-come alongside us like that, for 'tis their *standard operating procedure*. They would have seized us with *tractor-fields*, which be akin to grapplin'-irons, d'ye see? But I got me blow in first! Har-har-har! Arrogant an' proud they be, them little grey buggers, an' just as well for us, or they might a-been a trifle more *circumspect*. Har-har-har!"

"Shall I takes us down, Cap'n?" asked Bulbous Bill, interrupting the Captain's victory dance.

"Why, yes, Bill! With all despatch, now! There was just the two war-vessels here at the moment – I had intelligence o' that! Har-har! – but it be best not to let 'em have time to compose theyselves! Let us go down and finish this off as quick as we may!"

Bulbous Bill worked the levers on the binnacle and the frigate *Ark de Triomphe* corkscrewed abruptly and accelerated at a shocking rate towards the rusty-red surface of Mars. Nothing was felt inside the bubble, and the crew did not appear to notice the violence of the manoeuvre. They were assembling in the waist of the ship and on the foredeck, arming themselves with cutlasses, boarding axes, muskets and pistols. The marksmen were taking their positions along the rails, cradling their long-barrelled rifled muskets, their loaders standing by them with powder horns and pouches of bullets.

"Er, Bill?" said the Captain carefully.

"I be getting the knack o' this, I reckons, Cap'n!" said Bill, his jowly face creased with concentration and his lips drawn back in a snarl. He brought the frigate near to the surface without slowing down at all, and changed direction sharply so it was following the ground very fast at a very low altitude. The frigate whizzed over the red sands, the shock-wave of its passing kicking up a swirling rooster-tail of red dust behind it, despite the thin atmosphere.

"I reckons it be best if we a-come at 'em low, so we just pops up from over the horizon, belike," said Bulbous Bill. "This way they be confused, mebbe. Thinks we crashed or summat."

"That is a good idea! A very fine idea, indeed!" said the Captain. The red land of Mars unrolled under the frigate in a crazy blur. "But slow down before we hit their bubble, as we must slip ourselves through it quite slowly, d'ye see?" The Captain's voice was a little quavery, as he watched Bill's hands precisely moving the levers, and as saw how close they were to the ground, and how immensely fast they were moving.

"Aye-aye, Cap'n!" said Bill, through a gritted-teeth grin, and, under his breath, "Wheee-ooo! Har-har-har!"

"Arrh-har!" said Captain Greybagges, pointing ahead. A complex of buildings rose swiftly over the horizon. The huge bubble-field which covered the town was made mistily visible by the pink dust-haze of Mars. As Bulbous Bill slowed the frigate from its scorching velocity the buildings came closer, and were seen more clearly. Golden domes and palaces of brass, gleaming in the reddish sunlight. Spires, steeples, columns, needles, towers and minarets sticking up like stalagmites. Ziggurats and pyramids (quite small ones, but nicely made). Bartizans, bulwarks, bastions and barbicans, crenellated, with grey stone walls and ravelins. Nondescript multi-storied edifices of red-brown and orange stone. Flat-roofed metal warehouses, sheds and workshops. Ornamental parks and gardens, with fountains and statuary. The small town under the bubble formed a crescent around a large open red-dirt plaza, pock-marked with meteorite craters,

"Just kiss our bubble against their bubble, then just push on it," said Captain Greybagges. "It's the same sort of bubble, so it will squidge through."

"Aye-aye, Cap'n!" said Bill, and did just that.

"Put her down in that crater there, Bill! Near the edge o' the plaza, by that copper dome. It looks to be about the right size," said the Captain, pointing.

"Aye-aye, Cap'n!"

Bill wiggled the levers and the frigate *Ark de Triomphe* swooped down and settled into the crater, the 'bubble o' protection' fitting as neatly into the crater as an egg into an egg-cup.

"Switch off the bubble!"

Bill moved a lever and the bubble vanished with a '*tzzzzzing-pop!*' noise. The
Ark de Triomphe dropped slightly, and wallowed and swashed in the slopping pool
of sea-water, until Bill steadied it with a few deft twitches of the levers on the
binnacle.

"Ready, marksmen!" roared Captain Greybagges from the front of the
quarterdeck. "The toad-men will be first to attack. Don't shoot 'til yuz sees the
yellows o' their eyes! They do have big yellow peepers, so that'll be about two
hundred paces. Aim between them peepers, remember, for they will be wearing
breast-plates and helmets! Try not to shoot any o' them lizard-people. They are
smaller, and do have four arms."

"Aye-aye, Cap'n!" shouted the marksmen. Some of them knelt, or had kegs
or chairs to sit on, so they could steady their guns on the rail. Some lay on the
deck with their forearms pressed against sandbags, firing through the scuppers.
Some stood and rested their guns on ratlines. A few were in the cross-trees. Jack
Nastyface stood on the foredeck, where he could see all the marksmen and direct
fire, if need be. He raised his left hand in a loose salute to the Captain; his right
hand held a cutlass.

"Here they come! Here they come! Oh, lor' luvaduck! They be big bastards,
too!" shouted the topmast lookout, who had a spyglass. The toad-men were coming
out onto the red-dirt plaza from between the buildings, loping over the sand with
a flat-footed gait. There was silence on the *Ark de Triomphe*, so the *flap-flap-flap* of
the toad-men's green warty flat feet could be heard distinctly. They drew closer,
waving bludgeons and clubs, until their wheezing croaky breath could be heard
too. A marksman fired – *ba-bang!* – and a toad-man fell headlong onto the sand
and lay still, his bludgeon rolling away. The marksman immediately swapped his
discharged weapon for a loaded one and fired again. Now all the marksmen were
firing – careful aimed shots – and their loaders worked in pairs; powder-patch-
ball-ramrod-cock-prime, over and over again. The toad-men fell.

"Why do they not have firearms?" asked Mr Benjamin.

"Because they are too stupid, Frank" said the Captain. "They can obey simple
commands, but a gun requires a modicum of nous and a minimum of force to set
it off. They would shoot each other by accident, or look down the barrel and pull

the trigger to see how it worked, or some other foolishness."

The corpses of the toad-men had now piled up on top of each over, forming a wall which the last of them were doggedly climbing over. Several of the more-agile toad-men had almost reached the rim of the crater before they were killed, forming a grisly high-water mark. The toad-men's blood drained out into the red dirt to form pools; it was purple and thick, and it steamed slightly.

"I am sorry I must have them all killed," said Captain Greybagges, "but they are dangerous creatures and do not deviate from the orders that have been drilled into their thick skulls. One would have to kill savage guard dogs in a similar fashion, and I would regret that more, for even a rabid dog is a far more attractive animal than a toad-man."

The marksmen had stopped firing, as no living toad-men could now be seen.

"The lizard-people will try and attack now," said Captain Greybagges to Mr Benjamin. "They are much brainier than the toad-men, but have little talent for war, and even less liking for it. But they've been doin' just what they wuz told to do for a while, though, so we shall have to see which way they will go." He roared out to the crew, "Don't shoot the lizard-people, shipmates! Not unless I tells 'ee to!" He went to the quarterdeck rail, and waited.

"There be some creatures a-sneaking out from the alleyways, Cap'n!" the lookout shouted down.

"Thankee! Keep an eye on 'em!" the Captain shouted back, then waited some more.

Almost shyly, creatures began to come onto the plaza. This was a slow process, as each one seemed to be trying to hide behind every other one, so they spent much time milling about rather than moving forward. They looked like tubby lizards with stumpy tails, except that they walked on their two back legs and had four arms. There was a fair amount of arm-waving going on, as there seemed to be several serious disagreements taking place among them at any one time, as well as a surplus of arms to wave about. Their voices were like loud birdsong. They all appeared to be carrying weapons, but a strange assortment of them. One was carrying a weapon in each of its four hands; an odd-shaped silvery arquebus with a transparent red-crystal rod instead of a barrel, an engraved Spanish *miquelet* horse-pistol with a ball pommel, a Magdeburg crossbow (a heavy siege model with a *cranequin* built into its oak stock) and a long pike with a tattered *gonfalon* dangling limply from its cross-bar. Each of the lizard-people was similarly burdened, as though they had grabbed as many weapons as they could, so to appear intimidatingly warlike, but didn't feel very comfortable carrying them, or really know what to do with them.

Captain Greybagges stood at the quarterdeck rail and spoke in a loud and powerful voice, a voice of brass, the type of voice possessed only by a ship's captain, which can be heard at distances of up to half a sea mile, into the teeth of a Caribbean *hurricano* and over a *trommelfeur* of cannon-fire, yet not sound unduly forced or 'shouty'. The Captain spoke thus:

"Lizard people! Listen to me! You know me! You have seen me and my green beard before! I know you, too! You there, Pretty Polly! You too, Cheeky Boy! Joker! Squawky! Cutie Pie! Jemima! I don't speak your language, but some of you do understand mine! I know that well, for we have played cards together, you and I! You recognize the names I gave to you then, and which I call you by now! Translate my words for the others, if you would be so kind. I do not want to harm you! You hate the Glaroon as much as I do! Lay down you weapons, and you shall not be harmed! … I say it again … LAY DOWN THE WEAPONS AND YOU SHALL NOT BE FIRED UPON! *PLEASE* LAY DOWN THE WEAPONS! DO *PLEASE* LAY DOWN YOUR WEAPONS, *I BEG YOU!*"

A lizard-person bent down, dropped a clatter of assorted armaments on the sand and hopped back away from them. The other lizard-people did the same, as though to disassociate themselves from them - weapons? what weapons? They bumped into each other as they tried to back away from their piles of weapons. Hopping backwards they trod on others' piles of weapons, then jumped back away from those, too. There were collisions, and several tripped and fell over, and there was much angry chirrupping, squawking and arm-waving.

"Aah! Good! I would have been mortified iffen I'd had to kill 'em," said Captain Greybagges to Mr Benjamin. "They be diverting fellows … if a little clownish, betimes … GO TOWARDS … GO *THAT* WAY! THE WAY I BE POINTING! *OVER THERE!* IF YOU ALL GO IN THE SAME DIRECTION

YOU WILL NOT KEEP A-BUMPIN' INTO EACH OTHER!"

The lizard-people moved away, still chirruping and squawking and arm-waving, leaving the piles of weapons on the sand.

"That be the price o' an ill-considered policy o' divide an' rule, d'ye see? The Glaroon has the savage but witless toad-men to terrorise the lizard-people, an' the intelligent lizard-people to make sure the toad-men don't do anything too stupid. Each is a check upon the other, but when the toad-men are gone it all falls apart. There is a third factor, though …"

"Cap'n!" a cry came from the lookout. "Summat be a-going on up top o' the … whatever it is, the blue house … *there!* Little men got summat on little wheels up there!"

"Right on cue! The third factor. Little grey buggers!" said the Captain. On a flat roof some small figures were struggling with a device, which was indeed on little wheels. It was an assembly of shiny metal boxes, spheres and cylinders with coloured glass bulbs and tubes snaking around them, some of its components were glowing with flickering with green and purple light.

"Peter! Peter! Knock them down!" shouted the Captain.

"Turn the ship a little widdershins, Cap'n!" shouted Blue Peter from below in the gun-deck. Bulbous Bill fiddled with the binnacle, and the frigate yawed a compass-point anticlockwise, sloshing the water in the crater. There was a 'BOOM!' and a cloud of smoke from the frigate, and the glowing device was shattered into fragments. When the cannonball struck the device there was a bright flash of blue light and the small figures around it were blown in all directions, one of its little wheels bounced along the roof and sailed off the edge.

"Excellent shooting, Peter!" shouted the Captain.

"It was Torvald Coalbiter who laid the gun," Blue Peter shouted back.

"Keep yuz eyes open for any more o' their capers!"

The crew were disembarking. Some climbed out along the bowsprit, which projected over the crater's rim, and slid down a rope to the ground. There they grabbed gang-planks which were pushed out over the rails and quickly rigged them at prow and stern, and the pirates swarmed ashore onto the red sands of Mars. One pirate fell into the crater. The seawater pool had become rather polluted during the interplanetary journey, so when he climbed out over the crater's rim he was a source of much amusement. "Har-har, Jake Thackeray! Thou art all be-shat! Har-har!" shouted one of the old pirates gleefully.

"Less of the badinage, ye swabs! This ain't a picnic-party!" roared the Captain from the quarterdeck rail. "Yuz have yer tasks! Don't kill any people yer comes across, cuz' the people here be slaves. Don't kill any o' the lizard-people, either. Try not to kill the little grey buggers, but don't hesitate if yer has to, specially iffen they be carryin' any *strange devices*. Kill all o' them toad-men as quick as yer can. Off yer goes now!"

The squads of pirates trotted away across the red-dirt plaza, muskets on their shoulders and cutlasses in their belts. Captain Greybagges sighed and rubbed his face with his hands.

"Peter! Do please come up here!" Blue Peter came up from the gun-deck.

"Peter, can Torvald handle the gun-deck by hisself?"

"Surely he can. A good fellow is the Coalbiter!"

"Well then, you shall come with me. Give him his orders. I don't want no cannon-balls a-crashin' into the town unnecessarily, but anything suspicious an' he's to blow it to kingdom-come." Captain Greybagges scratched his chin thoughtfully.

"Bill, you must stay here and guard the ship. Lift her off again if you must to save her from counter-attack, but I don't think that be likely. The toad-men are mostly dead now. The lizard-people are prepared to accept a *change o' management*, har-har! The little grey buggers may yet be a problem, but there ain't so many o' them, and, though they be clever, they be not so sharp when took by surprise. Keep alert. The ship is under your hand."

"Aye-aye, Cap'n!"

"Mr Benjamin! Will you take the prisoners under guard and watch 'em? Over there on the sand, where they are standing about. The lizard-people and the little grey buggers both, but don't let 'em mingle or the lizard-people may twist the heads off the little grey buggers, as they have grudges. Take four men, that should be enough. Some o' the lizard-people speak the King's English, bless 'em, and you may be able to get 'em to help you watch the little grey buggers, iffen you makes it clear to 'em about no head-twisting, o' course. Do please be *polite* to them even if you are bein' forceful, *especially* if you are bein' forceful, for the lizard-people be good-hearted but they can be touchy. No need to be polite to the little grey buggers. Kick their arses if they are disobedient or contrary, but not too damn' hard, for they be weak and fragile creatures."

"Aye-aye, Captain!"

Blue Peter reappeared and he and the Captain clomped down the stern gangplank, followed by the six bully-boys. Mrs Miriam Ceteshwayoo and the island women were setting up a first-aid post, tearing bandages from old sheets on a trestle-table.

"Women's work, you are thinking, no doubt?" said Miriam sweetly. "Of course you are! Since you have not deigned to inform us of your plans, or our part in them, we must assume that we women must, as always, clean up after you. If my Peter comes back here and I have to stitch him back together then I will ..." One of the island women interrupted her, passing her another sheet to tear. Captain Greybagges opened his mouth to speak, but she was looking into Blue Peter's eyes. "Off you go now. Come back." She looked away and carried on tearing strips from the sheet.

Captain Greybagges touched Blue Peter's arm and they walked towards the town across the red sand, followed by the bully-boys. Blue Peter, with some difficulty, turned his thoughts to the business ahead. He remembered things the Captain and told him, and tried to put them in some order.

"Captain, you once told me of the Glaroon. Do you hope to catch him and take your revenge?"

Captain Sylvestre de Greybagges thought for a moment. Blue Peter noticed that the Captain's green beard was moving very slightly. Small ripples ran down it. Occasionally it fluffed up just a little, the way a cat's hair will do when it is scared.

"Yes, the Glaroon. I can sense his presence, but only very faintly. He is a Great Old One, so he can read minds, of course. This is useful to him, but irritating too, because of the relentless gabble of lesser beings' thoughts filling his ... his whatever it is he thinks with. He often rests in a chamber with thick walls made of osmium, or some such metal o' great price. A sort of quiet room, far from the noise and bustle. He is there now, sleeping, dreaming, or whatever it is that he does. I timed our landing to coincide with this, as his servants will be afraid to disturb him and face his wrath."

"I believe that you have laid your plans very carefully, Captain, with regard to time."

"Tis all timing," said Captain Greybagges fervently. "Everything is timing because everything is time. Some may say 'Aha! But what about space, eh?' but space is measured out in time, d'ye see? Why, it's three minutes walk to the pub! It's a hard day's ride to Banbury Cross! Three weeks to Port o' Spain, iffen the Westerlies stays brisk! Without time there'd be no space, because there'd be no measure of it. Time is everything, and every single thing is time. That's why I'm doin' all this, to be truthful. Because o' time! ... Well, that be one o' the reasons, anyway. The Glaroon is another one. I wish for revenge, and I shall have it. I don't believe he shall be woken, for then he would surely exterminate all the little grey buggers in his fury – blast them to atoms just by thinking bad thoughts about them - and the little grey buggers know that. So they will try to fight us, but they be *already* beaten because the real line o' defence was up in the sky above us, and we sunk their space-ships, and they aren't any good at fighting anyway. So we shall catch the Glaroon a-snoozing in his dream-chamber, trapped like a lobster in a pot."

They walked in silence for a while, two tall powerful buccaneers. One black as night, his face marked with scars, attired in bright silks trimmed with lace. One pink-faced with a green beard, clad in somber black broadcloth. The bully-boys had moved to flank them, three to each side, and were warily watchful, their muskets in their hands.

A small group of lizard-people came towards them, holding up all four of their arms in sign of surrender. Two of the little grey buggers were in front of them, being apparently herded towards the frigate floating in the crater. The lizard-people waddled past, stumpy tails swinging from side to side, some of them, presumably the more elderly, occasionally using their lower pair of arms to 'knuckle' with a gorilla-like gait. They all acknowledged the pirates with chirrups and squawks, and gave an impression of good humour. The two little grey buggers gave the pirates one glance of their large slanted oval eyes, nictating membranes flickering over the gleaming black surfaces, then turned their heads and walked on. Captain Greybagges spoke to the lizard-people cheerfully, and pointed them towards the crowd of prisoners being watched by Mr Benjamin,

"They are oddly charming creatures, I find," said Blue Peter. "They have aspects which surely ought to daunt a sensible and perceptive person. If they should chose to grapple with one, well, they have four arms to do it with, and the lower arms are obviously very powerful, They have a lot of teeth, *pointed teeth*. They have those *woogly* chameleon eyes, that you once described to me. But one's instinct upon seeing them is to smile and talk to them."

"I am very fond of them, Peter. When I was held here as a slave I think I should have gone mad, but for the lizard-people. They can be a comical sight, but don't be deceived by that. They have extraordinary talents. There are no mechanics and craftsmen better than the lizard-people, and some of them are astoundingly knowledgeable, true scholars. They love to drink, too. They love to gamble. They are musical, and love to dance and sing. They almost never mumpish or bad-tempered. How can one not like them? It is a good sign that they are surrendering, and bringing in little grey buggers, too. A very few o' the people here knew I was coming, so they are perhaps spreading the word to the lizard-people, who will not be unhappy to see the Glaroon fall."

They approached the town. There were few signs of war, only an occasional crackle of musket-fire came from among the buildings.

"Ah, still a few toad-men running about, I would guess, but otherwise things are proceeding as planned. What worries me most is that the lads will be distracted by the lust for plunder," said the Captain. "There aren't that many people and extramundane creatures in this town, really, considerin' its size. Most of it be treasure-houses or museums to store the swag that the Glaroon has looted from Earth's past ... *our* past. Our lads are good lads, but they still be pirates, or else I wouldn't have 'em on the ship, so the sight o' all that treasure a-glittering in heaps might turn their heads. The people here, the Glaroon's slaves, are also a kind of swag, stolen from our past, and some o' them might turn a young man's head, too, and some o' them might enjoy doin' just that. Them Borgia girls, fr'instance. They would consider it a downright insult iffen a fine strapping young pirate did *not* try to have his wicked way with them, the hussies, but that wouldn't stop 'em from slippin' a stiletto between his ribs, or givin' the poor sod a scratch with a poisoned ring, should he try to engage 'em in a bit o' slap an' tickle. I've told the lads over an' over that there ain't no need to pocket any trinkets or kiss the ladies, for we shall take the entire town in one swift move an' then do with it what we will at our leisure, but if they did not feel a powerful urge to rape, loot and plunder, why, then I would surely feel a little disappointed in 'em, really I would. That's why we must be here now, to keep things orderly, although I dare say there might be a couple o' brisk actions where the little grey buggers are bein' obstinate."

They came to the edge of the red-dirt plaza and halted by an elaborate fountain; limestone fauns and satyrs pouring streams of water from ewers and cornucopias into an oval basin. A rose-pink marble palace stood in front of them.

"Bloody ugly fountain, ain't it? All that nymphs-an'-shepherds classical nonsense ... Now, Peter, please take three o' the bully boys and follow that street there to the left. I shall go up here to the right. Just keep the lads to their tasks, and clap a stopper on any foolishness that yer sees. First we gets control, then we may relax a little, tell 'em that. Strictly business, an' no funny business, har-har! We shall clear each side o' the town back towards the middle and meet in the square. Break a leg, eh, Peter?" Captain Sylvestre de Greybagges slapped Blue Peter on the shoulder and strode off down a narrow alley, three bully-boys trotting after him.

Captain Greybagges was proved to be correct in his analysis. There were some brief but vicious fire-fights where little grey buggers had managed to rally a few surviving toad-men, but their resistance was weak, disorganised and easily overrun. The little grey buggers made a last stand in the central hall of a stately classical edifice with Doric columns and bas-reliefs of Greek gods upon its facades. The hall was filled with an assortment of statues, bronze armour and weapons and other ancient Greek and Macedonian relics. In the centre of the hall there was a chariot, made of wood and bronze and painted in bright colours. The little grey men had taken cover behind it, and put up a spirited defence. They had managed to get some of the silvery arquebusses to function, and the red-crystal barrels spat out bolts of pure heat, and several pirates were wounded with ugly burns. The pirates made attempts to move the chariot, but it was tied to a post with a large complex knot of hemp rope.

The pirates pulled back, and were discussing their next move, when Jack Nastyface lost patience. He seized the giant razor of Ali the Barber, which a pirate-squad had brought along as a sort of mascot, ran forward from behind cover and slammed it down upon the knot, which fell apart into strands. Jack shoved the chariot and, freed from its mooring, it rolled away to crash into a tall glass cabinet full of erotically-glazed Etruscan pottery. Jack Nastyface was then left exposed, and a bright fizzing bolt of red light punched into his chest, and he fell dead upon the parquet floor.

The little grey buggers were now open to the fire of the pirate marksmen, and surrendered, their silvery arquebusses clattering to the floor as they dropped them. Captain Greybagges strode forward, his face dark with anger.

"Who shot Jack Nastyface?" he roared. "Which one o' you little grey buggers shot that man?"

The little grey buggers showed no sign of understanding what the Captain had said, but they all moved away from one little grey bugger, leaving it standing alone. With a snarl, Captain Greybagges pulled a pistol from his belt and shot the little grey bugger, which was blown onto its back, a pool of blue-green blood spreading on the mosaic floor.

"You little grey buggers, if you be smart, will recognise that I be angry, and that when I be angry I shoots little grey buggers," he roared. "You wuz clever enough to know how to avoid the Glaroon's anger, so yuz best be clever enough to avoid mine from now on, or I swear upon my oath that I will shoot the damn' lot o' yuz!"

The little grey buggers stared at him with their big black eyes, then they all blinked their eye-membranes, as though in acceptance. Captain Greybagges turned away, and found Blue Peter next to him, his long-barrelled Kentucky pistol smoking in his hand; they had drawn their guns and fired simultaneously.

With the little grey buggers defeated and cleared away to the plaza, and the lizard-people happily surrendering and accepting a 'change of management', the people started to appear. Captain Greybagges had set up a command-post in a *belle époque* ballroom with horrible mock-roccoco *décor* of pastel-coloured plaster and gilt, where he directed pirates to escort groups of lizard-people herding smaller groups of little grey buggers to the plaza. A stocky fellow came to him, clad in boiled-leather armour and a helmet with a horse-tail plume.

"Why, Temujin! How pleasant to meet you again, old friend!" said the

Captain and embraced him warmly. They talked, while Blue Peter and Israel Feet continued giving orders to pirate-squads. The stocky man marched away, a confident swagger in his walk, although he had quite short bowed legs.

"He's a good fellow, is Temujin," said the Captain. "He's taken charge of the slave-people over on the west side. Got them to hide theyselves when the fight was still goin' on, and now he's gettin' 'em organised. One thing less to worry about. I've always liked the chap. I'm surprised that he had such a terrible reputation."

"Temujin?" said Blue Peter.

"Better known as Genghis Kahn, although he isn't the real one, of course, but a sort of copy."

Other people appeared, and the Captain dealt with them: "That was Aristotle, Peter. A heart of gold, but a bit of a bore, I'm afraid." … "Michelangelo di bloody Lodovico Buonarroti. Great artist, he's a copy of the real Michelangelo, but he can still whack out a sculpture fit to take yer breath away. Bit of an arrogant sod, though. I'm not sure whether I should keep him away from Mr Chippendale, or introduce them, if you catch my meaning." … "Helen o' Troy, Peter. The 'face that launched a thousand ships', and the bum that launched a couple o' thousand more, wouldn't you say? She's a great dancer, too. Nice lady." … "Oggie the Very Early Man. He can't take his drink – wasn't even invented in his day, was it? So he has an excuse, I suppose - but he has his good points. Right now I can't think what they are, though."

The Martian day is thirty-seven minutes longer than the Earth day, but that Martian day felt far longer than that, as there was so much to do. The sun was beginning to get low in the sky before Captain Greybagges was able to sit back and take his ease. Jake Thackeray had brought sandwiches, pies, cakes and bottles of cold lemon tea from the *Ark de Triomphe*, enduring many amusing sallies from the pirates along the lines of "har-har-har, Jake! I hopes that yuz have *washed yer hands*, har-har-har!" as he handed out the refreshments.

"Now there is something I must do, Peter," said the Captain, brushing crumbs off his black trousers.

"Go and wake up the Glaroon, Captain?" said Blue Peter.

"No, that can wait. He's snoozing in his chamber and the little grey buggers are all under guard. Even if he wakes he's still stuck in that chamber, and what keeps out the noise o' thoughts also keeps his thoughts in, so he be no threat for the moment. No, I have something else to do. Keep 'em in order here for a bit." Captain Greybagges got up and went.

Blue Peter thought for a short while, then decided that the Captain should not be wandering on his own, not with Glaroons still extant, even though the town was now secured and quiet. He checked that his pistol was loaded and primed, and followed him.

Captain Greybagges walked purposefully through the town, past gaudy palaces, small castles, thatched cottages with roses round the door, the jumbled-together architecture of the Martian capital (what is it called? thought Blue Peter). The Captain came to a large building of red brick, with tall windows and a grand sweep of steps up to its doors. He stopped for a moment, looking up at it, then trotted up the steps and went in. Peter followed him.

The interior of the building was quiet and well lit from the high windows. There were books everywhere. Bookshelves, row upon row, into the distance. Tables stacked with books. Books on lecterns. Books piled on the floor. Books, tomes, codexes, slim volumes, chapbooks, bouquins, folios, quartos, octavos, coffee-table books, text-books, dictionaries, magnum opuses, opuscules, manuscripts, handbooks, booklets, workshop manuals, scrolls, hardbacks, paperbacks, potboilers, classics, penny-dreadfuls, pamphlets, thesauruses, leaflets, bodice-rippers, blockbusters, atlases, bestsellers and incunabuli. All sorts of books, but no Captain Greybagges.

Blue Peter went up the stairs to the next floor. There was an open door. Blue Peter looked into the room. More books. A desk in the middle of the room with a shaded light. Standing by the desk, a tall slim woman dressed in a floor-length white gown, an Ionic *chiton*. She had a long serious face with an aquiline nose, large lustrous brown eyes and a mop of black hair in corkscrewing curls. She was beautiful. Captain Greybagges was facing her. Blue Peter recognized her as the model for the tiny figure next to the Captain on the quarterdeck of the ship-in-a-bottle in the Great Cabin of the *Ark de Triomphe*.

Someone nudged him gently, and he turned to find Miriam standing by him. She smiled, and indicated with a nod of her head that they should quietly leave. Blue Peter turned back. Captain Greybagges and the tall woman still faced each other,

"Hypatia!" breathed Captain Greybagges in a voice that quavered with emotion. "My Princess of Polynomials! My Queen of QED! My Empress of Exponentials! My love!"

"Sylvestre! The Capitan of my 'Eart!" She had a melodious voice with a Greek accent.

They stepped towards each other. Blue Peter noticed that the beautiful woman had fine green hairs on her forearms and on the backs of her hands and fingers. As she put her hands to his face Captain Greybagges's green beard *moved*, the long green strands swaying, reaching out to enfold her hands and entwine lovingly with the fine green hairs. They stood perfectly still, gazing into each other's eyes. Then a slight flicker of apprehension slid over Captain Greybagges's face.

"Why, you dirty ole goat!" the beautiful woman hissed. "You focked a bleddy witch, *you ole bastid!*"

Miriam grasped Blue Peter's sleeve and forcefully pulled him away from the door and quietly back down the stairs.

"I am glad that Hypatia is no longer angry with you," said Blue Peter, "and that she has agreed to be your wife."

"Showerin' her with baubles and trinkets o' great price merely caused her to laugh at me in a mockin' and contemptuous way. Abasin' meself and grovellin' alike to a poor sad fool pleased her greatly, but did not move her by more than the thickness of a hair, a very *fine* hair, too, such as might adorn the head o' yer beloved grandmother. Begging her to marry me was the only way I could mollify her," said Captain Sylvestre de Greybagges. "It has been quite successful, as a *stratagem*. I believe that in a couple of decades or so she may even consider forgiving me. Consider in a purely theoretical way, of course, as a problem in logic. She is no longer throwing things at me, or not very often, anyway, which encourages me to have these foolish hopes."

There was the sharp crack of willow upon leather, and a spatter of applause from the crowd at the cricket match.

"Oh, yes! Well played! Well played!" cried Captain Greybagges, clapping.

"I am sorry that the Glaroon escaped your vengeance, too," said Blue Peter. "That must have been painful for you."

"I didn't appreciate that the little grey buggers could launch him off like that without first awakening him. I did not know that his chamber o' silence was equipped as a saucer-craft, you see, so it did not occur to me that they could do that. When I saw the chamber fly out of the top of that tower I was so angry I nearly shot a couple of the little grey sods, but what good would that have done? Anyway, I suspect that I may never be able to have me vengeance upon him. I think that in many ways I have been merely the tool of Great Cthulhu in this affair, that I was but a small part in some political shenanigans of the Great Old Ones. They may have been glad to see the Glaroon deprived of power, but they would never have allowed him to be subject to the vindictiveness of a mere mortal. They have their position in the universe to consider. Such a thing might have given ideas to others."

There was another burst of applause. The wicket-keeper threw the ball high in the air to celebrate his excellent catch. The ball dropped down again into his gloved hands and he bowed to the crowd, grinning. The Captain continued.

"The Glaroon was, I think, becoming addled and corybantic in his dotage – even a Great Old One may become too old in the end - and thus a nuisance to the other Great Old Ones. I have heard that he is now in the keeping of Cthulhu in his palace at R'yleh. One might regard the whole business as similar to a manoeuvre to put mad old Lord Diddlewits into a nursing-home, so that he ceases to be an embarrassment to his family, and can no longer drink three bottles of Oporto wine before breakfast and shoot at the butler with a fowling-piece, as can sometimes happen in the best families."

"You have mentioned this Cthulhu fellow before, I remember."

"Great Cthulhu is a wily old cove, no doubt about that. I rather like him. When I was a slave of the Glaroon he was always decent to me. In some circles he has a grisly reputation, but that is mostly gossip, I think. There is a tale that you will go stark-mad if you merely go within a hundred paces of him, but that was only something his wife used to tell her girl-friends, the sort of affectionate calumny that wives are wont to say of their husbands. I had the story from Mrs Cthulhu herself, so it's surely the truth. I have stood right next to Great Cthulhu many times, and am I stark-mad? Their daughter, Miss Lulu Cthulhu, is a terrible scamp, but then she is only a few million years old, so barely in her teens by their reckoning."

The over came to its end, the bowler crossed to the other wicket, and the fielders rearranged themselves on the pitch, their shirts very white in the warm sunlight. Mumblin' Jake came and put a folding table between the two buccaneers, where they sat in campaign-chairs outside the boundary-mark, then came with glasses, a jug of ale and pork pies.

"Thank 'ee, Jake. Have a glass of ale yourself. Oh, is there any mustard? For the pie?" Jake brought a pot of mustard, and then sat under a tree with his ale, mumbling. They ate and drank in silence for a while.

"Anyway, I think that the Glaroon, with his mania for stealing things and people from Earth's past, was creating too many tears and rents in the fabric o' time, and the other Great Old Ones could not allow that. If this time-line of ours had collapsed from too many punctures, then everybody – the Great Old Ones included – would have been *inconvenienced* greatly."

"Will the damage to time heal itself, Sylvestre?"

"Yes, it will ... *in time!* Har-har-har-har! I apologise, Peter! I shan't do that again, for there are far too many opportunities for such levity when one speaks of time *all the time!* Har-har-har! Now I have on a somber face, I promise ... where was I? ... Yes, the damage caused by the Glaroon's saucer-craft ripping through the fabric o' time will mend itself as a wound will, if it be clean. I have been taking measures to clean the wounds, so to speak. Putting back the things that were taken, that sort o' thing. Means I've had to use the little grey buggers to crew a few saucer-craft, and so create a few small rips myself. In the same way, I suppose, that a wound must sometimes be trimmed with further cuts so as to heal better. *Debriding*, the doctors calls it. When that's done, mind you, there will be no further trips into the past by anybody, not if I have anything to do with it."

"The little grey buggers flying saucer-craft, Cap'n? Is that wise?"

"I've got the lizard-people keeping a weather-eye upon 'em, and the little grey buggers be the best at flying those things through time. Sideways through time, too, which can be rather *unwholesome* an' dismal. No, if trouble were to come, it would be from the Great Old Ones turnin' the little grey buggers against me, and my feeling is that I am doing pretty much what the Great Old Ones want, and saving them from having to do it themselves, so why should they? The little grey buggers are sharp enough to realise that, so they will obey me to keep the Great Old Ones sweet."

Captain Greybagges poured himself another glass of ale, drank deeply and wiped his mouth with the back of his hand. The bowler bowled, with an ungainly side-arm throw. The batsman slashed at the ball, and missed. The wicket-keeper fumbled and dropped it, cursing audibly.

"The healing process is already happening. When we were on the coast o' the Colonies we visited places and they were close together, and now they be far apart, hundreds o' miles. Nobody's noticed the ground shiftin' about, yet there it is. The Glaroon was doing' somethin' nasty around those parts, too. Solomon Pole told me about it when we met in Salem. Sol was shooting toad-men out in the barrens, with a great huge duck-gun on a punt, the sly fellow. That's all gone now. Whatever it was the Glaroon was a-doin', well, it ain't there now. Things are easing back to how they should be. The *disjunctions*, the cleavages, the gaps, the *lacunae* in the skeins of time will soon be of the past. They will be history. Quite literally *history*, too, as it will all hang together so prettily so that pompous old greybeards in mortar-boards will be able to write boring books about it, an' torture innocent schoolboys into learnin' it by rote as though it were holy writ."

Captain Greybagges took another pork pie. Blue Peter handed him the mustard-pot.

"Odd thing, Peter. Most of the Mars people - the slaves taken from the past, the Glaroon's historical menagerie – did not choose to go back to the time from whence they came. Oogie the Very Early Man did, but only because it was the only way he could stay sober, and he missed mammoth-steaks, too. A lot of them want to stay on Mars. They've spent their lives there, I suppose, if one discounts the false memories that have been put into their heads to make them think they are whoever it is they are supposed to be. It's their home, as much as anywhere is. Some of 'em surprised me, though. Aristotle is now running a *taverna* in Athens, down by the Piraeus docks. Says he should have thought o' doin' it years ago. The only proper work for a philosopher is bein' landlord o' a pub, he reckons. Temujin is trading carpets in the *souk* o' Stamboul, where his base cunning and native ferocity can be employed on a daily basis. An' Helen o' Troy ..."

"Is an actress here in London, and she now calls herself Nell Gwynne!" laughed Blue Peter.

"Good grief! How come you to know that?"

"I saw her at the theatre, only a couple of days ago. Guess who she was with?"

"I cannot hazard a guess."

"King Charles!"

"No! You jest! ... Well, yes, I can see how that might be. He does have an eye for the ladies, it's said, and Helen is certainly an eyeful."

"She is playing Florimel in Dryden's *Secret Love, or The Maiden Queen* at the Theater Royal. I took Miriam to see it, and it was a very droll entertainment. Helen, or *Nell* I should say, saw us in the foyer after the curtain came down, and sent for us to come back-stage, and there he was, the king of England. He was *incognito*, so I didn't recognize him – how would I know what the king looks like? – but that went well, as I spoke to him at first as a normal man, and I think he quite liked that. He is not unduly *stuffy*, for a king. Miriam and I are now invited to a royal garden-party next week."

"Upon my life, Peter! I once jested that you might end up as the king's Steward Of The Stool, but I never thought it might actually come to pass, har-har!"

"I suspect that King Charles wishes to shock his hoity-toity friends by showing us off to them as a blackamoor pirate and his fair Colonial wife – *quelle scandale!* - but I shall forgive him for that if the food and drink are *fit for a king*, and if no fool takes me for a flunky and gives me his cloak and hat to brush."

"I don't think there be much chance o' that, not if yer grins at the fellow with yer pointed teeth."

There was another outbreak of clapping, and the cricket-ball bounced over the boundary and rolled to Mumblin' Jake, who threw it to a fielder, who dropped it. Jake mumbled a curse, and drank some ale.

"Tell me about your adventures in Africa, Peter," said the Captain. "You found your home village, I believe."

"Indeed I did, and thank you once again for the loan of the good ship *Ark de Triomphe.*"

"Think nothing of it. You and Miriam needed a proper honeymoon, after all the kerfuffle, and what better one than a cruise?"

"I located the place of my birth quite quickly, to my surprise. It's a lot easier to find things if one can look down from the sky. It was pretty much as I had thought. My uncle had substituted his own son for me, the rightful chief of the tribe. My uncle was long dead, though, and my cousin is a decent fellow and an honest and upright leader of his people, so there was nothing for me to do, really. The thirst for revenge went from my heart when I saw how sorry and afraid my cousin was. My return gave him quite a shock, as you may imagine. I gave him some muskets, a keg of powder and a sack of musket-balls to help keep the slave-traders at bay, and we parted on good terms."

"I am glad of that," said Captain Greybagges. "To be still intent on settling a grudge would be beneath you, Peter, now that you are one of the wealthiest men in the world, har-har!"

"You vast hypocrite, Sylvestre! You yourself are *the* wealthiest man in the world now, and yet you still yearn to have your vengeance upon the Glaroon!"

"That be an entirely different kettle o' fish, Peter," said Captain Greybagges loftily. "The vile Glaroon made me wear *a little sailor-suit with ribbons*, and that is an insult not easily borne by a cap'n o' buccaneers. I would have fed him with little sailor-suits! I would've stuffed them down his gob with a cannon's ram-rod until all seven o' his eyeballs bulged like organ-stops, an' you may lay to that, I swears

285

it wi' a curse, look 'ee!"

Captain Sylvestre de Greybagges and Blue Peter Ceteshwayoo roared with laughter and clinked their ale-glasses together.

"I'm glad everything turned out well," said Captain Greybagges. "There were moments when I doubted they would, even with Hypatia helpin' me at every turn, and with such a fine crew o' reckless freebooters at my back. T'were touch an' go at times. Now me only worry is the little grey buggers."

"Why are they a worry, Sylvestre? I thought you had them tamed?"

"It be not so much the little grey buggers, as what they represent. I be tryin' to put things right, and that means healin' the damage caused by travel to the past. I have a deep suspicion, though, that the little grey buggers be from the future, an' that may be harder to fix up an' make ship-shape. The *really* worryin' thing is that they may be people like us, but from millions o' years hence, d'ye see? It may be our destiny to become little grey buggers, and I do not find that a comfortin' thought, for the sods have no sense o' humour. There be not an atom o' fun in any of 'em, the miserable bastards, an' that'd be a terrible fate for mankind."

Blue Peter considered this in silence. Mumblin' Jake mumbled something, and waved a bony hand. Captain Greybagges looked over his shoulder.

"Ah-harr! Here be the girls! ... Arrh! An' a passel o' the lads, too!"

Three four-in-hand coaches were pulled up onto the grass verge of the road behind them. The first coach was a fairytale carriage of pink enamel and gold-leaf with a coachman and postillion in sky-blue uniforms. Mrs Miriam Ceteshwayoo and Hypatia were stepping down from it, dressed in the pastel silks of that spring's Paris fashions, unfolding little lacy parasols against the summer-afternoon sun. Israel Feet and Madame Zonga tumbled from the second coach (a rakish speedy brougham, resplendent in burgundy with yellow pin-striping), both apparently the worse for drink, followed by Bulbous Bill Bucephalous and the chief of the island women, arm-in-arm. The third coach (a rented hack, its scarred panels dimmed by the dust of London's streets, driven by a beaming Mr Benjamin) was entirely full of drunken buccaneers, with drunken buccaneers falling out of the windows, drunken buccaneers on the roof and drunken buccaneers hanging onto the postillion's seat at the rear. They were lustily singing a pirate song, a ribald sea-chaunty of the most astonishing lewdness, which went like this .....

RICHARD JAMES BENTLEY, who happens to look the part of a salty English sea captain, has trodden many paths and worn many hats. From his early work as a dealer in dodgy motorcars, he progressed to being a design engineer on a zeppelin project. Computers then caught his attention and he authored a number of incomprehensible technical manuals before turning to fiction. He has lived in Switzerland and the Netherlands and now spins yarns in the north of England. *Greenbeard* is his first novel.